BENEATH THE NORTHERN LIGHTS

STORIES BY JONATHAN P. DAVIS

authorHOUSE®

AuthorHouse™
1663 Liberty Drive
Bloomington, IN 47403
www.authorhouse.com
Phone: 1-800-839-8640

Cover art by Todd Faris

Published by AuthorHouse   09/06/2012

ISBN: 978-1-4772-2440-3 (sc)
ISBN: 978-1-4772-2531-8 (e)

Library of Congress Control Number: 2012911088

CONTENTS

ACKNOWLEDGEMENTS vii

JED'S WILLOW 1

ASCENT 53

CONCERTO 107

COOGAN'S FOR SALE! 133

CHOICES 265

LEFTY'S GREEN ROOM 297

ACKNOWLEDGEMENTS

The best creations are those in which others share their talents to enhance an inspired foundation.

I'd like to thank the following people for their priceless contributions to helping me make this book an even richer and more meaningful achievement:

Jane Ricciardi and Anastasia Townsend, the perfect yin-yang of editorial consultants; their sweeping skills with fiction, logic, and language led to extra color, power, and resonance where I welcomed it most.

Todd Faris, an extraordinary cover artist who once again captured thematic essence with stunning impact and imagination; thank you, Todd, for an alluring and memorable invitation to the content within.

JED'S WILLOW

William Buxton slammed the dusty receiver against the pay phone. Then he hung it up for the fifth time since his current-model Toyota Camry XLE had broken an axle an hour before.

He walked to the edge of the old gas station's creaking front porch, placed his hands on his hips, and gazed across the gravel parking lot. Jenny looked up from where she sat on the Camry's hood with Mira sleeping in her lap.

She smiled and raised her eyebrows. He scowled and shook his head.

He jumped the two feet down from the porch to the lot and approached her.

"Looks like we're shit out of luck," he said. "Figures."

The stifling mid-July heat thickened by the minute. He slid a handkerchief from his back pocket and spread it over his oily face. Somewhere in the distance, the cicadas challenged the outnumbered crickets with their droning summer symphony. He returned the handkerchief to his pocket. The sinking sun's shadows hid the haggard circles that'd formed around his eyes.

He reached the car and leaned on balled fists next to her.

"There has to be *someone* who can come out and take a look at it," she said.

"Jesus, Jenny," he said. "We're in the middle of goddamn nowhere. We're screwed." He hung his head. "Damn it."

Jonathan P. Davis

He walked toward the dull two-lane road that sliced a swath through fields and farmland and the clinging stink of cow dung. At the edge of the parking lot, he stuck his hands in his pockets and looked in both endless directions.

One of the men sitting in a circle of lawn chairs at the far edge of the lot brayed behind him. William glanced over his shoulder.

There were five. All wore jeans, tee-shirts, and baseball hats. The one who'd laughed twisted the cap from a dripping bottle of Old Style and tossed it with a *clink* into the pile by the ten-gallon cooler in the center of the circle. He raised the bottle to drink but stopped when he saw William. He grinned and tipped the bottle in William's direction. William looked away and returned to the car.

"Great," he said to Jenny. "Three hundred miles south of Chicago and no mechanic." He checked the Rolex under his blue-oxford shirt sleeve: 8:13 p.m. "Looks like tomorrow's afternoon meeting is fucked, unless another county's tow truck drives by."

He slapped the hood with his palm.

"Bill!" Jenny said. "Easy. Mira's still sleeping."

He glanced through the windshield at his brown-leather briefcase on the back seat. Important people awaited its contents about the fates of Reliance State Bank employees after stock had fallen for a fourth consecutive quarter. The brass were going to lose their luster fast when they learned the information was trapped in southwestern Illinois.

William cracked his knuckles and leaned back on his heels. A sharp pain ran up the back of his right leg. He winced, removed the new Kenneth Cole shoe from his black silk-socked foot, and shook it upside down. The piece of gravel tumbled out.

"We may as well settle in," he said, "because this might be home for a night."

Jenny cradled Mira closer and kissed her forehead.

"We might have to sleep in the car," he said.

"Why don't you just ask one of them for help or a ride?" Jenny said, nodding toward the men in the lawn chairs. "They look like locals."

"Please," William said. "That's the last thing I need right now."

"Suit yourself," Jenny said. "Maybe I'll go talk to them."

"The hell you will," William said, standing straighter.

She rolled her eyes.

"Actually, I don't really mind it out here," she said. "It's peaceful . . . and quiet."

"Right."

She tilted her head at him. He hated that look: the one that said he should really learn to *just take it easy*. How nice it must have been for her to believe that a week held seven days and a day offered twenty-four hours. Listen though she might, she couldn't and wouldn't understand what it took to be *in charge*. To make influential *decisions*. To survive in a world of emotionally constipated bean-counters paid big bucks to pore over other people's mistakes.

"We wouldn't even be here if it weren't for your lunatic sister," he said. "Why did you let her con us into staying until this afternoon when you knew we had to *drive* back from southeast Missouri?"

"She needed us, Bill," Jenny said. "She's family. *We're* family. You know she's going through a bad time."

"She's *always* going through a bad time. She needs a dog and a priest, not us."

"You're being callous. Knock it off."

"What do you expect from her by now? Have you two ever heard the one about the definition of insanity? You know, doing things the same way and expecting different results? What more do *you* hope to learn from two divorces, three broken engagements, five kids, and a love affair with Stoli bottles?"

"She's family, Bill."

"She's baggage, and now I'm stuck in Shitsville because I agreed to help you with it."

"You're just in a foul mood. Take a chill pill."

"Take a chill pill." He smirked and kicked at the gravel. "If you hadn't shoved that map in my face, I would have seen the goddamn chunk of concrete in the middle of the goddamn road."

"Sure."

Her eyes still closed, Mira adjusted her position in Jenny's lap. Jenny kissed her head again.

A bell jingled over the gas-station door. A young, slim woman in a sleeveless flower-print dress emerged with a black plastic sack swinging at her side.

William watched her.

Farm-toned arms. Summer-blonde locks. Sin-red toenail polish. Shoulders tanned by days of work among the rows.

She descended the creaky porch stairs and swayed to the blue '87 Mustang convertible parked in front of the decrepit pump labeled UNLEADED. The knee-length hem of her dress lifted as she bent over the door to place the bag in the back seat.

William studied her calves and hamstrings.

He scratched his chin.

"You used to look like that, you know," he said through the side of his mouth.

Jenny giggled.

"What's so funny?"

"She's out of your league, Bill. Just because she's country doesn't mean she'd be starstruck by *you*."

He glanced back at her.

"No?"

The woman got into the car, backed out, and circled toward the road with a wake of white dust. She smiled at them both as she drove past them out of the lot.

Jenny *did* still look okay to him, even after eight years of marriage. And at thirty-six—seven years his junior—she could even still excite him too.

Sometimes.

But sustained desire no longer burned. Routine had parked its fat ass in their lives and smothered it. At least for him it had.

Yet he endured. He could have other women—many of them younger, feistier, and better equipped to please him—but he'd stuck with his wife because William Buxton was smart and exacting. Jenny was *safe*. He trusted her.

"If only all of us could be beauty queens after squeezing out an eight-pound object," she said.

He spun on her.

"That's *crap*, and you know it. What is it with people like you and the excuses? You could still look like that woman, even after *her*"—he pointed at Mira—"if you had any *discipline*. While people like you bitch and do nothing, people like me pay our dues to get what we want out of life."

"Whatever," she said, stroking Mira's hair. Mira mumbled and turned so that her mouth lay close to Jenny's breast, a B-cup that sloped beneath her short-sleeved blue shirt. "Since you're the disciplined one in the family, why don't you will yourself back to that pay phone and dial around for a motel. We're not sleeping in the car, *especially* not with Mira here."

"Hell, it might be good for her," he said. "This is a new age, remember? The era of gender equality? Isn't that what you've all been fighting for—to show that a woman can stomach anything a man can, even though you still want us to take care of you?"

He looked back at the men in the lawn chairs.

"You know what?" he said. "Maybe you're right. Maybe the townies over there have something to offer after all. Advice. Information. A beer."

He untucked his shirt and marched away.

The setting sun's lengthening shadows stretched across his path.

"I love you, Bill," Jenny said to his back, "but sometimes you can be a real jerk."

Two of the men saw him approach and alerted the others. Their laughter stopped and blew away with the same humid breeze that billowed William's shirt.

He slipped his wallet from his back pocket.

"Evening, gentlemen," he said at the edge of their circle.

The man to his instant right glanced back over his left shoulder; William saw only part of the side of his face. He wore a dirt- and sweat-stained St. Louis Cardinals cap low over his eyes, dusty denim jeans, and a red-and-black flannel shirt with the sleeves rolled up to the elbows.

"A bit warm for flannel, isn't it, friend?" William said down to him.

The man shifted in his chair and faced forward again.

"You need somethin', fella?" another said from William's left.

William stepped into their circle and looked around at them. They all appeared to have performed at least one oil change and humped to Garth Brooks songs in high school. William knew how to conduct himself among them: confidence and eloquence would always be elder statesmen amongst a ring of fools.

He removed two dollar bills from his wallet.

"I was going to ask if I might buy a beer from you," he said. "I could use the refreshment. I'd be happy to pay you for it."

He held out the bills.

"Shee-it," said the man straight ahead of him. He wore a dark-blue tee-shirt endorsing Jack's Racks of Ribs ("The Secret's in the Sauce") and a black baseball cap with the letters RAY stenciled in white. "Why don't you just go get yourself one from Mickey's fridge inside? S'colder than what we got out here."

The others chuckled. Two of them swigged from their beers.

"My name's William, Ray, and I'd rather buy a beer from you."

Ray leaned back, rubbed his chin, and looked him up and down.

"Hell," he said. "Why not, William?"

He rose and reached into the cooler. Ice cubes sloshed and rattled. He removed and held out a dripping bottle of Old Style.

William accepted the beer with his left hand and extended the bills with his right.

"This one's on me, William," Ray said, and sat down.

William's hand retracted. He folded the bills and slipped them into his front pants pocket.

"Thank you, Ray. That's very hospitable of you."

He glanced around the circle, twisted the cap off, and tossed it into the community pile.

"Would you men mind if I joined you for a few minutes?"

They looked at one another.

"Uh, sure, William," Ray said. "Donny, you wanna grab William a chair?"

"You can call me Bill," William said.

Ray nodded.

"Donny, would you get Bill here a chair?"

The man to William's immediate left stood, walked over to the fence-enclosed Dumpster a few yards behind him, and grabbed a folding lawn chair from several stacked against the right side of the enclosure.

"We keep a bunch of 'em over there," Ray said.

Donny returned with the chair, snapped it open, and set it between his and the man's to his left.

"You never know who might bop in for a chat and a cold one on a Sunday night, right Bill?" Ray said. "Sit yourself down."

"Thanks, Ray," William said. He squatted into the chair. It creaked but then held steady after he adjusted his weight.

"You men wouldn't happen to know of a roadside service, would you?" he said. "I didn't have any luck with the numbers I had. I broke an axle a little down the road back there. I asked the gas-station owner . . . Mickey?" Ray nodded. ". . . if he had any ideas. I called information too. No luck."

"Welcome to life in Tar Valley, Bill," Ray said. "Jess Paul has the only tow truck in town, and he don't work on Sundays."

"That's what Mickey said."

"Jess might have made an exception up until two years ago," Ray said. "But then he found Jesus, and now his Sundays belong to his family and the Lord. Lodging's pretty light here too. There's a motel out by Highway 50. S'about a twenty-five minute drive from here.

Maybe me or one of the fellas can take you out there . . . if we ain't too loaded, that is."

"That would be kind of you, Ray," William said.

"Ain't no guarantee there's a vacancy, seein' as how it's the only motel in this part of the county. But it's worth a try. You might want to call 'em first."

"That's sound advice. I appreciate it."

They eyed each other a moment.

"So where you from, Bill?" Ray said. He crossed a thick-booted foot over his knee.

"Chicago," William said. "North Shore."

"You folks surf up there?" said the man to his left.

William looked at him.

"Excuse me?"

"Don't mind Roger," Ray said. "He's already had about six of them Old Styles, and he's funny in the head to start with. Ain't that right, Roger?"

"Craziest bastard south of Macomb," he said. He flashed William a smile stained with nicotine.

The other men chuckled.

William looked at Ray again. He was tall—William guessed six-five or -six—and lean, maybe as light as one-eighty. His long legs shot from his pelvis and bent at bony knees that almost stood higher than his waist while he sat.

"Don't let us get under your nerves, Bill," Ray said. "We're just havin' some fun as we're apt to do. What you have here is quality entertainment on a Tar Valley Sunday, outside of what's on cable TV, or what might be on deck in the bedroom, if you catch what I mean."

"I think I do," William said.

The circle fell silent a moment. The man in the Cardinals cap sank another inch in his chair. William noticed he wasn't drinking.

"You guys lived here most of your lives, I take it?" William said.

Ray nodded.

"'Fraid so, Bill," he said. He swept his arm over his head and around the circle. "When your dad and most of the dads before him make a family in Tar Valley, chances are you'll do the same."

He twisted in his chair and pointed back at a red farmhouse with a soaring silo on the edge of a cornfield about a half-mile away.

"See that place?"

"Yes," William said.

"Shit like that gets into your head and your blood. You grow up here, you see, smell, and feel *everything*. You get so you can tell one neighbor's stink from another's, just by the way it acts in the wind. Everything talks to you down here, Bill. Even the corn standin' tall in the rain."

William sipped his beer.

"You look like a man who keeps himself busy," Ray continued.

William shrugged.

"I try to work hard."

"Ever sat in the middle of twenty acres for hours at night with nothin' but you and your thoughts?"

William shook his head.

"You get to know yourself," Ray said. "Well. And after time, in a place like this with other people just like you, you get to know them too." He sipped his beer. "Hell, I'll tell you right now that Todd here . . ."—he pointed left—". . . he still wears half a bottle 'a Brut to take his wife out to dinner at the diner. He's known her since grade seven. Ain't that right, Todd?"

"Eat my ass," Todd said.

William placed him at his own height—five-nine—but better built and ten years younger. He had blue eyes, fair skin with a few minor acne scars, and short, brown hair parted to the right. He wore brown-leather work boots, a gray tee-shirt with a red Budweiser logo on the chest, and acid-washed Levi's that frayed around the cuffs.

"You married, Ray?" William said.

Ray spit and laughed.

"Two times too many, Bill," he said. "Been divorced from the first six years and the second for three. But those ladies and I did produce four beautiful kids, and I gotta thank them both for that. Three girls and a boy, the oldest bein' eight now."

"Damn straight," Roger said. "Those are fine children you got, Ray."

"Thanks, Rog," Ray said. "Roger doesn't have any rugrats of his own, though him and Melissa get the blue ribbon for tryin'." He leaned forward and lowered his voice. "He ain't got enough pulp in his orange juice, if you catch what I mean."

"I do," William said. He raised his beer to drink and was surprised at how light it was. He nodded toward the cooler.

"Say, Ray, would I impose if I asked for another?"

Ray waved him off.

"Hell, no," he said. "This here's a community cooler so long as you help fill it once it's empty."

"I believe I can meet those terms," William said.

Ray rose and fished him another Old Style. William drained the last of his first and set the empty on the ground to the right of his chair just as the others appeared to be doing.

"How about you, Bill?" Ray said as William leaned back. "I take it that's your wife over there?"

William glanced over his shoulder. Jenny remained on the hood of the car with Mira in her lap while reading a paperback novel.

"Yes, that's my wife, Jenny," William said, facing Ray again. "And my daughter, Mira. She turned four in May."

"That's great, Bill," Ray said. He played with his bottle's peeling label for a moment. "Can't say there's anything better for a man than to have children with a woman he loves . . . and who's true."

"Speak for yourself," Donny said.

The others chuckled.

"You'll have to pardon Donny here," Ray said. "He's sore on the subject. You see, his wife ran off, along with his only son, to be with Jack Cooper 'bout three years ago. Bless his stubborn heart, Donny went to the county divorce court to try to get more time with Donny Junior and less money removed from his wages, but the legal bench doesn't view professional drinkin' as hard and focused work like we do. Lookin' for sympathy from that judge was like tryin' to get a rock to give you a ride across water."

"Piss off," Donny said. "That bitch screwed me royal without bein' fair and you know it. I shoulda shot her dead when I had the chance."

"Now, now, Donny," Ray said. "No need for talk like that, especially when there's a guest."

Donny scowled and sipped his beer.

"Well, all I know is Melissa would never pull that shit with me," Roger said, holding his beer in his lap with both hands. "That's because I treat her the *right* way. She don't need to prowl like a cat that ain't been fixed. It ain't what you did, Donny. It's what you *didn't* do that made her scoot."

Donny leaned left and pointed his half-empty bottle across William at Roger.

"How do you know, Roger? How do you know what she's up to when you ain't around? I don't care what any man says: ain't none gifted enough to figure out a woman's head. It's like when you *should* be gettin' mean on her, you're gettin' nice instead, maybe to make something right. Then while you're bein' nice, she's thinkin' less of you because you're not actin' like a *real* man should."

He retracted his bottle, drank from it, and relaxed in his chair.

"Deep down every woman wants a man who can *take charge*," Donny said. "A man with the bull-swingin' balls to not listen when she gripes about what she wants but can't get. Women fuckin' *love* a man who don't give in. It's just nature's way. Ain't nothin' any of us can do about it."

"Amen," William said.

Ray smirked: first at William, then at Donny.

"You're still off," he said to Donny, "but at least you're movin' in the right direction. They *do* got us, man"—he grabbed himself and gave a good yank—"right here. And I'll tell you something else that might ring your bell. They've known from day one that they're stronger. That's why we always get licked, even when we think we're ahead. It's been a *koo-day-ta* generations in the making. Hundreds, thousands 'a years they've let us run the circus while they shoveled the shit. Some even take a fist in the face and then smile when we say we're sorry. But they never forget: not *ever*. That's because they're smart, and they know a lot of us are just thin and empty glasses with a crack in the side. They bide their time until the crack is long and deep enough so that all it takes is a tap or a noise to make the glass break and fall to pieces."

He paused, thought, and sipped from his beer.

"In the end, no matter how tough he acts and how much ass he kicks, a king has to have respect if his rule is gonna last," he continued. "If he dumps on people too much, they'll turn on him, and he won't be a king anymore. We live in a new world, my friends. The wise will accept that we'll have to share it or else go live in the ocean."

Donny wiped his face with his hand. The others stared at the ground.

William sat straighter. Ray saw the spark in his eye.

"So you're speaking of a revolution, are you?" William said, crossing his legs. "You're saying that women have been preparing, patiently, to rebel against a dimmer opponent all of these years. Why do you suppose they chose *now* of all times to rise up? Why not a few hundred years ago, when, if really they're stronger, they could have prevented future women from having to suffer?"

Ray scratched his chin and then shrugged.

"Can't answer that one, Bill," Ray said, "any more than I can tell you why Donny's wife waited years to skip out on him, why my two marriages tanked but gave me great kids, or why Roger's wife thinks he's Don Frickin' Juan with a banjo." He reflected for a moment. "Maybe the answers lie in us. You and me." He gestured at the others with his thumb. "Them. Maybe *we're* different now. Or if we're still the same, they just stopped waiting for us to change on our own. We'd have to give them credit there. If it'd been us waiting for *them* to come around, they may have had a whole two weeks instead of a few thousand years."

"I don't mean to wear out my welcome too quickly," William said, "but I think we should *all* be frank in this conversation, which, by the way, is open and interesting, much to your credit."

"S'only way we know how to do it here, Bill."

"Of course," William said, and smiled. "You're right about one thing, Ray. We *are* different today. They're rebelling now because *we've* allowed them to. They might feel good about themselves, but they wouldn't have piss in a can if we didn't first set down the can to be pissed in. Power as I see it is a co-dependent relationship. On the one side, you have an influence that can impose its will over another's despite the other's resistance. The influence weighs too much for the influenced to avoid it without consequences. Resistance offers only the useless pride of upsetting a mightier foe, which leads only to pain or discomfort. Think of trying to stand up to Nazi Germany as a Jew or even telling off your asshole boss at the job you can't afford to lose.

"On the other side, power is what you *give* to another in exchange for something you want or need. The other has something of great perceived value to you, whether it be money, safety, sex, or the ability to give you more power. The desire for assets or benefits exceeds and replaces the will for self-determination. The other's influence over you then digs fox holes in your head and repels any of your attempts to reclaim control of yourself.

"Women haven't discovered how to overturn us, Ray." He leaned forward with his elbows on his knees. "They still need and depend on us. *We* are still the hunter-gatherers called by nature to provide. So what you're talking about is not a rebellion, or a revolution. It's a temporary redistribution in the percentage of women who believe they can change the natural order.

"The reason for that is that we, men, have let them believe that they have something for which we will sacrifice. But I guarantee you now that women will resume their roles before the current era comes to a close. You can toy with evolution, but you can't alter it. Women's drive for equality or even advantage will sputter. They've tried to add bad data to their hard-wired genetic codes. They weren't made to lead or control men. Not before, not now, not ever." He leaned back and sipped his beer. "It's that simple."

Ray stared at him with his hand over his mouth.

"It's clear you went to college, Bill," he said.

He winked at William.

"That's a whole lot of brain wind you're passin'. I'm impressed, 'specially since my nads are pumped from havin' finished high school. Hell, for all I know, you might already be thinkin' that if I ever had an idea richer than yours, it'd die of bein' so lonely. I'll lift my skirt to you there."

William shook his head: *I didn't mean it that way.*

"I ain't got a degree and a big-city salary," Ray continued, "but I still got eyes and ears. They tell me what I need to know. I can figure out the rest.

"None of this shit is about power, or evolution. It also ain't about Venus and Mars. It's about whether you can find and keep what's true in your life by first gettin' over yourself, and then bein' true to yourself. When it comes to us and women, the thoughts we have, and the choices we make, well, they have consequences."

Footsteps crunched on the gravel behind them. William turned in his chair. Still half asleep, Mira lay alone on the hood. Jenny mounted the steps to the pay phone on the porch.

William turned back around.

Ray watched Jenny making a call, sipped his beer, and squinted at William.

"I know what can happen when a man turns his back on what's real and true for what ain't," he said.

He scratched his cheek and gazed past William at the darkening sky.

"What time is it, Todd?" he said.

Todd checked the Timex on his left wrist.

"A couple frogs' dicks short of eight-thirty."

"Just in time," Ray said.

Ray looked toward the road. William twisted in his chair to follow his stare.

Jenny returned to the car. Mira still slept on the hood. Jenny removed a blanket and a small suitcase from the back seat and set them on the trunk.

"It's some coincidence that you're here when you are, Bill," Ray said, "because in just a few minutes, you'll have yourself a first-hand look at a long-standing Tar Valley ritual."

"Ritual?"

"You'll see an old man come walkin' toward us from that same road you came in on. His name's Jed Turner, as in Jedidiah H. He was born in Tar Valley before the Great Depression, and as far as I know, he ain't never been outside of it except to fight in war number two."

Ray rose to retrieve another beer from the cooler.

"Okay, boys," he said while sloshing the ice, "I think we're good for maybe forty-five minutes or so. Think we oughta stock up before Mickey closes at nine?"

"I'll grab another case in a few," Donny said.

"And of course I'll pay," William said.

Donny gave him a thumbs-up and a tight-lipped smile.

"And here's the funny thing about Jed's never leavin' Tar Valley except when the government ordered him to," Ray continued. "His farm sits right on the Tar Valley-Roquefort border. All he's got to do is step over the far west edge of his property and he's in another zip code. But he doesn't, and won't."

"Why do you suppose that is?" William said.

He glanced back at Jenny again. The suitcase was open. She folded the blanket and placed it inside. She then zipped the suitcase shut and returned with it to the front of the car. She set it on the ground and sat next to where Mira still slept on the hood.

"You guys gettin' ready to leave somewhere, Bill?" Ray said.

William rubbed his mouth and stared at the ground. His eyebrows furrowed.

He looked at Ray.

"Not that I'm aware of," he said.

"Okay, Bill," Ray said, "Whatever you say. Back to Jed and why he won't step two feet out of town. Some people just come to know and love a place. It gets into their blood, and their blood gets into it, and over time, they start givin' each other transfusions."

He sipped his beer.

William's eyes darted from Ray's to the Toyota.

"We *know* this place, Bill," Ray said. "Who's usin' what kind of fertilizer. The exact angle of the summer sun at two p.m. The price of every beer special at John Carmon's tavern on Center Street. The names, includin' the middle ones, of every child at the elementary school."

William looked at the slouched and quiet man in the Cardinals cap. It remained low over his eyes and still concealed much of his face. The others hadn't addressed him or mentioned his name.

"How about you, Bill?" Ray said. "You know that kind of stuff up by where you live?"

William shrugged.

"Is it necessary?"

Ray smiled.

"As for me," he continued, "I've spent my time outside of Tar Valley. Not much to the north, though. Been to Chicago only once, when my dad took me to a game at Wrigley Field. That trip plus a couple others through the collar counties were all I needed to figure out how people drift apart once they park their cars up there. It's not that they're bad people. It's just, well, a lot of them tend to start lookin' *in* a lot more. At themselves. *For* themselves. And when they do look out, it's usually to judge other people. They might act like friends and neighbors, but their hearts aren't always as you think you see 'em. That's because the cities and suburbs offer people more *stuff*, and the more stuff people have, the more they believe that deep down other people would want them to lose some of it. They also need to keep stackin' stuff, because that's what makes them feel safer."

William looked around. Each of the other men stared at the ground or their feet.

"The cities and suburbs also give them chances to hide if they lose somebody's trust," Ray said. "But not here. We might have land and space, but you can't go many places where someone won't find you, unless of course you move well out of town."

He swigged from his beer.

"Nope, when you betray someone down here, you gotta live close to your actions. Deal with 'em too, especially if you break someone's heart."

"Shut up, Ray!" Donny said in a loud whisper. "Here 'e comes!"

William turned around in his chair again. Jenny glanced at him and looked away. Mira, now awake, slid down to the ground and leaned against her mother's dangling feet.

And just beyond them both, William saw the tall, slump-shouldered elderly man emerging from the southbound lane. He wore a black felt hat, a dirt- and oil-stained white button-down shirt, faded denim overalls, and large, shuffling black boots. His right hand gripped freshly picked flowers.

"I appreciate what you're saying, Ray," William said. "You paint a nice portrait of small-town charm. But I'd like to contribute some reality. A man is destined to fail unless he's willing and able to change and learn through the years. If he's stuck as the same person in the same place for all of his life, he *will* get lazy, and complacent. He may as well commit suicide. Any man with self-worth will remove himself from whatever holds him back. That includes the bonds of small-town living. Maybe leaving Tar Valley is what that man must but cannot do. Maybe failure is his destiny."

"Another spunky choice of words, Bill," Ray said, "but they come from a man who looks like he's perhaps broken more hearts than's had done to his own."

William looked away, thought it over, and shrugged.

"Perhaps," he said.

"I sense you've stayed on the move most of your life," Ray continued. "You can't sit still for long. Too much to do. Too much to *achieve*. Am I right?"

William raised an eyebrow and shrugged again.

"You learned to think and speak real well. You practiced it too, on people. It's helped you win respect and opportunity. You've also been real careful about relationships. You don't let people get too close, or see too much, or they might figure out you're just a guy, like the rest of us. And if that happened, well, you might not be in charge all the time."

William simply stared at him.

"Only problem, Bill, is that a man in charge and on the go often forgets that we all need a place to call home. A place we know inside-out and belong to. One where a few people might even like us because we *ain't* fucking perfect, or bent on havin' everyone think we're important."

Ray sipped his beer.

"How far can a man run from himself, Bill, and for how long? If a man has to spend his whole life in one spot to learn just one goddamn lesson that means something, then so be it. It takes more courage to build a past and try to live with it than to cut the cord and leave it."

William smiled with his face but glared with his eyes.

Ray nodded toward the road. William looked back.

The old man had reached their latitude and was now crossing toward the opposite field. The purple-black sky offered just enough waning light by which to see him shuffle southeast toward a large willow tree next to a pond. Its drooping branches brushed and dipped into the water. He went beneath them and sat on the wrought-iron bench by the trunk.

He set the flowers next to him and removed his hat, revealing his sweaty, shiny pate. He wiped his brow with the back of his hand and turned sideways as if to speak to one who was already there.

The sky blended to black. An outer bulb protected by steel mesh flashed on at the upper right of the station's front door.

William glanced at the Toyota: its interior light had ignited as well.

Jenny removed her purse from the front passenger seat and slipped it over her shoulder. She then lifted the small suitcase with her left hand and took Mira's hand with her right.

They walked toward the road.

The men in the circle all watched.

At the edge of the lot, Jenny set the suitcase down and pulled up the handle to roll it on its wheels. They started heading north.

"Uh, you want to find out where they're goin', Bill?" Ray said.

William watched a little longer and turned back around in his chair.

"No," he said, and sipped his beer. "They'll be back. She just wants to see if I'll call her bluff. She's been losing the argument all day, so now she's resorting to her sixth-grade tactical plan. When in doubt, storm out."

Ray stared at him.

"You sure about that?"

William stared back.

"I'm sure."

"I hope they have good eyeglasses and pairs 'a walkin' shoes," Ray said, "because if she ain't lookin' to hitch a ride, I'm guessin' she might be bound for the motel out on Route 50 I told you about. Dark as hell along the way. Barely more than a rock to squat on too if they get tired."

William waved him off.

"Fuck it," William said. "She's pouting, but she's not *dumb*. Like I said, they'll be back. Mind if I grab another beer?"

"A'course not."

William finished his current bottle, set it down next to his other empty, and retrieved a new one from the cooler.

"Donny," Ray said, "you better get that case before Mickey shuts shop. Probably ain't open but another ten minutes."

"Yeah," Donny said. "I almost forgot."

William stood and removed a twenty from his wallet.

"Here," he said, extending the bill to Donny. "I said I'd cover it. Please keep the change."

"Why, thank you . . . Bill," Donny said.

He accepted William's cash and jogged away.

"I hope you're right about your wife," Ray said. "Because as a man who's been married twice, I'd say that if a woman takes more steps than will get her out of the front yard, she means business."

"Thanks, Ray," William said, "but once again, I'm not worried."

The men all sat and drank in silence for a moment.

"So what's with the old man and the willow tree?" William said.

Ray raised his hips from his chair and slid a pouch of Apple Jack from his right back pocket. He inserted a chunk in his mouth, gnawed on it, and spit into an empty bottle.

"Sorry, bad habit, I know," he said. "Started when I was sixteen. Ain't kicked it yet."

He spit in his bottle again: *pa-toonk!*

"As far as old Jed Turner," Ray continued, "from the looks of things, you might think they should call in the butterfly nets, the way he's sittin' there talkin' to air by himself beneath them droopin' branches."

William shrugged and shook his head: *I'm open-minded.*

"You'd think he was queer as Kool-Aid from a cow's teat, bein' all of eighty-plus years old and walkin' over two miles on tired legs out here from his farm. One night early on, when I was younger and a lot less patient, I even almost went over there to ask him what the hell his problem was. I mean, why couldn't the man just drive his old Chevy to the willow instead of walk the stretch slower than a snail. It just, I don't know . . . bothered me."

Donny returned with a case of Old Style cans and transferred them to the cooler.

"Thanks, Donny," Ray said.

Donny nodded, cracked open a can, and plopped back down in his chair.

"Then one day—and this is when I still lived at home, mind you—my dad got so sick of me chewin' it over that he pushed back from the dinner table and jerked his thumb for me to follow him outside. Out in the dooryard, he pulled up a couple of choppin' blocks and told me to sit. And it was then, while the sun finished takin' a dive, that he told me the truth about old Jed Turner."

William glanced back across the road. The full moon's reflection made a shimmering pirate-patch eye in the pond. The night and the tree now concealed the old man.

"That willow you're lookin' at over there, where Jed's sittin'," Ray continued. "Used to be called Lovers' Willow. Up until maybe 1975, if a man and a woman thought enough of each other, it was serious Tar Valley tradition for them to take the walk and sit beneath it. It meant their love was true and you could bet the family savings that they wouldn't split up any time soon. It was especially popular after war number two, when the boys who made it back dropped their bags and ran straight to the faces they'd spanked off to for as long as the metal rained down. My dad was just a boy then, but he told me it was somethin' special to spot a couple makin' the walk to the willow to say their promises. Was enough to bring a grown man to tears."

Ray spit into his bottle. Donny sipped his beer. Roger bit at his thumbnail.

William covered his mouth with his hand.

"Before his tour in the Pacific, Jed had been regular with a local named Jane McShaw," Ray continued. "My dad told me that they wasn't all hot and bothered the way lots of young people can be, always lookin' for ways they can make out or grab at where it feels real good. They were friends in the true sense. You saw it in their eyes and the way they spoke to each other." He paused to be pensive. "They were kind and gentle and respectful without all of the show that often comes with bein' in love. One would have to believe that they were gonna last a long, long time."

"Yeah, too bad she was a nut job," Todd said.

"Shut up, you ignoramus," Ray said. "Quit messin' with the goddamn story."

Todd smirked, gave him the finger, and drank from his beer.

"What idiot here meant to say is that most people knew that Jane had emotional problems. Her father was an unhappy guy that used to whack her now and then. That sure didn't help her much, but I also understand she was real-deal mentally ill. The head doctors would have argued she suffered from depression and anxiety both. If they'd had it back then, she probably could have used some of the Prozac or the Paxil or whatever shit they recommend besides cold beers nowadays to make people feel better.

"But love's a pill too, and it did wonders for Jane. Before she and Jed became an item, she mostly sulked around and kept quiet. In town, at home, at school. You know how folks with the depression have that *look*, like they're always waitin' for a storm that's still a few days away.

"That's until she met Jed when they were juniors in high school, 1943. He was probably the first boy who A, approached her for a conversation and B, had the patience not to judge her as most young people did. Of course he scared her at first, because she couldn't make sense of the attention. But he bided his time. Stayed friendly and consistent. And before long, they ate lunch together, walked home from school together, and listened to the radio and shared ice-cream sodas on the weekend. They even held hands out in public, so people knew they was a pair. Jane was, well . . . happy. The old-timers say they never saw her smile like she did when she was with Jed. She loved him. He was genuine to her, and he helped her forget the demons in her mind."

Ray spit in his bottle and wiggled his jaw to adjust his chunk of leaf.

"They graduated in June '44, and then Jed got his government notice. He wound up servin' in the Pacific. He didn't come back until September '45, after they'd given the Japs their double dose of radiation. One would think he'd have been ready to jump off that bus and see Jane standin' right there, not a feeling or memory out of place, her love for him ever the same."

He chewed on his leaf. William sipped his beer. Todd looked up at the stars.

"He *was* glad, and woulda stayed that way perhaps for all of time if one thing hadn't changed in Tar Valley since he'd left. That change was the August '45 arrival of Betty Deshayne, the niece of Buck Deshayne, who owned a few acres on the west end of town.

"From what my dad told me, Betty Deshayne fell from a beauty tree and took all the bark with 'er. She was a pure blonde thoroughbred and just nineteen years young to boot. *All* the boys noticed, and as you'd expect, the Betty Deshayne Hate Club built up fast among the other girls.

"What the guys didn't say around their wives and girlfriends sure made noise in the bars and pool halls and under open tractor hoods. The talk turned to who was gonna be the lucky bastard that got to her first. Bein' new *and* pretty, she liked the attention but didn't talk too much. She had that air of *confidence*. Like she knew she was the hottest ass in town but at the same time tried to act like she wasn't. She felt the stares and whispers and didn't mind them at all. Her mystery grew hair and legs of its own."

William glanced back at the dark, open, empty road.

Jenny still thought she was winning.

She wasn't.

"Jed Turner was the last guy in Tar Valley you'd expect to be moved by Betty," Ray continued. "He came from a good Christian family and wasn't prone to passion the way a lot of us are. He was solid. Upright. *Practical.* He understood that honest, stable, red-blooded friendship between a man and a woman was as hard to come by as a palm tree in Illinois. He'd been loyal to Jane from day one. Most believe he even behaved himself overseas."

He spit in his bottle: *spink!*

Roger helped himself to an Old Style from the cooler.

The man in the Cardinals cap continued to neither move nor make a sound.

"But goddamn if lust don't swing a fat bat," Ray said. "And on one early October afternoon, it squared up and smacked him good. Jed and Betty Deshayne locked eyes for longer than a comfortable second that day, and things would never be the same for a few different people."

Ray ran a thumb along the side of his spit bottle.

"Back then," he said, "on Saturdays, a lot of folks used to hang out at Joe Darby's drugstore in the middle of town. From late April until about Halloween, Joe would set up tables in front of his shop so people could relax and shoot the shit. They did just that until it got too cold to do so. Joe figured it'd be good for business if customers felt at home there, and for the most part, he was right, because they wound up buyin' stuff from him all day long.

"Some of them played cards for money, and while Joe didn't care for it, he kept quiet so long as they fed his register and didn't get too out of hand. Well, that one October afternoon, Jed walked from his family's farm to Joe's drugstore to buy himself a paper. There was a big poker game goin' on when he got there. Now, Jed wasn't a gamblin' man—his Christianity went against it—but he did like playin' cards. The fun for the gamblers had always been not to go after his money, but to see a Biblical man jump from Jesus to jacks for an hour or two. They also never had to push a dime his way, because he didn't make 'em pay when he won. Better yet, bein' an honest Christian, he ponied up whenever he lost.

"He joined the game after buyin' his paper. Won himself three straight hands and was about to take another when *she* strolled past them and through the front door. At first, Jed didn't look even though everyone else needed a reel to roll up their tongues.

"When she came back out, she stopped right next to Jed, most likely because he was the only one not payin' attention. He finally gave in and looked.

"Now he's screwed. He can't take his eyes off her, so he's in a panic. Don't know what to say or do. Scary thing is, she's lookin' at him too. Straight on. Smilin'. His heart's poundin' like a humpin' jackrabbit's. She pulls back that long, blonde hair, lets it fall, and of all the things the Lord would have her say, she asks him for a cigarette."

The other men snickered—all except the Cardinals fan, who remained low in his seat with his chin down.

"You believe that?" Ray continued. "So of course he says he don't smoke. Then he asks why don't she just go inside and buy her own. She says she's outta money after buyin' the stuff for her aunt's and uncle's pantry. So Jed, bein' a good Christian, he goes into the store and gets that girl her cigarettes. He comes back out and hands 'em to her. The fellas outside keep playin' cards but they're watchin' real close. She steps toward Jed with her eyes up and says that's the nicest thing anyone's done since she moved into town. She plants one on his cheek, whispers in his ear, and strolls away.

"The gamblers start laughin' and givin' him shit. And Jed, poor bastard, he had to be scared out of his mind. What would Jane say if the kiss got back to her? There he was, sittin' at a poker table with three aces in his hand and two sexy red lips on his face. The guys busted his balls to find out what she'd said to him, but Jed wouldn't tell. He only touched his cheek and stared at where she'd disappeared. I don't think Jed slept well that night. I don't think he's slept well ever since."

William looked back toward the willow. The old man remained obscured beneath it.

The gas station's front door opened. A fiftyish-looking man stepped out.

"Closin' up and headin' home, Mickey?" Donny said.

"Yessir," the man said. "I'll leave the porch light on for you boys."

"Thanks, Mickey," Ray said. "We'll be sure to clean up before we head home."

The man waved, locked the front door, and left the parking lot on foot.

"Mickey lives about a half-mile from here," Ray said.

William nodded.

How far had Jenny traveled by then?

He had to hold his ground, even if it meant she slept in a motel and they battled it out in the morning. He hadn't deserved her tantrum. Giving in would rubber-stamp her behavior.

Ray spit in his bottle. Roger set down his empty and grabbed another beer.

"So a few days passed after the kiss heard around Tar Valley," Ray said, "and things went bad for Jed real fast. He spent more time in bed, worked less on the farm. Cut back on his walks into town. He even stopped readin' the Bible. Worse yet, he put space between him and Jane. As often happens, speculation became rumors and then those began to act like the truth. And when half-baked truth spreads through a small town, it stays about as private as screwin' next to the pulpit on a Sunday morning. Of course Jane heard all of it too. The anxiety almost killed her.

"Now at this point, you might expect her to approach him about it directly. Loyalty and trust were on the line, and all over a pretty little missy who'd said thank you outside a drugstore."

Ray paused to pull the plug from his mouth. He plopped it on the ground next to his empties.

"The news about Betty and Jed had made Jane's heart move counterclockwise, and it messed her up bad. At the same time, Jane was strong and stubborn as folks with the depression often are and have to be. She didn't show how much she was slippin', at least not in public. People of course still stuck their noses in it, which stirred her up, but she did her best to hang tough. She also tried to see Jed as Adam fallen from grace and just as bound to make a mistake. And while beauty and charm were stacked up against her, she still had time and memories on her side, and those can still kick ass in the ring. She had the mind to consider that if their love was true, he'd come back on his own. If she tried to close in and hold on, she'd only push him away."

William rubbed his eyes.

Was Jenny walking, hitching a ride, or admitting her folly and returning to him?

"Two weeks pass without a peep from Jed," Ray continued. "Jane's tryin' not to melt down. She won't go after him yet, but she's scared enough to start sniffin' from the outside in from as close as she can. She talks to his friends and family. She learns that Jed *ain't* been sorting out his thoughts alone, but rather seein' Betty whenever he can. As to what they did when together, nobody knew, which made it ten times worse for Jane. It didn't bother her so much that Jed and Betty might be gettin' physical by now—women handle that a little better than guys do—but it did gnarl her good that she might be losin' his heart."

Ray paused and moved his tongue along the tobacco-chew side of his mouth.

"Another week without Jed makes Jane McShaw a wreck. Now people can tell she's dying inside, and worst part is, only Jed can bring her back to life. But Jed's head's out with the stars, so Jane's pain is long and slow. She looks bad, pale, sick, like she can't eat or sleep. She's losin' weight. She knows she's at a nasty fork in the road. Down one path, she can try to win him back with all she's got left. Down the other, she simply has to cut him loose. But to do that *well,* she has to write him off for real and, in theory, for good. She loses herself down one lane and Jed down the other. If you can't appreciate the pain of that choice, then you ain't ever been truly in love."

He reached into the cooler and fished out a beer.

"The story got thicker and deeper just around the time Jane decided what to do," he said, cracking open the can. "Jane got along nicely with Jed's sister, Kate, and it was Kate who knocked on Jane's front door one early evenin' mid-November. Kate told Jane that Betty's uncle, Buck, had been by the Turner farm the day before with his hat off and his head hung low. He'd apologized for stoppin' their dinner, but what news he carried was important. He'd known the Turners many years on account that his daddy and Jed's daddy's daddy had grown up workin' with earth and shit just like the rest of 'em had.

"Of course Mr. Turner let him in and sat him in the front room. Kate finished her dinner, excused herself from the table, and pretended to keep busy where she could hear their conversation. She picked up that Buck knew about Jed and his niece and that he was sorry about any trouble it might have caused. He'd approached Betty about it, but as he said then, young people get harder to talk to with every generation that follows.

"Main on his mind, and what he wanted to discuss with Mr. Turner, was that he'd also seen Betty with Tom Crockett. Now anyone who knew Tom Crockett, which was everyone, understood that was bad news in the brew vat. Tom was the toughest, meanest guy in Tar Valley. His father was an ornery human bottle of whisky, and you needed only glance at his mother to think that any time in her womb had to be hell. It also didn't help that Tom was big and built, even when he was a kid. He started kickin' ass when he was about ten or so, and by the time he reached fifteen, he was thumpin' on the *grown-ups* who pissed him off. The smarter folks stayed at least twenty feet away from him, especially when he became of legal drinkin' age. Those who did get in his way at the wrong time paid the hard price and quickly spread the word to the wise."

Ray sipped his beer and then pointed south with the bottle.

"The Crocketts lived on a big corn field you would have passed about two miles down on the west side. Wasn't a worse place you could imagine to live in. Tom's folks were nasty, like I've said, but all the same even they came to be afraid of him. Hell, some of the seniors around here today can tell you about a thump they took or a scar they still wear from bein' near Tom when he lost a hand at cards or dropped a beer because he was too drunk to hold it.

"Funny thing about Tom though, was that for all his rage and poison blood, he was quite a ladies' man. I've already said he was tough and dangerous, and we know the ladies love both, particularly when they're young. But he was a handsome guy too. I guess plenty of women liked him, although those who got close to him always came to regret it. Bein' who he was, he forced himself on a lot of them, and any men in their lives, brothers and daddies included, were too afraid to do much about it."

Ray paused again. Each of the rest of the men—including the quiet Cardinals fan—focused on a different point around themselves: the stars; a leaping cricket; a tree's rustling leaves; an old, bent beer-bottle cap on the ground. They could probably recite Ray's story by then, yet, William noticed, they acted as if they listened for the first time.

"Tom *did* have a soft spot in his heart for one thing," Ray said. "His tractor. He loved that machine more than anything. He washed it, polished it, tuned it up every few weeks. Christ, he even talked to it. The one way to pray for a peaceful conversation with Tom was to bring it up, because that was sure to lower the temp on the flames from his ears. It was a miracle of goddamn technology, he'd say. Genius made into metal to tame the wild and remove some of the pain from the laborer's ass. That red, hulkin' beauty did the work of a hundred men under a poundin' sun and didn't bitch once about it. She was big and strong and proud just like Tom, and she finished each brutal day coolin' off under the moon as if she hadn't worked at all. He loved that tractor because he understood it. They were both cursed *and* blessed because they were simple *and* powerful, and that same doo-al-i-tee made them lords in a court of smaller things.

"So you can imagine the fear it put into Buck. Tom and Betty had some kind of romance, and whether it was real, just sexual, or simply Betty teasin' one more boy, I'm not sure. What I do know is that Tar Valley's resident hurricane had a thing for her. He even brought her flowers and candy. And if you can believe this without soilin' your shorts, he penned a fuckin' *poem* for her, though I can't imagine it moved many mountains, as Tom was mostly illiterate.

"Buck wasn't as afraid for Betty as he was for Jed, which was why he went to the Turner's farm. He knew that if Tom cared for somethin' besides his tractor, he meant *business*. Betty had Tom on one string and Jed on another. The two were bound to be yanked until they met in the middle, and that couldn't be good for Jed. For the time being, Betty was wily enough to keep them unaware of the other even though much of Tar Valley knew some of the story. But when Tom *did* find out that Jed and Betty were *also* an item, there was gonna be a collision, and Jed was bound to bear the worst of it."

William scratched his chin and looked at his feet.

Could Jenny and Mira be road kill, or trapped in the back seat of a transient's rusty Chevy with stolen license plates?

"It worked out for Jed for a little while that Tom was his competition," Ray said. "Tom didn't have any real friends, just people he got drunk and started fights with, so he wasn't always close to rumors and inside information. Jed learned about Tom faster than Tom learned about him, but Jed was too whipped to keep his head. He couldn't steer clear of trouble and settle things as he ought to with Jane."

"And where exactly *is* Jane while all of this is going on?" William said, opening another beer. A slow and mellow buzz had kicked in. He liked it. It helped him . . . erase certain parts of his mind.

"I'm gettin' to that," Ray said. "The next part has always been the hardest to tell even though it all happened more 'n twenty years before I was a squiggle in my daddy's nut. It gets to *me* just thinkin' about it, so I can't imagine the hell it raises in Jed Turner's head."

He took a mouthful of beer.

"You see, when tragedy hits two people in love, a bubble pops and drops a load of wake-up that makes them decide how much their thing is worth it. No more games. No more la-la. You suck it up or move on. Jed's and Jane's moment of truth defined who loved who and how much. Jed's head was full of Betty, so by then he couldn't see Jane even if you slapped half-mile visors on his face. A hot chick can be worse than cocaine for the mind, and Jed kept goin' despite the skull and crossbones. He pitched Jane like a rotten ear of corn and stayed the course in his ronday-voo with a full-blown Crockett disaster.

"Poor fella. Sure we could talk about what an idiot he was and what he should or shouldn't have done, but then we'd be chock full 'a shit. We've all been there. We've all ignored the voice of reason that told us to haul ass from the fire in the hole. We've all walked through the high flames of hell for a beautiful woman who's nothin' but trouble.

"Christian though he was, Jed just couldn't get past his desire. Jane, on the other hand, couldn't think about anything other than *him*. By then, she'd already forgotten herself. She knew the whole deal about Jed and Tom and Betty, but she cared only of what might happen to Jed. She loved him with her soul, not her pride."

The Cardinals fan moved in his seat. William waited for him to show more life or speak, but the shadow-man only fell still again and blended back into the blanket of night.

"As I understand it," Ray continued, "a few days after Kate Turner told Jane what she knew, Jane went to Joe Darby's drugstore to pick up some stuff for her folks. The one thing I haven't yet told you is that back in those days, Joe also owned the only place to drink in town. It was right next to the drugstore. That's another big reason lots of the boys liked to play cards over there. You could enter the bar either by the main entrance or through batwing doors from the drugstore. Joe often let payin' customers bring beers out for the card games so long as they didn't wander off the property. The local police let his policy be. Sure, it was gamblin' and open liquor outside an establishment, but this is Tar Valley we're talkin' about. As you can tell . . ." He waved his arm in an arc. ". . . things are a little different down here. Hell, if it weren't for your axle, you probably would have lived the rest of your life without ever knowin' we're here."

William simply looked at him.

Ray raised his bottle in a toasting gesture and then sipped from it.

"Darby's old bar is Bob's Tavern now," he said. "Same building, probably right down to the original plumbing. I can't say I agree with how Bob's runnin' things, but that don't mean much to the story, so fuck it. Jane was in the drugstore when she heard a fight break out in the bar. Joe had heard it too, and he ran to check it out with the cash register's lower lip still wide open. Jane closed it for him and then went over to peek through the batwings. A bunch of tables and chairs were on their sides because of all the people who'd jumped to get away from Tom. His mood was worse than piss yellow. He was standin' in the middle of the bar, teeth bared, hair messed, spit flyin', tears runnin' down his face. He also had so much blood on him that you'd think he'd tried to dance with a cactus. He was holdin' the nub of a stick of lumber he'd used to work somethin' over real hard.

"Tom squatted, buried his face in his hands, and screamed so loud he could have grayed your scalp. He was shit-faced, but clearly he was angry too. Then he shot up, whipped the wood against a wall, and stormed out. When the coast appeared to be clear, everyone crawled out of their corners, paid whatever they owed, and split.

"Joe went to speak to the bartender. Jane went to the piece of wood on the floor. She picked it up and, lookin' it over, knew right then what'd made Tom so mad. And while it should have bothered her the most, she worried only for Jed."

"What did she divine from the wood?" William said.

Ray squinted at him, scratched his chin, and grinned.

"You mean what did she figure out from it?" he said. "Everything. Sometimes the truth can be easier to . . . dee-vine . . . in a town like Tar Valley.

"She put that bloody, splintered nub of wood in her bag of goods from Darby's store and left. At home, she unloaded her parents' stuff in the kitchen and then brought the bag up to her room. She set the wood on her bed and stared at it for a while, until she decided what she had to do."

"You didn't answer my question," William said.

Ray cocked his head and shrugged.

"About the wood and what it said," William said.

Ray sipped his beer and then dangled it over the end of his right armrest.

"That piece of wood had blood on it," he said. "But that's not what put a scare into Jane. Bein' surprised by blood around Tom would be like bein' surprised by pills in a porno star's purse. The wood also had streaks of red paint on it. Jane knew of only one thing in Tom's world that would have bled red paint, and she could think of only one reason why Tom would have made it bleed."

Ray drank from his beer again and gazed up at the moon.

"S'a full son of a bitch tonight, ain't it?" he said.

William looked up at it.

"Your wife and kid have been gone for a while," Ray said. "I wouldn't be offended if you took off right now to go find 'em." He paused. "It might, you know, be the right thing to do."

William glared at him. Then he relaxed.

"I'll determine that," he said. "Truth be told, Ray, they don't appreciate me. What they have. I give them everything, and they take it for granted. If this is how they want to behave, to treat me, screw them."

Ray's lower lip jutted out.

"Well, alright then," he said.

"They have no respect for what it takes to earn the life they enjoy," William said. "They'll come back, even if it's tomorrow, and I'll get an apology, because I'm their meal ticket."

Ray shrugged.

"You're the boss, Bill," he said. "Now, only one thing would have made Tom work over his tractor with nothin' but his bear paws and a stick of wood. Lovers' Willow."

"Lovers' Willow?" William said.

"Betty's double-dealin' would have made him kick ass, especially Jed's, for sure," Ray said. "But no way would it have turned him against the one thing he'd ever loved, the one true friend he'd ever had. Only somethin' big-time would have taken him over the edge.

"He'd found out about Jed and Betty, most likely by dumb coincidence, because again, he didn't really have any friends. But his bad news came with an extra-heapin' helpin' of piss-me-off. He'd also learned, Lord knows how, that Jed and Betty had plans for Lovers' Willow. That would be like findin' out that the bank's foreclosin' on your house and takin' the liquor cabinet too. Like I've said, Lovers' Willow used to be serious business here in Tar Valley. If a couple sat beneath it, they were tellin' themselves and everyone else that they were makin' a vow second only to the one before God. And as far as I know, almost every couple that made the walk to the willow stayed together the rest of the way. We still even have a few livin' seniors goin' on fifty, sixty-plus years after the altar.

"But just as the willow might bless a future, it could also curse one if you didn't give it the proper respect. At least, a lot of things sure seem to suggest it. I've heard of divorce, jail time, financial disaster, van rides to the state cracker house, and even suicide for those who turned their back on their pledge. Stuff that would make your dick pack its bags and hit the highway. Even thirty years *after* sittin' beneath the willow—a long time to honor a deal, in my book—the hell could rain down on those who divided.

"Betty hadn't lived here long enough to know how much the ritual weighed, and I'm not sure she would have cared if she did. I can only believe it was cute and charming to her. It also wrapped Jed that much tighter 'round her finger.

"And if that wasn't bad enough, she'd added *Tom Crockett* of all people to the goddamn mix. Worse still, she'd gotten him to open himself in a way that he most of all didn't expect. And though she might not have been evil in her ways—I don't believe most young flirts are bad people, just kind of stuck-up and naïve—she'd walked with both feet on his weakness. It'd made him lose his already limited mind, and as most of us have done, he took it out on the one he cared about most.

"Because of her, he beat that tractor hard. Dented it, chipped it, and *really* scuffed up the paint. Pulverized some knobs it needed too. And when he finally stopped to catch his breath, he stepped back, wiped his face, and realized what he'd done. What *she* had made him do.

"That's when he knew that what had happened to the tractor wasn't his fault. No, it was *them:* Jed and Betty and everyone else who had it out for him. To Tom, a million starry-eyed face-suckers could spend their whole lives under the willow and never feel the love that he did for his machine. Someone would pay hard for his loss. It was a scary thing to consider."

"Did anyone ever learn how he found out about Jed and Betty and the willow?" William said.

Ray thought for a moment.

"Maybe the Betty Deshayne Hate Club had helped to stir the pot," he said. "Maybe someone slipped a note in his pocket while he was passed out in the street. Who knows? Hell, maybe Betty herself had let it out so she could tighten her screws on him. I don't think it matters how he found out, because once the truth turns foggy and trust takes a hike, folks will chase whatever they're driven to know. The insanity of bein' suspicious don't ever run out of gas."

"So what did Jane decide to do?" William said.

Ray looked past him, across the road, at the willow's drooping, swaying, rustling branches. William could hear the old man weeping within them, even from the distance.

"The irony of it all," Ray continued, "is that the least guilty person received the hardest sentence. Jane McShaw had never hurt or been mean to no one. She hadn't lied, or led anyone astray. All she'd done is keep quiet, be patient, sit idle, and hope for the best.

"Like I told you before, she'd hit that fork in the road where people either hang on or let go. I also said that we lose down either path, which is what can make love so goddamn unfair. Jane knew three things." Ray held up his hand and used his fingers to count. "One, Jed had turned on her. Two, and the biggest smack in the face, Jed was takin' Betty to Lovers' Willow after barely a couple of months when he'd never made the offer to Jane after way longer than that. And three, somethin' bad was going to happen because of that event, and it was going to include Tom Crockett."

Ray paused again, longer this time. William finished his beer and fished out another. His increasing buzz had become even more important to him. It dampened the voice that said a real man wouldn't let his wife and daughter walk alone down an unlit country road. It whined for him to give in and hated him for being *in charge*.

Roger and Donny raised their arms to drink at the same time. Roger stopped, waited for Donny to finish, and then took his sip.

The men all looked down. Todd's mouth puckered into a tight, open circle. He made a single popping noise.

Ray looked at William.

"How you doin', Bill?" he said. "Hangin' in? We're close to the end of the story."

William nodded and forced a smile.

"I don't think anyone," Ray said, "Jane most of all, could have believed that she'd do what she did in the end. Most people knew about the shit-bag of problems she had because of the depression,

41

but few would doubt her character. Troubled and squirrely as she was, she'd still always walked a straight line, at least on the surface. Then again, I don't think anybody, you and me included, knows what's *really* inside of anyone until they're standin' tippy-toe at the edge of their personal drop-off.

"In Jane's case, she'd banked so much in Jed that she'd become dependent without even bein' aware. And when you throw yourself that far into another person only to have it not work out, it's twice as bad goin' back the other way, because now you got double the distance to cross to where you started from. You also gotta trudge through a flame-throwin' scumpit of bad thoughts and feelings. Self-doubt's a bitch when you take a risk on love and lose. The 'I told you so' smart-ass is right there in your head, waitin' to beat you down for even takin' the chance.

"It's bad enough for folks *without* the depression to take on the worst of what their minds can make up. Jane did have the curse, as we've established, so the demons jumpin' from her trees were three times as red and ready to piss premium gasoline. By then, she was too flat-out fried to fight back, so in the end, she did all she could do, and became one of them."

William's eyebrows scrunched.

"One of them?"

"One of the devil's recruits. He's always lookin' for talent, even if it's his to use for only an hour. He don't always need lots of time from us for his work, and it don't always take much to get us to sign up for the job. As we've covered, Jane couldn't hold on to Jed any longer. And try though she did, she couldn't let go of him either. Both her mind and her heart were splittin' right down the middle. Got so it took all her will just to get up to go to the bathroom. When people talked to her, even her family, she'd just stare into space, and wouldn't say shit.

"Despite her bein' catatonic, Jane *did* hunt down every detail she could about Jed's and Betty's upcomin' walk to the willow. And you can bet your 401-k that what she found out sounded even way more ugly when she played it back in her head. The depression likes to turn the volume high on bad news.

"Their walk would be more private. Where most couples were glad to do it out in the light and the open, Jed and Betty were gonna make theirs while most of Tar Valley was sleepin'.

"So a little after midnight one Sunday late November, with the Illinois chill snappin' the air, Jane knelt by her bed, prayed for God's forgiveness, and left her house with a brown paper bag. She crossed town by foot to Buck Deshayne's farm, slipped into the barn, and waited for Betty to come out of the house."

Todd clucked his tongue. Roger and Donny eyed each other and then sipped from their beers at different times. William looked at the shadowy man in the Cardinals cap.

"A little later," Ray continued, "Jed arrived at his and Betty's ronday-voo point. He waited, and waited, but Betty didn't show. He kept his cool. Figured Betty might have had herself a blonde moment and gone straight to Lovers' Willow. It bothered him some, because the walk to the willow itself meant as much as what was said beneath it. He cut her some slack knowin' she was still new to Tar Valley custom. Plus, his mind was still skunked with *hot chick,* and you're apt to let a lot of shit slide when you're wrestlin' with beauty on the brain. He set out on his own to meet her at the willow. Half the ritual was better than none.

"By the time he got there, Jed was probably wishin' they'd held off 'til spring. Tar Valley can get as cold as a sittin' polar bear's ass in late autumn and even worse in the winter, and it don't matter how bundled you are.

"Of course Jed thawed out fast when he got closer to the tree and saw Betty was there. It was just about done losin' its leaves around then. He forgot her *foe-pah* in a blink. She'd kept her promise, and the thought made him run the rest of the way."

Ray shrugged and cracked his neck.

"Damn, that feels good. Back and neck are startin' to team up on me."

He smiled at William.

"Guess the same can happen when you're hunched over a desk all day too, huh?"

William's face remained blank.

"About half the distance to the willow," Ray continued, "Jed sees a big 'n spooky shape cut into the moonlight from behind the tree. He drops to the ground to get a better view. It's Tom Crockett."

Ray sipped his beer.

"From there, the whole thing goes down at warp speed. Tom don't even talk or stalk. He just leaps on Betty and swallows her with them big-ass arms of his. Betty squeals and screams, so Tom clamps a paw over her mouth and nose. Jed crawls closer. Tom's squeezin' Betty so hard his face goes red and his muscles start makin' noises.

"She's still kickin' and strugglin' in spite of all. That's when he grabs her head like it's a melon on a stick and twists it with all the torque he's got. Her neck snaps, and her head falls limp and crooked. Tom lets go, and she falls to his feet in a heap.

"She's dead. Jed's freakin' out while flat on the ground. But what's he gonna do now? Run over there and kick King Kong's ass? He pushes himself up and takes off at top speed. Tom hears the poundin' feet and gives chase. He knows goddamn well that if someone saw what he did, he'll hang at high noon. Not even he could scare away justice when it came to cold-blooded murder.

"Tom was a powerful guy, but Jed was faster on foot. Tom couldn't and didn't catch up. Jed even managed to pull far enough away to hide in some thick shrubs and trees on the far side of the field back there." Ray jabbed his thumb over his shoulder. "He watched Tom lumber by, and when he figured it was safe to come out, he made his way back to the willow.

"Cryin' and shakin', he steps under the near-bare branches and squats down by Betty's body on the ground. He gathers her into his lap and rocks her, talks to her as if she can hear him. When it finally hits him she ain't never gonna wake up, he wails, pulls her head close to his chest, and rubs her head real hard."

Ray stopped to sip his beer. Todd glanced at William. Donny and Roger both stared at the ground.

"Jed feels somethin' wet in his hands. It's too thick to be tears, and it's too cold for him to sweat *that* much, so he sets Betty down and leans over to get a better look. He figures it out, and it messes him up so bad he can't even scream. He covers his mouth, backs away, and takes off even farther and faster than when he'd run from Tom."

Donny straightened his legs, pushed himself up, and went to the cooler.

He grabbed a bottle and returned to his chair.

"I think I'm near done drinkin' for the night," Ray said. "I still gotta drive my ass home."

"You sure?" William said. "You've had quite a bit."

Ray smirked.

"Maybe so, Bill," he said, "but if there's one thing I know on a Sunday night in Tar Valley, it's that the weekend shift of law enforcement has probably put away more beers than me. I ain't worried about gettin' pulled over, if that's your concern."

A weep escaped from the willow. The men all looked or turned toward it.

"Damn," Donny said, his voice low. "Sounds like Jed's havin' a rougher night than usual."

William still couldn't see the old man well, but he didn't need to: his sobs were proof he was there.

He faced Ray again.

"That's quite a story, Ray," he said. "And you're quite a story*teller*, I might add. I hope you won't find me rude if I ask if that's the end of it." He glanced back toward the road. "I have a couple of runaways I might have to retrieve."

He chuckled.

Ray looked at him through narrowed eyes and then nodded.

"Understood, Bill. They've been gone for some time. Let's hope they make it to the motel." He sipped his beer. "One way or another."

The others all stared at William quietly. He shifted his feet when he felt Ray's study of them.

"Those are some nice shoes you got there, Bill," Ray said. "There's an old sayin'—can't remember where it started—that you can tell a lot about a man just by the shoes that he wears. Take a guy wearin' boots with dried shit and dirt caked to the ankle. That's information. Ditto for a fella who wears shoes as nice and squeaky and clean as a virgin's ass after a shower. Folks look at them shoes and say now there's a man with style. Class. But sure as shit stays brown all day, that same guy might be tryin' to keep others from knowin' he's really on the run. From somethin'. Maybe himself. That's why he keeps 'em shined. All the time."

He paused and licked at his rear teeth.

"But the man who wears the shoes caked with shit, well, there's an honorable soul. He ain't in a race against time and the truth, which always smoke out a liar."

William sat straighter and folded his hands over his lap with his elbows on the armrests.

"It was Buck Deshayne who found Betty not long after dawn," Ray said. "He was on his way to the barn to feed the animals. Scratchin' his ass and pullin' up his overalls. Just inside the barn door, he noticed a foot stickin' out of a flat pile of hay. He swiped the hay away, and when he saw the face beneath it, he dropped, and sat on the floor for a while.

"He eventually phoned the sheriff. Back then it was Jack Closkey. About two hours earlier someone who wouldn't give his name had called and said Jack would find a dead girl at Lovers' Willow. Now of course they didn't have no caller ID or phone tracers in Tar Valley back in the forties, and I wouldn't be surprised if our thumbs are still high up our asses even now as I speak. Jack didn't know who made the call, but he did check out the story and find the body under the tree. So when he got Buck's bad news, he zipped right over. Wasn't in the barn five minutes when it all hit him square in the jaw."

Ray sipped his beer and glanced off to his right.

"Buck hadn't known what to make of what he'd found," he continued. "Because, you see, Betty's body didn't have a fuckin' scalp. Her face had been beat to hell too. When Jack and his deputy dug and sniffed around the barn a little more, they found a club, a hunting knife, and a roll of electrical tape in a bigger pile of hay not far from the body. That was when Jack pulled Buck aside and told him about Jane McShaw.

"The girl he found beneath the willow had shoulder-length hair. Blonde. Betty's color. Jane was brunette, and she usually kept the length about as low as her chin. And when Jack turned her chin to check for a pulse, the hair slid right off. The freezin' mornin' moisture had gone to work on the tape Jane'd used to keep Betty's scalp stuck to her head. It also made the dried blood tacky again." He paused. "You can imagine the unholy mess."

William remained quiet. Then he leaned forward with his elbows on his knees.

"Okay, I get it," he said, his eyes narrowing. "Jane was so twisted by heartbreak and indecision that she became Jed's pleasure and his punishment all at once. She couldn't let go, so she made herself into what he desired, Betty Deshayne. She also couldn't hold on, so she set herself up to be killed by Tom in order to be free from her pain and depression. And through that arrangement, Jed would be free from her as well, but he'd have to face what he'd lost, betrayed, and could never retrieve. That's why he returns to the willow on a Sunday, the day of his life's great tragedy. Jane and Jed might have been good people overall, but their common greed for love destroyed them, and bound them together forever. Interesting moral. Very touching."

Ray smiled at him.

"You could see it that way, Bill," he said. "Or you could look at it as I do. We can't ever see all the way into anything. We live on faith: in God, His angels, ourselves, one another. We take death-defyin' risks when we open ourselves to be hurt or betrayed, but we got no other choice down here. Otherwise, we'd have to face how alone we really are, and then there'd be no sense in livin', wouldn't you say?"

William raised his eyebrows and shrugged.

"We had all better pray that we stay true to what *is* true," Ray continued, "lest we *all* be damned. Jane McShaw wasn't born a killer any more than I was born one stable over from the baby Christ's. But she had a flaw as we all do, and it took her to an ugly breakin' point that kicked her clean from the yard of faith I'm talkin' about. She became somebody, some*thing,* that no one could have ever guessed about her. Her heart was broken by hope in another person. It was enough to unlock the gates of her own holy hell, and more people than her had to pay for it. That could be me and you too, Bill. Or someone we know and love."

William rose from his chair. The movement combined with the beer in his blood almost knocked him over. He shook it off and steadied his balance. He slid his wallet from his back pocket and slipped out a twenty-dollar bill.

"Gentlemen, I appreciate your time, the story, and most of all, your hospitality," he said. "You've been friendly and welcoming. Please enjoy part of next Sunday's get-together on me."

He placed the bill on the cooler and set an empty bottle on top of it.

"Where can I dispose of my empties?" William said.

Ray waved him off.

"Don't sweat it, Bill. We'll take care of it."

William smiled.

"Thank you, Ray."

He glanced around the circle once more. His back to the porch and his body slouched in his chair, only the Cardinals fan remained non-distinct in the faint light from the bulb by the door.

"I have quite a journey ahead of me," William said. "I've got a stray wife and child, a broken-down car, no place yet to stay, and a board room that will surely be pissed off in Chicago. Wish me well."

"Can I give you a lift anywhere, Bill?" Ray said. "Maybe down the road there, to see if they might still be on foot?"

William regarded him.

"No thank you, Ray. But thank you for asking. Good evening, gentlemen."

He nodded. Ray and Donny nodded back. Roger pumped his fist once. Todd held up two fingers. The Cardinals fan did not move.

William aimed for the road.

The old man still cried from beneath the willow.

William stopped and turned around.

"Ray, about your story," he said. "You never said what became of Tom Crockett."

The other men exchanged glances. Ray finished his beer and set down the can next to his army of empties. The Cardinals fan rose, stood for a moment, and then walked away from the circle.

A draft of ice-cold air pimpled William's skin. He watched the shape disappear into the dark and open field behind the gas station.

"Tar Valley took care of its problem," Ray said, "just as my body or yours will deal with a wound or infection. Life can be hurt but in the end is meant to heal and be clean."

He leaned back in his chair. His long, spindly legs spread a little wider.

"Tom got what he deserved. I guess you could think of those who flushed out the infection as Tar Valley's white blood cells, huh, Bill?"

William said nothing.

"But just because the dead are dead doesn't mean they're not around," Ray said. "They get lonely too, and homesick. Even on a Sunday night with nothin' goin' on but beers and conversation."

William furrowed his eyebrows and looked toward the field beyond the gas station.

"It's a tragedy," Ray continued, "what can happen when we turn from the truth and get taken by pride and desire. Even the best of us can fall, and will." He followed William's gaze at the field. "And sometimes the debt of a sin ain't never fully settled . . . among the living, or the dead."

Ray's intent but tranquilized eyes became darker and mildly dangerous.

"What about you, Bill? You square with the truth in your life?"

William maintained eye contact until he no longer could.

He turned and aimed for the road again.

When he reached it, he ran: past fields and farmland and cow dung that clung to the summertime air. All around him, the night creatures droned in discordance from their shadow-cloaked places of hiding.

He heard raspy, labored breathing: his own. He stopped. Sweat soaked his armpits and stained his button-down shirt. His brand-new Kenneth Cole shoes had also flown from his feet, probably a quarter-mile back. All that remained were blood-soaked holes in tattered black-silk socks.

He wanted to sit, to rest, to gather his breath and his thoughts, but he knew there was no time.

He would have to continue to run—to run and run and run—until he could no longer hear the weeping that followed through slow-moving wind.

ASCENT

*L*ove is mercy without conscience, Ranyana remembered.

He'd memorized the line by Tatiki Wallaha written shortly before the poet's execution.

"Ranyana!"

The sergeant's spittle speckled his face. Arms flat to his sides, Ranyana clicked his heels.

"Sir!"

His voice echoed into the hangar's farthest corners. The platoon was statue-still.

"Straighten up!"

Ranyana imagined he was a pillar and acted like one.

The sergeant slid to the next soldier in line.

Once finished with roll, he handed his clipboard to a junior officer and strolled to the front center of the platoon. He clasped his hands behind his back.

"The Regent has directed the army, the police, and the national guard to step up security around Mount Takusha," he said, his voice as crisp and hard as state-issued bed sheets. "Violations of the Public Disorder and Fornication Statutes are surging. Transgressors will now be apprehended and charged without questioning."

Ranyana's face remained riveted forward.

"Security will be doubled at the mountain," the sergeant continued. "It will also be deployed at additional points of surveillance."

He stepped forward, pivoted, and walked slowly to his right.

Ranyana saw the glint in his eye.

"The Regent has authorized deadly force in the event a deviant resists or flees arrest."

He stopped. His booted feet *clacked!*

"Fall out!"

The soldiers marched in formation to the exit. Before he stepped outside, Ranyana looked up into the Regent's almighty eyes watching from the portrait on the wall.

*T*he days were long and boring, but it could have been much worse. He could be working civil espionage or bloody border patrols rather than standing idly under stifling heat at the mountain.

Ranyana took a small sip of sanitized water from his canteen, re-capped it, and looked out at Bahdran's modest skyline. The roughest part of the Regent's Great Revolution had ended before Ranyana was born, but the capital of Demarqua still suffered from its hangover. Violence, poverty, and zealotry remained as common as bad plumbing and long nights without electricity.

He turned around, shielded his eyes from the sun, and craned his neck to see the mountain's cloud-covered peak.

He once again imagined the prophet, Kwatakan, abandoned there as a baby by his shamed and unwed mother. Miraculously, the child had survived among the wildlife, dense foliage, and steep and rocky terrain: proof that Baruna had divinely intervened to guard and teach him for a *purpose.*

At least that's what the scriptures proclaimed.

They also put forth that on Kwatakan's twentieth birthday, he descended from the mountain with the precepts Baruna had issued to save all pagans and sinners from ruin.

And just as Baruna predicted, His holy words sparked wars and persecution and, ultimately, the death of the prophet. But Baruna had also promised Kwatakan that the messages he left behind would inspire others to complete the book he'd begun.

In the finished book—which Ranyana had first read cover-to-cover before age twelve by law—Baruna called upon the young to use the mountain, as Kwatakan had, for the worship, deep thought, and meditation that led to a mature and spiritual life.

It was the holiest place in the faith. None but students in training could step foot on it.

The religion spread and prospered for centuries. As to when it first began to lose its grip, Ranyana knew little: the unpopular sections of national history had been revised many times. He gathered mainly that it started when the first Western feet arrived in the latter nineteenth century.

More would follow with big money and bigger ambitions.

Their principles compromised and their hearts fat with greed, Demarqua's monarchy first accepted and then condoned the cultural overthrow.

The white faces continued increasing well into the twentieth century. They flooded the land for inexpensive trips in geographic luxury. Their changing ideas and fashions came with them.

Alcohol appeared. Sultry music swam through dark and smoky bars. Curfews went away.

Businesses sprouted and boomed. Commercial billboards proclaimed from new buildings.

Dissenting and opposing opinions flowed from various presses.

Momentary virgins caroused. Unhappy marriages ended. Homosexuals emerged from their closets.

Restrictions became ghosts of a faraway past.

Self-determination began to feel better than faith.

And then one day, years later, as if out of a fog or a dream, a hooded monk appeared. With Kwatakan's book tucked in his arm, he announced his belief that Demarqua needed to be cleansed.

The reigning monarch didn't agree.

The monk recruited enough converts to ignite a civil war that he won. He anointed himself the Regent, and Demarqua became his to purify.

Only Mount Takusha stood in the way of his total control.

Aware of their constraints, students in spiritual training recognized the mountain for the immunity from him that it was. *Baruna* had declared they must be left alone up there. Not even the Regent could interfere.

It was an old and festering problem his own religion wouldn't allow him to fix.

Ranyana hadn't been on the mountain since completing his own training two years before. Students had taken advantage of its hands-off sanctity then, but their transgressions paled before those typical of the current "criminal" class. Something more restless and reckless and bold had been brewing among the modern-day youth. They were spending more time among the mountain's most private locations—and pushing the limits of what they wished to experience.

He himself had never dared to wander from its "authorized" areas. He hadn't even known where the secret places could be. Only lately, as more whispers made their rounds, had he learned where students might go to recite memorized forbidden books by candlelight under the heavy cover of trees; lie naked in groups on grass made lush by streams and waterfalls; and smoke fragrant bowls of sangreet before making passionate love.

He looked toward voices to his right. Several soldiers were arriving to relieve others from posts positioned at twenty-meter intervals.

The mountain's entrance log that morning had listed 171 names. Recently, if 200 entered, 185 might return before curfew. Those who came down later or even the following morning received expensive citations from steel-eyed police.

Ranyana had never missed curfew while in training. Those from his class who did had paid for their extra freedom with the hefty fine on the ground and their parents' beatings at home.

Each one he'd questioned afterward had told him it was worth it.

The soldier from the station to Ranyana's right approached him.

"What are you doing, Maleko?" Ranyana said. "Get back to your post."

Maleko stopped and looked around.

"I don't see any officers," he said, grinning and lighting a cigarette. "Do you?"

Ranyana shrugged.

He glanced at Maleko and then out again at Bahdran.

Western office buildings still stood next to and across from mosques that Kwatakan himself had helped to build. Dirty compact cars crawled through cluttered streets. Citizens scurried in Regent-mandated dress codes: dark-blue shirts and pants for schoolboys (light-blue robes and headdresses for schoolgirls); brown robes for male students in training on the mountain (yellow robes with hoods for the females); black robes and headdresses for single women; white robes and headdresses for married women (violet stripes on the shoulders if they had children). Single and married men wore what they wished as long as it wasn't "profane" or "irreverent to God."

The police moved about in light-green uniforms. Most soldiers wore dark-green fatigues.

The Regent's "politicians" were always clad in clerical robes or imported suits depending on the setting.

"I hope some of them don't come down *this* time," Maleko said.

He smiled and exhaled smoke through his nose.

"I *hope*."

He slid his rifle from his shoulder and hefted it twice.

"I *hope.*"

Ranyana looked back up at the mountain.

Low clouds had moved in to help conceal the sin.

R anyana watched the sun splash the dark-purple dusk with red and pink and orange. His fatigue weighed more than his body: he'd been standing guard for almost twelve hours.

According to the mountain's main-gate attendant, all but six from the day's log had returned. Ranyana looked at his watch: 7:52 p.m. Eight minutes until curfew.

The surveillance helicopters had reported no illicit conduct in view, which meant such conduct was certain.

What might the last six be up to, Ranyana wondered, when they knew the cost of 8:01?

He looked up at the lump that loomed against the twilight.

Somewhere beyond his sight, tongues touched softly in wet and playful kisses; warm bodies pressed in guilt-free embraces; minds relaxed and expanded with illegal herb; hearts and minds absorbed the forbidden words of Wallaha.

How many secrets did—could—the mountain hold? Millions. Maybe billions.

His heart began to pound.

If the Regent couldn't stop the young on the mountain, then they in truth were greater than the Regent, and closer to Baruna without him . . .

No.

He was losing his focus. The scriptures said he could not find God on his own because of his sin and his ignorance. He needed discipline and self-restraint accessible only through the divine. He needed chosen intermediaries who could lead him closer to the prophet and the Father.

Intermediaries such as the Regent.

He had to regain control of his mind.

He thought of Trunaya. She and her family would be waiting at his house with his family when he returned from duty the following evening. The table would be set with the soft beef, couscous, shredded cabbage, green olives, hot tea, and fresh bananas they had brought. She would stand and smile at him with wobbly brown eyes and cheeks like brown balloons.

He would then smile back and remind himself that he loved her: loved her even though she had only a slight idea of who he really was.

He would love her because their families had decided that he should.

Besides, if he used his imagination correctly, she could become more attractive with time.

They—he—might not feel right for the first few years. But at least they would be prudent. Structured. Predictable. Passions could not pester them and potentially drive them apart.

What *was* passion, anyway? The scriptures likened it to a match that blackened paper hearts for the wind to rend and scatter. It was the devil's back-pocket slingshot used on easy targets.

Yes, he would make his marriage work and scoff at his desires if only to spit at what was unreasonable.

He glanced at his watch again: 7:58.

The soldier at the station to Ranyana's left raised his hand and made circles with his index finger. Ranyana nodded and motioned to Maleko. They both jogged toward him.

"The remaining six haven't returned yet," the other young corporal, Baledo, said to them. He gestured with his head toward the mountain. "They're probably still getting off."

"I say we stomp on their faces and scrape them from our heels," Maleko said. He looked directly at Ranyana. "No one will question us."

Ranyana held his stare for a moment and then turned to Baledo.

"We have direct orders to apprehend if we see a violation of statutes," he said. "We're not authorized for summary executions. Not for curfew."

Baledo glared at him with Maleko's same intensity.

"We have our orders," Ranyana said.

Baledo smirked at him and then looked up at the mountain. Its silhouette swallowed the sky.

"They deserve to die," he said. "They mock us."

He looked at Ranyana again.

"They mock *you.*"

Ranyana checked his watch. The second hand ticked past 8:00.

He looked beyond the electrified fence and saw no one through the thickening dark.

Then he heard a female voice.

He stepped closer to the fence and saw the yellow robe about fifty meters from where he stood. The other five latecomers—three males in brown, two other females in yellow—followed the first girl along the path to the entrance gate. One of the boys brushed dirt and burrs from his robe.

Baledo strode to the fence with his rifle held out in front of him.

"You're past curfew!" he shouted.

The six students stopped and looked in his direction.

The girl in the lead left the main path and approached them until she was a few meters from the fence.

"We're sorry," she said.

Ranyana gained a clearer view of her. His pulse quickened.

"We were praying and lost track of the time," she said.

"Right," Baledo said, taking another step toward the fence. "You're just as deceitful as you are selfish and stupid. Get out of there before I shoot you dead right now."

The girl remained graceful and calm.

"We're sorry," she said.

"You infidels had twelve hours to *pray*," Baledo said. "Or not."

Ranyana continued staring at her: about five-foot six; slender but for extra weight in places that became her; green eyes that proved Western blood in her stream; long, black hair that spilled over her shoulders; small but sculpted breasts that pushed against her cotton robe; dark skin made darker by her days on the mountain.

He imagined tracing her lips with his fingertips. He wondered how her inner thigh would feel beneath his gliding hand.

One of the males—slightly younger, well built, passably handsome—came up beside her. He referred to her as Martika. Their robes brushed, and their pinky fingers almost touched.

"Get to the gate before I kill you," Baledo said.

Martika nodded at him and then looked at Ranyana.

Ranyana's heart beat even faster. His mouth turned into paste.

He looked away.

She returned to her group, and they continued down the path to the entrance. Ranyana, Maleko, and Baledo followed a few steps behind them along the fence.

The soldier at the main gate screamed at them. Two police officers walked over, cuffed them, and led them to an armored truck.

"That's new," Ranyana said. "Citations *plus* detention for curfew?"

Maleko glanced sideways at him.

"It's excessive," Ranyana said, his voice a little lower.

Baledo grabbed his arm and spun him around.

"Did you just say *excessive?*" he snarled. "They defied God *and* the law!"

"Baledo," Ranyana said, softer than intended. "I believe we're . . . we're . . ."

"We're what?"

Baledo's right hand clenched into a fist at his side.

"Nothing," Ranyana said.

Maleko gripped Ranyana's left shoulder.

"You must be careful about what you think and say," he said.

Ranyana watched the students climb into the back of the armored truck.

"You're right, Maleko," he said, his mouth still sticky-dry.

Baledo stared him down a moment longer. His body relaxed but his eyes still burned.

The soldier at the entrance closed and bolted the gate.

The truck left the area and headed for the city.

Two other soldiers strolled over to Ranyana's group. One whistled with two fingers at another truck with an uncovered flatbed. The driver waved through the open window, pulled a U-turn, and drove around to them.

They all jumped into the flatbed. Baledo slapped the side of the truck twice. It spat black exhaust and sped away.

With the tepid night air washing over his face, Ranyana closed his eyes.

Smiling, inviting, her green Western eyes glassy like a cat's, Martika filled his mind.

Before it could embrace her, it went dark and silent, leaving Ranyana only with the knowledge of sin.

R anyana studied the dot of light overhead.
At first, he thought it was a pulsating star. But it was only an army patrol plane prowling the sky.

"It won't be long before they all understand," Baledo said from his position on the other side of the entrance. "Every single one of them."

They'd been transferred to external security at the detention center after completing their shifts at the mountain. Two hours remained in Ranyana's eighteen-hour workday.

"They will understand that there is one god, one Regent, and one law in Demarqua," Baledo continued. "No one stands above." He saw a bug by his foot and stepped on it. "Those who don't obey will bear the consequences. And they'll have no one to blame but themselves."

An armored car with a manned turret rolled by on the street in front of them.

"What about you, Ranyana?" Baledo said.

"What about me?"

"*Do* you believe in the law?" Baledo said.

Ranyana paused.

"Why would you ask me such a thing?"

Baledo paused as well.

"I think you know why."

Ranyana didn't respond.

"I wonder, Ranyana," Baledo said, lighting a cigarette, "whether you too would rather spend your time on the mountain. Whether your speech is down here, but your heart is up there."

Ranyana turned and charged at him.

"What are you getting at, Baledo?" he said, staring hard into his eyes. He almost stood on Baledo's feet.

Baledo exhaled through the side of his mouth and smiled.

"I saw the way you looked at her, Ranyana."

Ranyana's jaw clenched.

"If anyone wishes to question my loyalty, it can be the Regent himself."

"Oh, really?" Baledo said.

"Yes, really."

Baledo looked down and then back up.

"If your loyalty must be verified by the Regent himself, then it stands in even greater doubt."

Ranyana continued to glare from an inch away. Baledo's face was stone. Then he smiled.

"Go to hell," Ranyana said, returning to his position.

*H*e lay in bed at home the following night, eyes wide open, pillow soft beneath his head. He could not sleep despite his heavy head and aching body.

Trunaya's meal had been filling, and for that, he could appreciate her.

He closed his eyes and turned his head to the left on the pillow.

Baledo would soon cause him problems. He would begin by turning other soldiers against him. His suspicion might then spread enough to alert the lieutenant.

It was just a matter of time. Ranyana wondered only whether the tension would tighten before or after his wedding three months away, soon after his twenty-first birthday.

He tried to rest—to sleep. Once halfway under consciousness, he saw his wedding-day bride swim up through his thoughts. He received her and raised her veil. When he looked into her face, he did not see her chubby cheeks and wet but winning smile.

He saw the girl from the mountain: Martika, with the flowing black hair and Western eyes.

He twisted over and felt behind the bed's headboard for his tattered copy of Wallaha's last book of published poems. He slipped it out, lay back, and held it up in front of him with both elbows on his thin mattress.

Of course the poet had had to die. According to what Ranyana understood, he'd been a tolerant liberal who believed more in free thought and expression than in the edicts of an abstract and invisible deity. Wallaha *had* offered a place in his mind and even his heart for God. He'd even spoken of a yearning to find and understand Him. But he would not blindly obey a doctrine dictated by people in power, and for that stance, he'd earned the purest hate of the Regent.

Wallaha had extended lengthy olive branches to the Regent. They included letters explaining he respected the Regent's laws, beliefs, and authority as long as they did not rob him of his human right to *think*. But his entreaties would never touch their target.

The Regent charged him with "crimes against the state." And in the end, he gave Wallaha's mind the freedom to think apart from its body at the bottom of a bloody basket.

All of the poet's work was banned and, wherever possible, destroyed. Possession of it became a severe offense with harsh penalties.

And yet the writing remained: buried in dirt, stashed under floors, boxed away in secret corners and alleyway shadows.

Slipped behind bed headboards as well.

Ranyana held the aging book closer to his face and inhaled its illicit hope. He loved the musty smell.

Dofnaya, his younger brother by two years, stirred in his bed on the opposite side of the room. Ranyana slipped the book beneath his bottom.

Once sure Dofnaya still slept, he lit a small candle on a dish from under his bed. He slid lower on his sheets, opened the book, and flipped to his favorite of the poems, "War and the Judgment of Love":

> Man wages war to free the oppressed
> yet lavishes the trigger men
> spilling beautiful blood for ideals
> that breed lies for perpetual power

and the greed that is its mistress
Love is the only ideal
that will not kill for an imperial god
dreamed by thugs in ceremonial dress
preaching hope but promising fear
Only love refutes a fascist faith
and makes a master a servant
Love is the only perfect rebellion
Love is mercy without conscience

Ranyana read it again. He wiped a single tear from his eye, closed the book, and returned it to its hiding place.

He went to sleep. Within his heretical dreams, he made love to an emotion with green and glassy eyes.

Ranyana!"

Ranyana stood straighter in front of the sergeant.

"Sir!"

"Step front!"

Ranyana stepped out and stiffened even more.

"The lieutenant will speak with you."

The sergeant spun around and strode toward a door at the far end of the hangar. Ranyana fell in behind him. He looked back at Baledo, who remained a rod facing forward. Another officer resumed the morning's roll call.

Ranyana followed the sergeant into a dark hallway that passed several closed doors before ending at the lieutenant's office straight ahead. The sergeant knocked twice and identified himself.

"Enter," the lieutenant said from the other side.

The door opened. The sergeant motioned for Ranyana to pass.

He walked into the office. The door closed behind him. The sergeant's footsteps retreated.

An armed soldier stood by the doorway to Ranyana's right. The lieutenant sat with his back to them in a swiveling black-leather chair before a broad and meticulous desk.

Ranyana glanced around the room in front of him: four horizontal wall shelves lined flush with military books and binders; display cases decked with medals, plaques, and certificates; the portrait of the Regent.

He did not see Kwatakan's book.

The lieutenant turned slowly around. He wore mirrored sunglasses and chewed an unlit cigar. He plucked it from his mouth and pointed it at the two chairs facing his desk.

"Sit," he said.

Ranyana sat.

The lieutenant returned the cigar to his mouth and stared at him.

"It has come to my attention that you recently interfered with a fellow soldier's duty at the mountain," he said.

Ranyana looked at his twin reflections in the lieutenant's lenses.

"Is this true?"

Ranyana sat straighter. His right hand wore the swelling from the punch he'd thrown at Baledo the day before. He'd swung hard and missed, hitting the edge of Baledo's helmet with his now tender first knuckle.

The lieutenant leaned forward and set the cigar to his side on the edge of the desk.

"I did respond to inappropriate behavior, sir," Ranyana said. "I saw a fellow soldier violating protocol. He was harassing a spiritual student. Grabbing and groping at her, to be more accurate. When I believed it would only get worse, I acted in the honor of the military." He paused. "Even in light of the increasing . . . problem, we are still professionals."

The lieutenant slammed his fist on the desk. The cigar moved, as did an expensive pen.

"Who are *you* to decide on anything? Do *you* establish the code and issue the orders?"

Ranyana remained silent.

"Tell me where you learned that an army corporal is free to ad-lib right and wrong. I want to know."

Ranyana slumped an inch.

"Do you have any idea what would happen to Demarqua if corporals started believing they could make these decisions?"

The lieutenant leaned back, returned the cigar to his mouth, and turned it once.

"I should re-assign you right now," he said. "Maybe to a border."

Ranyana swallowed thickly.

"May I speak, sir?"

The lieutenant shrugged.

"I wasn't trying to step outside my rank, sir," Ranyana said. "I was upholding our beliefs and our integrity as Baruna would have it. The soldier had been improperly touching a girl. Beyond being unprofessional to the army, such behavior is condemned by the scriptures themselves. You have my full respect and apology, but I stand behind my actions."

The lieutenant stared at him through his mirrors.

"A girl," he said. A corner of his mouth went up. "You mean *your* girl. The one you want to lie with. The one other than your wife-to-be."

Ranyana stirred.

"Sir?"

"You know exactly what I'm talking about."

Baledo—what speed.

"Your wedding is, what, three months away?"

He leaned forward again and folded his hands flat on the desk. Ranyana's reflections grew larger.

"What you're doing and thinking is dangerous," the lieutenant said. The cigar stayed steady, even when he spoke. "I advise you to wise up *fast* before you bring shame to your family."

Ranyana looked down.

"May Baruna forgive me," the lieutenant said, "but if I had my way, I'd pack the base of the mountain with bombs and light the fuses myself. Sacred or not, it's a disgrace to all of us now."

He removed the cigar from his mouth and rolled it in his fingers.

"You're still young and stupid, so I'll allow you to redeem yourself," he said. "If you succeed, you'll be forgiven and this will be forgotten."

He pointed at Ranyana with the mouth end of the cigar.

"And if you blow it . . ."

Ranyana waited for the rest. It didn't come.

"You're not an individual, corporal. You're an extension of a greater whole that knows what's best for you, both here and in the hereafter. You owe it the loyalty of your soul."

Ranyana nodded.

"I understand," he said.

"That girl who excites you," the lieutenant said, leaning back again, "is the daughter of a *street-sweeper*. A peasant with a head full of shit from having read too much Wallaha. He's worthless, and he'll find a bed in a grave before long. As for his daughter, she's just another liberal slut hiding in a state yellow robe. She will never contribute to Demarqua. She's far too free in her mind."

His mouth turned down. He pointed with the cigar again.

"You will track her," he said. "Like a fly on an elephant's ass. You will watch her every move, and you will find one that justifies what you will do."

He leaned farther forward. Ranyana's reflections became garish cartoons.

"You will do your duty discreetly, and without conscience."

He leaned back and placed his elbows on the armrests of his chair.

"You will never be questioned. I personally will see to that."

Ranyana looked away.

"Do you understand your orders?"

Ranyana looked back at him.

"I understand," Ranyana said.

"Dismissed."

The lieutenant reached for the top manila folder from the tray at his desk's right corner.

The soldier behind them opened the door.

Ranyana stood, saluted, turned, and left.

The Regent's painted eyes followed him closely, even after the door had closed.

anyana looked at his watch: almost noon. He'd been at his post for four hours. Martika's group had arrived early to the mountain and been among the first to sign in. He'd watched them enter and then make their ways up using the trails and ropes and stairs.

He thought of her father. A street-sweeper, the lieutenant had said.

Worthless, and he'll find a bed in a grave before long.

Ranyana wanted to ask Baruna if taking life was okay as long as it was done for a state set up in His name. He'd used his fists and even fired his gun since joining the army. But he hadn't yet spilled any blood.

Could he?

Of course he could.

Anyone could. Especially if God's front-office reps approved of it.

The sun continued to bake in the sky. He wiped beads of sweat from his brow.

Might Martika be perspiring too—enough so that she had to remove her robe?

He thought of her breast, beaded with moisture, pressing softly against his cheek.

Damn you! a voice screamed within his head. *Are you* trying *to lose your soul?*

And yet thoughts of her had begun to crowd out even Baruna. In his dreams, she'd walked toward him, naked, perfect, her hair blowing gently in wind-brushed filaments over her shoulders. Her green and glassy cat's eyes lit the space between them. She smiled as if she knew him well.

And when she reached him, she held out her hand and spoke to him.

Ascend with me, Ranyana.

He accepted her hand, and his feet left the ground. They soared, until the squares and lines and bumps beneath them disappeared.

He laughed with her, because she made him happy.

He held her hand tighter and pulled her closer to him. Her silky hair tickled his face. He opened the door to himself and welcomed her in, but she was already there, where he'd made her a home without telling her how, or when, or why.

Higher and higher they rose, much too far for the Regent to reach.

They came as close to Baruna as they imagined they could. So close that . . .

Ranyana heard voices from the main footpath. He spun around and glanced at his watch.

Martika and her group had come back down—hours early.

He took several steps along the fence to survey them.

"Don't leave your post, Ranyana!" a voice barked from behind him.

He stopped and turned around.

"Go back to your station, Maleko."

Maleko stopped within a meter of him.

"Don't do it to yourself," he said.

"Don't worry about me," Ranyana said.

"It's only temptation. See it for what it is."

Ranyana looked back at the main gate. Martika's group was signing out and leaving.

A jeep cleared security and approached the mountain from the access road. When it arrived at the main gate, a soldier jumped out and walked toward Ranyana and Maleko.

"You're not scum like them, Ranyana," Maleko said. "You belong to something greater. You understand the faith and the law. There's hope for you."

"You're relieved from your post," the soldier said upon reaching Ranyana. "You're to report to your next assignment. I'm here to replace you."

Ranyana stared at him.

"Lieutenant's orders."

Next assignment.

The Regent's eyes were everywhere, surely even watching him now.

Martika's group had reached the access road and was heading toward the city.

Ranyana nodded at his replacement and jogged to the idling jeep.

"Bahdran," he said to the driver.

He jumped in. The jeep sped away.

Once in the city, Ranyana directed the driver to drop him off at an intersection he randomly specified. He'd have to blend into the masses and wait for the group to walk the distance that remained from Mount Takusha.

Even with his lead time and vantage point, he wasn't sure he'd find her: too much sun, too many blocks of swarming activity, and especially too many people. He saw dozens of yellow robes.

He stood and watched a while, but did not see her. Deciding she might have already passed him, he picked a direction and moved in it.

He searched for close to an hour, wandering the cluttered streets, peering into doorways and windows. At some point, he stopped and wiped salty grease from his face with the sleeve of his jacket. Some of the film slipped into his eyes and stung them. When his vision cleared again, he saw her. Saw *them*.

They stood outside a café two doors from the corner of the intersection he faced. The boy who never left her side handed her a drink in a cup and sipped from his own. They chatted and then walked to Ranyana's left.

He jogged toward them, stopping traffic, and slowed when he closed to within ten meters. They paused at the next intersection, waited for the light to change, and crossed with the pack of pedestrians.

He followed them through the streams of color-coded clothing.

They continued straight for several more blocks until the human congestion started to thin. Ranyana dropped back a few meters and fell in behind two older men in plain clothes.

The students turned right around another corner. He reached it just in time to see them disappear into an alley. Two middle-aged women in their white attire noticed with disapproval.

At the mouth of the alley, he gazed into its darkening length. A canvas curtain hung from a pole about halfway toward the back. The students were already behind it.

Unless he pulled back the curtain, he wouldn't be able to witness a crime. According to the lieutenant's current spin on the law, being alone, unmarried, and unattended would be cause enough for disposal.

But it wasn't yet just cause for *him*.

Maybe if he waited long enough, they'd emerge, and there'd be no reason to kill.

He remained at the mouth of the alley, which he gauged to be about twenty meters deep. The street was mostly empty but for a few passing cars and the white-attired women walking away.

Five minutes. Ten.

The canvas curtain didn't move.

He stepped into the alley.

Rotting, baking trash in a garbage can slapped him with a hot hand of stench. He held his breath and moved farther in. As he came closer to the curtain, he heard their first muffled noises: soft kissing, rubbing fabric, low tones of conversation.

He threw the curtain aside.

They both looked up with a start. She sat on the boy's lap on a discarded sofa riddled with stains, holes, and a few punched-through springs.

"What are you doing here?" Ranyana said. His voice died against the warm and damp brick walls.

She slid from her companion's lap and, mindful of a spring, sat next to him. The boy looked at him with frozen eyes.

"I said, what are you doing here?" Ranyana repeated.

He wondered if she even recognized him. She appeared to try: her green and glassy eyes glowed at him through the heavy, humid shadows.

He slipped his rifle from his shoulder and pointed it toward their feet.

"This is illegal," Ranyana said. "Don't you know that?"

They only stared at him.

"Do you even care?"

Martika looked at him calmly. The boy took hold of her hand.

"I am military," Ranyana said. "What if I were police?"

She looked at him even more intently. He saw the spark of recognition.

"What will you do with us?" she said. Her voice was soft but steady.

"What *should* I do?" he said. He raised his rifle from foot- to knee-level. "What do you believe you *deserve?*"

She looked down, thought, and then looked up again.

"I believe we deserve to be free," she said.

Ranyana squeezed the rifle.

"*Free?*" he said. "It's not enough that you run wild and do as you please on the mountain?" He glanced at the boy, who remained rock-still. "That you indulge with no regard or respect for your god, your country, *or* yourself?"

She almost smiled.

"What is your name?" she said.

His red mind blinked and dimmed.

"My name?"

"Yes," she said. "What is it?"

"That's not important," he said. "I am here in the name of Demarqua and its honorable leader, the Regent."

"What about Baruna?" she said.

"Baruna?"

"Yes, Baruna. Aren't you here for Him too?"

His rifle changed levels by inches: up, down, up, down.

"That goes without saying," he said.

"Are you going to shoot me?" she said.

His finger tensed on the trigger.

"Should I?"

"It doesn't matter if you do," she said.

She stood and stepped forward, toward him.

He stiffened and pointed his gun at her face.

"Don't move," he said.

She hesitated, searched his eyes, and then stepped forward again. Slowly, she reached for the nose of the rifle. When Ranyana did nothing, she guided it away from her.

"My name is Martika," she said.

He backed away, spun around, and kicked a garbage can. It rattled and fell over, spilling a sludge of fruit and vegetables.

"You belong to Demarqua, don't you understand?" he screamed. A cat scampered from behind a caved-in cardboard box. "You are not your own. You are bound to the law and the faith. You cannot write your own morals!"

"I can't?" she said.

"No!" He stepped closer to her. "They have been written *for* you!"

His eyes blazed. Beads of sweat rimmed his lips. His knuckles cracked as he tightened his grip on the rifle.

"The Regent and Demarqua exist only in your mind," she said. "If you decided today they don't exist, they no longer would."

"And then I'd be headless in a shallow grave," he said. "It's blasphemy!"

He shoved her back with his rifle.

"You have a *death wish!*"

Her eyes remained emeralds at rest in the shadows.

"You're completely ruled by your fear," she said.

He pointed the rifle at her face again.

"*I warn you,*" he said. "Your life is in my hands right now."

"Is it?" she said.

"You are an immoral slut!" he said. "Couldn't you fornicate enough on the mountain? Are you so depraved that you can't wait an hour without sneaking into a filthy alley for more? Have you no decency, or dignity?"

"We . . ."

"No! Shut your mouth!" He swung his rifle toward the boy. "I want *him* to answer this time!"

The boy raised his palms and held them out.

"Please," he said. "We are sorry. We only wanted to be . . . together. We are . . . in love."

Ranyana sensed tears behind his own eyes and hated them.

"*Love?*" he said. "*Love?* All you know is the lust in your heart. You are lost . . ." He looked back and forth between them. ". . . and you must be saved from yourselves."

Ranyana aimed the rifle back at Martika.

"We are weak, and full of sin, and incapable of making good choices for ourselves," he said.

He brushed his cheeks against each shoulder to make sure that no tears had escaped.

Martika noticed. Her eyes softened even more.

"We are foolish, and victims of our selfish desires," he continued.

The rifle lowered a couple of inches.

"Do you realize what we'd become if all behaved as you do?" he said.

"Yes," she said. "We'd be ourselves, and our hearts would lead us to God according to what we already know, because God is already in us. We don't need the Regent or anyone else to tell us where to find Him. God is closer than the Regent and even Kwatakan would have us believe."

Ranyana felt the blood draining from his face.

"Evil lies," he said. "The lieutenant was right. One cannot think and feel and speak as you do. You must be suicidal."

"Perhaps," she said, "but if I was meant to die by your hand, I wouldn't be breathing or speaking."

He gritted his teeth, lowered the rifle, and backed away.

"You're as presumptuous as you are reckless," he said.

"Then kill me if you must," she said. "I will still be free. I will also have forgiven you even before my heart stops beating."

He aimed at her again and pulled the trigger a hair's space from clicking.

She closed her eyes and waited.

The rifle dropped and hung loosely in his hand by his side.

She closed the distance between them and placed her hand flat on his chest.

His head slumped forward.

She slid her arms around him. He smelled her hair and felt her breasts against him. He wanted to touch them, but not because of desire.

"Let go of their control of God over you," she said close to his ear. "Baruna is not theirs to give or withhold."

"Why are you saying this to me?" he whispered, his chin still down against his chest.

"Because you want to ascend," she said.

His head shot up. He pushed her away.

Her demeanor did not change.

"I can see it in you," she said. "I saw it at the mountain. You are already free. You're just terrified of being discovered."

His face darkened.

"*Leave!*" he screamed at her companion. "*Now!*"

The boy stayed still. Ranyana strode over to him, yanked him up by the arm, and shoved him toward the daylight end of the alley.

The boy looked back and forth between Ranyana and Martika.

"*Go!*"

The boy ran. Martika moved forward to follow. Ranyana grabbed her arm.

"No," Ranyana said. "You wait. You will leave separately and not be seen with him. This never happened. I never found you here. Do you understand?"

She brushed a long, loose lock from her face.

The boy turned left at the sidewalk.

Ranyana and Martika stood quietly.

"Now you go," he said.

She took several steps past him and then stopped.

"I . . ."

"*Go!*" he said.

She spun and ran away around the alley's right corner. Ranyana waited several minutes and then left the alley as well.

Once out on the sidewalk, he squinted under the fresh blast of sun and looked to his right. When he saw no sign of her, he began to walk, unhurried, back into the crowds that moved like colorful ants for miles beyond the base of the mountain.

*H*ours after his time alone, Ranyana entered the flickering shadows of his family's quiet house. His mother had lit many candles.

He closed the front door behind him and stepped farther into the small living room. She sat on the floor, weaving another blanket she'd try to sell to those who already owned too many. Her stack of unsold finished work still cramped half of one wall.

With his rifle still slung over his shoulder, he leaned down to kiss her. She did not look up but moved stiffly to accept his lips on her forehead.

She continued with her work. When still she didn't speak, he turned toward where his brother ate from a bowl at the table on the other side of the room that served as their kitchen.

"Dofnaya," Ranyana said.

His brother made eye contact and then continued eating in silence.

Ranyana slipped off his rifle and set it against the side of the tall, plain, near-empty shelving case to the right of the front door. He removed his helmet, placed it on one of the shelves, and joined his brother at the table.

"Where were you today?" Ranyana said. "Weren't you supposed to be on the mountain?"

Dofnaya spooned more couscous into his mouth. A few grains fell to the table.

"The mountain is for heathens," he said without looking at him. "I can do better with the scriptures by myself."

He finished chewing and swallowed.

"I am not an infidel, like some."

He glared at Ranyana.

"But wouldn't you have been missed at sign-in? Won't you be reported?" Ranyana said.

Dofnaya laughed once: a harsh, brisk burst of air that shot a grain from his mouth.

"Don't be stupid," he said. "You *work* at the mountain. You know its reputation as well as I do. Do you really think they'd send for me now?"

"Maybe not," Ranyana said. "But the law still calls for . . ."

"Damn the law, and the mountain," Dofnaya said. "Come to think of it, damn you too."

He hunched over his bowl again.

Ranyana's face tensed up.

"Do you mind, Ranyana?" Dofnaya said. "I'm trying to eat."

Ranyana hesitated and then slowly stood from the table. He took off his coat and bullet-proof vest and moved with them to the short hallway to the two small bedrooms at the back of the house.

The door to his bedroom was closed. He stood before it and listened. His breathing quickened. He turned the doorknob.

A thin sheet of vertical moonlight sliced in from the room's only window on the opposite wall. It split the floor between his side of the room and Dofnaya's. He stepped in.

"Close the door, Ranyana," his father said from the cloak of shadow in the far right corner. He sat in the room's single chair, which he himself had made of unfinished wood.

He drew from his cigarette. The crackling cherry glowed orange against his face.

Ranyana shut the door.

His father struck a match, lit the candle in Ranyana's little dish, and set it on the foot of Ranyana's bed. He then held up a paperback book and waved it.

"Your brother found this behind your headboard this morning," he said. "He thought I should see it too."

He lowered the book and thumbed through its pages.

"This is hard for me to believe or accept, Ranyana."

Ranyana remained silent and still.

"How dare you!"

His father whipped the book at him. It bounced off his upper arm and fell to the floor.

"*Wallaha?* In *my* house? Do you understand the *danger* you've invited?"

He drew deeply on the cigarette and then set it in the dish.

"What have I done that would make you betray me this way?" he said. "Have I failed you as a father?"

Ranyana's mouth and throat felt as dry as the Demarquan desert.

"No," he said softly.

His father rose, walked over to him, and retrieved the book from the floor with his left hand. He held it to Ranyana's face.

"Then *why*, Ranyana? Why the sin? Why the *lie?*"

Ranyana licked his lips. His tongue was a slab of paste.

"It's . . . only a book, Father," he said.

Before Ranyana could flinch, his father's heavy, open right hand smacked his face. Ranyana fell back to his right and almost hit the door.

"*Only a book?*" his father said.

Ranyana touched his stinging cheek and then moved past his father to sit on the edge of his bed. He leaned forward with his hands clasped and his elbows on his knees. The dish tilted toward his weight.

"Why must we be so afraid of ideas, Father?" he said.

"Because our ideas are who we are inside," his father said. "They must be the right ones or we will suffer and be damned."

He took a step closer to him.

"Wallaha is pollution of the mind and soul. You know this, Ranyana."

Ranyana looked at the book in his father's hand.

"Then why have a mind at all, if we can't decide for ourselves how to use it?" he said. "Why didn't Baruna just make us all empty and simple, and interested in nothing but Him? Why even allow us to consider anything else?"

His father held the book over the candle and let the flame lick at it. Ranyana watched it catch fire.

"You never said those things or asked these questions before, Ranyana," his father said. He continued moving the book to help the flame eat more of it.

"I'm only trying to be your honest son," Ranyana said. "I do not love you, or my country, or Baruna any less because I ask and say these things. They are simply thoughts I have."

"Your thoughts," his father said, "are not entirely yours. They are too weak to stand alone, just as mine are. We need the scriptures, and Kwatakan, and Baruna. We need the Regent."

"But we are not the Regent," Ranyana said. "So how can we think as he does? How can he think like we do? Baruna made each of us to be unique in His image, did he not?"

"He did make us in His image, yes," his father said. "And left to our own thoughts and devices, all we do is try to soil it."

He let the book burn until less than a third remained. He then blew out the flame and threw the charred nub to the floor.

"I fear that it might be too late, Ranyana," he said. "I'm afraid you've read enough of this garbage to poison your brain for good."

"I am fine, Father," Ranyana said.

His father stared down at him.

"Words," he said. "Just words. You've already shown me you can lie, and hide a secret."

"I would have had these thoughts and asked these questions with or without the poet," Ranyana said. "All he is or was to me is a voice that expressed how I already feel. I am your son, and a child of Baruna, but I am also a person. I am human, and capable of reason. I can . . . imagine."

"That's enough, Ranyana!" his father spat, pointing at him. His index finger jabbed at the air. "We've had our private conversation, and this is where it will end. I'll hear no more such nonsense from you ever again in this house."

"If that is so, Father," Ranyana said, "if I cannot be who I am, and if my only destiny is to find God through one man or one book, then I am already no longer living."

"*Damn you, Ranyana!*" his father screamed. He leaped at him.

Ranyana shot up from the bed, wrapped both arms around his father's torso, and drove him against the opposite wall. A ceramic figure fell from the single shelf above Dofnaya's bed and smashed on the floor. Ranyana wrestled his father down and pinned him until he stopped fighting.

"Damn you," his father said in a raspy, labored voice.

The door flew open and whacked against the wall.

Dofnaya pounced on Ranyana and clamped his neck in a rear-naked choke. Ranyana let go of his father and pushed back with his legs. He and his brother twisted on the floor in the middle of the room. Dofnaya tightened his hold. Ranyana's face contorted as he battled for air.

He reached up with both hands, cupped the back of Dofnaya's head, and pulled with all his might while he squirmed. He wiggled free, punched his brother in the jaw, and shot up to his feet.

"*I hate you!*" Dofnaya screamed from the floor.

A splotch of blood appeared at the corner of his mouth.

Ranyana looked at his father, who now sat with his back against the wall.

Footsteps approached from the hall. His mother came to the doorway but did not enter the room.

"The Regent is the Regent because he demands with force and fear that we regard him as such," Ranyana said.

He looked from his father to his mother to Dofnaya, who had risen and now sat on his own bed. The candle still burned on Ranyana's; it hadn't tipped during the fracas.

"We all agreed," Ranyana continued. "And once we did that, we *obeyed.* And once we obeyed, his identity grew stronger. So did our fear of the fiction he is. He is no more fit to interpret the truth than we are. *We* are truth as Baruna speaks it to each of our hearts. *We* celebrate Him by how we love and think and dream and create. He proves Himself through us, and through Him, we discover who we are. Baruna is beautiful, and so are we. If we cannot communicate with and through Him as ourselves, then our existence amounts to nothing."

Ranyana looked at all of them again. Even in the room's concealing candlelight, he could see the disgust in their eyes.

"Ranyana," his father said, "if you insist on speaking and acting this way, then clearly you are full of pride and defiance. And if that is true, then you are not my son, and I cannot mourn whatever happens to you."

He fought to his feet and leaned forward with his hands on his knees and his bottom against the wall.

"The word is the word," he said. "You cannot add to it, subtract from it, or use it as you choose. It is the *only* truth. Your mother and I raised you in the right way. We can now only pray for you. And if it is God's will not to answer our prayers, then we will beg Him to forgive you."

The room fell quiet again. Ranyana looked at his brother, whose eyes had become even more sinister.

"Tell us now," his father said, "if you have anything else to confess. As long as you live in this house, your secrets are our secrets. Their consequences belong to us."

"I have no more, Father," Ranyana said, looking first at him and then at his mother in the doorway.

Martika's eyes flashed on like green headlights in the middle of his mind. They flooded him with shame.

"I am angry with you, Ranyana," his father said, "but I'll love you until you make it impossible. You *must* choose, here and now, to clear your head of this nonsense before it opens the gates of hell upon this house."

His father stood and approached him.

"If you continue to defy the law and the truth," he continued, "you'll leave me no choice but to turn you into the authorities myself. And then you will also have to bear the guilt of having broken my heart."

Ranyana stared at the floor.

"I'm sorry, Father," he said. "You are right, and I am wrong. I will correct my thoughts and beg for Baruna's forgiveness."

His father embraced him.

"I love you, Ranyana," he said. "I know you'll do what's right and make me proud."

Ranyana half-hugged his father around the waist.

"I won't fail you, Father," he said.

His father squeezed him once more and then left the room. He guided his wife away from the doorway.

Ranyana looked from his brother to the candle still burning in its dish on the bed. Their father's cigarette was now a blackened butt.

"What happened to you, Ranyana?" Dofnaya said. "When did you decide you want to die?"

Ranyana glanced at what remained of Wallaha's book on the floor.

"Maybe I already have died," he said. "You too."

Dofnaya sneered.

"I pity you," he said.

He rose from the bed and walked toward the door. He stopped at Ranyana's side.

"May God have mercy on you," he said.

He left, closing the door behind him.

"Without conscience," Ranyana said, with less than the breath of a bird, to the dim and empty room.

He blew out the candle and set the dish on the floor.

He lay down on his bed. When sometime later his thoughts decided to leave him alone, he closed his eyes, and fell to sleep.

*T*he banquet room was not one he'd ever afford, let alone be permitted to occupy. Yet it welcomed him as if familiar.

He glanced around at the seated handsome people in their formal suits and gowns. They laughed and smiled and chattered. Teeth flashed. Eyes and diamonds twinkled. More lances of light shot from silver serving trays bearing food and decanters of wine.

The long and narrow table in the center of the room offered fresh fish and meats and cheeses from one end to the other. Ranyana also saw fruits and herbs and vegetables; olives and couscous and rice.

Tambourines and stringed instruments came to life, inciting the celebrants to rise from their chairs. Ranyana watched their pleasing bodies respond to the music. Across the room, Trunaya lifted her veil and beamed at him.

He finished his wine, stood, and approached her through the dancing crowd. With every step, she became more attractive and endearing to him. He loved her as a friend and lusted for her as a lover. As he moved closer, her unspoken voice filled his head: *I love and understand you, love and understand you, love and understand you.*

The wedding guests parted in his path to form an aisle from him to her. Seconds stretched into minutes without counting. Faces blurred. All sound slowed and distorted.

The room rumbled. A column of light punched through the ceiling and landed in a perfect circle between them.

"May this union be blessed by God and the prophet," a deep voice bellowed from above. "May your home prosper as the scriptures promise to those who seek and follow the truth."

The wedding guests fell to the floor and prostrated themselves. Only Ranyana and his wife remained standing.

Ranyana looked up and squinted at the radiant light. It bathed and warmed him with hope.

He embraced his wife and kissed her as hard as he could.

Smiling, still holding her tightly, he drew his face back.

Her skin bled from her bones like melting wax. Matted clumps of hair fell away from her scalp. Her mandible unhinged. A tongue thick with sores shot from her mouth.

Fuck me, Ranyana, FUCK ME!

He shoved her. She cackled and groped for his groin. He spun around to run, but the guests had formed a wall of themselves to trap him in. Trunaya's gown slipped from her shoulders to the floor. She plucked off her nubby, mosquito-bite breasts and held them out to him.

Have me, Ranyana! Take what's filthy and yours!

He tried to run to his right, where the wall of people was thinner, but the floor provided no friction. He ran faster and faster in place until he started to scream.

He glanced back over his shoulder.

The skeletal monster came toward him in long and bony strides.

Have your whore as well, Ranyana! it said in Martika's and Trunaya's voices combined. *Isn't that what you want? Isn't that what ALL men want? A virgin to live with and a slut to sleep with?*

The tongue licked side to side and then fell to the floor from the skull.

Come to us, Ranyana!

He tried running harder but still he could not move.

The speech behind him became deep and muddy, sped up like a tape in fast forward, and then slowed down again. It sounded tinny and ambient, like an announcement blared from an old speaker high on a pole.

He listened closer to the inflections within the scratchy echoes—and identified the Regent.

All sinners go to HELL! You should have listened to your leader, listened to your leader, listened to your . . .

The light retreated into the ceiling. The hole above closed and the chandeliers shattered, drowning the room in deep shadows. Jagged glass rained down, scattering screaming people.

Decanters toppled and emptied themselves onto the floor. The wine became a hissing river of boiling blood that ran around Ranyana's feet.

He closed his eyes and prayed although he couldn't be heard: "Forgive me, forgive me, forgive . . ."

His eyes snapped open.

He looked up the barrel of his own rifle. His brother looked down the other end of it.

"Dofnaya," Ranyana whispered, not moving. "What are you doing?"

His brother's ropy jaw muscles flexed within the faint moonlight from their one small window.

"You no longer belong to this family," he said. His finger tightened on the trigger. "You are worse than scum."

Ranyana did not breathe. They both remained corpse-quiet.

Then, his eyes wide open, Ranyana said:

"Do it."

Dofnaya kept the rifle stiff and level at Ranyana's face.

They stared at each other. Neither knew how long.

Dofnaya lowered the gun and took a step backward.

"There is no rest for the infidel, Ranyana," he said. "The righteous will destroy you, or you will destroy yourself."

Still holding the rifle, he turned and went to the door.

"No one will defend a traitor," he said over his shoulder.

He left.

Ranyana lay rigidly for a while, thinking. At some point, he swung his legs out of bed and sat on the edge of it. He lowered his head and rubbed his face with his hands. When he looked up again, his father stood just beyond the doorway: a silent, ominous half-shape in the dark.

The shape watched him a little longer and then, like a phantom from a dream, it went away.

*H*e approached the mountain for duty the following morning and knew that something had changed. Soldiers swarmed like bothered bees by the entrance. Many carried H4 Yanzers—the corporals called them H4-Ya's—a high-end assault rifle that weighed less than eight pounds and fired more than a thousand rounds per minute. It was used almost exclusively by the Regent's elite special forces. A corporal would wield it only during a go-for-broke offensive.

Ranyana still carried a standard-issue automatic rifle. No one had told him about the H4-Ya's. From what he could see, he was the only soldier without one.

Jeeps and trucks sped, turned, and stopped to drop off more men. Orders like bullets zipped through the air. Helicopters whizzed and whirred above the mountain.

"Ranyana!"

Maleko was running toward him.

"The Regent's pissed off," he said, slightly out of breath. "Looks like he's through with the mountain. As of six a.m. he authorized invasion."

"But what about immunity?" Ranyana said.

"What about it?"

Clacking feet came toward them. Ranyana and Maleko stood straight and saluted the captain.

"You two are in the air today," he said. "Get moving."

"Sir!" they responded in concert.

The captain glanced from Maleko's H4 Yanzer to Ranyana's standard gun.

Ranyana awaited a comment. The captain looked at him longer, and then he strode away.

Ranyana and Maleko jogged to the marked vehicle that would take them to the landing field. They jumped into the back with the dozen or so soldiers already there. Ranyana reached up and grabbed a rail of the truck bed's overhead frame.

Once beyond the access road, the truck cut and wove through traffic for several kilometers until it reached the turn-off. The truck slowed, gained clearance, and then sped up again. When it stopped, the soldiers emptied out and sprinted to the waiting helicopters.

Two officers in sunglasses broke them into their groups. Ranyana, Maleko, and two other soldiers boarded their bird. Their pilot and co-pilot gestured at them, and then the copter took off.

It swung toward the mountain, which always seemed closer than it was because of its size. Ranyana looked out at it through the copter's open cabin. The wind blew hard on him but did not feel any cooler. He wiped his sweaty face on the sleeve of his jacket.

The co-pilot twisted in his seat.

"We're going in close!" he screamed over his shoulder. Ranyana noted his insignia patch: sergeant. *"Real close, so be real fucking ready!"*

Ranyana nodded once.

"Close enough for a kiss and a picture!" the co-pilot continued. He laughed. *"Kill if you feel like it!"*

Ranyana looked away. He felt dizzy, and faint. He thought he might even throw up.

Mount Takusha grew slowly larger with their approach. Its lush vegetation and serpentine streams and footpaths came into even greater relief.

Ranyana had never seen the mountain this way.

Its beauty broke his heart and made him feel small.

He glanced around the cabin; no one paid attention to him, not even Maleko, who sat against the cabin wall with his H4 Yanzer pointing straight up between his legs.

Ranyana looked out at the mountain again. Clouds formed fluffy smoke rings around its peaks of varying heights; waterfalls spilled over cliffs into private pools below; trees and flowers splashed and dotted their bumpy, uneven canvas with color; animals lounged, ate, hid, and slept within their self-contained worlds.

The co-pilot slipped from the cockpit into the cabin with a pair of binoculars.

"Look!"

He shoved them at Ranyana and pointed to a circular clearing of grass surrounded by thick and leafy trees.

Ranyana took the binoculars and held them up to his face.

Right away, he saw the naked young bodies running and rolling on the grass despite the copters they had to have heard and perhaps even seen.

They didn't know the scriptures had stopped protecting them.

"Look at that!" the co-pilot said. *"We hit them first!"*

Ranyana counted four of them: two boys, two girls. One of the boys chased one of the girls and pulled her to the ground. He climbed on top of her. She wrapped her legs around him.

Ranyana's heart beat faster.

"They're yours!" the co-pilot shouted into his ear.

Ranyana lowered the binoculars and looked at him.

"We'll lower you into the trees! You'll take care of them, and then we'll come back for you!"

The co-pilot grabbed a backpack and shoved it at him.

"It's got everything! You know what to do!"

The helicopter swung from the clearing and then circled back, flying lower to where the trees grew even thicker. The co-pilot threw out a rope ladder.

"Go!" He slapped Ranyana on the back. *"We'll see you after they're dead!"*

Ranyana slipped on the backpack, secured his rifle to his body, and climbed down the ladder, which disappeared into the branches below. When he reached the bottom rung, he chose his branch, straddled it, and tugged on the ladder. The ladder rolled up, and the copter flew away.

Holding a higher branch for support, Ranyana walked along his branch toward the trunk. He removed the binoculars from the backpack's side pocket and looked out toward the clearing.

The view wasn't clear enough for a shot. He maneuvered around the trunk and used several more branches to move to the next closer tree. After finding the position he needed, he raised the binoculars again.

The one boy remained on top of the girl he had chased. They were now making love.

The other two, also still naked, stood talking just a few meters from the writhing bodies.

He stared at the prone boy's contracting back and clinching buttocks. The girl hooked her heels in the bends of his knees. She pulled herself up beneath him and kissed his shoulder.

He lowered the binoculars and looked off to one side.

He raised them again.

The girl was guiding the boy's mouth down to her breast.

Ranyana dug into the pack and located the long-range scope. He fastened it to his rifle and then hung the pack by a shoulder strap from an overhead branch.

When he trained the scope on the students again, the two who were standing shifted their positions, giving him an even better look at their faces:

Martika, and her constant companion.

He focused on the other two. Yes: he now recognized them as well. He'd seen them coming and going with Martika at the mountain.

He shifted the scope back toward her.

Damn her. Their encounter in the alley had amounted to nothing.

She would continue to be who she was, and do what she did, and believe as she believed.

She's just another liberal slut in the guise of a convert.

He took aim at the boy grinding on the girl on the ground.

Another liberal slut hiding in a state yellow robe.

Far too free in her mind.

His finger moved on the trigger but didn't apply any pressure.

She will never contribute to Demarqua.

He continued to stare through the scope.

The girl wrapped her legs around the boy's waist. The boy posted himself on one arm.

Decent people—spiritual people—did not conduct themselves this way.

Maybe they were just still too young and immature. Maybe they would improve after completing their training.

Or maybe not.

Ranyana drew his head back from the scope and looked off to the side again.

The students in the clearing were darkened by forces that Ranyana and Trunaya would and could not know. *Their* union would be wholesome and safe. Practical. *Responsible.*

Baruna would bless them. The scriptures said so.

Ranyana pressed his eye to the scope and aimed the rifle.

Martika put her hand on her companion's arm.

Ranyana pulled the trigger.

The bullet punched the prone boy in the back. He rolled off of the girl.

She screamed.

Ranyana shot him again.

The girl screamed louder.

Then he shot her.

Martika and her companion sprinted for the trees. They left their robes in crumpled heaps behind them.

Ranyana kept his rifle trained on them until they disappeared.

He slipped the rifle over his shoulder and removed the walkie-talkie from the backpack.

"Corporal A-1-5 to pick-up, do you read me, over," he said into it.

"Sergeant X-1-3, over," the co-pilot said after a couple of crackles.

"Mission accomplished, over," Ranyana said.

More screeching static.

"Drop-off point inside fifteen, over."

Ranyana returned the scope and the talkie to the backpack, cinched it shut, and began working his way to where the copter would meet him.

About halfway back, he stopped.

A humid yet still pleasant breeze pushed past him and rustled the leaves. A distant waterfall scattered hissing droplets of sound that formed a faint mist in his ears.

He looked up, beyond the overhead branches. Two eagles encircled the sky right above him. He watched them glide in wide arcs that signed their wings on the air.

Minutes later, he heard the first whirs of the rotors. He balanced himself, re-secured his gun and pack to his body, and completed his way to the drop-off point. The copter came into view—a bulky mosquito that swelled as it came toward him at a downward angle.

When the copter idled overhead, the co-pilot threw down the ladder and waved. Ranyana snatched the bottom rung and climbed as the copter slowly turned around. The co-pilot pulled him in at the top.

"Took care of all four!" Ranyana said.

The co-pilot nodded and smiled.

"Just nailed six before we got here!"

Maleko and one of the other two soldiers gave Ranyana a thumbs-up.

The copter accelerated. Raising his binoculars, the co-pilot leaned out and looked back toward Mount Takusha.

Ranyana thought to grab him, but the co-pilot's face had already changed.

He yanked Ranyana by the arm. Ranyana almost fell out of the bird.

"What's that, corporal?"

The co-pilot shoved the binoculars at him and pointed out of the cabin. Ranyana held them up and aimed them at the mountain.

The two dead bodies remained naked and still in the grove.

Clutching their robes against their chests, two distant, tiny figures were running toward the trees. Ranyana watched them plunge into cover again.

He lowered the binoculars, looked into his lap, and handed them back to the co-pilot.

"Two of your dead sure look good, corporal!"

The co-pilot shoved him, hard, back into the cabin.

Ranyana did not look at him, nor at anyone else. All eyes but his may as well have been the Regent's.

He sat alone and apart from them and rode the rest of the way within the judgment of silence.

*T*he lieutenant had been staring at him silently for a while, chewing on his unlit cigar.

Ranyana glanced up at the mirrored reflections of the two armed soldiers standing to either side of the door behind him.

The lieutenant chewed harder and leaned forward. Ranyana and the soldiers became bigger in his eyes.

"We have ourselves a . . . *situation,* wouldn't you agree, corporal?" he said.

Ranyana said nothing.

"A *grave* situation," the lieutenant said.

He plucked the cigar from his mouth and spat a bit of leaf to the side.

"What am I to believe about you?"

Ranyana looked down.

"Well?"

Ranyana looked back up.

"Sir," he said.

"Sir, what?" the lieutenant said. "Have you nothing to say for yourself? You're dangerously close to being branded a traitor."

"I . . . shot to kill," Ranyana said. "I struck down two infidels for the Regent and Demarqua."

The lieutenant returned the cigar to his mouth.

"Of course you did," he said. "But according to intelligence I now have, at least one infidel is still standing, isn't she?"

Ranyana started to speak but stopped.

"If you killed two, why did you say four?" the lieutenant said. "Why did a sergeant in the air see the other two running to safety?"

The lieutenant chewed on the cigar several times.

"More important, why did your *assignment* come back down from the mountain alive?"

His mouth tightened and then smoothed into a smile.

"Don't answer," he said. "Doesn't matter. We collected your friends at the gate. In fact, they're here in the building right now."

Ranyana's head turned slightly sideways. His eyebrows went up.

"They're close by," the lieutenant said. He stood, set the cigar on the edge of his desk, and straightened his multi-medaled coat. "Come on, I'll show you."

He walked around the desk and looked down at Ranyana. Ranyana rose from his chair.

One of the soldiers opened the door, and the lieutenant walked out. Ranyana followed. Both soldiers fell in behind him.

The group crossed the hallway into the hangar. Staying several strides ahead, the lieutenant aimed for another hallway on the far side. Ranyana felt the stares of the soldiers who watched.

The opposite hall was darker and longer. Halfway down, the lieutenant opened a door to his left. He motioned for Ranyana to enter.

Ranyana stepped in. Martika and her companion sat in steel chairs at a plain table bearing the tales of the room's many former occupants: dried blood that hadn't fully faded; chinks, gashes, and gouges made with both dull and sharp instruments; ominous, desperate words inscribed with who-knew-what. Baledo stood in a corner with his rifle against his shoulder.

Martika looked up at Ranyana.

"You will take them outside and complete your assignment," the lieutenant said from the doorway.

Martika's companion slumped forward and rubbed the back of his head with both hands.

The lieutenant removed a .22 caliber Ikotona automatic handgun—an officer's gun—from inside his jacket. He handed it to Ranyana and nodded toward Baledo.

"Your comrade will ensure that you finish the job," he said. "And if you can't, he will."

Baledo stared at Ranyana with red-rimmed eyes.

"At which time he'll also have my orders to finish *you*," the lieutenant said.

He turned and left with footsteps that echoed. The two soldiers remained outside of the room at either side of the door.

Baledo stepped from the corner and gestured toward the door with his rifle.

"Up," he said. "Let's go."

Martika rose slowly, looked at Ranyana, and stepped out. Her companion stood and left as well.

Ranyana and Baledo looked at each other across the room.

"Well?" Baledo said.

"Well, what?" Ranyana said. "Let's be done with it."

Out in the hallway, Ranyana pointed at Martika and then to his left.

"The exit at the end of the hall," he said.

She and her companion started to walk.

Ranyana remained a few steps behind. Baledo trailed him closely; Ranyana could almost hear his eager breathing.

The students reached the exit door and stopped. Martika looked back at Ranyana.

He pointed the lieutenant's gun. It felt efficient in his hand.

"Outside," he said.

She searched his eyes, and then obeyed.

Ranyana followed them out into the alley. He did not hold the door for Baledo, who caught it with his forearm before it shut.

"Ten steps to your left and then face the wall," Ranyana said.

The sun felt heavier now. Ranyana wiped his face against the arm of his coat.

At the end of their steps, the lovers looked at each other. They mouthed words that Ranyana couldn't decipher. Then they faced the building.

"Redeem yourself," Baledo said. He stood halfway between Ranyana and the door.

Ranyana strode up behind the students and pointed the gun at Martika's head.

He spun around and pulled the trigger.

The first bullet missed Baledo. The second and third punched through his forehead.

Baledo dropped.

Ranyana fired again, and then again.

He turned toward the students.

"Look at me," he said to them.

They did.

"If I let you go, tell me what you will do," Ranyana said.

They glanced at each other. Martika's companion nodded at her.

"We know a man," she said. "He lives at the edge of Bahdran."

They looked at each other again. Her companion nodded once more.

"He can get us to the border, if we pay the right amount. It doesn't mean we'll get there."

Ranyana's gun hand fell to his side.

"Now is your time to try," he said.

They stared at him.

"May Baruna watch over you," he said.

Martika walked to him and gently touched his face.

Ranyana placed his hand on top of hers. He held it momentarily, and then removed it.

Still looking at him, she backed away. Her companion took her by the hand. They ran to the end of the alley and around the corner of the building.

The door behind Ranyana flew open.

"Drop the gun!"

One of the lieutenant's two soldiers burst into the alley with his rifle up. The other soldier followed, dropped to one knee, and aimed his rifle as well.

Ranyana raised his left hand and bent slowly to set the gun on the ground with his right.

The standing soldier snatched the walkie-talkie from his belt and spoke into it.

A minute later, the lieutenant stormed outside. He looked from the soldiers to Ranyana to the body on the ground.

"Face the wall, corporal," he said.

He picked up his gun from where it lay near Ranyana.

Ranyana approached the wall.

He waited for the bullet that would turn out the lights. And as he did, he dreamed, but not of gods and government, or even of passions he'd never be able to feel. He dreamed only of where he might go now that his term in the hell that men insist on was over.

A form of paradise came into view in his mind—one he recognized and understood—but he couldn't yet hear its welcoming music: his ears were too full of the sound of beating wings, like eagles' wings, circling the air over the mountain in a sky as clear and as blue as his conscience.

CONCERTO

*T*he people walking the dark, rain-slicked sidewalk beneath the apartment building at 101 East Rooker Street stopped in harmony. They'd heard the sounds of love from beyond a third-story window.

It carried down to them, inviting them to listen. Each looked up toward the consummating notes dancing through the raindrops.

The woman in the living room of apartment 321 tightened her one-handed grasp of the neck. Her other hand guided the bow across compliant strings that knew what her fingers could do. Tears welled in her eyes with the approach of their crescendo.

The strangers beneath the window glanced at one another. One man touched another man next to him; a teenager didn't return her headphones to her ears; a homeless woman smiled and continued pushing the shopping cart that carried her life.

The phone rang in apartment 321.

Anita Juergen put down the bow and set the cello on its stand in the corner. She wiped her brow with a small, white hand towel.

The phone continued to ring. She didn't answer. The caller hung up and tried again.

She crossed the room and picked up.

"Hello?"

"Anita."

"Hello, Monte."

"I need to see you right away. It's important."

She glanced at the lamp table's digital clock.

"It's almost midnight."

"I know, I know. But I really have to see you. Talk to you."

"Just tell me now."

"No. It'll be better if we speak in person."

She bit at her thumbnail.

"Ten minutes—tops."

The other line went dead. Anita returned the phone to its cradle.

Monte arrived in less than fifteen minutes on foot; he lived only three blocks away. He stepped in and ran a manicured hand through his rain-slicked hair.

She looked him up and down.

"Have you ever seen it rain this much?" he said. He shook himself off like a dog. Flecks of musky water peppered the planks of the floor.

"Hey!" she said. "I have to mop that up, you know. Ever heard of an umbrella?"

"Who needs one . . . ," he said, kicking the door shut with his heel. He pulled her toward him. "When I know I'll be wet with love here anyway?"

"If only you could speak as well as you play," she said, resisting his embrace.

"Do you mean with the violin, or with your nether regions?"

"You said you needed to talk. I said you had ten minutes."

"Maybe it's better if we just get down to business."

He kissed her neck.

She pushed against him harder. He hugged her tighter and licked her earlobe.

She relaxed.

"You're right," she said, making her neck more available. "Stop blabbering and kiss me."

He shoved her against the wall and tore at her shirt.

"Be careful," she said. "This blouse is new."

He ripped it down over her shoulders, popping two buttons and stretching the fabric. The bra was the next to go: he placed his mouth around her nipple.

He moved her to the sofa and onto her back. Then he turned off the lamp, undressed the rest of her, and pinned her shoulder with a thin, muscular arm.

The cello watched from the corner.

"What was that?" Monte said, pushing up.

Anita shifted beneath him.

The skin of their stomachs stuck softly together with sweat.

"What was what?"

"That scratching noise."

He rose with his knees still on the edge of the sofa cushion and looked around the darkened room. He recognized only Anita's basic accoutrements: lamp table, coffee table, two chairs, some prints of musicians and musical notes on the wall, the cello in the corner.

"Never mind," he said, and mounted her again.

It hated the sounds that they made: so selfish, atonal, no soul. The beast attacked her from above as if to steal her breath. Splinters like tears rained within its hollow body. One of its strings reached the knife edge of breaking when . . .

Monte finished.

He lit a Salem for Anita and a joint for himself. They moved and sat side by side.

"So what was so important that you had to rush over and tell me?" she asked.

Their cherries glowed in the dark.

He inhaled, held the smoke, and exhaled slowly.

"I forgot," he said.

Anita looked forward.

The cello stood still in the corner.

They continued smoking in silence.

Monte extinguished his joint with wet fingertips and returned it to a small zip-loc pouch in his pants pocket. Then he got up and dressed.

Anita crossed her legs and folded her arms over her breasts. She held her cigarette away from her in the V of her right index and middle fingers.

Monte paused at the front door and glanced over his shoulder. She couldn't see his face.

"Thanks," he said, and left.

Anita lay flat and buried her face in her arms. Monte's musky scent still filled her nose.

She wiped a tear from her eye.

Still naked, she rose from the sofa and padded down the hallway to her bedroom. She slipped into her white cotton robe.

Back in the front room, she turned on the lamp-table light and plopped into the loveseat. Her head fell back. She listened to the wet traffic and the sleepless city outside.

Her eyes returned to the cello.

Had it moved since she'd placed it there, before Monte came over?

She rose and walked over to it. Kneeled on the floor before it. Ran her fingers along the curves of its body. The cello sighed in her mind.

She stood and stepped back to look it over again.

Her heart skipped. She moved closer.

A light, shallow groove, almost one inch long, had been etched into the hardwood floor. It started where the cello had been and ended where it now was.

She returned it to its original place, turned off the light, and went to bed.

A nita removed the cello from its case just as Monte arrived. The Civic Auditorium's performance hall swelled with the jumbled and discordant notes of orchestral tuning.

He passed the cellos without looking her way. She watched him stride with his case to his chair among the violins.

She didn't love the *man,* she reminded herself as he began chatting with the younger blonde who sat next to him. She loved him for what he *could* be, if only he'd let her help him find that. All he had to do was provide the answers to the riddle she'd allowed him to be.

He removed the violin from the case in his lap. He said something. The blonde woman smiled and laughed. She gave him her rosin: he'd forgotten his.

Anita's face went red.

A baton rapped on the lectern. The tuning and chattering stopped. Attention went to the front of the stage.

Jacques Fortier, the conductor, cleared his throat. The instruments' last dying notes floated to the dome of the roof.

His voice betrayed his size. To Anita, he looked like an older Mickey Rooney but spoke like a lighter James Earl Jones. She'd also never seen a single hair move within his combed goatee: not even beneath the force of his breath.

"We will begin with Monte Stanton's original Violin Concerto in D Minor,'" he said.

Anita glanced at Monte. He did not look at her.

The musicians positioned themselves and awaited Fortier's cue.

The soft, lulling notes to the concerto rose and picked up tempo. Swaying back and forth with his eyes closed, Monte tapped and drew his bow across his strings. He then effortlessly flowed into the melancholy measures he'd shared and discussed with Anita so many times when they were alone.

The orchestra followed his lead.

Anita felt a crippling cocktail of grief and respect. She gripped the cello's neck harder than she knew she could. Each graceful saw of his bow sliced her even more deeply.

Beneath her poised fingers, the cello's strings tightened.

She held it closer to her and rubbed her cheek gently against its neck.

Monte finished his piece with a flourish. The other musicians broke into applause. He stood and nodded toward each section.

Fortier stepped down from the podium, walked toward the violins, and bowed in Monte's direction.

"A superb rendering of the material, as is to be expected," he said.

He returned to the podium, raised his arms, and led the orchestra into Mendelssohn's "Concerto in E Minor."

Anita stared at Monte as she feigned to play her part.

He remained fixated on Fortier's baton and jerking, sweeping arms. The blonde beside him leaned closer as they performed. Anita watched her watch him for a sign that he noticed her too.

She wanted to cry.

Monte was . . . perfect. Beautiful, charming, gifted, maybe divine.

She cursed herself. She had to focus. To contribute to the language of tones all around her. It was the only speech that made any sense.

She summoned the patterns of play she'd drawn in her mind during relentless hours of practice: the long and short draws of her bow, the subtle shifts in pitch and volume, the press and release of the strings.

She tried to perform. The cello resisted.

"Please, please," she whispered to it within their whirlpool of sound.

She stroked it and squeezed it tighter between her thighs.

She drew her bow above the bridge. The cello gave her a sound like a tack across a blackboard.

The piece continued with no knowledge of their miscarriage.

The music reached its crescendo and concluded.

The musicians relaxed and moved in their chairs once it was done. Some murmured. Others wiped their faces and foreheads.

"Let us move into Dvorak's Cello Concerto, featuring Anita Juergen," Fortier said from the front.

Anita's breathing stopped.

Her preparation didn't concern her: she'd put in almost thirty hours that week. It was her blasted . . .

The cello's end pin slid beneath her. The instrument lurched to her right. She caught it before it could slip from her grip.

"What's wrong with you?" she said close to its neck. "Why are you being like this?"

"I do love it when you play this one," the cellist to her left said with a smile.

The woman winked and patted her arm.

Anita's stomach tightened.

The auditorium went quiet. Fortier rapped his baton.

She stared at the floor, and then, like paperclips drawn to a magnet, her eyes found their way back to Monte.

With his bow in his lap and his violin cradled loosely in his left arm, he grinned.

The blonde beside him glared at her.

Anita searched his expression.

He shrugged.

Anita swallowed paste and ran her fingers along the cello's neck.

"Please," she whispered to its scroll. "Play for me."

Fortier rapped his baton again. Feet shuffled. Weight shifted as the musicians resumed their positions. Fortier raised his arms, paused, and rocked into his direction.

She glanced at Monte again.

His face confirmed what both of them knew.

She was going to fail.

The piece's opening multiple measures played their ways toward her solo.

She had to do something—think fast.

She closed her eyes.

Her father, kneeling next to her chair as she bumbles through her exercises. Neither hands nor cello obey.

She shoves the instrument away. He catches it.

She dashes past him and up the stairs to her bedroom. Slams the door and dives onto her bed.

He knocks and lets himself in. She won't look back at him; her heart is too full of shame.

His footsteps brush the carpet. The edge of her mattress sinks with his weight. A warm hand touches her back.

Don't give up on it, he says. *Just think of it as though it's your friend, and your friend has been hurt, and asked you to make the pain go away. If you make your friend feel better, your friend will remember the love you gave, and give it back to you when you're sad and alone and afraid.*

The love you share will find you again. It will search for you and find you, because love does not forget.

She stares at him through blurry tears. His face is patient and calm. He gently strokes her hair.

She scrambles up and hugs his neck. Holding hands, they return down to the living room. She smoothes her skirt and sits in the metal folding chair before her silver music stand.

He watches from a corner while she tends to a friend. The healing continues as she plays, and within an hour, she and her friend sound as they should. She smiles at her dad and kisses her cello.

Anita opened her eyes.

Countdown to concerto: four more measures and closing in fast.

She straightened in her chair and positioned her bow.

"I'm sorry, my love," she said to the cello, drawing its scroll closer to her mouth. She ran her left hand up and down its neck and strings and fingerboard. "You are not alone. I am here for you."

Its strings began to respond. She felt new warmth between her thighs.

They played, and played, and lost all knowledge of time.

And when it ended, all fell silent around them, returning her to the sea of gaping eyes.

Fortier leaned over his lectern until it appeared that he might fall. Leaving his baton, he stepped down, walked to where she sat, and stood with his hands clasped in front of him.

"That was . . . holy," he solemnly said, and then began to clap.

The rest of the orchestra joined him. Chairs screeched as they moved for the standing ovation.

Blushing, Anita stood and took a bow with the cello close to her body.

Monte remained still in his chair.

"Thank you," she said to the cello. She kissed its scroll; Monte saw her do it. "Thank you."

*H*e clenched his fist. His fingernails dug half-moons into his palm.

For one blind moment, he considered hurling his $25,000 David Burgess violin at any one of the cretins who praised her.

How pathetic they were, and easy to be swayed.

He'd like to see her do it again; he'd quit playing for good if she could.

His hatred heated her cello.

When she felt it too, she looked at him, and smiled at his beautiful rage.

*A*nita let herself into her apartment and set the cello in its case against the inside wall. Her sopping umbrella cried on the hardwood floor to the kitchen, where she set it down open to dry.

She filled a kettle and put it on the stove.

Once out of her damp, clammy clothes and into her robe, she sat on the front-room sofa, thinking about music and Monte. The kettle whistled minutes later.

She returned to the kitchen and made her instant coffee.

After blowing on the steam from the cup, she stood still, and listened to the silence.

Back in the front room, she set down her coffee and lit a candle on the lamp table.

She looked at the rain-flecked cello case by the door.

It simply stared back at her. Simple, vulnerable.

Hers.

She reached into her robe and ran her hands along the curves of her breasts.

She moved closer to the case. When she stood a foot from it, she ripped open her robe and slid her hands down her stomach. Her fingers slipped into her panties and slithered through her silken hair to the place that wanted to be pleased.

Her eyes closed. Her mouth parted.

She opened her eyes.

The cello case was still closed.

Her loosened robe fell to the floor.

The uncovered window peeped at her. She snatched her robe from the floor, threw it back on, and hurried to close the drapes.

The room fell pin-drop quiet but for her breath and heartbeat.

She rushed to the cello, kneeled before it, and ran her palms up and down the case.

"My dear," she said, "my love."

She removed the cello and bow and carried them carefully to the front room.

She took off her robe and sat naked in her practice chair. She drew the cello closer to her body and kissed its scroll with wet, parted lips and the tip of her tongue.

She drew the bow across the strings.

It tried but struggled to play: would she banish it to a corner if the beast returned to make its awful noises?

She rubbed her breasts against the back of its body.

"Please," she said, "I want to be with you. I have more to give."

The piece she attempted sounded off-key, so she tried changing compositions: maybe it'd respond to something else. When its impotence remained, she set it against the wall.

"What?" she said, standing before it, tears creeping up on her eyes. "What do you want from me? What do I need to do?"

It only stared ahead.

She lay face down, next to the coffee table, on the gold and maroon area rug. She buried her face in her hands.

Maybe she'd been wrong.

Way too bold and confident.

She shouldn't have made Monte feel threatened. Surely he'd make her pay.

Plus, she was talking to a *cello*. Without her clothes on, even.

Her sobs raided the room.

Something yielded.

A scratching sound, like a pin on wood.

She rolled over and looked at the cello.

"Is that you?" she said.

It continued looking at her from its position against the wall.

"*I'm sorry!*" she said. She crawled up to her knees, sat on her heels, and clasped her hands between her thighs. "I admit that I've been wrong and selfish. I need you to forgive me. You are all I have. *We* are all we have."

It remained a block of room-temperature ice.

She smiled, wiped the tears from her face, and crawled over to it.

"Now, now," she said, pulling it gently toward her. She pushed the coffee table against the sofa and laid the cello on its side on the rug.

"It's going to be okay."

She turned off the lamp, bathing them both in candlelight.

The rain ran in sheets down the covered front window.

She moved her practice chair closer and positioned the cello between it and the coffee table. Balancing herself on her hands with the chair to her left and the table to her right, she bent down into a half-squat and straddled the dip between the cello's upper and lower side halves.

The cello warmed between her legs.

She pulled her hair over one shoulder, licked her lips, and began to move back and forth in teasing, tickling brushes.

Her hips quickened with the same light but steady movements—back and forth, back and forth, a quick shift left and right. She cupped one of her breasts with her hand.

She looked left at her arching back in her swaying silhouette on the wall.

She glided faster, faster, faster. Her straining, screaming thighs were trembling.

She threw back her head.

Seismic moans escaped her mouth.

Shuddering, out of breath, her hair now dangling over her face, she rolled onto the rug and lay next to it.

"Yes, I can," she whispered to its scroll, ". . . yes, I do love."

*T*he telephone awakened her.

She looked sideways at the cello and then rose from the rug to answer.

"Hello?"

"Anita."

She closed her eyes.

"Yes?"

"It's *me*."

She glanced back at the cello.

"Now's not the time, Monte," she said. "I'm sleeping."

An extended pause.

"*Sleeping?* I'm glad one of us thinks that nothing's wrong."

"Nothing *is* wrong. I'm fine."

"*You're* fine. I see. Well that's fucking grand." Another pause. "Why are you acting like this?"

"Acting like what?" she said.

Another pregnant pause.

"Why did you leave without saying a word? And why didn't *you* call *me* after being so goddamn rude? I've been sitting here all night like an asshole, waiting for you. You owe me an apology."

"I'm through with you, Monte," she said.

The line fell quiet again: the many Montes were calling an emergency meeting.

"Don't say anything you might regret, Anita," one of them said. "*Please.* I . . . love you. You know that, don't you?"

"No," she said. "I don't." She looked at the cello again as if afraid she might disturb it. "Our relationship is bad for me."

Another Monte snickered.

"What?" he said. "Do you think you're *better* than me? Do you think I *need* you? I *don't*. I could call any of five other women *right now.*"

"Then why don't you?"

"Listen closely," he said, and now she heard the panic in his anger: she'd officially inconvenienced him. "At the end of the day, *you* need *me,* and one good rehearsal can't change that.*"

"Monte . . ."

"Shut up—I'm talking. Let's get something straight. Your head's pumped up right now. When it pops—and trust me, it will—you're going to be sorry about this conversation. *Very* fucking sorry."

She looked at the cello again.

"I'm coming over," Monte said, "so put on something I'll like. Something that will help me . . . forget."

He hung up.

She set the phone down on the lamp table and returned to the cello.

She lay down and touched it gently, but the spruce of its face was already cold.

*H*e knocked only once: a crisp, no-nonsense sound.

Anita cinched the belt of her robe, strode to the door, and stopped just short of it.

"I know you're right there, goddamn it," the voice on the other side said, "so open up before I get *really* upset."

She remained where she stood.

He knocked again—harder.

"Anita," he said. "I'm not fucking around. Open it."

A moment of silence.

"Go away, Monte. I don't want you here."

She heard only her breathing and her clicking throat.

He kicked the door. It rattled.

"Open the door, Anita, or so help me God, I'll break it down."

She looked at the phone.

He kicked the door again.

When still she didn't move, he placed his forehead and hands against the door.

"Anita, darling, please," the softer, slightly muffled voice said. "You just . . . I'm just very upset right now. I really need to talk to you. I need to see your face."

More silence.

"Please, Anita. I swear, it'll only take a few minutes. I . . . don't want to leave things like this. I care too much . . . we've . . . shared too much. If we have to end it, let's at least do it in a way that lets us still be friends."

She didn't speak.

"We still have to see each other every week," he said. His voice dropped even more. "Let's not make it uncomfortable for either of us."

She stared at the door for close to a minute.

"Five minutes tops, Monte," she said, "Anything longer than that, I call the police."

"That's all I need," he said. "That's all . . . we need." A pause. "I promise."

She hesitated, stepped forward, and undid the lock.

The door burst open. Monte plowed past her through the doorway.

Anita closed the door and turned on the lamp.

"Speak up, Monte," she said, turning to face him. "I said five minutes. Use them well."

He looked her up and down and then went to the kitchen. The refrigerator opened. A cap came off a bottle and clinked on the counter.

He returned with a bottle of beer.

"Take it off," he said. He sipped the beer and wiped his mouth with the back of his hand.

She crossed her arms over her chest.

"Excuse me?" she said.

"Did I stutter? I said take it off. *The robe.*"

She smirked and shook her head.

"You're so pathetic," she said. "I gave you your chance. Now get out or I *will* call the police."

Monte sipped the beer again.

She moved for the phone.

He shot over and grabbed her wrist.

"Not so fast," he said.

He set the bottle next to the phone on the lamp table.

She tried to pull her arm away. He gripped it harder.

"You're hurting me, Monte," she said through gritted teeth.

He jerked her closer to him.

"*You* hurt *me*, so I guess that makes us even," he said.

He untied her robe and opened it with his free left hand.

He stared down at her breasts.

"Yeah," he said, "that's what I like."

He cupped her right breast and rubbed her nipple with his thumb.

She tried to shove him.

He laughed.

"Don't even bother," he said, his breath now low and hot and heavy. "I'm not going anywhere."

He ripped the robe from her body and buried his face in her neck.

"I hate you," she said.

"Well, I *like* you," he said. He licked her ear lobe. "A lot."

He let go, stepped back, and picked up his beer.

"We're going to have fun," he said.

He took a sip and studied her.

"Get down on your hands and knees," he said.

She didn't.

He made a fist and held it to her face.

"I said get down on your fucking hands and knees!"

She winced.

"I'll kill you, so help me," he said.

She glanced at the cello, which still lay on its side on the rug, and then back into his burning eyes.

"Do it!"

Slowly, she crouched and did as he said.

"Now move so I can see it."

She obeyed. He drank.

He finished the beer and set it back down with a *clank!*

She looked over her shoulder. He was removing his clothes.

He kicked the back of her leg.

"Don't you fucking look at me!"

She faced forward.

Moments later, he gripped her buttocks with his slight but powerful hands and rammed her with all of his weight.

She grimaced: her body shook with his force.

The loveseat blocked her view of the cello.

Monte began to pump even harder. Somewhere far away from her, skin was smacking against her.

She tensed and crawled toward the loveseat with Monte still inside of her.

"Oh, yeah," he said. "You scoot, you little bitch." He slapped the side of her leg.

She scrambled up to her feet and leaned with both hands on the back of the loveseat. Monte pulled down on her shoulders and adjusted his angle.

"Yeah, yeah, that's how I like it."

She blinked to clear her eyes.

The cello's end pin pointed right at her.

The love you share will find you again. It will search for you and find you, because love does not forget.

She tried to squirm away. He threw one arm around her waist and yanked the back of her hair.

He gnashed his teeth close to her ear.

"Where do you think *you're* going?"

His pumping sped up: he'd brought himself close to relief.

The cello gleamed in the lamplight.

Anita raised her left leg and donkey-kicked his thigh with her heel. He cursed and let her go.

She lurched forward. Her right hip slammed into the loveseat. He punched her in the back.

She dropped and scurried toward the cello. Monte grabbed her ankle just before she reached it.

She spun on her rump.

Hands clenching, his penis still erect, he rose and loomed over her. His wiry muscles tensed and rippled. He drew back his right fist.

"Damn you," he said.

"D-don't come near me, Monte," she said, raising her legs to strike again. The room was shifting in her head. "P-please, j-just leave."

He took another step closer.

"*What is it with you?*" he said. Spittle flew from his mouth. "Why can't you just *do what you're told?* Why do you have to make it so goddamn *difficult?*"

Another step forward. Her right heel bumped his left thigh below the red spot she'd given him.

"Leave me alone, Monte. It doesn't need to be like this."

"Oh yes, it does," he said, leaning toward her. "And you have only yourself to blame."

She coiled her right leg and sprang her heel into his knee with a *smack!*

"*Ow—goddamn it!*"

He buckled, clutching his knee, but balanced himself.

"Alright, that's it," he said, his whole body flexing. "No more nice guy."

He lunged down at her with both fists swinging.

She fought him with a flurry of bicycle kicks. Her left heel hit his face. Red specks spattered the rug. He backed away with his hands to his nose.

Blood flowed from his nostrils and poured around his mouth. A rivulet ran into his teeth.

"Oh, Anita," he said.

He darted to the kitchen. Drawers ripped open. Utensils rattled. He returned with a stainless steel butcher's knife.

She shot up and backed up. Her bottom bumped into the cello, knocking it over.

"Boy," he said, stalking her in a half-crouch; he was no longer erect. "This is too bad, Anita."

He continued creeping forward. Lamplight flashed from the blade. His blood made a thin and dotted trail on the floor.

"We crossed a line," he said, slowing his pace but keeping the knife extended. "I'm going to have to kill you now."

"Good luck," she said. Still facing him, she bent and felt behind her for the cello. "Your blood and fingerprints are everywhere. You'd never get away with it."

"Yes I will," he said. The blood had formed a gory goatee; it splattered from his mouth as he spoke. "And I'll be doing you a favor. You're pathetic and lonely and ready to die."

He raised the knife and charged at her.

She spun and grabbed the cello by its neck with both hands. Then she shot up and swung it around with all of her strength.

The back of it smacked into Monte. He staggered, lost his balance, and fell.

She drove the end pin into his chest.

He screamed and pushed it out of him.

With one final burst, he snatched the cello and threw it down. He jumped and stomped on it, breaking the bridge, releasing the strings, and smashing what he could of the wood.

Out of breath, bleeding from his nose and chest and feet, he sat on the floor and looked drunkenly at Anita. Then he lay down.

Now on her knees on the rug, her arms across her chest, she watched him fade away.

She gathered what remained of the cello and held it to her breast. Her tears dripped onto its broken wood and loose strings with pindrop-quiet *plinks,* sounding the notes of their final concerto.

"You're lucky to be alive," said the plain-clothes detective. He was sitting on the edge of the loveseat and leaning toward her with his hands on his knees.

Anita noted his close-cropped hair, olive skin, and neatly combed moustache.

"You must be one hell of a fighter," he said.

He scanned the room again.

"Looks like the instrument had a rough night too. That your work, or his?"

He thumbed at where Monte's corpse remained flat in its blood. Investigators moved around it as they processed the scene.

Anita tucked her legs tighter beneath her on the sofa and continued staring forward.

"Mind if I smoke?" he said.

She shrugged.

He produced a pack of cigarettes from inside his overcoat, slid one out, and offered it to her. She glanced at it and shook her head. He popped it into his own mouth and lit it.

"Ashtray?" he said through pinched lips.

"No."

"Hey, Rollie," he said over his shoulder. "Let me have that if you're done with it."

A twenty-ounce Styrofoam cup with a bottom half-inch of cold coffee appeared by his ear. He snatched it.

Anita shivered once although dressed in the jeans, socks, and sweatshirt she'd thrown on before the police had arrived. Voices murmured; digital cameras flashed; men wrote notes and spoke on their radios.

"Now I know you've been through a lot," the detective continued, "but if you can, I'd like you to walk me through exactly what happened, from the beginning."

He ashed his cigarette in the cup, returned it to his mouth, and fished a notepad from an outer coat pocket. He set it on his knee.

She studied his face: handsome, though if he kept living hard, his early wrinkles would begin marking his age like rings in the trunk of a redwood. Like many men, he obscured his softer side with vacant pupils and a veneer of *I'd rather talk about sports.*

"If you can't talk much, I understand," he said. "Maybe you could start with why he came after you in the first place."

She looked away, and then back at him.

"He knew I was in love with somebody else," she said.

"You'll have to excuse me," he said. "I don't mean to be cavalier. It's just there's a naked, partially mutilated dead man on your floor. Where was your 'someone else' while all of this was going down?"

Anita thought for a moment.

"He was here, but he's gone now."

The detective ashed in the cup again.

"Well, where would he be?"

"Nowhere," she said. "He's not coming back, and no one will find him."

"I see," he said. He set his notepad on the lamp table and leaned back in the loveseat. "Some fella to leave you to deal with this all by yourself."

He stared at her. When she offered him nothing else, he rose and let her be.

T he pattering rain dampened Anita's hair from shifting directions. She pulled her raincoat's collar around her neck and ran the rest of the way to the awning of the music store.

The door opened with a tinkling bell. A college-aged girl looked up from the thick, worn paperback she read behind the cash register.

"May I help you?" she said.

Anita smiled. "Just browsing for the moment . . . and drying off. Thank you."

The cashier smiled back and returned to her book.

Anita strolled down the store's single long lane. She walked past drums, guitars, keyboards, and brass instruments to the string instruments arranged against the back wall.

A second college-aged girl watched her survey the cellos until she focused on a particular one.

"A full-size used Stradivarius copy," said the clerk, approaching with her hands behind her back. She wore her hair in a ponytail and her glasses high on her nose. "Are you a serious player?"

"I perform in the city orchestra," Anita said. "I've been playing for more than twenty years."

"I see," the clerk said. "Well . . ." She laughed nervously. "It can perform, but it _has_ seen better days. For a professional, we have some models over here that . . ."

"I like this one."

The clerk half-smirked in the event Anita was putting her on.

"Uh, okay," the clerk said. "Although . . ."—she leaned toward Anita and lowered her voice—". . . if you want my honest opinion, it's a little overpriced for its condition. We do offer better choices for not much more."

Anita lifted the cello from its display stand and inspected it further: a blemish on the body, one stiff tuning peg, a hairline crack in the neck, strings in need of changing.

"Thank you," she said, "but I believe I'll stay with this one."

The clerk smirked again, still waiting to be let in on the joke. Anita's face remained straight.

"Do you need a case for it?" the clerk said.

"Only if it's the original one that came with this cello."

"I'll see what I can do."

The clerk disappeared into a back room. She returned minutes later with a scuffed and weathered white fiberglass case.

"You're in luck," she said. "We'll include it with the price of the cello."

Anita brought the cello in its case to the front register. And as she opened her wallet to finish the sale, she heard a voice like her father's deep within her thoughts. It reminded her that for every shadow, there is a light; for every pain, an equal pleasure; for each dissonant sound, beautiful music; and for the wounded, there is a loving friend.

COOGAN'S FOR SALE!

"*T*oo much," said the sweating young man with the sunburned face. He leaned forward with his eyebrows turned down.

The brown-skinned merchant grinned. He loved haggling with the Americans: they always bitched about price as if he didn't know where they came from.

"Too much?" he said, his English crisp and clean from decades of watching BBC on satellite.

He lifted the gold-plated compact from the fading green vinyl–covered folding table between them and rubbed a weathered thumb over it.

"Do you understand that people in power would offer me riches—-or kill me—-for it?"

"Then why haven't they?" the young man said.

Now the merchant's eyebrows turned down.

"Because I conduct my business very carefully," he said. "I know too well what could happen if this fell into the wrong hands. Catastrophe, like few have seen."

"Yeah, but fifteen hundred American dollars? You think I carry that kind of cash?"

The merchant barely controlled the glint in his eye.

"Fifteen hundred is fair," he said. He set the compact back on the table. "*More* than fair."

The young man fingered a triangular flap that had torn away from the tabletop.

"I'll give you nine hundred," he said.

He looked away from the merchant and around the cluttered booth. The space measured perhaps 12' wide, 20' deep, and 9' high but felt ten times smaller because of the jackpot of junk and trinkets packed inside: leather whips, old swords, fake-metal necklaces, handmade chess sets, tarnished brass and copper plates, flimsy tee-shirts with cheap iron-ons of cartoon camels. A corrugated tin roof provided modest protection from the pounding North African sun, which still baked the air among the mounds of merchandise.

Most tourists would never find the booth unless told exactly where to go, and perhaps by someone they'd never want to meet again. Inconspicuous, inconvenient, it hid itself from casual browsers in a remote corner of the sprawling bazaar.

The merchant picked up the compact as if he meant to stow it away again.

"Nine hundred," he said in a soft, amused snort.

He stood and stared down at the young man.

"Go back to your air-conditioned hotel room," he said. "And if you want to enjoy the rest of your time in our country, you're really going to need some sunscreen."

The merchant patted his own face with a soiled handkerchief. He then turned toward the hanging white bed sheet serving as the curtain to his "back office," where he always retreated when pretending to hold firm on a deal.

"Wait," said the young man.

The merchant stopped.

"Twelve hundred."

His back still turned, the merchant smiled. He faced him again slowly.

The young man motioned for him to sit down. The merchant paused for effect and then walked back to the table. His shoulder bumped a horse saddle.

"Thirteen-fifty," he said, and sat.

The young man's blue eyes blazed within their wet and reddened white flesh.

"You'll find none other like it in all the world," the merchant continued. "Its magic once inspired epic songs and stories, even worship. But as I've explained, those powers work only *once* upon being first opened by a *new* owner. After that, they are spent until the item changes hands again through me."

The young man stared without expression. More sweat beaded on his face.

"The new owner alone will determine how it performs. If the magic is intended for someone other than you, it remains equally useful, depending on whom you have in mind to give it to."

"You can hold up on the hocus-pocus pitch," the young man said. "*I* know this could be a hustle. But the guy who got me drunk and sent me here said there was something to it. I probably pack more magic in my boxer shorts. But what the hell? I'm on vacation, and it sounds interesting."

The merchant's face remained blank.

"And if it really is what you say it is, I believe I can put it to good use." He leaned closer over the table. "Very good."

He leaned back again.

"If it is not what I say it is," the merchant said, "then you may return it to me and I will pay you twice what you paid me for it."

The young man crossed his arms but pulled his hands away: the armpits of his short-sleeved white Izod were soaked.

"Okay," he said. "Thirteen-fifty."

The glint in the merchant's eye flared up again.

He held out his hand. The young man shook it.

"Deal," the merchant said.

The young man fished his roll of cash from the front pocket of his khaki pants. The merchant rose and moved to a small counter close to the curtain. He wrapped the purchase in a thin cloth and slid it into an old white paper bag with green vertical stripes.

When he returned, the cash lay in large bills on the table.

He held out the bag. The young man reached for it, but the merchant kept it a few inches beyond his grasp.

"Remember what I told you," the merchant said. "Its magic will work only once for the new owner the first time he or she opens it. You must not forget this. After that, it has no power until it finds its way back to me. And it will. It always does."

The young man's arm dropped into his lap.

"Whatever you say," he said.

The merchant's brown eyes focused and hardened, creasing his face.

The young man stood and grabbed the bag. The merchant did not resist.

"Thank you," the young man said. "If it's not what you say it is, I *will* take you up on the offer. Even if it means I have to ride donkeys to get here."

"Trust me, sir," the merchant said. "One way or another, *you* will not come back."

The young man straightened.

"Let's hope not," he said.

The merchant watched him stuff the bag in his backpack and leave.

Outside the booth, the young man slipped the pack on his back and retraced his route: two ninety-degree bends and a long lane that returned him to the bazaar's writhing mass of bodies.

He pinballed his way through proprietors, snake charmers, musicians, contortionists, and very careful prostitutes. The sun's lengthening shadow stretched over the sternly standing mosque towers strewn across the ancient terrain.

He spotted an exit gate in the bazaar's enclosing stone walls. Once beyond them, he jumped into the first of the long line of taxis idling by the curb.

He spoke the name of his hotel. The driver nodded.

Seductive strings and jangling tambourines played from the cracked and dusty radio. The young man slipped off his backpack, set it in his lap, and gazed out the grimy back-seat window.

The taxi cut in front of another car. Breaks squeaked.

They wove their way through more traffic like a blunt and slippery needle. Extra horns voiced their opinions.

The oncoming evening grew one shade darker. The young man closed his eyes and leaned back his head. Just as he did, foreign words of religion boomed from distant speakers that felt larger than the world.

*H*ank Coogan turned up the collar of his new Marc Jacobs overcoat and shoved his hands farther into its pockets. *Damn* it was cold out. But he wasn't about to give in to January in Chicago: no fucking way. He'd lived through sixty-one

Windy City winters, and if he had his way, he'd tell sixty more to piss off.

He should have scheduled the 5:30 meeting with Ron Shanahan in his rat's-ass near–West Side neighborhood for another day. Any day but *this* day. *His* day.

He looked up at the twinkling Chicago skyline in the near distance. How he loved the city: its energy, its variety, its architectural majesty. Its Grade A–meat professional women who made bedroom eyes for the almighty dollar. And, of course, its exclusive network of professional boys with access to plenty of cash.

But the goddamn weather, especially winter, well, that could go straight to hell.

He buried his chin deeper into his coat and began hopping and shrugging for warmth. The sub-zero wind chill had already molested him through the gaps in his tailored suit. Now it wanted his ears as well. He clamped his gloveless hands to his earmuffs.

The night smacked him with another icy blast.

He cussed.

His BlackBerry Pearl Flip 8230 cell phone rang.

"Jumpin' Jack Christ," he said.

He fumbled in his right coat pocket for it and flipped it open, silencing Sinatra's "My Kind of Town" ringtone.

"Yeah," he said.

A taxi with its light on cruised past him: the fourth he'd seen in the last ten minutes.

"Where the hell are you?" he said.

He watched the taxi slow and stop at the intersection one block up. Two people climbed inside.

"A traffic jam? Are you fucking kidding me? Do you realize it's like two degrees out here and that I'm waiting in it for you like an asshole? You said six-fifteen!"

He looked to his right across the street. A black man with a bad eye, a bum left leg, and dirty dreadlocks walked down the sidewalk in his direction. Hank looked away.

"I don't care if you're in line to meet the Pope! Get your ass over here before my nuts fall off!"

He flipped the phone shut and shoved it back in his pocket. The man had stopped and now stood directly opposite him.

"Scyuse me, suh," the man said, stepping from the curb. His limp, crooked foot scraped and rolled over street debris and chunks of filthy, frozen slush.

"Sorry," Hank said. His glare of contempt had worked as garbage repellent before; maybe it would do so again. "No money."

Another warm, available cab sped through the space between them.

The man slid toward him a couple more steps. Hank could hear the foot's awful dragging even through his earmuffs.

Hank leaned over his curb and looked both ways for any sign of Rich: nothing yet. When he stepped back up, the man was only a dozen feet away.

"Scyuse me, suh."

Hank's jaw clenched.

"I said no money! Get lost!"

"Scyuse me, suh," the man continued. His bad eye floated in its socket like a moist golf ball with a brown stain on it. "Kun yew tell me war izza neggs buzzdob?"

His arms flat at his sides, the man still stood outside of the typical six-foot personal-comfort bubble (it was actually nine feet for Hank, unless he was getting laid or hamming a deal). A thin stream of clear snot ran from his left nostril and gathered along the top of his lip.

Hank's face relaxed a little. He pointed to his left.

"About four blocks."

"Tank ya, suh," said the man. "Gawd blezz yew."

He turned and dragged his leg back across the street. When he reached the opposite curb, a car whizzed past behind him and stirred his tattered clothing.

Hank looked left again: a pair of familiar headlights approached. Seconds later, a used but attractive Nissan Pathfinder pulled up to the curb. Hank stepped into the street, rapped on the passenger-side window with two knuckles, and gave Rich the finger.

Hank's new commercial real estate agent, an office-tenant representative, waved and grinned. The Pathfinder's power locks opened. Hank slid into a cocoon of blowing warm air and soothing music by Coldplay. Once seated, he smoothed his pants from thigh to ankle.

"I'm sorry, Hank," Rich said. "Traffic really was a mess. I almost considered jogging here."

"Save it," Hank said. He glanced at his watch. "One more minute, and you would have been out of a job."

Rich shifted in his seat and forced a smile.

"Y . . . you're just kidding, right?"

Hank cocked his head toward him.

"Yeah." He folded his hands in his lap, then: "Or no. Maybe. Just drive. And turn the heat up higher. If my balls clink even once, they're gonna break."

Rich's smile faded.

Hank cackled and slapped him on the thigh.

"Had you goin', you bastard!"

Rich laughed unevenly and tried to grin again.

"Good one, Hank," he said. "Okay, we still have time to make it to the hotel. I'm sorry. I really apologize. The traffic really was . . ."

"You already said that," Hank said. He blew in his hands and rubbed them together. "I hate these goddamn award ceremonies. The food better be good . . . or at least I better get some pussy, eh?" He smiled and elbowed Rich. "Eh?"

"Right . . . ," Rich said. "Pussy."

Traffic opened a little in front of them. Rich hit the gas.

"Rule number one to make it in this business, kid," Hank said.

Rich nodded, his eyes still on the road. He'd learned early to anticipate Hank's impromptu switches to mentoring mode.

"Be a man of your word. Always do what you say you're going to do——and then make sure you get fucking paid for it."

Hank looked out at the buildings rolling past his window.

"You listen to what I tell you," he said, "and maybe someday they'll give *you* an award for dressing well, selling information, and drinking top-shelf liquor."

Rich nodded again. Hank laughed, and then fell silent.

The hotel came into view several blocks later. Hank's name ran across the large liquid-crystal display sign at the foot of the drive to the entrance. It reflected in reverse across the Pathfinder's windshield.

Rich pulled into the parade of late-model cars leading to the front horseshoe.

Up ahead, a white-haired man in a long, green coat handed a bank note to his valet.

"Goddamn it," Hank mumbled.

Rich looked sideways at him.

"That's Howie Frank," Hank said. "Total fuckstick. Whatever you do, don't even try to bring any of his deals into my firm, or I'll sling your ass. Tight-ass Jew drives a BMW M6 Coupe, and I'll bet he tipped a dollar."

Rich shrugged and nodded.

The Pathfinder reached the horseshoe. The chandeliers dangling from the arched ceiling cast sparkling chips of light that crackled in the winter air.

A valet opened their doors. Hank and Rich climbed out. Hank tipped with a ten-dollar bill.

They walked side by side toward the entrance.

"Hank," Rich said, "don't people usually tip *after* they get their cars?"

"Sure," Hank said. "If you're a middle-class stiff who clips coupons."

He opened one of the glass doors and gestured for Rich to enter first.

"You can forget what you learned from your church and your parents," Hank said, following him inside. "All that matters out here is the green, and you better be ready to flash it, even when you can't afford to part with it."

Rich looked back at him. Hank winked.

They stepped onto the lobby's thick, lush carpet. It sank beneath their feet.

"Hank!"

"Aw, Christ," Hank muttered.

Howie Frank strode toward them from their left and stuck out his hand.

Hank looked at it.

"Hello, Howie."

Howie dropped his hand and hugged him. Hank clapped him once on the back.

"Good to see you, Hank," Howie said. "And congratulations. Broker of the Year and Lifetime Achievement in the same ceremony. How many dicks you suck for that?"

He chuckled and slapped Hank on the shoulder.

Hank glanced at Rich.

"Everyone's but yours, Howie. I'd have to be able to find it first."

Howie snorted.

"Tooshay. Who's the rookie?"

"Rich Swanson. He's one of my new office reps. He's about as green as that wrinkled bill you gave your valet."

Howie laughed again.

"I'll bet your boss didn't tell you he's a comedian too."

"No, Mr. Frank," Rich said. "He didn't."

"Well, it's a pleasure to meet you, Rich."

They shook hands.

"And don't you believe a word of what this wily bastard says about me."

A late-twenty-something woman in a matching charcoal-gray coat and skirt appeared beyond Howie's shoulder. Rich studied her quickly: broad shoulders; wavy brown hair; a soft, round, pretty face; toned legs that flexed beneath cream-white stockings as she moved.

"Did I see you in a *Pathfinder* outside, Hank?" Howie said.

"Very funny," Hank said. "You think I'd drive a piece of shit like that?" He winked at Rich, who forced a laugh. "It's my chauffeur's. Blame the help."

Hank saw the woman Rich was watching and elbowed him in the ribs.

"Say," Howie said, stepping closer to Hank. His breath smelled of late-lunch onions mixed with recent Listerine. "Any word on the situation over at Marks, Lincoln, and Stratham? The street says they might dissolve the partnership."

Hank stepped back and stuck his hands in his pockets.

"Any reason you want to know?"

"Just wondering," Howie said, smiling.

"You mean you don't want to know if they'll stay together when the lease expires next month?"

Howie shrugged.

"Well, let's just say the partnership *does* break up," he said. "Would you still represent all three of them, or just one or two?"

"Come on," Hank said. "You know better than to ask me that."

"I *do* have an accounting firm that would love that space, Hank."

"Nice try."

Hank tugged on Rich's arm and motioned forward with his head.

"Good seeing you, Howie. Rich and I are going to keep moving here." He started leading Rich away. "Give my best to Rebecca and the girls."

"Sure, right."

"Damn, Hank," Rich said once Howie was well behind them. "This place is *crawling* with hotties."

Hank smirked.

"Too bad you're married, kid."

"Too bad we're *both* married."

"Whatever."

They strolled halfway down the main hall to the banquet room and stopped at the coat-check window. A young woman in a white blouse and a red vest exchanged tickets for their coats. Hank winked at her and tipped her a ten. She smiled.

He guided Rich to the mini-bar to the left of the banquet room's double doors.

"What're you drinkin', kid?"

"Uh . . . I'll have a Sprite."

"A Sprite? Get serious. What're you drinkin'?"

"Um, I have to drive, don't I?"

Hank slung an arm around his shoulder. His slight paunch pressed against Rich's hip.

"Shut up. You like beer, wine, or the real stuff?"

"I guess I'll have a Miller Lite."

Hank snickered, let his arm drop, and slid his billfold from his back pocket.

"Bonas nochays," he said to the Hispanic bartender, who looked Hank up and down. "Give the lady here a Miller Lite, and I'll have a double Johnnie Black on the rocks."

He paid for the drinks, tipped a ten, and led Rich into the banquet room. They maneuvered through the small colonies of networking agents just inside the doors and turned right toward the welcoming table. Two women sat behind neatly lined rows of folded and alphabetized white cards with table numbers on them.

"Well, hello there, Kimberly," Hank said to the one on the left. "Don't you look stunning."

"Thank you, Hank," she said. "It's a pleasure to have you here . . . and to see you honored."

"It's a pleasure to *be* here, Kimberly," he said. "Let's have a drink later."

They eyed each other a moment. Rich glanced back and forth.

"I'll take my card and the one for my ugly date here," Hank said, slipping his arm around Rich's shoulder. "Rich Swanson."

She located their cards and handed them to them. Hank looked at his.

"Looks like we're at table two," Hank said. "Right in front for the pony show. Guess that means I have to behave."

He clapped Rich on the back.

Rich followed him through the growing mass of expensive suits and dresses and shoes. Hank stopped several times to accept hugs and handshakes.

"You go grab your seat, kid," he said. "I'm gonna catch up with a few more people."

"Sure, you bet," Rich said.

He wove through and around more laughing, drinking, chatting people until his empty table came into view. He sped toward it and gladly sat down.

He tried to appear unaware of himself. He'd been with the firm for only six weeks, so he didn't really know any of the agents but Hank, let alone tenant reps from other companies. Scanning the banquet room, he spotted four co-workers he recognized. One had been genial and genuine. Another had welcomed the chance to ramble on about sports and money with no interest in what Rich had to say. The other two didn't even pretend to offer more than a pleasant veneer.

His watch read 6:57 p.m.: three minutes from the start of the ceremony.

He fidgeted with the two-sided program card that'd been set on his plate. Behind him, a short, balding man in a navy-blue suit squirted from a small crowd and climbed the four steps to the stage. He scurried to a decorated podium centered before a large and smooth white screen. He tapped on the mike to ensure it was live.

"Excuse me, everyone . . . hello . . . hello . . . testing, testing . . ."

A few people looked up toward the stage.

"Ladies and gentlemen, please find your seats. The program is about to begin. Please . . . find your seats."

The groups dispersed and the chairs began to fill.

"Hello . . . hello . . . it's wonderful to have you here for the seventeenth Annual Excellence in Chicago Real Estate Banquet. We have an exciting evening ahead of us, so we ask the last of you to please, find your seats."

All of Rich's co-workers but Hank made their ways to the eight-chair table. Once they were seated, Rich felt an intense stare from his left. He glanced over at it.

"Hello, Chad," he said.

The other nodded. Rich knew little more than that his name was Chad Harwick and that he managed the marketing. He also sometimes supported the administrative staff, which struck Rich as peculiar. Rich had also guessed him to be close to his own age—around twenty-seven or -eight.

Rich looked around at the other name cards: Brian Wilcox, Tad Dexter, Nick Papanicholas, Ezra Klein, Mitchell Parsons.

Hank arrived moments later, his lips wet with laughter and scotch. He greeted each agent with a wink, a "hey," or a handshake, nodded curtly at Chad, and sat down.

The room's lights dimmed. Quieting murmurs continued and then died.

The short, balding man opened the program with a monologue on "the unprecedented era of opportunity" in Chicago commercial real estate. Demand "exceeded supply at levels that spurred healthy competition and profitability without prompting cost-prohibitive rates per square foot." Coincidence and circumstance had "lined up for a confluence of expiring leases among the city's most prestigious professional-services firms." Developers were "investing greater resources into more efficient and attractive spaces" that would "prolong the current spike in absorption activity."

A slide show of corporate ads and banquet sponsorships flashed on the screen behind him.

Rich looked over his shoulder.

The woman he'd seen in the lobby was sitting two tables over and one row back to his right. She noticed him and smiled.

The other agents at Rich's table remained focused on the presentation. Hank drank his second double scotch and gestured at people nearby.

Rich slid sideways in his chair for a better view of the stage. As he turned, he glanced left again. Chad's face now looked more strained and white.

Rich shrugged at him: *You okay?*

Chad nodded once and sipped the last of his cranberry juice.

The man on the stage finished his speech. Several different people then presented the evening's slate of distinctions: Architect of the Year,

148

Developer of the Year, Interior Design Firm of the Year, Property Management Company of the Year, and so on.

Hank also rose to accept his Office Broker of the Year award. Once on stage, Rich noted, he became instantly composed and articulate in spite of the two double scotches. He even managed to shed a tear of gratitude, which he wiped away for effect.

Hank *loved* Chicago, the greatest city on Earth. It had been the cradle of his lifelong ambitions. The yeast that had leavened his dreams. A bottomless reservoir of opportunity for those who were willing to dig.

More important, he could not have succeeded without his employees, or the city's diverse and talented commercial real estate workforce. He thanked them all . . . he was truly honored . . . God bless.

Tuxedoed waiters served the dinner's multiple courses. Water pitchers emptied and filled.

Was Rich the only one who saw Harwick becoming even more pale?

Redevelopment of the Year. Build-to-Suit Project of the Year. Property Representative of the Year.

Rich wanted to go home.

Two of the agents at his table whispered to each other. The others stared straight ahead. Hank looked at Rich, pretended to fall asleep, and laughed.

Development of the Year. Retail Broker of the Year. Project Manager of the Year.

Rich glanced back at the brunette again: she still smiled at him. He turned away.

Multi-Family Development of the Year. Special Achievement of the Year.

Chad now looked pissed off as well, and the piss appeared to be pointed at Hank.

A middle-aged woman on the stage introduced a man behind her as "a stalwart visionary and a developing legend in Chicago commercial real estate." Rich joined the applause but not the half-room ovation.

Hank turned toward Rich and mouthed *he's an asshole*.

Rich grinned.

His parents had always asked him what he'd planned to do with his degree in philosophy. I don't know, he always replied. Think. Analyze. Try to understand the human condition.

Yes, son, his dad said, but will the cashier at Taco Bell give you a Gordita out of respect for your knowledge of Socrates? Life is about *economics*. Nobody cares how deep and intelligent you are—unless of course they can make money from it. I love you, son, we both love you, and we want you to be happy doing what you enjoy, but understand that starving artists are no longer cultural heroes. It's better to have income than to be interesting. Read Plato and Aristotle until you can't move because your thoughts are so heavy, but, please, for your own sake, consider *what you're really going to do with your life*.

And so here he was, the age of thirty in sight, wearing a suit he could barely afford, sitting next to a mythical millionaire and five go-getters who surely banked six figures each. (He didn't imagine Chad earned a nickel over forty-five grand, but that was a-whole-nother story.) His stipend of $27,000 beat begging for food, but he'd have to start scoring the "sexy" commissions Hank had dangled during his interview if he and Dawn were to stay in the city. She'd been earning the bigger bread for too long.

He didn't let himself dwell on the details lest he become anxious or depressed. In Hank, he'd signed up for a come-and-go-as-you-please-but-you-better-make-your-numbers system. Making those numbers would require nine-hour days of cold-calling prospects and schmoozing "important," impatient, and extremely high-paid Republican vote-givers being licked by at least ten other lapdogs for the office-tenant agency.

He'd done the math early. Nine hours a day x 5 days a week = 45 hours. Forty-five hours x 52 weeks = 2,340 hours. $27,000 ÷ 2,340 hours = $11.54 per hour. *Gross,* before Papa Sam claimed his cut. Without commissions, he would have fared better as a fast-food restaurant manager. He'd also accepted Hank's terms that he pay back 50 percent of the total stipend he'd received once the "real money" started "rolling in."

The job offered no retirement plan. The health insurance would provide a Band-Aid for a gaping wound. He'd have to work out his own taxes on the commissions as well.

Rich looked once more around the table at those who had "made it" in the business. Each but Chad drove a luxury car, wore nice watches and high-end suits, and surely paid a stately mortgage. A couple might even indulge in trim on the side to season their rote American family lives.

But it couldn't be all like that? *Some* in this profession respected more than money and the rush of the deal. *Some* considered spiritual puzzles, mind-expanding ideas, and humankind's complexities.

Some prayed in private and found achievement in compassion for their fellow man.

Right?

The brunette's blue eyes still beamed through the dim space between them.

The ring on his left hand felt heavier.

A waiter set another glass of cranberry juice in front of Chad, a statue of white in his seat. Tad Dexter whispered something to Brian Wilcox.

". . . thirty-plus years in the business," said the voice from the lectern. "He was a major player in three successful partnerships before beginning his own firm five years ago. He has closed more multimillion-dollar deals than anyone in the game, and he still holds the Chicago commercial real estate record for the single largest office-tenant transaction. You know him, you can't resist him, and you can't help but admire what he has done to and for our great profession. Ladies and gentlemen, fellow real estate professionals, without further ado, I present to you the honorable recipient of this year's Lifetime Achievement Award, Mr. Hank Coogan."

The banquet room erupted in applause. Plates and silverware clinked as people pushed back from their tables to stand. Hank winked at Rich, rose, and swam through the adoration toward the stage. Hands clapped him on the shoulder and slapped him on the back.

Up by the podium, Hank shrugged and waved forward with both arms as if to say *get outta here.*

The ovation continued. Rich's hands became tired. Chad clapped wanly from his seat.

Hank hugged the presenter and then stepped back to accept his award. The words "Lifetime Achievement Award Winner—Mr. Hank S. Coogan" loomed in large letters on the screen.

The applause settled. People returned to their seats. Hank approached the microphone.

"Wow," he said. "What do I say to that? You're too kind. This industry has been too kind. Those of you who know me understand my passion for Chicago real estate. I would serve no other city but this one. Chicago is, and always will be, our country's beating heart. From manufacturing to professional services, *we* are the workers, the dreamers, the innovators. *We* represent the backbone of the modern entrepreneurial spirit. *We* offer the highest-caliber people and companies from the country's most precious land.

"To accept this award from my peers is to validate a dream that began when I was a young teenager working at my father's Back of the Yards butcher shop. I watched him toil ten hours a day, seven days a week, to make an honest living. I watched him selflessly strain to ensure my mother, brother, and I never lacked the basics we needed. He was even able to put my brother and me through junior college.

"But from the moment I realized that the ground beneath my father's shop might someday be worth three times more than the business itself, I saw my life's path open in front of me. The indomitable American spirit consumed me and possessed me. I knew that I could want more, do more, have more. The American dream *still* inspires me. I have succeeded in creating wealth for myself and others by applying myself to help other people get what they want. It's that simple, folks.

"*You* can achieve as much by following two enduring principles. Number one, be a good *listener.* You have two ears and one mouth for a reason. And when you do talk, choose your words carefully. Share wisdom, solve problems, and confirm what the other has said to show you understand. Otherwise, do us all a favor by saving your breath."

Chuckles rippled through the room.

"Secondly, always, and I mean *always,* follow through on your word. Your good name is your greatest asset. Treat and preserve it like gold by being honest, reliable, and consistent."

Hank paused and looked down. When he raised his head, a tear glistened in his eye.

"And so before I step down from the stage on this most memorable evening, I ask humbly that you not praise or elevate me beyond this moment. I would prefer that you regard my achievement as a tiny flame for igniting your own professional fires." With one hand, he held up the award, a miniature glass skyscraper on a cherry-wood base with an engraved brass nameplate. "May each of you become a blazing light for someone else. This award stands for so much more than one man. It speaks for *you,* for *us,* and for the American dream. I thank you."

The room erupted in applause again. More plates and silverware clinked as chairs moved back from their tables. The whole room stood for the ovation—except for Chad, who'd left his seat.

Rich scanned the room on tiptoe. He spotted Chad's head weaving through the crowd toward the exit to the hallway.

On the stage, Hank hugged his presenter again and then made his way back to their table. Several people grabbed at him or tried to shake his hand.

The applause settled. Everyone sat back down.

"Christ, I thought I was going to piss myself up there."

Hank set his award on the table, slapped Rich on the back, and shook hands with the other agents. Then he too sat down.

"Alright," he said toward Rich. "Let's end this fucking thing so I can get another drink."

A tall, gray-haired man strode to the lectern and made a few more announcements.

Rich glanced down at his program card: the show was almost over. The words from the stage became a blur to him. He stared into space and thought about Chad, Dawn . . . the brunette who wouldn't stop looking at him.

". . . and for those of you who would like to stay to network, the banquet room will remain open for another forty-five minutes. The cash bars at the east and west sides of the room will also serve for another fifteen minutes. Thanks to all of you for attending. We wish you a spectacular year in Chicago commercial real estate!"

Half the room clapped. The crowd dispersed. Easy jazz spilled at a low volume from the room's surrounding speakers.

"Sweet Joseph and Mother Mary, I need a scotch," Hank said, rising from his chair. "How about you, Regina? Want me to fish you another lite beer and put a nipple on it?"

Rich smiled and shook his head.

"No thanks, Hank. I better be getting home. I'm in good shape to drive."

"Suit yourself," he said.

Tad and Mitchell aimed for the bar. The other three agents shook hands all around and then left to go home.

Just as Hank made his own move toward the bar, welcome-table Kimberly and another woman grabbed him by either arm.

"Congratulations, Hank," Kimberly said. "You looked great up there. And the speech—simply amazing."

He smiled.

"Do I know you?" he said to the other woman.

"No, you don't, Mr. Coogan," she said, holding out her hand. "I'm Katherine. I wanted to introduce myself. I'm one of your biggest admirers."

"Oh, really?" Hank said.

Rich placed her in her early thirties. About five-seven, a nice halfway between heavy and thin. Red-haired Irish with fair skin, fine features, and sprays of light freckles.

"Oh, yes," she said. "I'm a new office-tenant rep at Wilson and Kohlmeier. I work with Kimberly. I've heard and read so much about you."

"I see," Hank said. He could smell both of them now: sweet, suggestive, maybe even open for *business*. He shook her hand. "It's a pleasure. I'll have to give Jimmy some hell for not making me more aware of you. He and I go back fifteen, sixteen years."

She bit her lip and looked down.

"I gotta get goin', Hank," Rich said. "I want to get some decent sleep and maybe come in early tomorrow. I'm sure Dawn's waiting up for me too."

"Excuse me, ladies," Hank said.

He took Rich by the arm and guided him a few feet to the side.

"You sure you don't want to stay for this?"

He glanced toward the women.

"Could be fun. Bar's still open, and it looks like they want to *talk*."

Rich laughed nervously.

"It's tempting, but I really do have to go, Hank," Rich said.

He slid his arm from Hank's grip and started to turn.

"Congratulations again, Hank," he said, backing away. "I'm really glad the night went well for you. See you tomorrow."

"You're such a good boy," Hank said. He winked. "A *nice* boy. We'll talk more about the Katz and Fowler situation sometime tomorrow."

Rich waved once and spun toward the exit. A scattered queue had formed to file out of the room. He fell into place at the back of it.

He saw several more attractive women close to his age, as well as a few other grayer, heavier, or more masculine ladies.

He focused on one in particular: mid-forties; thin at the waist but thick in the thighs; a light mustache; long, well-maintained brown hair; a sense of current fashion.

Watching her gab with two older men—one tall and thin, the other medium-height and overweight—he wondered how Dawn would look in twenty years.

He made his way closer to the door. He now stood behind two forty-ish men who looked either Greek or Italian.

"Rich!"

Howie Frank approached from his left with a taller and much more fit blond man.

"Got a second?" he said.

Rich nodded.

"Mr. Frank," he said, extending his hand.

Howie shook it.

"Nice ceremony, huh?" Rich said.

"It was a fat bag of gas out of somebody's ass," Howie said.

Rich didn't reply because he didn't know how. Howie cackled once and slapped him on the shoulder.

"It was what I expected, except for maybe the community head they gave to Hank. Then again, they'll blow me too if I finish up with another few years of shady deals and kissing the right people's asses. Don't tell him I said that, of course."

Rich blushed.

"Rich, I'd like you to meet Ron Munson," Howie said. "He's one of my firm's top agents. Been with us four years."

Rich held out his hand.

"Rich Swanson."

The blond man shook it and nodded once. His blue eyes glowed within his lightly tanned face.

"Looks like you went on vacation somewhere," Rich said.

"Tunisia," Ron said.

"Nice."

"Say, Rich," Howie said, stepping even closer to him. Rich inched away. "I can tell you're a good kid. You might have a hard time in this business at first—we all do—but if you can hang in there and get over the hump, you just might like it. Usually takes at least a year. Maybe even two."

"That's what Hank said."

"Right . . . Hank. I'd like to talk to you a little about Hank."

Ron sipped from his clear drink with clinking cubes. His eyebrows tensed. He looked left and right.

Howie slipped his right arm around Rich's shoulder. Ice rattled in the near-empty Cuba Libre in his left hand.

"How do you like working for Hank?" he said.

"Uh . . . fine, I guess. Looks like it might be a good opportunity for me. He's obviously big in the business."

"So they say," Howie said.

He raised the drink to his slippery lips and sipped. His arm fell from Rich's shoulder.

"So people feel the *need* to say. But let me tell you something, Rich . . ."

He went silent and scanned the room. Hank and the two women had wandered to the bar to the far left of the welcoming table.

"Hank's been in this business a long time," he continued. "It's made him wealthy. Now, I hope you take this for what it's worth. I've been at it about as long as he has. And after you put in that much time, well, you're able to *see* things. About people. Call it instincts. And right now, mine are telling me that you're a good kid who got into this because he needed the money and didn't know what else to do. It's all over your face." He smiled. "You're easy to read, kid. You might need to work on that."

He dried his drink. His left hand dropped to his side. The empty glass dangled by his fingertips. Rich looked him in the eyes and then at the floor.

"Now," Howie continued, "I'm sure I could catch holy hell for saying this, but there's something I like about you, so I'll say it anyway. Watch yourself over there. At Hank's firm."

Rich put his hands in his pockets and continued looking at the floor.

"Do what you gotta do and learn what you gotta learn," Howie said. "But mind who you trust. Think hard about who's on your side, and you'll be okay."

Rich looked up.

"Mr. Frank, I appreciate your concern, but honestly, I'm not so sure we should be having this conversation," Rich said.

Howie lifted his empty glass toward Ron.

"Ron, another Cooba Leebray, please?"

Ron accepted the glass, eyeballed Rich, and then strode away toward the bar.

Howie adjusted his pants at the waist and tried to stand taller.

"I've known that son of a bitch since you were a kid," he said. "I know what he can *do* to people. I also know that he likes himself a lot more than he likes you. He'll use you for as much as you can give him, and if he decides that's not enough, he'll dump you. Either that, or he'll frustrate you until you quit." He put his hand on Rich's upper arm. "Sorry, but I've seen him do it to people a lot tougher than you."

"Well," Rich said. "Thank you for the warning."

He held out his hand.

"It's been a pleasure, Mr. Frank. But I really do have to get on home now."

Howie considered the hand and then shook it.

"I mean it, Rich," he said. "You might not believe me. Hell, we don't know each other. But I do have your interests in mind. If you ever run into trouble over there, you come see me. I'm sure I can help out."

They looked at each other. Rich studied his red but focused eyes.

"Right," Rich said. "Thanks."

Ron returned with Howie's drink and a bottle of water for himself. He uncapped it and took a swig.

"So, Howie," he said after swallowing, "how long do you think he'll last with shithead?"

Howie laughed and almost spilled his rum and Coke.

"Fuck it," Howie said, clapping Rich on the shoulder. "Let's forget the whole conversation. Go on home. I'm sure you and Hank will work out just fine."

Rich looked back and forth between them.

"Right. Good night, Mr. Frank. Ron."

He turned.

"He's a lying, selfish bastard," Ron said to his back. "He deserves whatever's coming his way."

Rich left the banquet room and didn't look back.

In the hallway, to his right, several people crowded the mini-bar for one more drink right before it closed. Several others spoke in small groups. He made his way to the coat-check window, handed the girl a two-dollar tip, and spun with his coat to leave.

In stride, he glanced left, and saw him: back to the wall, hands deep in his pockets, head hung low, face a pensive scowl.

Chad.

An inner voice told Rich to not stop moving.

"Rich."

His head twitched toward the voice.

Chad glared—through him.

Rich approached.

"What's up?" he said. "You okay, man?"

Chad straightened. His eyes could have been Ron Munson's: blue, intense, burning, deep set.

"I didn't even want to be here," he said. "But Hank had an extra ticket because Alex Powell had to bail on it. Hank didn't want to waste it, so he pretty much told me to go."

"Aw, come on," Rich said. "It's not that bad. You got a free meal, didn't you?"

He patted Chad on the shoulder.

"Come on, let's go home."

Chad didn't move. He looked down, his face pained, his body tense.

"Seriously, Chad, are you okay?"

Chad looked up. Tears were close behind his eyes.

"I don't know how much more I can take."

"Take what?" Rich said.

"Working for *him.*"

"Why? What's wrong? What happened?"

"I know you haven't been with the firm that long," Chad said. "But you'll learn. About him."

Rich glanced right, toward the lobby and exit.

"I hate my job," Chad said. "And now I'm starting to hate my life."

"Come on, Chad," Rich said. His face began to warm. "It's never that bad. Let's go." He touched Chad's arm. "Let's go home."

Chad pulled his arm away. His eyes narrowed to slits.

"I'd like to see *you* work eight or nine hours a day, five days a week with fictional budgets. I'd like to see *you* spend half of every day dealing with pissed-off vendors chasing little invoices four months old. And how about spending the other half fighting off agents busting your balls because their deal announcements aren't making it into the trade pubs? Or trying to explain why their business cards aren't being printed on time?"

Chad wiped his face with his shirt cuff.

"It has nothing to do with *me.*"

Rich looked around. No one appeared to be listening, but two different men had begun to notice them.

"Let's go," Rich said. "Let's take this outside."

"It's freezing out there," Chad said.

"Well, we'll stand in the lobby then."

Chad pushed away from the wall and retrieved his coat from coat check. Rich headed down the hallway. Chad followed a few steps behind.

Once near the front desk, they stood under the chandelier light twinkling from inverted bowl–like ceilings. Other business events had ended at around the same time, depositing dozens of extra bodies into the lobby.

"This whole night's been weird, Chad," Rich said. "You should have heard what this one guy just said to me about Hank."

"Hank's a liar," Chad said, his jaw clenching.

Rich laughed lightly.

"This gets better by the minute," he said. "I thought he was the man of honor tonight."

"That's because he knows exactly who to scam and how so that he gets what he wants and looks good doing it," Chad said. "He's a dick."

Rich looked him in the eyes and then down at the floor.

"Interesting evening, to say the least," he said. "I guess I should probably get going."

"I can't even place a fucking classified ad," Chad said, his face still red. "We're months behind on our bills with the real-estate rags. But somehow, he still manages to collect his five-figure commissions and his first-class lunch and travel expenses less than a week after he turns in his paperwork. It's bullshit."

"How can that be?" Rich said. "How can he run a business like his if he's not paying his bills?"

Chad's face relaxed a bit.

"Because Hank's a master of the grease game. He might be the best in the city. He's in tight with the people who can keep a cash flow running for *him*. And he couldn't give a shit about anyone who's waiting on him to pay. They just have to hold their place in his line. It's been a tight year, tighter than usual, so whatever comes in goes straight into his pocket first. After that, he'll sign the checks for the agents' commissions, which as you know are a fifty-fifty split with the firm. After that, he'll pay the administrative salaries, including mine, out of his line of credit. It's almost maxed out, and it's a big one too. After that, he pays the rent and utilities—late. And anything after that goes to the invoices, which were about six inches high the last time I saw them in Vera's office."

"Jeezuz."

"Yeah," Chad said.

Rich shook his head.

"This is strictly confidential. What I'm telling you."

"Of course," Rich said. He looked at his watch. "Alright, man. Long day. Time to go home."

"I don't mean to dump anything on you," Chad said. "I just needed to get some of this off of my chest, and you seem like a good enough guy."

They stood silently for a moment.

"Okay, Chad," Rich said, extending his hand. "See you tomorrow."

Chad shook it.

"See ya," he said.

Rich slipped on his coat, adjusted the collar, and headed for the doors.

Just before he stepped outside, he heard one man say to another that Hank Coogan was his hero.

*H*e hated the smell. It invaded his young nose from the packaged cuts on the prep tables and the sides that hung from cold steel hooks all around him. It was the worst in summer, when the thick Chicago heat baked the earth and steamed the air. The Midwestern temperatures always *had a taste for the meat, some of which gave in to stink and rot despite his father's efforts to keep the microbes out.*

Henry begged his father, Frank, not to make him go back there, into the freezer. Not today, when the mercury groped for one hundred, the skin felt slicked with oil, and sweat pooled like piss in the crotch. Not today, when the power had gone out and much of the meat at the front of the shop had to be rushed to either the freezer or boxes of ice. And once those spaces were full, Frank had been forced to gamble the rest of it in non-refrigerated display cases. They could only hope they'd lose just some of it to the seasonal rape.

The power came back on. Eager families streamed in for the beef, lamb, pork, and chicken for their summertime barbecues. Frank and his wife, Verona, ran the counter and register while Henry and his brother, Kevin, brought the meat from the back to the front of the shop.

Henry stepped into the freezer, which still huffed and puffed and chugged to return to the low-thirty degrees that it needed. The thermometer just inside the door read forty-one: better than the forty-four he'd recorded earlier.

He looked down the lane of sides to be cut, quartered, and served: the bulky remains of the beasts that'd been slaughtered somewhere down Halsted's Back of the Yards. He stared at them, as he always did, and imagined their eyes filling with the reflections of their gore-drenched executioners.

He wondered how, or if, their expressions had changed when the blade slashed across or the hammer slammed down so they could be skinned and pulled apart for pleasant family meals in the park.

Dad wanted the cuts Kevin had stacked on the back prep table.

Henry would have to cross through the meat again.

The horrible, dead, and quiet meat.

A blast of cold air slapped him from a vent to his right near the ceiling.

He jumped, and then laughed at his nerves.

He heard a groaning, rocking sound.

His head jerked around.

Had the sides begun to move?

No: that was silly.

He stepped farther into the twenty-foot lane between him and the table.

He walked, and walked, and walked, but gained no distance. The floor beneath him rolled as if he were on a conveyor.

He began to jog toward the table. When that brought him no closer, he ran.

He ran and ran, and crossed no more than six inches. His heart pounded. Sweat soaked his face in spite of the cold. His stomach lurched and threatened to empty. He broke into a sprint.

But still he covered no ground.

The meat rocked all around him—back and forth, side to side. The hooks creaked and croaked. And when Henry tried to turn left or right, the sides collided in defiance.

He moaned. The meat now swung to strike him, a card-carrying conspirator in the death for appetite.

He whimpered. Not a single piece of meat was still. Even the prep-table cuts slid from their boards to the floor and slithered toward him.

He cried out. The meat would have its revenge for the thousands of pounds his family had bought, cut, sold, and even discarded if it went bad: the ultimate waste of a life.

Someone had to account for the murder.

Four cow sides slammed into him at once.

Henry screamed and fell down. When he tried to get up, he slipped and fell again because of the slime with which they'd caked him. He rose and fell and rose and fell. Their noise morphed into laughter that mocked him, telling him it's what he deserved.

He lay on his back. Tears ran down his face and mixed with the goo that slicked it. The sides closest to him tried to release themselves: they wanted to finish their work and crush him in a pile.

He shut his eyes and waited. This is how it would end, and maybe it was justice after all: the toiling Irish butcher's thirteen-year-old Irish runt found dead in the cooler. In his one pair of brown leather shoes and one pair of fading brown corduroy pants. Killed by what they had killed to make their living.

The meat stopped moving and went silent. When Henry opened his eyes, his father and brother stood over him with their hands on their knees.

Henry remained flat on the floor and stared at the ceiling. When they asked him what was wrong, why he had screamed so they could hear him from the front of the shop, he began to laugh. He laughed so hard that tears streamed from his eyes once again.

He pointed up at his father.

It's you, Dad, it's you! It's you it's you it's you and this shitty butcher shop that isn't worth the ground it's standing on. It's you because of this. Because you work too long and break your back for meat.

Well, not me, Dad, Henry said, and his father stood up and stepped back. Not me, not ever. I'm going to be somebody, and I'm going to do it without slimy hands and old clothes. I'm going to be rich and powerful, and I'll live where I want and drive what I want and have the best in life, because I deserve more than this. Damn you for being a slave to the meat! Damn you, damn you,

". . . damn you!"

Hank shot up from his back. The cool, red satin sheet slipped from his skin and pooled around his waist. Beads of sweat had formed around his hairline.

"Hank? Hank, are you okay?"

Kimberly rolled over and touched his leg.

"Yeah, yeah," he said. He put his face in his hands. "Just a bad dream." He lay back down. "Jesus."

He turned toward his night table and grabbed the digital clock: 1:47 a.m.

"You better get going," he said.

Kimberly snuggled closer to him. Her small but lively breasts pressed against his arm and chest.

"But it's so *comfortable* here, Hank," she said. "Can we at least go one more round?"

He looked past the end of the bed toward the black and starless abyss beyond his large bedroom window. Fifty-two stories down, Lake Michigan continued to slosh through winter by stirring in its glacier-cut bowl.

Kimberly spun over and straddled him.

"Come on," she said. She ran her smooth, red-nailed hands down his chest and over his paunch. "One more treat for Kimmy and then Kimmy go home."

He felt himself getting stiffer and smiled in the dark. It would be his third performance in the last ninety minutes: not bad for sixty-one and no Viagra. Sharon, his wife, would have called him Christ or Santa Claus if he'd laid the pipe three times in a *month*. Three times in one day would be humping proof he'd been building his endurance, well . . . somewhere else.

Kimberly rode him carefully, slowing down when she sensed he was near and speeding up when he appeared to calm down. Hank and Sharon observed them from Martinique in the framed 3" x 5" photo on the night table by Sharon's side of the bed.

"Okay," Hank said when they were done. "*Now* you have to go home."

He placed his hands on her hips.

She tapped his nose.

"If you say so."

She climbed off of him and slid from the bed. He watched her lithe yet curvy body as she gathered her clothing within the moonlit room.

He crossed his hands behind his head on the pillow.

"You need cab fare?" he said.

"So chivalry isn't dead, after all," she said, slipping on her skirt.

Hank studied her silhouette as she stuffed her nylons in her purse. Her breasts barely moved as she leaned forward. His groin grew stiff again.

She pulled up the zipper on the back of her skirt and straightened it around her waist. She then put on her bra and blouse, leaving it untucked.

"I might be just an office-tenant rep on the up-and-up, but I can still afford public transportation," she said, smiling.

A lock of hair fell onto her forehead. She blew up at it.

Hank grabbed his money clip from his night table. He removed a twenty, rolled it into a skinny tube, and flicked it at her.

"Take it," he said. "It's the least I can do for *that.*"

She picked it up and tossed it back on the bed.

"For real," she said. "I'm good."

"Did I ever tell you how much I love my life?"

"No," she said. "How much?"

He threw down the bed sheet so she could see.

"This much," he said.

"That's a lot," she said. "I'll need to use the restroom before I go."

Hank pointed left through the dark.

"Over there."

He closed his eyes and let his head fall back against the pillow.

She glided through the shadows toward two white doors set a few feet apart on the wall.

A door latch clicked. A few seconds of silence followed, and then:

"My God, Hank . . ."

His eyes shot open. Adrenaline raced through his veins.

NO!

How could he have been so *stupid?*

He'd *never* left his special closet unlocked—except for that morning. Sharon was in Florida for the week, and he'd let it slide after sipping coffee in it for a while before going to work.

Just this *once* he'd relaxed on a detail. Even worse, he'd let the little head steal the wheel from the big one when he brought Kimberly home.

He forgot about the closet.

Now it served him goddamn right.

Still naked, he bolted from the bed toward the almost half-open door.

"Don't go in there!"

But of course it was too late. The light from the closet's overhead bulb spilled into the bedroom.

He opened the door wider and looked at Kimberly's back. Her head turned slowly side to side.

Hank stepped into the closet behind her.

"Well, what do you think?" he said.

She couldn't speak: the well-organized fortune of cash, bonds, precious metals, luxury items, and high-end menswear had taken her breath.

At 10' wide and 18' deep with an 8' ceiling, it could have been a comfortable bedroom. The left wall started with a 2' x 4' display case containing designer watches arranged vertically, top to bottom, left to right, in alphabetical order: names such as Cartier Santos, Geneve, Gucci, Movado, Rolex.

Following the watches were four more glass display cases mounted equidistantly from one another on the wall; each presented carefully prepared and labeled rings and jewels. The bottom edges of the wall displays aligned perfectly with the top horizontal plane of the standing watch case.

Hank had devoted the remainder of the left wall to gold bars, foreign bearer bonds, and strapped packs of fifty- and one-hundred-dollar bills, stacked left to right in that order. Each stack was two feet high and level against the wall.

To the right of the stacks, at the end of the wall, stood a 2' x 4' steel vault with a Harman Kardon MAS 102 stereo system on top of it.

The master's throne, an oak captain's chair, faced them from the closet's back wall in the aisle's perfect center. The stereo's speakers aimed out toward the door from stands to either side of it.

Along the right wall ran Hank's regal array of attire: a different gray, black, or blue designer suit for each day of the month; an aristocrat's supply of shining dress shoes, many of them black Italian leather; perhaps a hundred handsome ties; a couple dozen pressed white shirts monogrammed with Hank's initials; a small wall-mounted glass display case holding engraved gold cuff links; and a 30" x 44" maplewood bureau for his socks, underwear, and casual clothing.

Kimberly gasped.

"Hank . . . ," she said, barely above a whisper. "It's Fort Knox in here."

She reached toward the case with the cuff links. Before she could touch the glass, Hank grabbed her wrist and pulled it away.

"Don't touch that!"

He let go of her hand. She drew it to her chest. He squatted to a stainless-steel box on the floor. She looked down at his folding love handles and slightly spread ass crack.

"I better go now, Hank," she said.

He removed a white cloth and a spray-bottle of glass cleaner from the box and worked on the glass until it squeaked.

"Hank, don't worry," she said, her voice still soft. "I didn't touch it."

"You *almost* did," he said, and wiped it again.

He leaned back to observe it.

"Okay," he said. "I think it's okay now."

"I'm going to go now, Hank."

Kimberly turned toward the door. He shot up and squeezed her shoulder.

"You're not to say *anything* about this to *anyone*," he said. His eyes were dark and red.

Kimberly, a few inches shorter than Hank, looked up into his haggard face. The overhead bulb added weight to the skin sagging over his cheekbones.

"I won't, Hank," she said. "I promise."

"I'm not kidding," he said. "If *one word* about this gets back to me from anyone, I'll see to it that your life in this city turns into hell."

He let go of her shoulder.

She stepped back.

"Hank, is that a threat?"

"No, I wouldn't call it that," he said. He adjusted his scrotum, which had been sticking to the inside of his leg. "A stern advisory would be more accurate."

"Not that I would say anything," she said, "but my status at my firm *is* secure. I get along well with Jimmy and Lewis. They like how I perform and I don't think they would ever . . ."

"Doesn't mean shit. A few moves by me and you're *done*. They go back longer with me than they do with you. They both owe me fucking big time too, especially Jimmy. So if I tell them you're no good, then believe me you, you're not."

He smiled.

"You're also assured a lawsuit-proof reason to lose your job."

Kimberly looked down.

"I won't say anything, Hank," she said.

She walked out of the closet and back into the bedroom. Hank followed and locked the door behind him. He grabbed his black Ralph Lauren terry velour robe from the back of his reading chair, slipped it on, and tied it snugly around his waist.

"So, you still want that cab fare?" he said.

She pulled her purse around her shoulder. The wine buzz had dragged the last of its muddy boots through her bloodstream. Awareness of poor judgment began.

"Good night, Hank," she said, and left the bedroom.

"Thanks for letting me bust a few nuts!" he yelled at her back.

The front door opened and closed.

He crossed the bedroom to the window and looked out. Although he couldn't see it in the cold, black night, he sensed the lake, out there, all around him, a quiet, gaping, deep-throated maw in the dark. He stared out at it for some time, and when the abyss began to bore him, he turned around, and went to sleep.

R ich Swanson unfolded the maroon linen napkin and spread it in his lap. Reed & Barton silverware clinked on china. Ice cubes splashed from crystal carafes pouring into crystal water glasses. Ringing cell phones and eager conversations formed a lunchtime mosaic of sound.

"Ever been here to Frank's Fishery before, kid?" Hank said, reaching for his water glass.

A white-uniformed busboy ran over with tongs and a dish of lemon slices.

"Lemon, sir?" he said.

Hank set down his glass.

The busboy remained frozen with a slice pinched by the tongs.

Hank's right hand tapped and drummed on the table.

"Well?" he snapped.

The busboy laughed nervously and set the slice carefully in the glass.

"I'm sorry, sir," he said. "I didn't hear you say anything."

"Do I need to say something?" Hank looked at Rich. "Christ."

The busboy blushed and leaned toward Rich.

"Sir?"

"Yes, please," Rich said.

He held his glass up and received his slice.

"Thank you very much."

The busboy nodded and scurried away.

Hank watched him stop at another table.

"Idiot. Bet he makes six bucks an hour."

"Actually, I believe it's less than that," Rich said. "I think he depends on tips from the wait staff and bartenders too."

"Whatever," Hank said. "Set your sights low and that's what you get. So what do you think of this place?"

Rich scanned the nearly full room of white men and a few white women. He did spot an Asian woman sitting with two men in the far back corner. The restaurant's patrons all sat in groups of two to five at circular tables with heavy, white tablecloths and a thin central vase with one white rose and one red rose.

"Pretty nice, Hank," Rich said. "Ritzy."

"It's like I've been telling you, kid," Hank said. "If you want to make the big bucks, you've got to *spend* the big bucks and be where the big bucks are. A lot of million-dollar deals have gone down right here in this very fuckin' room. I'll bet I've made almost half my fortune in places like this."

"Alright," Rich said. "I think I can live with fine seafood for lunch and Chef-Boy-Ar-Dee for dinner."

Hank's face darkened. He spread his napkin in his lap and shifted in his chair.

"Is that supposed to be funny? Are you bitching about your stipend? Christ, I'm buying your lunch, aren't I?"

Rich's face and neck turned red. He slid his one-sided menu from the table.

"Of course not, Hank," he said. "I'm very grateful for what you pay me while I'm learning the trade. So, what would you recommend?"

"I already know what I want," he said. "The lobster bisque for starters and then the Chilean sea bass. You might like the Alaskan halibut or the roasted salmon."

"How's the filet mignon or the prime New York steak?"

"I wouldn't know," Hank said. "I don't eat meat."

Still looking at his menu, Rich laughed once. His skin's fading red flushed again when he felt the weight of a stare.

Rich lowered his menu. Hank glared at him.

"You were just kidding, right?" Rich said.

More silence. A longer look.

"You don't eat meat?"

Hank shook his head.

"Oh, well, that's interesting," Rich said. "I would have put a fine steak among the things you enjoy. My apologies." He reached for his water with a slightly shaking hand. "What made you stop or not want to eat meat?"

"None of your business," Hank said. "Fish is okay. Just nothing that walks, runs, crawls, or flies."

"Got it," Rich replied. "How about sweets?"

Hank leaned back and patted his paunch.

"What are you, a smart ass?"

A waiter strolled over.

"May I bring you gentlemen something to drink?"

"Belvedere on the rocks," Hank said. "Rich?"

"Coke, please."

"I should have figured," Hank said. "I'll start with the lobster bisque too."

"A Belvedere on the rocks, a Coke, and lobster bisque," the waiter repeated. "I'll be right back with your drinks and your soup."

The waiter darted away. Hank leaned toward Rich.

"Now, let's get down to business. You've been with us, what, a couple months? You haven't opened or closed any deals, but I don't really expect you to yet. First rule is don't get discouraged. The good news so far is that nothing's been your fault. Especially when that jag bag Bob Harrington decided to extend his current lease without renegotiating. Six fucking months that asshole was telling me he planned to move the firm to that sexy new space over on Adams I had locked in for him."

He licked at something inside his mouth.

"Shit like that will happen. Don't sweat it. It gets a lot easier to swallow once you're swimming in the cash from other deals."

He tapped his fingers on his lips and stared into space for a moment. Rich noticed he wasn't wearing his wedding ring.

"I've got two new deals that I'm going to bring you in on. Good ground-floor stuff for a kid like you. But one thing's important and don't make me say it twice: *I* take care of the hairy stuff. If anyone starts pressing, or bitching, or getting feisty, you kick them over to me. You follow through on everything else and keep me informed about all of it. Your paperwork and even your e-mails run past me before they go anywhere else. Clear as Christ so far?"

"Clear."

The waiter returned and set their drinks in front of them.

Hank reached for his immediately.

"Sweaty Jesus, do I love vodka for lunch."

Rich sipped his Coke.

"You can probably already tell I'm a hands-on leader," Hank continued. "You'll learn faster that way. This business can be trickier than talking to a gay transvestite when you're piss-drunk." He sipped his vodka. "Okay, the first is a fifty-eight-hundred-square-foot lease renewal for an IT firm on LaSalle. The landlord's talking five years at eighteen bucks a foot triple net, and we're talking four years at sixteen plus five bucks per foot in tenant improvements per lease year. Now, this guy's ass is so tight that he might have to crap through his nose, but he likes our clients in his building. They're a bunch of stiff-backed drones, but they're also quiet and polite and they pay their bills on time. The owners and managers also talk to the landlord a lot, so he's cozy with them. We might have to settle at sixteen-fifty or seventeen a foot, but we should be able to talk him down to the four-year lease. We'd consider five years if our client had room to expand, but the extra space isn't there. The firm is growing and making more money than a South Side parish, and they'll need a bigger building soon.

"Now the second deal's a little different . . ."

"Hank!"

Rich and Hank both turned in their seats. A thin, tanned, fifty-something man in a dark-gray suit strode toward them with his arms spread. He reminded Rich of the actor George Hamilton.

Hank stood from his chair. His lap napkin fell to the floor. The two men embraced with a *clap!* and then let go to shake hands.

"Maury, you son of a bitch!" Hank said. "How the hell are you?"

"A lot better than you, I hope," the other replied. "How about you, you bastard? How's Sharon?"

"She's great, she's great. She's at the house in Sarasota with Amy and Andrew right now. Soaking up the sun, just like you. Where in Christ did you get that tan?"

"Saint Thomas. Eight days."

"With Annette?"

"Only if I was supposed to be buried there." He winked at Hank. "Who's the boyfriend?"

"Oh, sorry," Hank said. "Maury, this is Rich Swanson. One of our new tenant reps."

Rich pinned his napkin to his lap with his left hand and stood halfway up to shake Maury's hand with his right.

"Pleased to meet you, sir."

"I'll tell you right now, Rich," Maury said, "don't listen to a goddamn thing this guy tells you or you'll be working deals for hand-job shops over on Taylor and Halsted."

"Someone's gotta do those deals while you're going blind in the booths," Hank said.

"Yeah, with your mother pulling my crank," Maury said. He slid his arm around Hank's shoulder. "Great to see you, buddy."

He looked down at Rich.

"You couldn't have a better boss in Chicago. Hank's a good man and a better broker. Stick by him and you'll do well in the business."

Rich smiled and nodded.

Maury hugged and squeezed Hank again. Hank kept his arm around Maury's waist.

"I saw you across the room and wanted to say hello," Maury said. "Sorry I didn't get back to you last month about the Waterman Brothers thing. It's been a nut house over at the firm lately. Let's schedule a lunch and talk about it. Have your secretary contact mine."

"Whatever you say, hot shot," Hank said. He patted him once on his still-flat belly.

Maury clapped him on the shoulder. The two men let go of each other.

"Nice to meet you, Rich," he said, half-waving as he turned to leave.

"Likewise, Maury," Rich said from his seat, but the other didn't hear. He'd already grabbed another person.

Hank sat back down. When he realized his napkin had fallen to the floor, he kicked at it until it disappeared under the table.

"That's Maury Wilson," Hank said. He lifted his vodka and sipped. "He's a managing partner over at J.B. Granderson."

"Whoa," Rich said. "They're big time, aren't they?"

"Bigger than big time. He moves and shakes when and where he feels like it. You get in with those guys, and you're a fucking made man in this town. Fast."

"Wow," Rich said.

Rich held his water glass by the stem on the table and looked at his hand.

"I'll see to it that you do," Hank said.

Rich looked up at him.

"Just work hard, listen to what I say, and stay loyal to me. You'll get in with them and everyone else that matters."

The waiter arrived with Hank's soup and set it down.

"I need another napkin," Hank said.

"Certainly, sir," the waiter said. He moved away briskly.

"So what were we talking about?" Hank said. "Oh yeah, the deals I'll have you work on. By the way, how are you doing with those leads I gave you last week?"

Rich looked at his hand and the water glass again.

"Not so good," he said, rubbing his thumb over a slowly running bead of condensation. "I called every name on the list, and no one called me back. I even wrote to them using that e-mail script you gave me. Nothing on that either."

"No surprise," Hank said. "They're just playing hard to get. This business is sort of like chasing pussy, kid. They want to give it up, but not too fast. They want to see you dance and play for it first. As long as they know you're one of mine, they'll eventually lie down and spread their legs. Just give it time and be persistent. And whatever you do, don't get too eager or you'll chase away the pussy for good. When did you make your last call?"

"Yesterday."

"Alright. Just put the list in a drawer for a week. Then *I'll* place a couple calls to lube things up a little. You still might have to play the game after that, but you should be getting some action inside a few weeks."

"Sounds good."

The waiter returned with the basket of rolled napkins. Hank took one and spread it in his lap.

He leaned over his soup and slurped a few spoonfuls. He then picked up his vodka, pushed back from the table, and crossed his legs.

"Now, before we get back to your two new deals," he said, "why don't you tell me what Howie Frank and his crony Ron Munson were talking to you about at the banquet last night."

Rich's face flushed.

"Sorry?"

"Don't play dumb with me," Hank said. A spark flared in each of his dark-green eyes; Rich couldn't tell if they had pupils. "I've been in this for over thirty fucking years. I have x-ray vision through my kneecaps and an eye in my asshole too. So tell me what they said about me."

"Uh, nothing, Hank," Rich said. "Just small talk. He was asking me how things were going at the firm. Congratulated me about you too."

Hank leaned forward and set his drink back on the table.

"You're a lousy liar, kid," he said. "You better work on your poker face if you want to bag deals in the big time. Otherwise you can go back to grooming dogs or whatever you did before you came to my firm looking for a better life. Now tell me the truth. I'll know if you're bullshitting me."

Rich reached for his Coke and swallowed a gulp. He set it back down and looked at Hank with both hands flat on the table.

"Okay, Hank," he said. "They pulled me aside and warned me."

"Warned you?"

"Yes. About you."

The sparks in Hank's eyes brightened. A hurried waiter breezed past behind his chair, causing a hair to fall out of place. Hank fixed it.

"What was their warning?"

"He . . . he just said I should watch myself. That I should learn what I can from you but not trust you."

"That's it?"

"Yes."

Hank sipped his vodka and licked his lips.

"You're lying. Keep talking."

Rich stared at him. Hank's face was granite.

"He said that if things ever got too hairy for me at the firm, I could see him and he could help me out."

Hank smiled.

"Is that right?"

Rich looked away.

"That's good to know," Hank said.

Their waiter returned. Hank held up his empty vodka glass and rattled it.

"You know what to do."

The waiter accepted the glass.

"Of course, sir. And have you gentlemen decided on lunch?"

"Chilean sea bass," Hank said.

Both he and the waiter looked at Rich, who hesitated, then:

"Alaskan halibut."

"Very good," the waiter said. He scooped up their menus and spun away.

"That was pretty unethical, wouldn't you say?"

Rich raised his eyebrows.

"The waiter?"

"No," Hank said. "The Jew bastard. Howie Frank."

Rich neither spoke nor moved.

"I've been sharing this city with that fat-lipped fuck for a long time," Hank said. "Like a saint. Two-faced prick. Just goes to show. What people say and what people do are almost never the same. You'll meet a lot of posers, Rich. They'll act straight and pretend to like you during a deal, especially if they can smell the payday. Don't ever forget that."

The waiter returned with his second Belvedere and set it down.

Hank picked it up.

"Now about those two deals we were talking about . . ."

Rich looked intently at Hank and listened to more "vital" information about dealing with landlords and tenants. About strategies for predicting future space requirements.

Hank lowered his voice as if someone might be straining to hear. He spoke of occupancy rates and net absorption and concessions at something-plus dollars a foot.

Rich listened, and listened, and heard some more.

Hank halted to answer his cell phone.

The waiter served their food.

Rich gazed across the manicured merchants of elite information. They bartered their knowledge, ideas, and connections, all so they might annex more dollars to their personal kingdoms.

On the sidewalk outside the front window, a black homeless man accepted a couple of coins from a woman.

Hank's phone conversation continued. Knowing he'd been forgotten for the moment, Rich began deleting Hank's soulless facts from his head, and asked himself if he still knew who he was.

"*R*ich?"

Dawn rubbed her eyes and sat up against the backboard of their queen-sized bed. Rich stared at her from the rocking chair in the opposite right corner. The large bedside clock's glowing-green digits mixed with the moonlight, making him look like a phantom.

"Rich, what's the matter? Why are you up?"

He remained silent and still.

She slid out of bed and crossed the floor to kneel by him.

She took one of his hands and held it in both of hers.

"Honey, what's the matter?"

He rubbed her cheek gently with his thumb.

"Why did you marry me?" he said. "Why do you love me?"

She drew his hand to her mouth and kissed one of his fingertips.

"Because I love you."

"But why?"

"Because . . . I don't know. I just do."

He slipped his hand away and leaned back in the chair.

"But I barely make any money. And I still don't know what to do with my life."

"You're only twenty-seven," she said. "I'm making enough for the bills. You'll earn more soon enough."

He paused and studied her.

"But that's not the way it's supposed to be," he said. "*I'm* supposed to be the breadwinner."

He leaned forward. His head fell into his hands.

"I'm a failure."

Dawn sat back on her heels and smoothed her white-cotton nightgown on her thighs.

"Stop being so hard on yourself," she said. "We'll be fine."

"But what if someone else came along . . . who could give you all you wanted *now?*"

"I wouldn't do anything."

"But what if I really never want more than to just pay my bills and be *me?* What if I don't ever get us a big house with kids in the yard?"

Dawn looked at the floor and thought for a moment.

"Then I'd help you pay them. Your bills."

Rich slid down to his knees and joined her on the floor.

Dawn guided his head down to her breast. He closed his eyes and listened to her breathe.

"I love you," she said. "I wouldn't want to be with anyone but you."

He wrapped his arms around her waist and buried his face in the lap of her nightgown.

*H*ank poured himself another scotch from the crystal decanter on the bar and plopped back into his favorite front-room leather chair. Sharon glared at him from the matching sectional sofa.

"Christ! Why do you keep looking at me like that?"

"You're despicable," she said.

"Nice to see you too. I really missed hearing you bitch about your easy life."

He hiked up the chair's foot rest and sipped his drink.

"How was the weather in Florida?" he said. "Did Amy and Andrew have fun?"

"Don't change the subject," she spat. "What did you do while I was gone?"

"Oh, nothing," he said. He set his drink on the end table to his left and slid a cable-TV guide from the chair's right magazine pouch. "Just work. Still breaking in the new kid. Good kid. Smart. Not sure yet if he has the brass, though. He might cut and run before he makes any real money."

Sharon's eyes steamed in their sockets.

He looked at her blankly.

They'd met when she was a front-desk secretary for a firm on his cold-call list during his days selling office supplies door-to-door. At first, she'd been a polite but immovable block of ice. But holy hell, had she been a *looker*. Better yet, she came from a conservative, upper-middle-class Episcopalian household, and that usually meant *stability*.

After four months of follow-up, she finally agreed to coffee and pie. That led to greater access, and pretty soon, they were making out. Then they got naked—a lot—and marriage became a matter of time.

With the right woman at his side, one who believed in him, he left door-to-door sales for business real estate. The kids arrived a few years later. Hank busted his ass and rose through the ranks of city firms. They started living well.

His *real* drinking showed up a little after that. The high-paying partnerships and flagrant affairs pulled up the rear.

Sharon had hated his changing behavior at first. She'd even threatened to leave.

He learned he could shut her up for a while by writing prescriptions of cash and vacations.

Sharon's eye beams heated the air. He smiled. Hell, she *still* looked pretty good, even at fifty-seven. He'd never tell her so, but he liked her Sarasota tan and sun-bleached dirty-brown hair. At five-six, one-forty, she could still turn a middle-aged head. And she still knew how to dress.

But all assets considered, she couldn't compete with the pieces of ass to which he still had access. It wouldn't even matter if he flashed a Hollywood spotlight on his wedding ring. The parade of quality trim would continue to play for him with seventy-six trombones.

"What about your banquet?" she said, crashing into his thoughts.

"Oh, that?" Hank shut the cable guide and tossed it on the floor. "That was fine."

"Didn't anybody ask or wonder why your family wasn't there for your lifetime achievement award?"

Hank scratched his chin.

"No. Not really."

"And I'm sure you were in no hurry to explain that your wife would rather soak in a lake of hellfire than watch you booze up and chase younger women again."

"Please, Sharon. Don't start. I'm not in the mood."

She rose, walked past him to the bar, and returned to the sofa with a Southern Comfort and lime juice. The light from the overhead studio track shone in white slivers on her recently polished red fingernails.

"When is it enough, Hank? When will you have closed enough deals? Made enough money? Had sex with enough young women to prove your virility? I'd really like to know."

Hank's head fell back against the leather chair's cushy headrest. He looked down his nose at her and sneered.

"You're one to talk," he said. His drink now lounged in the loose grip of his right hand, which dangled over the armrest. "You could have left a long time ago. But you couldn't bear the shame. Or what you'd be leaving behind, even with a decent settlement."

He sipped his drink and let his arm fall limp again.

"You see, your problem is that you love your free ride more than you hate being my wife, and that says a fucking lot. You're basically accepting payments to stick around. I guess that could qualify you as a wife-for-hire, if not something worse I won't say."

"Damn your soul," she said through clenched teeth.

"Soul?" he said. He chuckled and crossed his ankles the other way. "Don't get moral on me, Sharon. This isn't about what's right and wrong. Never was. It's about who has the balls and the will to live well. Enjoying life doesn't always sign you up to be a great person. You know that, so cut the shit. There are those who go out and *get,* and those who play nice and watch it go by. Who settle for doing without. Well, if that makes people feel like good Christians, that's fine with me. In the meantime, I'll take what life has to offer before I'm six feet down with the beetles up my ass."

He sipped his drink.

"I am who I am, you know how I am, and you bought into all of this a long time ago."

He rattled his ice cubes.

She glared even harder and started to tremble.

"I did love you once," she said, and stood. "I might still love you, if you were a lovable man."

"So how are Amy and Andrew?" he said. "They have fun?"

He swished more scotch in his mouth, savored it, and swallowed.

"They're the only thing that reminds me you're human," she said. "How you managed to love and care for them is a mystery I'll never solve."

She walked over to him.

"Dare I say there's hope for you yet?"

She set her drink on his end table.

He watched her reach into the left pocket of her white pants. She placed a small object next to the glass with a *clack!*

"You might want to return this to the owner," she said. "I found it under my pillow."

He stared sideways at one of Kimberly's earrings.

She picked up her drink and spun away. A puff of air slapped him. The kitchen's swinging door moved back and forth, and then fell still again.

Hank pulled the foot rest back into the chair with his legs, scooped the earring from the table, and strode over to the bar. He poured another scotch, went to his den, and closed the white French doors.

He dimmed the infernal lighting, lit two candles, and turned on the Sony stereo in the in-wall bookshelves. Luciano Pavarotti swelled from the speakers.

He sat at his polished-oak desk.

After a while, he retrieved the stereo's remote control from the desk's top right drawer. A couple of clicks changed the music to the melancholy acoustic-guitar pieces he preferred when he just wanted to stare into the air and think.

For once, he needed someone to consider *him*. Someone who could understand *his* struggles.

Nobody cared about *him* until they needed something from him.

But that was fine. He could take it, because he saw through it all.

He removed an 8.5" x 11" frame from the tall right-bottom drawer and stood it in front of him on the desk.

"Hi, Dad," he said.

He sipped his scotch and set it back on the coaster to the right of the frame.

The handsome, brown-haired son of Irish immigrants smiled at him from his frozen black-and-white moment from the late forties. A neighboring merchant had taken the picture of Frank Coogan in front of his new butcher shop just after the bank had approved his loan. Its doors would open within weeks, his face and posture revealed, and society would find out fast what a Mick with a Mission could do with twelve hundred square feet and a dream. All sturdy five-feet-eight of him gleamed with innocent pride. He would now work for and answer only to himself. Thick forearms bulging from rolled-up shirtsleeves told that he was ready to get to business right *now*.

Hank leaned closer to the picture.

He slammed his fist on the desk, moving the frame and stirring the ice in his drink.

"Goddamn it, Dad! Nobody gets it. I *deserve* what's mine! I *paid* my fucking dues."

He straightened the frame.

"We all have our reasons for doing what we do. All of us. You did too."

He slipped his hand around his drink but didn't raise it.

"Look at you, for Christ's sake. You busted your ass and walked a straight line. And for what? To barely break even."

He drank.

"What was your reward? Stress-related heart problems. Dead at fifty-two."

He wiped the one tear from his eye.

"Well not me. No way. I won't do that to myself."

He drank again, leaned back, and looked away from the picture.

"If we're going to live, and I mean *really* live, we all have to wear moral shit stains at some point." He looked back at his father. "And if God doesn't like it, it's because He never went one-twenty down a lone stretch of highway in a Jaguar XJ Super V8 with a hot piece of ass riding shotgun."

Another sip of his scotch.

"I can't help that I was chosen to succeed. It was just my destiny."

He set down the drink, lifted the frame, and held it before him with both hands.

"Sorry, Dad. Maybe you get it by now."

He kissed the thin glass covering his father's image.

"Good night, Dad. Thanks for the talk."

He returned the frame to the drawer, finished his drink, and turned off the stereo.

He extinguished the infernal lighting but did not leave the den.

The French doors remained closed and protective. He stared through them at the empty front room and, standing alone in the dark, listened to the listless silence of his palace high above the lake.

W eeks passed, and then months. Winter gave way to spring and its occasional sunshine.

With Hank's guidance and pull, Rich Swanson closed his first two office deals on his own: a small advertising agency and a smaller personal-injury liability law firm. He proudly—and quickly—gave the $4,120 in two commission checks to his wife, who continued to love him and pay the bulk of their bills.

In early April, he'd withdrawn from his modest life savings to take her to Miami. For four balmy days, they'd walked, dined, and shopped along Ocean Boulevard. One night, as the beautiful people caroused and the soft, billowing wind rolled in from the ocean, he'd sat on their hotel-room balcony and reflected on what he'd learned by multiple means at Coogan Commercial Real Estate so far:

Hank Coogan earned an annual average of $700,000 in salary and commissions from the firm and undisclosed millions more through private investments and capital ventures.

Coogan Commercial Real Estate had collected $4.2 million in commissions the previous year. After subtracting Hank's earnings, it paid its fifty-fifty split to its twelve office agents (not including Rich, who earned his four grand in the current year), Rich's $27,000 stipend, and a total of $257,000 to its five administrative employees.

On paper, that left $1.47 million to cover the firm's $1.8 million in taxes, loans, legal fees, outside service fees, monthly utilities, marketing expenses, and annual rent for its Loop-based office.

In Chad's department, most vendors had not been paid in months. Coogan Commercial Real Estate also did not discriminate when choosing who would suffer the pangs of collection. While the firm's principal lounged in luxury, dined with distinction, and retired to his Sarasota beach home six times a year, a South Loop printer chased payment of a five-month-old invoice for two new sets of business cards ($137.50). A small-time real estate magazine pursued $47.24 for a classified ad it had run for one of Coogan's agents the previous fall. An independent broker of printing services lost his biggest client thanks to $7,782.46 that Coogan owed but would not pay.

Chad spent at least two hours per day fending off furious vendors or seeking replacements for the growing list of those who refused to work with him.

Both the phone and electric companies had threatened to cut off service three times in the last nine months.

Hank Coogan had slept with one of the two female office agents who reported to him.

Some of the other agents were okay guys, or at least that's how they appeared one inch beneath the surface. Writing all of them off as shallow and greedy had been convenient for Rich at first. But in time, he unearthed the exceptions. Some of them loved their wives, read good books, and thought of life beyond the dollar. One even went to church—and prayed. While the top performers could sometimes resemble well-dressed and -mannered sociopaths, the "lower" earners revealed no need to control everything. They might even do a favor for *you.*

Hank Coogan was a tidy housekeeper at work. Every item had its place. All file drawers had their labels. Tirades had been known to follow a stray pen on a break-room table or a loose paper that'd fallen from its folder. Both Martha Stewart and Hitler's National Socialists might have appreciated his office equally.

How could anyone work for a man such as Hank? Rich believed the agents could take him or leave him as long as they made their money because of him.

The "overhead" staff, on the other hand, remained at the mercy of those who "paid the bills." An agent's request required instant attention; a support person's question might go unanswered for weeks. Large-commission requisitions arrived at accounting the night before checks were to be cut; countless memos had asked for at least five business days. Marketing materials were *demanded* from Chad, who delivered only through a dwindling supply of patient vendors.

For Rich, each day among the deals in motion clarified why certain people could generate wealth while creating nothing. They worked hard on knowledge and relationships until reaching their positions of advantage.

And yet he'd committed to dress like them, talk like them, carry himself as they did.

He had bills, and beyond money, only God had greater power to convert a man.

Sitting alone on the hotel balcony, listening to the sounds of nightlife, he'd wished that every dollar in America would just crinkle up and blow away.

Rich turned the corner toward his office. Chad stepped out from his own. Rich almost ran into him.

"Jeez, man!" he said. He placed his hand on his jackrabbit heart. "Don't do that to me, Chad."

"Sorry," Chad said. "I was actually just coming to see you. Can I speak to you for a moment? In my office, in private?"

Rich scanned the short hallway. Out of sight, around a corner, Tad Dexter griped to Mitchell Parsons about a landlord's tenant-improvement proposal.

"Sure, Chad," Rich said. He stepped into his office.

Chad closed the door behind them. Rich seated himself in one of the two chairs facing the desk. Chad sat down in his own.

"What's up, Chad?"

"I just needed to talk to someone I can trust," he said. "I can't discuss anything with *them*, and I think Vera's tired of hearing me bitch. She has enough of her own problems."

"No problem," Rich said. "What's on your mind?"

"What do you think?"

"Hank."

"Asshole," Chad said.

He slid a paper-stuffed manila folder from a desktop vertical sorter and set it on the desk between them.

"Know what these are?"

"Invoices."

"About fifty of them. Some are ready to file for Medicare. I've stopped giving them to Vera for now. She's still dealing with the other fifty or sixty I gave her a while ago."

He held one up.

"This one's for one of Hank's full-page deal announcements in *Crain's Chicago Business*. Three months old. We'll probably pay it this fall."

He held up another invoice.

"See this one? Fifty bucks. Seventy-two days old. I won't tell you what it's for, but it's ridiculous."

He stuffed the invoice back into the folder.

"It's out of control. *He's* out of control."

"I don't get it," Rich said. "How are we staying in business?"

"Because he's brilliant in an idiotic sort of way," Chad said, leaning forward. His eyes were dark. "He knows *exactly* who to pay by when to keep the ship floating and his image clean with the right people. He also knows who'll wait as long he wants them to while he takes care of himself."

Rich looked down, into his lap, and then back up.

"So . . . what are you going to do?"

"What *can* I do? I've been looking for other jobs."

Chad sat back and stared at his screen saver, a photo of a mosque tower in a desert city at dusk.

"What I wouldn't give to just get away from here. To be *happy.*"

He looked straight at Rich again.

"Why do we do this to ourselves, Rich? Why do we drag ourselves to jobs we fucking hate? We think we're free, that we have choices, but we're not, and we don't."

Rich thought quietly for a moment and shrugged.

"I'm still trying to figure that out, Chad."

Chad lifted the bulging folder and shook it above the desk. A few invoices almost fell out.

"Is it worth it, Rich? Is it *worth it?*"

"I've asked myself that question a thousand times, Chad."

"I wake up in the morning, and the first thing that I do is hate my life. Hate it. I think about the whole day *here,* working for *him,* cleaning up *his* mess, taking shit from *his* vendors, having him bitch at *me* about what's not done when he knows I *can't* do it because of him. All while he lives large, looks good, and gets drunk with the in-crowd."

He paused to wipe spittle from his lips.

"You know what Vera told me? Last week we collected a one hundred thousand–dollar commission on one of his deals, and fifty thousand of it went straight into his pocket, even before the payment had a chance to clear. She cut the check, right there, while he watched,

196

with a stack of unpaid invoices on her desk right in front of him. He didn't even look at them. Just took his fifty grand and walked out the door."

"Yeah, that's messed up," Rich said. "But it is his business, and this is just how he runs it. Not much we can do."

Chad sneered.

"I don't care," he said. His glassy eyes became a darker red. "It has to stop. It's not right. Why does everyone have to suffer and wait in order to take care of his lifestyle?"

"It's bullshit, I know," Rich said. "But we probably can't get too idealistic about it. At least not while we're in here."

"I wish someone would just take him down. Beat his ass. Ruin his reputation. Something. Jag-offs like him get away with way too much."

Rich stood. Chad looked up at him.

Since joining the firm, Rich had never seen him smile. Not yet.

Chad stood as well.

"Tell me, Rich," he said. "If you were to take your own guess, what do you think will happen to a guy like Hank in the end?"

Rich looked down and then back up.

"I think he'll keep having fun until he has to own up to himself." He paused. "And he'll probably be the one who decides when that'll happen. From what I've seen, he doesn't give a shit what most people think about him. He won't feel bad until he's ready."

Rich glanced toward the door.

"I have to get back to my office. Have to make a few calls. You alright? Gonna make it through the rest of the day?"

Chad's eyes softened although they still were red.

"I'll make it," he said. "Always do."

Rich shook his hand and then turned for the door.

"I've liked you since I met you, Rich," Chad said to his back. "I hope this place doesn't change you. I hope you stay who you are."

Rich paused with his hand extended toward the doorknob.

He glanced sideways, over his shoulder, and then let himself out.

*T*he closet door opened. Sharon stepped in with her right arm behind her back.

Beethoven's Ninth Symphony enveloped her.

Legs crossed, eyes dazed and pensive, a glass of scotch in his hand, he sat in his oak captain's chair.

"Hank?"

He looked up as if someone had leapt from a bush.

"Christ!"

He pointed a small remote and lowered the volume.

"I knocked first," she said, "but you had it up too loud again."

"What do you want?"

She slipped her arm from behind her back and held out the phone.

"You have a call."

He stared at it as if it were a gun.

"It's a woman," Sharon said. "A younger woman."

He rose, set his scotch on a display case, and snatched the phone from her.

"I hope it's on mute," he said.

She smiled.

"I'm meeting Martie for dinner and drinks. Maybe a movie too. A couple hundred should do."

Hank glanced right at his immaculate stacks of cash.

"What, you already spent the hundred you took from me yesterday?"

Color drained from what remained of her tan.

"What do you mean?" she said.

"You know goddamn well what I mean."

He shifted the phone to his left hand and grabbed the top pack from the hundreds with his right.

"There's a note missing from this," he said. "Are you stupid? You know I still count it."

Her smile faded.

"You're psychotic," she said.

"No, I'm alert, and you're a goddamn thief," he said. "*This* is why I have to keep it locked. Christ! I can't let slip for a *minute,* not even to take a *piss* one door over! Good God, Sharon."

She folded her hands in front of her waist and looked down.

"It's so predictable that I can't even find it in me to get angry at you."

He slid two hundreds from the pack and held them out to her. She hesitated, and then reached forward to take them. He yanked them back at the last second.

"The least you can do is apologize."

"May I please just have the damn money, Hank?"

"Yeah, right," he said.

He threw the bills into the air. They fluttered and landed askew on the carpet.

She bent down and picked them up.

"Now get out of here," he said.

She clutched the bills with both hands, looked once more at Hank, and left.

"And shut the fucking door!"

Footsteps brushed against the bedroom carpet. The closet door closed.

Hank hit the mute button on the phone.

"Yeah, Hank here," he said.

"Hank?"

Hard-wired instincts jump-started his heart and stepped on the gas.

"Kimberly?"

"Yes," she said. "I'm sorry to bother you, but I really need to speak with you. It's best if we meet. Tomorrow after work, if you're available."

"Christ. What in hell are you doing calling me on this line?"

"I'm sorry, Hank. I tried your cell a few times. It couldn't wait. We have to talk."

He suddenly felt as if he leaned forward, arms spread, from the top of a skyscraper.

"This had better be *real* important, Kimberly."

Silence like drying cement, then:

"It is."

"I've got three ball-buster meetings tomorrow."

"It'll only take a few minutes," she said. "I promise. I can meet you at O'Hanahan's. Six-thirty."

"Too early."

He closed his eyes and rubbed them with his free hand.

"Fine," she said. "Seven then."

He puffed his cheeks and exhaled.

"Alright," he said. "Seven. And if you get there before I do, order me a Johnnie Black." A pause. "On the rocks. Please."

The other line clicked and went dead.

Hank hit the OFF button. To his left, his hanging suits loomed like headless Hanks, any one of which he wished he could be: anything to escape the feeling that something was about to go south.

*T*he day from hell warmed up for Hank Coogan minutes after he pulled out of his luxury condo building's private parking garage.

A nasty accident on Lake Shore Drive had halted traffic with hazardous timing. The home-to-office trip typically took thirty-five minutes through mild congestion, so he'd left at 7:45 a.m. to arrive around 8:20. He and Mitchell Parsons would then prepare for their 9:00 meeting with the three managing partners of The Langford Associates. The high-end accounting firm was about to renew a five-year lease on 3,500 square feet in an area of the Central Business District where the rates for Class A buildings gave commercial agents erections. Only Hank's firm and Howie Frank's still had a shot at negotiating with the property-management company.

Hank rolled down his window and stuck out his head. The accident had attracted an ambulance, two firetrucks, and four flashing squad cars.

The drive became forty minutes, and then fifty, and then sixty.

His heart thumped. Panicked and pissed, he abused his cell phone calling his firm.

The partners were impatient sons of bitches. They wouldn't care why he was late.

Mitchell would have to provide an Academy Award–winning stall.

Seventy minutes.

Eighty.

He couldn't even pull off onto any of the exits into the Loop. They were already clogged with cars moving like leaves in a gutter during a drizzle.

"Christ hates me," he mumbled.

The car clock hit 9:15.

He already knew the story. The partners would leave in five more minutes, and the deal would be dead. The huge commission would be heading for the Jew a few blocks away.

He threw his black Lexus SC430 in park, shoved the door open, and climbed out.

Horns honked. A few people cussed out of their windows.

He tossed his suit coat into the car, loosened his tie, and walked several feet down his lane of stagnant traffic.

He stopped and held up both middle fingers.

"FUCK YOU, MOTHERFUCKERS! YOU PEOPLE FUCKING SUCK!"

More horns honked. A Hispanic man stared him down. A white woman called him an asshole. A black man smiled and laughed with bouncing shoulders.

Hank returned to his car, climbed in, and closed the door.

The car clock's digits advanced. Traffic still strained to inch forward.

"Good morning, Mr. Coogan," Helen, the front-desk receptionist, said when he walked in at 9:38.

He walked past her and cut through the few agents milling in the front hallway.

His office came into view. He saw Mitchell's back through the front glass wall.

"I don't want to talk about it," he said when he got there.

Mitchell was on his cell phone. He glanced at Hank mid-sentence and nodded.

Hank plopped in his chair and slammed his brown-leather briefcase on the desk. A metal-mesh tray of papers fell to the floor. Mitchell's cup of coffee followed it down.

"Son of a bitch!" Hank said.

Mitchell ended his call and flipped the phone shut.

"Hank, it's oka . . ."

"Mitchell, please. Just get the fuck out and leave me alone for a while."

Mitchell bent and picked up the cup.

"I'll have someone clean it," Hank said.

Mitchell slid his left hand into his pocket. The empty cup dangled by its handle from his right index finger. He looked at Hank a moment longer, opened his mouth to speak, and then left.

Hank let his head fall back against the headrest.

The phone's red message light blinked incessantly.

"Of course," he mumbled.

He leaned forward and tapped the speaker button. Once logged into voice mail, he paged through and deleted the flotsam of complaints, questions, and sales calls until one message made him stop. He replayed it three times:

"Mr. Coogan, this is James Dubrowski from Superior Signage. I'm calling again on the eighty-three hundred you owe for multiple signs we made and installed for a number of your commercial-property listings, especially in River North. A few of these invoices are more than six months old. You had promised to pay most of this off by last week, and as of today, I've still received nothing. You've consistently reneged on our payment terms, and you're no longer returning my calls. I'll be by late this afternoon to discuss this situation with you personally. Thank you. Good-bye."

"Dick face."

He deleted the message and clicked off the phone speaker. He spun around to check e-mail at his computer behind his desk.

A knock made him turn around again.

"Christ, what is it?"

Chad Harwick stood in the doorway.

"Hank, do you have a moment?"

"Do I look like it?"

"I'm sorry, but, well, it's just that I need to speak with you. Ezra has asked me to put up a sign at a new loft-office listing over on Erie, and Jason wants to order new business cards."

"So?"

"Well, I'm afraid we've run out of vendors."

Hank's face tightened.

"What the hell are you talking about?"

"I'm saying, I've used more than a dozen sign and printing companies in the city and even a few from the suburbs. None of them will work with us now. I've even tried calling some new ones up by Waukegan and down by Calumet, but they've either ignored my calls or said they can't accept our projects."

Hank stiffened in his chair.

"Are you being a smart ass?"

"No, I'm not."

"What did you say to Ezra and Jason?"

"I didn't say anything. I said I'd look into it."

"Well, find a goddamn printer and a sign company and keep your mouth shut. Get them what they asked for."

"Hank, I think we're running out of options."

Hank leaned forward and scowled.

"Get on the fucking phone and call fucking Nova Scotia if you have to."

Chad looked down, away, and then back at him.

"Hank, with all due respect, do you understand what I'm saying to you?"

"Get out of my office," Hank said, spinning back around to face his computer. "Those requests had better find homes by tomorrow."

Chad stared at the back of his chair.

"You're still here," Hank said.

Chad left.

Hank checked his watch and then his schedule on Microsoft Outlook. Meeting with Richard Thompson / Morgan & Smith Financial / Dearborn / 11:00 a.m. Another expiring lease, another big firm, another fat commission if he could represent and work out the deal. He had about an hour to re-review his notes and the firm's documents before consulting Thompson.

His stomach flipped.

He stood and looked at the floor where his metal-mesh tray had fallen.

Both the tray and its contents, including his notes, remained sprawled—and soaked with coffee.

He grabbed his favorite Mont Blanc pen and whipped it against the wall. It cracked and fell onto a filing cabinet.

His phone rang. The front desk's extension flashed on the caller ID. He tapped the speaker button.

"Yeah."

"Hank, there's a gentleman from Superior Signage here to see you," Helen said.

Hank laughed to himself.

It was an old trick. He knew it well. Tell them when you'll be there and show up at another time.

"Tell him I'm busy."

She put him on hold. A few seconds, then:

"He said he'll wait." A pause. "As long as necessary."

Hank looked at his crippled pen. Then he exhaled once, hard, through his nose.

"Christ. I'll be right up."

He strode out of his office and went to Chad's.

"Hey," he said, leaning through the doorway. "Need you. One of your people is here."

Chad turned around from his computer.

"Who? What do they want?"

Hank scowled.

"Don't ask me questions like that. You know what he wants. Let's go. Follow my lead and cover my back."

Chad stood and walked out with him. Hank remained several paces ahead.

When they arrived at the front desk, James Dubrowski rose from the black-leather lobby sofa. He held a semi-thick folder of papers.

"Mr. Coogan."

Hank looked him up and down.

"Can I help you?"

"Yes, you can," Dubrowski said. He looked back and forth between Hank and Chad. "I left you a message this morning. I'll assume you received it."

Hank glanced at Helen. She pretended to read the contents of an open three-ring binder.

"Let's go into the conference room," he said.

The three men moved past the reception desk to the conference room on the left halfway down the front hall. Inside the room, Rich Swanson looked up from the documents he'd spread at the far end of the Italian-marble table for twenty.

"Oh, hi, Hank," he said. "I was just reviewing the deal for . . ." He saw Chad and Dubrowski standing just outside the door. "Uh, you need me to leave?"

He stood and gathered his papers. Hank walked over to him.

"Stay for this one," he said under his breath. "I want you to see how it works."

Rich nodded. He stacked his papers neatly, set them to his right, and sat back down. Hank gestured for Chad and Dubrowski to enter.

"James, this is Rich Swanson," Hank said. "He's one of my office-tenant representatives. He's going to sit in on this meeting."

"Nice to meet you," Rich said from his seat.

James waved curtly and looked back at Hank.

"Whatever suits you," he said. "The sooner we can work this out, the better. I'd really rather not have to be here."

"Please, please," Hank said, pulling a couple of chairs away from the table. "Make yourself comfortable."

Dubrowski chose his chair and set down the folder.

Hank circled around to the other side of the table, where he sat across from Dubrowski one seat to Dubrowski's right. Chad sat two seats to Dubrowski's immediate left, between Dubrowski and Rich.

"So," Hank said, leaning forward with his hands flat on the table. "Sounds like you have a problem with some invoices."

Dubrowski opened his folder.

"No, Mr. Coogan, *you* have a problem with some invoices."

He placed his palm on the top sheet of paper.

"Eight thousand dollars' worth. Now, I don't know where you come from, maybe that's not a lot of money to you, but it is to me and my business. We're a small outfit, Mr. Coogan. We're feeling the missing eight thousand."

Hank rubbed his chin and winked at Rich. Dubrowski didn't see him do it.

"How much we owe you again? Exactly?"

"Eight thousand two hundred and ninety."

Hank pushed back from the table, crossed his legs, and folded his hands in his lap.

"Tell you what, Jim . . ."

"It's James."

"Tell you what, James. If we can settle at sixty-five hundred, I'll walk straight over to Vera's office and have her cut a check right now."

"But that's not how much you owe me."

"It's what I'm offering to give you if you want to resolve this today."

Dubrowski's eyes narrowed.

"Why don't you pay me sixty-five hundred now and the balance in thirty days?"

Hank's face hardened.

"I've made you an offer, Jim." He paused. "Let's settle this now."

Dubrowski grinned and shook his head.

"You're asking me to discount eighteen hundred after you've made me chase you for months."

"Look, Jim," Hank said, "I want to wrap this up as much as you do. You think I enjoy this? Sixty-five is my offer, and you get paid today."

Dubrowski closed the folder and leaned back in his chair.

"I've worked with your kind before, you know," he said.

He glanced to his left: first at Chad, then at Rich. Both looked away from him.

"I know what you must think of me," Hank said, "and what you might feel compelled to do or say when you leave. But before you get carried away, let's set a couple things straight. First, I am a reputable man, and this is a reputable business. I'm truly sorry if I caused you and your business any discomfort. That was not my intent. We do our best to fulfill our debts as any firm with integrity would. We've been waiting on several large commission checks. A few major deals also fell through on us this year. We can't pay you until we get paid. You know how it goes.

"Secondly, I'm going to buckle up with my marketing director . . ." Hank gestured toward Chad, who looked up, surprised. ". . . and see if we can improve some of our procedures with our vendors, particularly the sign companies. Chad's system is okay overall, but a few things are getting crossed up, and unfortunately, they're slowing down some of our payments even more."

Chad's hands clenched into fists.

Hank leaned forward and met Dubrowski's stare.

"So what do you say, Jim? Do you want the check?"

Dubrowski sat back. He looked at Hank a moment longer and then threw his hands up.

"Done," Hank said. He turned toward Chad. "Chad, would you please have Vera issue the check?"

Chad's eyes became slits.

"Please?" Hank said, smiling.

Chad rose and glanced at Rich.

"I'll be right back," he said, and, trembling, left the room.

Silence settled over the remaining three men.

"So, James," Hank said. "How you think the Cubs will do this year?"

Rich listened to them small-talk about struggling hitters and bush-league relief pitchers and underperforming millionaires. At some point, their conversation faded out for him.

These men both owned a company, but clearly one of them was making the rules. He did so because what he presented identified a *greater man.*

Rich tried not to laugh. Just the other day, as he'd washed his hands in the men's room, Hank had entered a stall without saying hello. He'd unbuckled his pants, dropped the seat with a *clank,* and then blown moist air through his ass before filling the bowl with a *splat!*

Less than fifteen minutes later, Rich watched him pull rank and raise his voice in a tense, full-capacity meeting. People heard and feared and obeyed.

And yet the smell he'd left in the stall was the same as most others deposited there.

Chad returned with an unsealed #10 company envelope. He handed it to Hank, who slipped out the check, looked it over, and signed it. He put it back in the envelope and pushed it across the table.

"There you go, Jim," he said. "Done deal."

Dubrowski slid the envelope toward him and cracked it open with his thumb and index finger. Then, without expression, he put it in his folder and stood.

"Thank you," he said.

Hank rose and stuck out his hand.

"Sorry for the inconvenience."

The hand hung suspended. Dubrowski looked at it.

Color trickled into Hank's face. Rich and Chad glanced back and forth between the two men.

Dubrowski finally shook it. Then he left the room.

A few seconds later, the lobby door opened and closed.

"What a fuckwad," Hank said. "You see the way that asshole was looking at me? Loser. He's lucky I gave him anything."

Hank moved for the door. Rich scooped up his papers and followed.

Chad remained standing behind them.

"You coming, Chad?" Rich said.

Hank slowed before reaching the doorway and turned around.

Blocking Hank's view of him, Rich gestured to Chad with his head: *let's go without any trouble.*

Chad's hands balled into fists at his sides. His neck muscles became steel cords.

"What the hell's the matter with *you?*" Hank said.

Chad shoved past Rich and rushed to within a half-foot of Hank's face.

"Why'd you lie about me?"

"Lie about what?" Hank said, ignoring the speck of spit that'd landed on his cheek. His shoulders tensed and his face began to twitch.

"About the system, Hank," Chad said; Rich thought he might head-butt him. "About your invoices being my fault."

Hank looked away and laughed through his nose.

"Oh, that," he said. "That was just bullshit. We had to give him some kind of excuse, right?"

Chad stood even closer.

"Now," Hank said, "back the fuck off, because you're two seconds from losing a job."

"But you embarrassed me for something I didn't do," Chad said. He did step back an inch.

Hank's eyes became burning slits.

"You trying to *tell* me something, kid?"

Chad tried to hold Hank's stare but glanced away.

"Well, let me explain something to *you,*" Hank said, jabbing at Chad's chest with an index finger but not touching him. "You think that guy cared whose fault it was? He wanted his goddamn *money*. That's it. He was done with us a long time ago. This isn't about honor and respect and integrity and all of that bullshit. Your *good name* doesn't weigh in here. What he says about *me* can hurt us way more than what he might think and say about *you*. I said what was right for the business."

Chad's face softened but his body stayed stiff.

"My reputation matters to me," he said, his voice slightly shaking. "The truth matters to me."

Hank's poking-finger hand fell back to his side.

"I'm glad it does," he said. "But when that jagdish goes to his networking breakfasts and Toastmasters circle jerks or wherever else he presses palms to raise a buck, do you think he'll want to bury you, or me?"

He jabbed a thumb into his own chest.

"*Me.*"

Hank clapped Chad on the shoulder and stepped backward.

"So let's just drop this fucking thing and get on with the day."

He turned toward the doorway.

"It's not okay," Chad said.

Hank stopped and slowly faced him again.

"Look," he said. "I've had a shit day, and it might get even worse. So don't call me out on a decision I made for *my* firm where *you* work. You'll lose this one, so let it go."

Chad looked away and battled the lump in his throat.

"I'm not happy here, Hank," he said.

"You're not *happy?*" Hank spat. "Since when did my business exist to make you *happy?* I pay you a salary with benefits. I even gave you a Christmas bonus. You have a clean office and all the coffee you can drink. Are you telling me you need me to hold your hand and tell you you're special on top of that?"

Chad stood straighter, cleared his throat, and relaxed his shoulders.

He looked at Rich. Rich shook his head.

"I want you to stop making messes that I have to clean up," Chad said.

Hank stepped toward him.

"What?"

"I want you to listen to me when I talk to you," Chad continued. "I want you to turn off your ridiculous cell phone for the five minutes per month you *let* me speak with you about the job I do for *your* company."

Hank's jaw clenched. His eyes ignited.

"I want you to stop spending money you don't have or don't intend to pay. I want you to give me the first of the six-month reviews you promised me when I joined this company three years ago. I want you to quit reprimanding me when I don't know how to lie for you. But

213

most of all, Hank, I want you to stop being a fake, shallow, insecure asshole."

Hank's face turned close to crimson, but then drained just as fast.

He stepped back and smiled.

"You have exactly fifteen minutes to pack what you can and get out of here," he said. "We'll box the rest and send it to you."

"That's fine with me," Chad said. "I'll be filing for unemployment tomorrow."

"Humor yourself," Hank said.

He glanced at Rich.

"I have an eyewitness to your blow-up here. I *had* to fire you, kid. You won't collect shit."

He shook his arm to slide up his sleeve and check his watch.

"You better get moving," he said. "If you're here in fourteen minutes and forty-five seconds, I call security to help you out."

Hank left the room.

Rich and Chad stood in silence. Rich put his hand on Chad's shoulder. Chad stared at the floor.

"Don't let it get to you," Rich said. "You'll be better off somewhere else."

"Maybe," he said, looking up at him. "But I'll still know he's in the world. And that's no good."

He patted Rich's hand and removed it from his shoulder.

"Thanks for being a good guy, Rich. Maybe I'll see you around."

He left the room as well. Rich remained still, and listened to the heavy footsteps moving away.

*T*he young man finished his pint of Guinness and clacked the empty glass on the ring-spotted bar inside O'Hanahan's Tavern and Grill.

"Another, please," he said toward the bartender, who pretended not to hear. He flirted with a redhead a few stools to the young man's right.

"Another, please!"

Leaning on the bar with both hands, the bartender excused himself from the girl and grabbed the empty glass.

The young man fingered the gold-plated compact he'd set next to his coaster. He rubbed his thumb over it. Picked it up and rolled it in his palm. Put it back on the bar and spun it like a top.

He'd wanted to open it hundreds of times since buying it several months earlier, but never more so than now.

The bartender semi-slammed the fresh pint of Guinness in front of him. Creamy, caramel-colored foam spilled over the lip and ran down the side of the glass.

"You want a tip, or not?" the young man said.

The bartender returned to the redhead.

The compact gleamed in the beam of a ceiling light above it.

Open me, it said to his mind.

So far, he'd managed not to surrender to his curiosity—and its quietly persistent command.

Open me.

The merchant had told him it could be done only once.

Once, and then its "magic" would be spent.

He caught his reflection in the mirror behind the shelves and pyramids of liquor bottles on the opposite wall.

Who am I? the reflection said.

He looked back at the compact.

Who are you? it said. *Open me.*

He considered it, hard, for a while.

The head of his pint had settled.

He fished in a pocket of his nylon zip-up spring jacket on the stool next to him. He slipped out his cell phone and dialed a number.

"Hi, Rich," the young man said after a couple of rings. "It's Chad. Listen, can you meet me for a few after work? I'd like to discuss something with you. It's important."

A pause to listen.

"Yeah, we can have a beer, and I can run it past you. It won't take long."

Another pause.

"Great. What time? Six-thirty? Great. Thanks, Rich."

He hung up and returned the cell to his jacket.

The compact continued to gleam.

No, he would *not* open it. Not now, and, he realized, probably not ever.

He'd looked at himself in the mirror a few more times. The face that looked back had explained that the mystery belonged to somebody else.

*H*is back to the world beyond his office door, Hank stared at the glowing computer screen in his slightly dimming office.

Kimberly's e-mail remained open in its window. Hank read it, and read it, and read it again. He had half an hour until she completed his bitch of a day:

Hank-

See you O'Hanahan's 7:00

Will save your seat please try not to be late.

Have another appt. 7:45 and we have lots to discuss.

The sooner we start the sooner we're done.

Kimberly

He folded his hands under his chin and watched the computer's clock count down: 6:27, 6:28, 6:29. When it reached 6:30, he stood, turned everything off, and looked around his quiet office. His plaques, awards, and professional certificates stared blankly back at him.

He heard two of his agents chatting before leaving to go home.

His normally incessant cell phone lay dead on his desk.

He scooped it up, snatched his sport coat from the post in the corner, and, he hoped, entered the last lap of hell he'd have to run before sleep.

Springtime's cooling evening air trailed Rich into O'Hanahan's Tavern and Grill. He patted down a few wind-mussed hairs. The immediate room had already filled with a mix of regulars and after-work boozers. Some sat in cozy, dark-colored booths with stained-glass partitions and brass posts and railings. A few drank pensively alone on bar stools. Others sat in twos and threes, chatting and laughing.

Rich spotted Chad hunched over his glass at the bar. He strode over and tapped him on the shoulder.

Chad jerked in his seat and spun around.

"Sorry," Rich said.

He pulled back the stool to Chad's left and sat down.

The bartender's redhead swayed her way out of the bar. The bartender folded the written-on napkin she'd given to him, slid it into his back pocket, and looked at Rich.

"Water with a slice of lemon, please," Rich said.

The bartender reached for his beverage nozzle.

"So what's up?" Rich said.

Chad showed him the gold-plated compact.

"This is what's up."

Rich regarded it.

"What is it?"

"It's what I wanted to discuss with you."

"It looks like a woman's make-up thing."

Chad shrugged.

"I still don't know," he said. "All I know is that it's old as hell."

He turned it upside down to reveal the Arabic characters.

"The guy I bought it from told me it could be opened only once."

"Only once?" Rich said. "What does that mean?"

The bartender set Rich's water down in front of him. Rich tipped him a dollar.

"It means what it means," Chad said. "Remember when I was away on vacation back in mid-December?"

Rich thought for a second and nodded.

"I was visiting some friends in Morocco," Chad continued. "A couple are missionaries, and a couple others are just working there on visas. They're all Americans. One night, while I was having a drink at a bar by myself in Casablanca, me and this Arabic guy who spoke English started talking. He bought me a few more drinks, and we wound up shooting the shit for quite a while. I eventually told him about my problems. Back here, at the job."

He drank from his beer.

"Then we both did a shot of rum, and I went from buzzed to fully loaded. He got kind of quiet, and began, like, staring at me in this funny way. Like he *knew* something about me . . . even more than what I'd told him. His face was smiling, but his eyes were serious. It was weird, but I was too wasted to make a big deal out of it." He paused. "Then he said he knew of somebody. Somebody who solved problems like mine."

Rich shifted on his stool and looked forward. He caught his reflection in the mirror on the opposite wall.

"He said I'd find this guy at a market in Marrakech. It'd be packed with tourists and vendors. Lots of junk and food for sale. Every kind of entertainment for tips you could think of."

He paused again.

"He also told me most foreigners would never find the booth I needed unless one, fate wanted them to, and two, they had the right map.

"And so, while we were sitting there, hammered, in that smoky Casablanca bar, he wrote the info on a napkin. And dyin' if I'm lyin', the guy knew his stuff. I found the booth no problem."

Chad placed the compact in his palm.

"When I got there, I told the vendor my problem, and he sold me this."

Rich stared at it.

"How much?"

"More than I wanted to pay," Chad said. "But he said I could return it for a double refund if it didn't . . . perform as guaranteed."

"So it was kind of expensive," Rich said. The compact had begun to entrance him.

"Expensive enough," Chad said, and swigged from his pint again. "I bought it with my Christmas bonus from Hank. He gave it to me early. Late November, so I'd have it for my vacation. What a guy.

"Fifteen hundred bucks. Fifteen hundred for three years of hell with no raises or reviews and all that I could take of his crap. I spent just about all of it on this. I was going to give it all right back to him with a special gift of my own."

Chad looked sideways. Their eyes met.

"My way of saying keep the tip, you cheap, ungrateful bastard."

Rich stared at it a few seconds longer.

"Can't say I'd know what he'd do with it," Rich said.

Chad smirked and looked away.

"I'm not going to give it to him."

He gulped the rest of his beer and rapped his knuckles on the bar.

"Another Guinness, my man!"

The bartender, about twelve feet to their right, stopped wiping the bar. He glanced at Chad and poured another glass.

"I've thought about this for a while, Rich. I've had this thing for months and haven't opened it yet. The guy who sold it to me was probably duping me anyway. Fleecing me with hocus-pocus. For all I know, it's full of dead bugs or something."

He rubbed his thumb over the top of the compact.

"But, I don't know. There's always that chance he was telling the truth. There's something different about it I can't quite explain. It almost . . . talks to me somehow. Like it wants me to know what it is. What it can do."

"So what are you going to do with it then?"

Chad turned in his stool and faced him. Rich saw the beer at work in his eyes.

"Give it to you."

"To me?" Rich said. "What would I do with it?"

"Whatever you want."

The bartender set Chad's fresh pint in front of him.

"Thanks," Chad said.

The bartender moved away and resumed wiping the bar farther down.

"I just don't want it any more. I've held on to it because I was mulling over when I was going to throw his money back in his face without him even knowing it."

He set the compact on the bar between them.

They sat silently for a few seconds.

"I've given my anger at Hank a good ride," Chad said. "But now I think I just pity him. You take away all of his money and his posse of shady professional cowboys, and he could have been another no-name wearing three pairs of pants and talking to himself beneath the Wacker bridge."

He stifled a burp with his fist.

"I don't have a job, but I have my . . . peace." He blocked one more burp. "I'll find a job."

Rich slid the compact toward him.

"I don't know, man," he said. "I'm not sure if I want it."

"Then I'll leave it here," Chad said. "If you don't take it, someone else will, and they won't know what it is or where it came from. At least you know something about it."

They both looked down at it, gleaming in the light that fell between them.

"If the universe has any justice at all," Chad continued, "and I think it does, then any magic it might have will work like it's supposed to. I think I believe that now."

Rich looked at the compact a little longer.

"Maybe Dawn would want it," he said.

"Maybe," Chad said.

He downed another mouthful of Guinness; his buzz was cruising nicely now. "Or maybe you'll want it. For what it can do. Could do. Should do. I dunno."

They looked at each other again.

"Or maybe you'll give it to . . . somebody else."

"Weird, man," Rich said. He picked it up. It felt heavier than it appeared. "This is weird. This conversation. The whole day. The last few months. I've been feeling out of sorts for a while. Like I don't know what I'm doing . . . or who I am."

"Well, *I* think I know who you are," Chad said. "You might still have some things to work out, some decisions to make. We all do. But you seem okay to me. Whatever's comin' your way, you'll handle it. The right way. From truth. You're not for sale."

Rich looked away and rubbed his chin.

"How do you know that?" he said when he looked at Chad again.

Chad's eyes were now red and slightly bulging.

"I don't," he said. "I'm just taking a stab. When you get down to it, no one really knows anybody. We all have something secret we don't show."

One more sip, and then he slid the pint away.

"That's it. I'm done."

He wiped his mouth.

Rich clapped him on the shoulder.

"You're an intense guy, Chad. Maybe that's why I like you."

Chad exhaled through his nose and ran both hands through the sides of his hair.

"Okay," he said. "Tank's full, head's empty. Time to go." He leaned across the bar and waved his hand behind it. "Check, please!"

The bartender half-grinned. He rang the receipt and placed it face down on the bar in front of them. Chad flipped it over, scanned it, and set it back down with cash on top of it.

"Life *is* intense, Rich," he said, standing up from his stool. He pulled on his jacket. "And we're all messed up, some less, some more so than others. Run from anyone who claims to be normal."

He stood straight and stuck his hands in his pant pockets.

"Intensity is how we burn through the bullshit to find what really matters. If you run into people who keep things light and easy and choose to live on the surface, just remember they're wearing boxers to an armored battle."

Rich laughed, looked down, and nodded.

Chad removed cherry-flavored Chapstick from his right pocket and applied it unevenly to his lips.

"So what are you going to do now?" Rich said.

"*Right* now? This second? Go home. Watch TV. Take a nap. Maybe wake up and play some video games. Tomorrow, maybe look for a job. Or maybe I won't. Haven't decided."

Rich turned in his stool to face him.

"You'll be fine, Chad. Put me down as a reference if you need one."

"You're a good man, Charlie Brown," he said. "Let's grab lunch sometime."

He stuck out his hand. Rich shook it.

"Stay in touch," Rich said.

"Last thing," Chad said, starting to turn away. "What's the difference between a man and a monkey?"

Rich glanced to his right, considered it, and shrugged.

"I don't know," he said. "What?"

"A monkey looks in the mirror and sees a monkey."

Chad threw his arm up, waved once, and left O'Hanahan's Tavern and Grill.

Rich looked back down at the compact, which he still held. Chad was right: there *was* something off (or *on?*) about it. It felt even heavier now. His arm had also started to tingle.

He dropped it into his sport coat's right pocket.

The ice in his water had almost melted. He took one more sip and chewed on a shrinking cube. Then he too left the bar.

When he stepped out onto the sidewalk, he saw Chad's back disappear around a corner a block down to his right.

A light Windy City breeze tousled Rich's hair and billowed his coat. He looked up at the springtime sky and the towering man-made wonders that tried but failed to reach it.

He headed left, toward the Brown Line El train that would take him close to home.

Across the street and bit farther down from O'Hanahan's, a woman collected a ticket from a parking-garage attendant and slipped it into her black hand purse. Before she crossed toward the tavern and grill, she paused to compose herself: for her now uncertain future, and for the news she knew Hank Coogan would hate.

*H*ank stepped into O'Hanahan's and, at first, felt a rush of relief. He couldn't see her anywhere.

Maybe she'd been held up or, better yet, changed her mind. He didn't need or want to spend any time with her. Not even if her only goal was to give him a smile and a hummer.

He just wanted to be with his Collection and a bottle of Black.

The whole ride over had been Act II of *Cut Coogan's Nuts Off.* Morgan & Smith's Richard Thompson had torn him a new one over the coffee-ruined documents earlier. He then called again later to make sure it stayed ripped open. Hank had apologized at least five times, but his regret had only grown the hand for the spanking.

Hank scanned the room again and still couldn't see her.

He could leave right then.

"Hank!"

He winced.

Kimberly waved at him from her stool at the bar.

He scowled, nodded, and moved toward her.

"Hank," she said when he reached her.

"Kimberly," he said.

He looked at the scotch set before the empty stool next to hers.

He slipped off his sport coat, folded it neatly, and placed it on the empty stool next to his. He slid onto his seat.

"Damn it," he spat after a sip of his drink. "This isn't Johnnie Black."

"I asked for that, but they were all out of it, so I ordered Red instead. It's still Johnnie Walker, right?"

"But I don't like Red. I like Black."

"Forgive my *faux pas.*"

He took another sip.

"So what's so important that you needed to see me here?"

He looked over at the bartender, a young and surely vagrant smart-ass in jeans. The bartender sensed Hank staring at him and stopped rinsing glasses.

Hank sneered. The undisciplined assholes who worked the service industry so they could do drugs, sleep late, write poems, and play in bands could all go straight to hell. Men who made livings wore *suits,* goddamn it.

"I'm pregnant."

Hank almost dropped his drink.

"What?"

"I said, I'm pregnant."

He stared at her, hard, and then drank half of his scotch.

"I was three weeks late on my period," she said. "I took a test a few days ago. It came out positive."

"Kris Kringle Christ," he said under his breath. "Aren't those things wrong sometimes?"

"I went to the doctor too, just to be sure. She said she was sure."

"How do you even know it's mine?"

Kimberly's eyes darkened.

"Don't give me that line, and don't play that game with me, Hank. You're the only man I've slept with in the last two months."

"But I banged you just that one time—well, after that other time, of course. The one we said we wouldn't discuss."

"Right," she said, and he noticed she drank only water. "We *had sex* a second time, which once again proved my horrible judgment. But we did have sex. When I was ovulating."

"What? You don't use birth control?"

"I'm pregnant, Hank."

He finished his scotch.

"So, why are you telling me this?" He set the glass on the bar. "What do you want *me* to do about it?"

They sat quietly for a moment. The bartender looked at Hank, who nodded.

"I think we should keep this baby, Hank."

"We?"

"Yes," she said. "I'm thirty-two now, not eighteen. My conscience demands that I have it. We can decide how we're going to raise it, or we can put it up for adoption."

"Christ hates me," he said, turning in his stool to face forward.

The bartender set another scotch in front of him. Hank picked it up instantly.

He rubbed his face with his other hand. When he looked straight again, he saw himself in the mirror on the opposite wall.

His reflection wanted to ask him a question. A direct and personal one.

He tried to ignore his own haggard face, but it wouldn't leave him alone.

Look at me.

I am looking. What the hell do you want?

What do I want? I want you to answer the fucking question. You know the one I'm talking about too. You've done just about every damn thing in your life but answer it. It's time, tough guy. Time for you to look me in the eye and tell me who I really . . .

"I'm sure you'll want to keep this a secret," Kimberly continued. "And I promise that I will, until it starts to show. After that, I'll have a reason ready to go. I'll say it was a donor, or someone who agreed

227

to make me a mother. My family and closest friends know I've always wanted kids."

"Right," Hank said. He finished half his drink. "You'll crack. And when you do, you'll demand things of me. Like money. *Especially* money. Lots of it. Hell, you might even ask me to *be there* for you."

"Get over yourself," she said. "I believe you'd be there for me about as much as I believe you want this baby. But *I* want it. All I ask is for you to be civil and to provide some basic financial support. We can arrange something without getting ugly about it. You can even put it all in writing, to protect yourself, and I'll sign it."

He loosened his tie. Then he laughed.

"Man," he said. "If it weren't for the ten other ways I've already been bent over today, I might actually flip out. But I can't feel anything right now, so keep it coming. You're on a roll."

"I'm sorry, Hank," she said, crossing her legs and straightening her skirt. "But you had to know. Of course you had to know."

Hank's reflection blew a wet two-finger whistle.

Hey! Tough guy!

"If I can trust you on this, and if you're fair about it, I won't say anything to anyone," she said. "I won't come after you for more than what we agree on. Like I said, we can put it in writing, and I'll sign it, and you can keep it with your . . ." His head snapped sideways. ". . . in a safe and private place. It will stay our secret as long as we honor the terms."

She leaned toward him. Her eyes became arrowheads.

"But I swear to you, Hank, if you try to worm your way out of this, or work your connections against me, so help me, I *will* find a way to respond."

She leaned back again.

"But I don't think that'll be necessary. Not if we're both adults about it."

She folded her hands on her top thigh.

"I know where I stand and how I'll conduct myself," she said. "The rest is up to you."

Hank had barely heard a word: the reflection was still barking and whistling at him.

"You can do the right thing," she said. "The simple thing."

Psst! Hey, buddy . . . over here! Whatsa matter? Still scared of your own goddamn face?

"You can't keep it, Kimberly," he said, turning and looking at her. "You *won't* keep it."

His shoulders relaxed.

"And you're in no position to dictate terms to *me.*"

I'm talking to you, asshole!

"This is a minor mess we can pin on one indiscretion. It happens. I can't say I'm happy about it." He held his drink with both hands. "I have two kids of my own, and I love them. Very much."

Her face tried to stay steady but dimmed.

"I appreciate your wish to have a baby. I truly hope you do someday, with the right man. And I hope he takes great care of you. But your baby cannot, and will not, be mine."

Man, are you one big bag of sh . . .

"I was in the mood, you were available, and what happened, happened. I'm not a perfect person. Some might even say I'm a bad man." He sipped his drink and leaned toward her with a hand on his knee. "But *nobody* gets to taste it all without wearing at least a little dirt. I enjoy more than most people because I'm not a slave to worthless morality. Why should I be? Why should *you* be? The reason so many people wind up struggling and hating themselves for it is because they care too damn much about what other people think about them. I don't. I can't."

He scratched his lip with his thumbnail.

"I don't need you to accept me. Hell, I don't even care if you like me. I don't have the time. Or the energy."

He placed his hand on her shoulder.

"You'll get over it."

She looked down and away.

"I'll take care of the expenses. I also know of a clinic. A very private one. Excellent outpatient care. It's up by Milwaukee."

She removed his hand from her shoulder.

"I'm having this baby, Hank. Even though it's yours."

Kee-rist . . . ever read any Shakespeare, Einstein? "To thine own self be true, and it must follow, as the night the day, thou canst not then be false to any man." Repeat that and I'll give you a dollar.

Hank straightened in his stool and looked across at the mirror. He winked at his reflection.

"I'm sorry, but you're not having it," he said without taking his eyes off of himself.

"I am, Hank," she said. "You might control your business, and your family, and maybe even lots of other people, but you don't and won't control me."

He looked at her again.

"Kimberly, my dear," he said, smiling, "I hate to say it, but . . . I do."

"Hank, I already said no one would know about this."

"*I* would know," he said.

He tightened his tie under his neck again.

Much better. Damn if he hadn't felt like a balding tire rolling over glass gravel until about two minutes ago.

"Call me tomorrow," he said. "I'll give you the number and the physician's name for that clinic by Milwaukee. After you make your appointment, let me know how much it will be, and I'll give you what you need. I'll cover your travel expenses too."

"No, Hank."

"Yes, Kimberly. And if you give me a hard time, I'll complicate your life in ways you couldn't imagine. I do hope you have your kids someday. But it can't be like this. Not with me."

"I'll sue you."

He laughed and leaned against the bar with his elbow.

"No, you won't. You won't because if you do, you'll unleash a holy nightmare. So please, work with me on this one."

She glared at him. Her hands began to tremble.

"And let's say you *did* get something from me in court," he continued. "You'd forget about it before you could enjoy it. You'd be too busy trying not to kill yourself after I was done with you."

"You're awful," she said. "How do you live with yourself? Do you even have a soul?"

He looked down, shook his head, and smiled to himself.

She wiped a tear with her still-trembling right hand.

"I wouldn't expect you to understand," he said, looking up. "Hate me hard if it'll make you feel better. This is simply personal *business*, and I have to treat it that way."

"I can't believe I even slept with you again," she said. Her nose was starting to run. She reached into her hand purse for a tissue. "I must be insane."

Hank rattled the cubes in his glass.

231

"How much longer do you want to drag this out?"

She didn't answer.

He finished his drink.

"I'm ready to get the fuck out of here."

She dabbed at her nose with the tissue.

"Look," he said, nudging the empty glass away from him on the bar, "if you remember one other thing about me, remember that I told you this: there are three kinds of people in this world. Those who have a will to power, those who want to bake cookies for their neighbors, and those who have an illusion of balance because they fall in between.

"Those with a will to power steer changes and shape the future. They get goddamn wealthy too. The cookie-bakers hang on to pets, religion, and Hallmark cards to keep themselves from jumping off of bridges. The in-between group is just a bunch of lobotomized sleepwalkers. At least the cookie-bakers believe in something and stand up for it."

She sniffled and then wiped away another tear.

"You think I use and manipulate?" Hank said. "What about *you?* You think you're a nun or something? What was *your* agenda? Why did *you* ever want to sleep with *me* in the first place?"

The bartender gestured to him. Hank held up his hand and shook his head.

"Nobody serves up the clam like you did unless they want to control you, destroy you, or get something out of you. You slept with me because you wanted a blank professional check you could cash later on. Why the hell else would a good-looking young broad like you dick an out-of-shape goon like me? Don't even think about passing judgment on me. You're no better than I am."

"Why are you doing this, Hank?" she said, softly.

He leaned back and folded his arms across his chest.

"Because you're just like everyone else, including my wife," he said. "You're vultures waiting to swoop down on what's mine."

A sob escaped her throat. She covered her mouth with her fist.

"I can't believe some of the things you say," she said. "Everyone has good inside of them, even you. Why are you so afraid to be a real person?"

Hank instantly glanced at the mirror. His reflection had no comment.

"I don't sprinkle the truth with powdered fucking sugar so you'll like it more," he said. "It's too bad you can't see that's actually the decent thing to do."

"All I'm asking for is a *little* support. I mean, just what you have in your closet alone . . ."

His face tightened and darkened. He pointed at her face.

"Don't you speak about that. Not here, not now, not *ever*. Not even from your death bed, or God help me, I'll fix you even worse than if you follow through on this other business you want to lay on me."

The bartender stopped talking to a woman ordering a Stoli and cranberry juice and looked at them.

Kimberly sighed. Her eyes remained red, but her tears had almost dried.

"Of course, Hank," she said. "You'll fix me like you do anyone who disagrees with you." She drank from her water. "Or who even comes close to exposing who, or what, you are."

She dabbed once more at her eyes and nose with her tissue.

"Did you hear what happened to Howie Frank?" she said.

"Yeah," Hank said, leaning back to sit straight. He smirked. "Too bad."

"That lawsuit's going to really hurt his firm," she said.

"It's a goddamn shame."

"I heard it was a breach of contract, right?" she said. "He leaked information about one of his high-end tenants to the landlord, and it cost the tenant something like a million dollars on the lease."

"Yep," he said. "That's what they say."

"I wonder how the tenant found out," she said. "I can't imagine that Howie would have said anything to dig himself such a hole."

His smirk became a smile.

"Well, Kimberly, it all comes back to that whole thing about reaping and sowing. He's been stacking himself a tall and steaming heap of shit with that mouth of his. He doesn't think carefully enough about who he pisses off."

He winked.

"Right," she said, and looked down into her lap.

She slid from her stool and straightened her skirt.

"I have to get going."

She adjusted herself some more.

"Me too," Hank said. "I'll be in touch with that name and number you'll need. And Kimberly?"

She stopped moving.

"I am sorry," he said.

He stood and hugged her. Her arms remained pressed to her sides.

When he released her, she scooped her purse from the bar, draped her light formal coat over her arm, and left.

He returned to his stool. The bartender strode over and stood before him with his hands on his hips.

"Something to eat, sir? Some mini-burgers or chicken wings?"

Hank looked at him.

"I don't eat meat," he said. "I'm leaving soon."

The bartender rapped a knuckle on the bar and whisked away to serve a man in an expensive blue suit.

Hank stood, slipped on his sport coat, and looked around the room. He didn't see anyone who might have recognized him.

When he stepped outside, a light Windy City breeze tousled his hair and billowed his coat. He looked up at the springtime sky and the jagged line of skyscrapers full of money yet to be made.

How naïve God had been when making a man. In His haste to have a Mini-Me, He'd ignored His creation's gift to devise. Tall buildings were but feathers that tickled the chin of a greater master plan. Earth offered only a lounge for diversion before man opened a Starbucks on Alpha Centauri.

And before long, he'd be dealing office space in the heavens as well.

Hank crossed the street to the parking garage.

Kimberly pulled out as he walked in. She glared at him to no avail: his thoughts belonged to how a commercial brokerage might fit into the ether.

"What's that?" Dawn said.

She bit into her first square of the Tombstone cheese pizza Rich had baked as soon as he'd arrived home a few minutes before her.

They both looked at the compact on the four-seat glass dining-room table. Dawn sat across from him.

"Guy at work gave it to me," he said. "Chad. I think I've mentioned him before."

"Prob-ab-wee," she said.

She leaned over her plate with a string of melted cheese hanging from her mouth to the slice. Steam rose from the uncovered sauce. A splotch fell and splatted on her plate.

"Hot-hot!"

She set the square back on her plate to cool.

"Why'd he give it to you?" she said. "Looks like a woman's compact."

"I think it is," he said. "And then again, it isn't."

He turned it over.

"Look at these characters on it," he said. "Arabic."

"So? Arabic makes it not a woman's compact?"

"No, that's not it." He squinted at it. "There's something else about it. Something . . . different. I can't put my finger on it yet. I think it's how it feels when you hold it, like it's gaining weight. And I could swear it vibrates when you carry it close to your body for a while, like in your coat pocket."

Dawn shrugged and picked up her pizza again.

"Plus it's what Chad said about it," he said. "It can be opened only once."

"Only once? What's that supposed to mean?"

"Well, it *can* be opened more than once," he said. "A thousand times, if you want. But its . . . uh, magic works only the first time."

Her eyes widened and then narrowed.

"Magic?"

"Yeah," Rich said. "Magic. That's Chad, not me. He bought it from some guy in Morocco who said it has special powers. Supposedly, they kick in when a new owner opens it. Then it goes back to, well, no powers. Just a regular compact. Until it starts another cycle, however that works."

She raised her pizza to her mouth while reaching for the compact with her other hand. Rich grabbed it before she could touch it.

"Hey . . . !" she said.

"Sorry. I just don't want you to screw around with it. We don't understand it yet."

She set her pizza down and leaned back in her chair.

"What's there to understand? It's a woman's compact from another country. Big deal."

He rubbed his thumb over the Arabic characters. The longer he looked at it, the more certain he became that a detail had changed.

"It is a big deal," he said. "This thing *could* be magic. I'm starting to wonder."

He scratched his chin.

"You haven't carried it or spent time with it yet," he said.

"Come on," she said. "You don't really believe that voodoo stuff, do you? That's probably just what that Moroccan guy told him so he could add a few hundred bucks to the price."

He picked it up and held it before his face.

"There's only one way to find out if it's true," she said. "Open it."

His head jerked toward her.

"Here? *Now?*"

"Yeah," she said. "Why not?"

He looked at it again. Damn it: something else had changed. Had the characters shifted within the length of a glance?

"Jeez, Rich," she said, smiling. She took two bites of her pizza and brushed her hands over her plate. "I know you can be sensitive and cerebral, but I don't remember ever seeing you this jumpy."

"It's . . . it's this thing."

"Well, what are you going to do with it? Just stare at it?"

A pause.

"I don't know yet," he said. "I'll have to think about it for a while."

"You could always give it to me," she said.

He half-smiled at her.

"I'd have to think about that too."

"I love you," she said.

"Love you," he said.

She finished her pizza and then reached for another square from the pan on a steel stand in the center of the table.

"Well, if you decide to give it away, or can't decide, I'll take it," she said. "I'm sure I could put it to use."

He held the compact closer to his face. Something *was* off. A squiggle of a line *had* moved. Somehow, he sensed that *all* of its characters wanted to rearrange into another message.

He set it back down on the table.

"I don't know how much longer I can take the firm, Dawn," he said.

She took a bite, chewed, and drank from her glass of water.

"It's gotten a little better, hasn't it?" she said. "I mean, you're getting better at it, and you've closed a few deals in the last couple of months, right?"

"Yeah," he said. "But that's all crap. I hate it."

"Is it the work, or is it Hank?"

"Both."

He could swear the air around the compact was vibrating, but Dawn paid no attention; he knew what was on her mind, love him though she did.

"You've tried other things and didn't like them either," she said. "You also made a lot less than you do now. What, nine, ten bucks an hour at some of those places? You may not love your job, but welcome to reality, Rich."

"*Reality?*" he spat. He leaned back with his arms spread and his palms turned up. "What the hell does *that* mean? The world was real before *we* got here. Before six-dollar beers plus two-dollar tips at Wrigleyville bars and ten-page registries at Crate and fucking Barrel. This isn't real." He waved an arm around their recently painted dining room. "This isn't real. *We* made this up. People. We imagined it, and now we're slaves to it."

She sighed, leaned forward, and rested her face in her hands.

"There you go again, Rich. Your idealism can be charming, and it's part of why I love you. But we're only going to get older, and our bills are here to stay. At least now you have a chance to make some decent money if you stick it out. Maybe even *big* money, in spurts. Money that could free you up to do the things you want to do, like read and write. Your job is just a means to an end. *Our* end."

The standard call to reason issued from her eyes. He shook his head once and snorted softly.

"It's all bullshit," he said, almost under his breath. "And I don't care about the money. Screw the money."

She took another bite of pizza.

"I'm sorry you feel that way," she said. "Just don't give up again. This could work out for you. For us."

"Maybe it won't," he said.

"Don't be like that," she said. "We're not living with our parents anymore. We have debts and obligations. Your happiness is important, and I'll do everything to help you find it. But you need to keep a steady income. We both do."

He slammed a fist on the table. Dawn flinched. The pizza rack rattled.

"What? You want me to piss away my time, doing boring, meaningless work with shallow, selfish people while I wither away inside, all so we can pay for shit we don't really need?"

"We need food, shelter, and clothing, Rich."

"Eat from Whole Foods, live in Lincoln Park, and dress in clothes from Banana Republic?"

"I enjoy some of those things, Rich," she said, "and I happen to like where we live. We deserve it. *I* deserve it. Why not? I work hard. What's wrong with wanting more for ourselves? We should feel blessed. We're not living beyond our means, and we're not being vain."

"I don't care," he said. "I know there's more to life than this. There's also way more to *my* life than working for Hank Coogan."

She closed her eyes, sighed again, and fell silent for a moment.

"Alright, Rich," she said. "Suit yourself. Look for another job if you're really that miserable. Just please keep earning somehow."

She finished her square and stood with her plate.

"You know I'm behind you, always," she said. "But I can't carry it all on my own."

She moved around to the back of his chair and placed her hand on his shoulder.

"I love you," she said. "Eat some more and relax. Tomorrow's another day."

She ran her hand once through his hair and then left him alone in the room.

He soon heard the kitchen faucet running. An old, familiar sadness swam into his heart.

He held the compact to his face again.

"What are you?" he said, his voice just above a whisper.

It remained silent but eager, still yet oddly vibrant, beneath the dining-room light.

Words of truth that still had to hide filled his head. He wanted to release them, to rid himself of their weight, but didn't dare, especially not to Dawn: at least not yet.

And among those words that only he could hear, with an instinct he could never explain, he believed the compact now commanded to be opened.

*B*eyond *the white walls with the one skinny window, past the quiet computer and the dormant desk, an entire world surged with passionate energy.*

Writers wrote. Artists dreamed. Singers sang.

Boaters fished. Farmers sowed. Jungle hunters looked for food.

Winds blew. Tides swelled. Trees grew and spread their leaves.

In the meantime, the young American male strained for stacks of dollars within his 14' x 14' office with the one skinny window. He made calls; wrote e-mails; studied numbers, contracts, and charts; pursued possible leads through the Internet and contact-management software.

The beautiful, surging world beckoned him with slivers of sunlight that slashed through his one skinny window. He worked until that light went down and the ghastly glow of fluorescent bulbs made the dark efficiently pale.

Filing papers. Filling out forms. Staring at a screen. Tip-tapping on a keyboard. Reading legal bullshit. Making love to the chair with his ass.

Pay the mortgage, fill the tank, shop for processed food. Seek entertainment on weekends.

Bleed green for healthcare and taxes.

Save the couple million he was supposed to have for retirement.

His phone dangling from his hand with the receiver pressed to his ear, the young man listened to the blather of someone he didn't respect but whose business he needed.

The compact stared up at him from the desk. He stared back at it.

Then he heard the sounds, like the strings of Arabic ouds coming undone but maintaining their music. Floating, drifting, swimming, their seductive notes surrounded him.

He hung up the phone before the client finished a sentence.

The compact's characters curled and swirled and shifted heights and shapes. Then, slowing and spilling as if desert sand, they arranged themselves into symbols he recognized.

Two words. Two simple words with a loaded request:

Open me.

"No!" he screamed.

Open me.

"I won't!"

Open me.

The command engraved itself into the air.

Open me.

When still he would not move, the room began to rumble. A sterling-silver pencil cup tipped over. Some of its contents rolled to floor.

The room's four walls moved counter-clockwise. Faster, and then faster.

Open me.

The walls stopped moving. He ran to the one skinny window and pounded on it with his palm. He jumped and flailed his arms. No one noticed from the dozens of windows facing his own from the opposite building. Those who lived behind them remained glued to their tasks and technology and strategies for making more money.

He looked back at the words in the air.

Open me.

Outside, clouds like black blankets wrapped the sun and darkened the sky.

Open me.

The room rumbled harder again. The young man fell to his knees.

"No! I won't, goddamn you! I don't need to, because I know who I . . ."

"Rich, Rich! Wake up!"

His eyes snapped open.

"Rich!" Dawn said. "You were having a bad dream!"

He raised his hand to his face and covered his eyes.

"Man," he said.

He rose, swung his legs over the side of the bed, and leaned forward with his elbows on his knees.

Dawn crawled up behind him and placed her hands on his shoulders.

"What were you dreaming about? It must have been bad. You woke me up."

He stood, went to the rocking chair, and sat down.

"I know what I'm going to do with the compact," he said.

He ran a hand through his hair.

"What?" she said.

"I'm going to give it to him." He paused. "To Hank."

She scooted to the edge of the bed, sat Indian style, and played with the ends of her shoulder-length blonde hair.

"I love you," he said.

Her head tipped up a little. He rose from the chair. She straightened where she sat and backed up on her hands in response to what she thought he might do.

When he reached the bed, he looked down at her.

She wet her lips and reached out for his stomach. Her fingers fell just above the waistband of his boxer shorts.

"I love you, baby," she whispered.

She pulled his boxers down to his knees. He slid them off and stepped out of them.

They both removed her nightgown. She lay flat with one knee up.

He remained still. She reached up for him.

"Come here," she said.

Goddamn it, I have to come out and say it. I have to let her know the . . .

He climbed on top of her. She lifted her legs and rested her heels against the backs of his knees.

He looked into her face, but the shadows shaded her eyes. He hoped she couldn't see his.

He pleased her first without pleasing himself; he could wait.

When it was his turn, he groped and gripped and grunted. Tears ran down his face to the edge of a change he hadn't allowed her to see. He buried his face in the pillow, and in her breath against his ear, he could almost hear her say good-bye, my friend: farewell, and don't forget me.

"What in Christ is that?"

The compact lay in the center of the immaculate desk between them. It gleamed in the sunlight from the window.

"It's a gift," Rich said. "For you."

"What the hell do I need a gift for?"

Hank sat back in his chair with his arms on the armrests.

"Besides, it looks like it's for broads. What do you want *me* to do with it?"

"Whatever you wish," Rich said. "It's for you."

"I don't get it," Hank said. He leaned forward with both hands flat on the desk. "What are you up to?"

"I'm not up to anything, Hank. I just thought you might appreciate it."

Hank slid the compact toward him.

"Looks like it might've cost a few bucks."

Rich shrugged and smiled.

"A few," he said.

Hank looked at him askance with narrowed eyes.

"Cut the shit," he said. "What's in it for you?"

"Nothing's in it for me. Seriously. Somebody gave it to me, and I didn't need it. I offered it to my wife, but she already has one."

Hank remained silent. His eyes were darkened slits.

"You seemed a logical choice," Rich said. "You like nice things."

Hank stared at it.

"It *does* look like real gold."

"It is."

Hank turned it over. One eyebrow went up.

"You already had my name engraved on it?"

Rich's eyes widened. He leaned forward.

Hank held it up, but Rich saw only the looping, squiggly Arabic characters.

Screw it: something had appeared, and he'd have to play along.

"It was the least I could do," he said. "I wanted to make it a little more special. Actually, make it yours. Really. I hope you can put it to use or at least enjoy it as a collectible."

Hank's head jerked slightly. His face tightened.

Rich smiled again.

"Or hell, if you don't want it, maybe your wife will."

Hank remained tense a moment longer and then relaxed.

"I still think it's funny," Hank said. "Off-center. But it's a nice gesture, Rich. Thank you."

"My pleasure, Hank."

Rich stood and stuck out his hand. Hank shook it firmly.

"Think of it as my way of saying thank you for all you've done for me," Rich said. "You've shown me quite a few ropes. I wouldn't have learned so much so fast without you. You've done your best to give me . . . opportunities."

Hank leaned back and crossed his legs.

"Anytime. That's what good leaders do."

"Well, you are a leader, Hank. No argument there. As they say, you *are* Chicago commercial real estate. I'm fortunate to be here, with you, learning from the legend."

"I'm effective only if you're succeeding, Rich. I want *you* to be the best alongside me. Now go make some money."

Hank winked at him.

Rich nodded and turned to leave.

"Hey, Rich . . ."

Rich stopped and spun around.

"If you're not busy at around three-thirty, why don't you come back to my office. I have a new deal in the works, and I'd like to get you in on it."

"Sure, Hank. You bet."

He nodded again and then left.

Hank looked at the compact on his desk.

Did it shine more brightly now they were alone?

He stared at it—harder.

It *was* odd.

It was also beautiful. It must have been precious to someone, somewhere, sometime.

He leaned toward it with his ear.

Had the thing been *whispering* to him, or did he just need a drink?

Cockle-doodle-Christ, he'd been stressed out lately.

Rich gave him the gift for a reason. He still didn't trust what it might be.

But then again, why worry? Rich was a decent kid: painfully easy to read. If he had a motive, it had to include putting more brown on his nose.

Hank turned the compact over and rubbed his thumb across the engraving of his name.

He chuckled: a sound that hit the walls and died.

He had to chill out. It was as simple as that.

The gift was good. *Fine.*

He slid his brown-leather briefcase from beneath his desk. Tilting it toward him in his lap, he entered the dual combinations and clicked open the latches to either side of the handle.

He swiped the compact from the desktop and placed it inside.

Was it humming?

Had his hand tingled when he touched it again?

"You are one interesting little bitch, to say the least."

He closed the briefcase and placed it against the side of his desk.

He would get to know his new prize better later that evening, when he introduced it to his Collection.

The light spilling from the bottom crack into the outer hallway suggested Sharon was home. Hank inserted his key and carefully opened the door.

"Sharon?"

No answer.

He moved farther in and looked around.

She'd left the entrance-hall lights on, but wasn't home. Probably out shopping, drinking, or stuffing her face with her name on *his* credit card account. Definitely talking bullshit somewhere with her spoiled and lazy friends.

He closed the front door and went to the front room. The day's mail was on the end table next to his chair.

"Sweet baby Jesus and a Jell-o bowl of Jehovah."

He'd told her at least ten times not to put it there.

He flipped through the bills and junk mail, including a real-estate rag he didn't read unless he'd placed an ad.

The Johnnie Black was calling his name from the bar. He changed into some casual clothes and hurried back. He poured it, set it down next to the mail on the end table, and plopped into his chair with his briefcase.

He clicked it open.

"Man, are you queer."

He removed the compact.

"Come on. I want you to meet the family."

He closed the briefcase, set it on the floor, slipped the compact into the pocket of his slacks, and strolled with his scotch to the kitchen. The blue digits on the microwave clock above the stove read 8:02 p.m.

He paused to sip his drink and then continued toward the master bedroom in the back.

He stopped.

Sharon had closed the bedroom door.

Why?

She almost never did.

He opened it.

"What the . . . ?"

She'd cleaned and straightened the room. She'd even made the damn bed.

Didn't make sense. What about the mail on the table?

Rome had to be burning somewhere.

He crossed to his closet, entered the combination in the small panel above the doorknob, and let himself in.

He flipped on the light and turned on the stereo. *Madame Butterfly* emerged from the speakers.

Once seated with his scotch in his captain's chair, he slid out the compact and held it up.

"Welcome to the family, you little bastard peter-pecker."

He turned it over to look at the engraving again.

"You've got to be kidding me."

Looping, swirling Arabic characters had taken the place of his name.

"What is this shit?"

He swallowed half of what remained of his drink.

"Don't play games with me. What'd you do with my name?"

He lowered the compact until his hand rested palm up on his leg.

"Don't get too proud of yourself. You're not the first to try to mess with my head. Fuck you."

He scanned the walls to either side.

"Now, the question is, where do you go? I don't collect women's shit, you know. You sure as hell wouldn't be here if the kid hadn't handed you over."

He finished his scotch and set the glass to his left on the floor.

"Maybe dad'll have some ideas where to put you. What do you say about that, tough guy? Should I go ask my da . . ."

The characters had changed once more. He moved the compact closer to his face.

"*What?* Who am I?"

He raised his hand to hurl it against the half-closed closet door. A shock ran up his arm and froze it. He gasped.

When feeling returned, he lowered his hand and read the engraving again:

Open me.

"Alright. I'm not *crazy*, you know. So *knock it off!*"

He looked around the closet.

"Is this *you*, Dad? Is this *your* idea of a joke? Do I look like I'm laughing, goddamn it?"

The music quieted for a measure.

Open me.

He closed his hand around it, waited several moments, and then peeked at it:

Who are you?

He shut his eyes. Opened them:

Open me.

"Christ almighty!"

He stared at it, and somewhere in his crumbling, cobwebbed soul, a heavy vault door grated and rumbled.

"Oh, my . . . ," he said softly, his voice trembling. Tears pooled in his eyes.

Open me.

The characters arranged themselves into the palm-sized image of a desert with towering sand dunes. A dot among them became a man on a camel approaching from an endless horizon.

Who was he, and why could Hank see him?

A pair of eyes emerged from over the desert. Dark, watchful, *total,* they loomed above the lonely traveler—and out at those who saw him. Hank sensed neither good nor evil in them; they were simply *there,* as old as the universe and as young as the day it was born.

Open me.

Hands shaking, chest thumping, the sadness of truth now flooding his heart and his mind, Hank Coogan held up the compact half an arm's length away.

And opened it.

Fine dust puffed out in a powdery mist.

It had no pad: only the shallow, silver indentation where it should have been.

Only that, and the mirror.

He tried to resist it although he knew it was pointless. Slowly, with a remorse that screamed in his ears 'til they rang, he looked into it.

He leaped up from the chair.

"Oh, Amy, Andrew . . ."

It started in his feet and raced up his legs.

"Please God, forgive me . . . ," he said, and then his mouth locked shut, and the compact fell to the floor.

ich stared out at the bank of windows of the building next door. E-mail subject lines stacked in his computer screen.

The phone rang and rang. Its red light continued to blink. Callers were kicked into voice mail.

Someone knocked at his office door. He spun around in his chair.

"Hey, Rich, got a minute?"

Tad Dexter leaned through the doorway in a vertical push-up position.

"Uh, yeah," Rich said. "What's up?"

"Sorry to bother you." Tad flashed his Colgate smile, exercising his smooth, moisturized face. "You haven't heard from Hank, have you?"

Rich glanced at the clock in the monitor's lower right corner: 12:47 p.m.

"No, I haven't."

"Me neither," Tad said. "Neither has anyone else. We've been trying his cell phone all day. I'm just checking around before we have Helen call him at home."

"Nope. Nothing over here."

"Right."

Tad studied him a second.

"It's not like him," he said. "He can be a private guy, but he almost always lets at least one of us know if he's late or won't be here."

Rich shrugged and shook his head.

"Don't know," he said. "Maybe he got tied up. Or maybe something's up with his family."

"Well, we'll see," Tad said.

He moved a few steps into the office.

"Say, that's some real shit that went down with Harwick the other day, huh?"

"You mean Chad?"

"Who else?"

"Yeah, that was too bad."

Rich looked down.

"You were there when it happened, right?" Tad said.

"Yes, I was."

"Well, if you ask me, Harwick had it coming to him. He was a hard worker, pretty good at his job, but he was a little off. In the head."

"Off?"

"Yeah, like too intense. Like he was going to blow any second."

"Blow?"

"Yeah, as in postal. You ever notice how quiet he was? Either that, or pissed off. He had that *look,* like he hadn't been laid in a couple of years."

Rich remained silent a moment.

"I can't say I blamed him," he said.

Tad crossed his well-toned arms over his chest.

"Why? What do you mean?" he said.

"I mean Hank put him in a lot of bad situations. He was helpless half the time."

"Like what?"

Tad's eyes widened. He put his hands on his hips. His latissimus dorsi expanded like bat's wings beneath his blue dress shirt.

Rich tried not to smile. He was looking into the past, when Tad surely chugged beer bongs with other cheering, chanting, squeaky-white yups in the basement of their parent-funded animal house.

"I probably shouldn't discuss it," he said. "It's not my place to say."

"Well, whatever it was, I'm sure Hank had his reasons. He's a straight shooter, and Harwick had problems. He wasn't a happy guy."

He took another step toward Rich's desk.

"Hank's a little rough around the edges," he said. "And let's face it . . ." He glanced back over both shoulders. ". . . he has a bit of an ego. But get past the flash and the hard-ass, and he really is a good guy. He loves what he does, and he cares like hell about the firm."

Rich placed his elbows on his armrests and folded his hands over his lap.

"I'm sure he does, Tad."

"I guess we all have our reasons for what we do."

A moment of awkward silence.

"Well, hey . . ." Tad clapped his hands once. "If you hear from the big guy, let me know. I need to talk to him."

"I will," Rich said.

Tad smiled, pumped his fist once, and left.

Rich resumed staring out his window.

The phone continued to ring unanswered.

Knuckles rapped on Rich's door. He opened his eyes. He didn't know what time it was.

Helen, the front-desk receptionist, stood in the doorway. He rubbed his face.

"Hi, Helen," he said.

It was 4:17 p.m.

"Hi, Rich," she said. "Sorry to, uh, interrupt you, but I'm making my final rounds to see if anyone's heard from Hank."

"No," he said. "I haven't."

"I tried his cell at least five times, but all I got was voice mail. His wife's been calling here from home all day." She crossed her arms and leaned a soft, plump shoulder against the door sill. "It's strange. It's almost like . . . something might have happened to him."

Rich sat up in his chair.

"I hope not," he said.

She looked down and then up.

"I guess we'll just have to keep trying him. I'm sure there's an explanation."

Rich smiled at her.

"I'm sure there's a good explanation," he said. "Please let me know if he calls you."

"Certainly."

"On a separate note, I'll probably be leaving soon," he said. "I'm not feeling so well."

The corner of her motherly mouth turned up.

"I didn't want to say it, but you don't *look* so well," she said. "You're a little bit pale."

She stood straight. Her arms fell to her sides. She smiled.

Rich liked her; she was one of the few he would miss.

"I think I'll go home," he said. "Take care of myself."

She smiled even wider. Freckled crow's feet formed at the corners of her eyes.

"Okay. Good night, Rich."

"Good night, Helen." He held up his palm and waved. "See you on the way out."

"Of course."

She left.

Rich looked at his computer screen, where the stack of black subject lines continued to pile. He closed the program, shut down the computer, and turned off the monitor.

The phone's red voice-mail light continued to accuse him.

Rich looked up from the office-lease documents that he almost killed himself to care about.

Helen stood in the doorway. Her face appeared even more aged by concern.

It was 9:47 a.m.

He had already gone home, scanned the newspaper, eaten dinner, watched TV with Dawn, gone to sleep, woken up, showered, swallowed a bagel and two cups of coffee, and taken the El back to work. The correct day may as well have been yesterday—or the day before.

"Good morning, Helen," he said, forcing a smile.

"Still no word from Hank," she said. She clasped her hands in front of her waist.

"No?" he said. "Nothing here either."

His phone rang. They both glanced at it. His voice-mail light remained a bright, blinking red.

"Well, Mrs. Coogan is here, at the office," Helen said. "She said the police have been notified."

"The police," he said.

Open me.

"She's asked to see you."

"Me?"

"Yes. Shall I tell her to come in?"

"Uh, yeah, sure," he said. "Send her over."

Helen nodded and left.

The phone rang again. He looked at the caller ID: Howard Sommerbaum, a current client still chasing him about the proposal that lay on his desk. Rich had tried to review it but could never get past the first page.

The phone fell silent. The relationship had to be in jeopardy now.

He looked up.

Sharon Coogan stood in the doorway.

"Rich? Rich Swanson?"

"Yes," he said.

He'd never seen her before except in the framed family photo on top of one of Hank's filing cabinets. Rich found her good-looking despite minor heft around the middle thanks to her age. Tanning beds and equatorial sun had also begun to leather her skin. She had nice hair, pretty eyes, full lips, and charming smile lines. Full, curving bosoms heaved above a reasonable waist. Her wardrobe spoke of her status as well; Rich could smell Hank's money even from where he sat.

She stepped in and stood halfway between the door and his desk.

He rose and gestured for her to sit down.

"Please," he said. "Make yourself comfortable."

"Thank you."

She dropped her purse from her shoulder and sat in the chair facing Rich to his right.

They looked at each other for a few seconds.

She crossed her legs and set the purse on the floor.

"You know by now that Hank's gone missing," she said.

He nodded.

"I must have called his cell thirty times in the last day and a half," she continued. "And Helen's probably already sick of hearing from me."

257

He nodded again.

"At first, I thought Hank was just being Hank . . . sort of. He *has* stayed out late or not come home before."

She waited to see if Rich detected what she meant; he didn't.

"Nothing felt seriously wrong until late last night. That's when I had that *feeling,* like an anvil falling from a roof. I just knew that something had happened to him." She looked into space; her eyes glazed over momentarily. "No. To be truthful, I think I knew the moment I came home to find him gone and the door to his . . . closet . . . open."

Rich covered his mouth with his hand.

"That never happens, Rich. *Never.* And then there's what he'd added to his . . . collection."

His hand moved away from his mouth.

"Collection?"

"His fortune. He kept it locked in our master bedroom closet. It's been building all these years . . ."

She looked away. He tried to read her eyes but couldn't.

"He loved it more than anything, you know," she continued. "More than me." She sat straight with her hands pressed between her knees. "Maybe not as much as he loved Amy and Andrew. I know he loved it more than God. What am I talking about? I don't think he even believed in God. The only thing that *might* have meant as much is this firm."

He still had no idea of what she was talking about. He wasn't sure if he cared.

"He *always* kept the closet secured. He didn't even trust his own wife to be near it."

Rich heard tears forming and wanting to follow.

"Vainglorious son of a bitch," she said under her breath.

Her eyes softened although her face remained hard.

"I'm sorry, it's just . . ."

Rich gently waved her off.

"Don't worry, Mrs. Coogan."

She wiped the corners of her eyes carefully with a long-nailed middle fingertip.

"I've seen him do and say a lot of strange things through the years, but the latest trumps them all," she said. "Would you believe that man had a life-sized, solid-gold statue made of himself?" She spoke as if oxygen drained from the room. "I mean, he was a miser, but of all things . . ."

"I'm sorry, Mrs. Coogan," Rich said. "Are you saying Hank wasn't home when you got home and has been missing ever since, but you found a life-sized gold statue of him in his closet?"

"Yes," she said. "That's what I'm saying. All five-foot-ten of him in heavy, shining, solid gold. I couldn't believe it."

Rich leaned back, folded his hands over his lap, and looked at his screen saver, a picture of him and Dawn from their Miami vacation.

"Mrs. Coogan," he said, "is it just me, or have we been talking about Hank in the past tense?"

They looked at each other. Did they understand—dare say, *hope*—something neither could say out loud?

"You'll have to forgive me, Mrs. Coogan, but I have to ask. Why did you choose to tell me all of this? I mean, we've never met bef . . ."

She held up one hand to silence him and bent to her purse on the floor. She removed the gold compact and placed it on his desk.

"I found this by the foot of the statue," she said, "and not far from an empty tumbler with melted ice in it. It had your name on it."

"*My* name?"

"Yes," she said. "Look for yourself."

He picked it up and turned it over:

Nothing but the loops and squiggles of Arabic characters.

He closed a fist around it and pulled it toward him on the desk.

"It *is* yours, isn't it?" she said.

He hesitated, then: "Yes. Thank you. I must have left it with him without knowing it."

"That's why I came here, to meet with you," she said. "When I saw the compact with your name on it, I felt I should return it and talk to you. It seemed there might be some connection. I thought you might have . . . answers."

He thought deeply for a moment.

"I think I understand," he said.

"Wouldn't surprise me if the selfish bastard was up to something," she said. Her gathering tears had abated. "He's probably on his way to an underage bimbo and an offshore bank account in French Polynesia or someplace like that. He probably has a new identity too. I wouldn't put it past him. Maybe that's why he's been building the U.S. Treasury at home. He was plotting his time to escape."

She thought.

"No, probably not," she said. "There's no way he'd leave behind his firm, the condo, and most of his collection. The mere thought of losing that much would have him running home."

"I still believe there's an explanation, Mrs. Coogan," he said. "Heck, maybe he'll call or show up as soon as today."

She grabbed her purse, stood, and slipped it over her shoulder.

"Maybe," she said.

Her thoughts drifted. She straightened and pretended to smile.

"Or maybe not," she said.

She extended her hand.

"It was nice to meet you, Rich. Hank spoke well of you. He said you were smart." She paused. "A good kid."

She smiled.

"That was nice of him to say," Rich said.

He stood and slid the compact into his pants pocket in one motion. Then he shook her hand.

"A pleasure, Mrs. Coogan."

"Call me Sharon."

He nodded.

She moved toward the door, stopped at the doorway, and half-faced him.

"I like you, Rich," she said. "You have a way about you. A calm. You listen. After so many years with someone like Hank, I can spot a good guy from a mile away."

She rocked on her right foot.

"I like you," she repeated.

"Thank you, Sharon."

She looked down and then back up.

"I wonder how much that gold statue is worth," she said.

Her eyes brightened; Rich didn't believe she was aware.

"I'll bet it's worth a lot," she said.

He shrugged.

"Bye, Rich," she said.

"Bye."

Mrs. Hank Coogan left.

Rich walked over to the window and gazed out for a while. No one passed his office, almost as if each of them knew, like he did, that he was alone now, and he would never see them again.

*T*he sweating young man with the sunburned face leaned forward. His eyebrows turned down.

The Arab merchant grinned.

"You have something for me?" he said in close-to-queen's English.

Rich wiped his face against his shoulder.

"I do," he said.

He placed the gold-plated compact on the fading green vinyl–covered folding table.

The merchant glanced down at it.

"I'm curious," he said. "How did you find me?"

"I just did," Rich said.

"Of course. They always do. The young man I sold this to—how is he?"

"He's fine, as far as I know."

"Then he did not open it?"

"No. Someone else did."

"I see," the merchant said. "And how is *that* person?"

Rich looked around at the jamboree of junk packed into the booth. He could almost hear each long-forgotten object praying for a new owner to resurrect it by paying for it again.

"He is . . . as he should be," he said.

"Yes," said the merchant. "Of course. That is what it does. That is what it will forever do."

Rich rubbed his gummy, oily face against the shoulder of his off-white tee-shirt.

"You look out of place, my friend," the merchant continued. "You've never been to Morocco before?"

"No," Rich said. "Been here about four days."

He fingered a triangular flap that was torn away from the tabletop. The merchant studied him.

"What would you like in return for this item?" the merchant said.

"What do I want?" Rich said. "I thought it was yours."

"No, not at this time," the merchant said. "It was purchased from me, and I've not yet bought it back."

He held up an arm and swept it around at his mounds of merchandise.

"If you do not require cash, may I suggest we make a trade? You see I have many choices."

Rich scanned the booth from side to side.

"No, I don't think so," he said. "That won't be necessary."

The merchant leaned forward. His eyes were half-sized eggs with firm, brown yolks.

"That's because you haven't looked closely," he said, "nor let me describe what I offer." He flashed a conspirator's smile. "You might be surprised by what could be right for you here."

Rich glanced around once more.

"No," he said. "No, thank you."

"Cash then?"

"No, thank you. I'm okay."

He placed his palm on his pants pocket. He'd cashed out his bank accounts and childhood savings bonds before leaving the States. A reasonable amount remained in his pocket and hotel-room safe. Enough to survive for a while.

"Willing to turn down even extra money, are you?" said the merchant. "But I still cannot accept this item without an exchange. It is not proper and dignified business. It would upset . . ." He paused to monitor Rich's expression. ". . . the balance that guides us all."

Rich looked down at the compact.

The balance that guides us all.

He wondered what Dawn was doing now.

How she was.

How much he might have upset the balance of their lives.

"You can have it back for ten bucks," he said.

The merchant looked deeply into his eyes.

"Deal," he said.

He stuck out his hand. Rich shook it.

The merchant disappeared behind the hanging white bed sheet in the back and returned with a maroon vinyl zip-pouch. Back at the table, still standing, he counted out the exchange in Moroccan dirhams. Rich accepted the bills and shoved them into his pocket.

"I would have paid you more," the merchant said.

"Consider it a deposit into the balance," Rich said. "My balance."

The merchant scooped the compact from the table and dropped it into his pouch.

"I wish you well," he said. "Thank you for your business."

Rich rose and turned to go. He almost ran into another white man who entered.

"Pardon me," the other said, grabbing his arms. His accent was British.

"Sorry," Rich said. "I should have watched where I was going."

The merchant removed the compact from his pouch and placed it back on the table. The new man stared at it.

The merchant smiled at Rich.

Rich left. When the booth was well behind him, he stepped back into the sprawling bazaar. Its swarming, hustling mass soon swallowed him once again.

CHOICES

"**Y**ou can love someone without liking them, you know."

The man smiled. His dimples sank further into his salon-tanned cheeks. He leaned against the bar and rolled the stem of his martini glass between his thumb and index finger.

The much younger woman smiled back. He stood, she sat. He liked how the white light from the art-deco bar counter flashed against her straight, moist teeth and diamond-stud earrings.

He also liked her hair: rich, black, fragrant, chin length. He stood a little closer.

"How is it possible to love without liking?" she said.

She finished her own martini and gestured with her glass to the bartender, who was looking at her. He glided over. His trim pectorals twitched beneath his tight, black v-neck short-sleeved shirt.

"Another?"

"Cosmo, please," she said.

He nodded. She watched him move away to make it.

"Haven't you ever been obsessed with someone you hated?" the man continued.

"What does obsession have to do with love?" she said. "It doesn't."

"Of course it does," he said. "You can't love someone unless you've obsessed over them at some point."

"Not true," she said.

"True," he said. He took a small sip of martini. "If you really think about it for a minute, you'll know exactly what I'm talking about."

She'd already decided he was handsome: nice eyes, solid chin, kissable lips, facial lines in all the right places. Distinctive streaks of gray within his brown hair as well.

She leaned on the bar with her right elbow and held her right hand with her left.

He spread his shoulders. His chest expanded, stretching his black Armani sport coat over his open-neck white button-down shirt. He also wore a white tee-shirt underneath.

"You're in good shape for your age," she said, looking him up and down from chin to waist.

The dimples went deeper.

"How old do you think I *am?*" he said.

His eyes traced her naked shoulders above her strapless black cocktail dress. He tried not to stare at the firm and shallow cleavage beneath the Swarovski buckle.

"Forty-seven," she said. "No—forty-eight."

"Close enough," he said.

"Am I right?"

"Close enough." He put his non-drink hand on his hip. "What about you? You can't be over thirty."

The bartender returned with her Cosmopolitan. He set it on the frosted-glass coaster in front of her.

"Twelve dollars, please," he said.

The woman reached for her monogrammed Yves Saint Laurent clutch handbag.

"I've got it," the man said, touching her arm.

He slipped a money clip from his black slacks and gave the bartender a ten and a five.

"Keep the change," he said.

The bartender nodded and smiled. His thin and well-shaped bicep moved as he accepted the cash.

"So am I right?" the man said.

"About what?" she said. "My age?"

"Not a day over thirty."

"Close enough," she said, and sipped her drink.

"That's a nice bag," he said. "Where'd you get it?"

"Michigan Avenue," she said. "That's a nice coat. Where did *you* get it?"

"Michigan Avenue," he said. "What do you do?"

"I'm a personal trainer," she said. "What do *you* do?"

"Bull," he said, and winked. "Personal trainers don't buy bags like that. What do you do?"

"How presumptuous," she said, winking back at him. "I'm the assistant vice president of Firmer Firms."

"I've heard of it," he said.

He finished his martini and set the glass on the bar.

"You help the high-paid white collars get back in shape," he said. "Law firms, investment firms, accounting firms, what have you."

"Yes," she said. "We customize workout programs for professional-services representatives. Should I assume you're not a white collar?"

"Senior creative director at Needleman and Ross," he said.

"That's still white collar to me. A firm."

"We're an agency, not a firm."

"Right," she said, her eyes twinkling. "You handle some of the big insurance and telecommunications companies, right?"

"Among other things," he said.

"So, senior creative director," she said. "Sounds like responsibility."

He shrugged. "It's a nice paycheck."

"A lot of people beneath you?"

"Some. Writers, designers, art directors, production managers."

"Wow."

"It's a lot of meetings and management, let me tell you," he said. "I haven't seen a forty-hour work week in years."

"I can imagine," she said.

"Then there's the travel to present to the clients," he said. "New York, L.A., Denver, San Francisco. I've seen conference rooms the size of the Senate chamber. A lot of knee-sucking too. The CEOs with the eight-figure salaries like to be stroked."

She laughed.

"I guess you're not married," she said.

The bartender returned with another martini for the man and took the empty glass.

"Still cash, sir?" he said.

"You know, let's open a tab," the man said, grinning at the woman.

He handed the bartender one of several credit cards from his wallet.

"What makes you say that?" he said, looking back at her. "That I'm not married."

"Well, obviously, you're either at the office or on the road," she said. "That would have to be rough on a marriage. Even more so if there's children, unless they're grown up."

She sipped her drink.

"Besides, being gone, and . . . so good looking and successful, you must have a lot of, well, *choices.*"

His grin grew larger.

"What about you?" he said. "Why aren't you married?"

He took her left hand and held it between them.

"No ring," he said.

She gently slipped her hand back.

"I'm sure you have choices as well," he said. "A woman as charming and beautiful as you."

She shrugged.

"Men ask me out sometimes," she said. "I go out with some."

"Nothing serious?" he said. "You must be dating boys."

She set her drink on the bar, crossed her legs, and folded her hands over her top knee.

"Define a boy."

"I don't know," he said. "A guy, young guy, who wants to impress you so he can get into . . ." He reconsidered. "One who loves to have fun but hates to commit. A show-off who doesn't know what a woman *really* wants."

"And what does a woman want?"

He sipped his martini.

"Strength. Humor. Confidence. Intelligence. Sensitivity. Emotional and financial security. Someone who can both calm and excite her."

"You skipped humility," she said.

"Right," he said. "It's a long list, and a boy doesn't have a chance with it."

"Certainly you would know."

He nodded and chuckled.

"You didn't really answer the question," she said.

"Which one?"

"Whether you're married or not."

"You answered it for me, didn't you?" he said.

He noticed a thirty-something professional man caressing a woman's arm at the far other end of the bar. The man said something close to her face. She laughed and flipped her hair.

"Let's not talk about marriage," he continued. "It's a specious concept."

"I like that word, specious," she said. "Although sometimes I confuse it with spurious."

"They both work for me," he said. "Marriage is specious *and* spurious."

"Okay, then," she said. "If you're not married, then you've been through a divorce."

He rolled his eyes and smiled.

"I'm glad I'm talking to a palm reader," he said. "It's better to be single. Trust me."

"But that can get so . . . *lonely,*" she said.

"Sure," he said. "But at least you wake up each morning with possibilities. The sex when it happens is way better too."

"Why can't sex be good in a marriage?"

"Same thing, same grind, over and over, day after day, year after year," he said. "No one, and I mean no one, can keep it going that long. We weren't made for the monotony. Marriage kills the sexual instinct."

"Well, I can't argue with you entirely there," she said. "But there's still something we get from the vow. Each of us needs to be loved by a friend who chooses to be there."

"Well, there are animals better at it than we are," he said. "Ostriches mate for life, and I'm sure they don't bitch about it like we do."

"How do you know?"

"Because I've been to the ostrich farm on Washington Island off the tip of Door County."

"Well, I still think marriage is the most important idea that we have," she said. "Monotony's not so bad when you're seventy-five and slowing down."

"Depends what kind of seventy-five-year-old you are," he said.

"If only love and lust weren't mutually exclusive," she said.

"Screw love," he said. "Lust is more fun."

"Maybe so," she said, "but the best lovers can be horrible friends. What makes them so good in bed is the same thing that messes up your life when you're out of it."

Glasses clinked a toast somewhere off to their left.

"Well, that might be," he said, "but it doesn't change the fact that love and monogamy are pipe dreams of churches and too many movies. It's unnatural. No matter what we think on wedding day, we all need to move on at some point. To live and experience something else." He sipped his drink and moved his lips to rub the moisture from them. "Everyone figures that out a few years in. If they don't, it's because deep down they're desperate for the safety and the validation. One person can't possibly provide all that we need all of our lives. Especially as we get older."

"You speak like a man," she said, smiling, "and you should have been a polygamist. It's *especially* when we get older that we need someone with us. Ever heard of loyalty? Companionship?"

"They're nice thoughts," he said, "for people too afraid to date."

She laughed and sipped her drink.

"How did we get into this conversation?" he said. "I hope it's not killing the vibe."

"The vibe?" she said.

"Uh, yeah. You know. We're both here to have fun. Meet people. *Connect.*"

"Isn't that what we're doing?" she said.

"Yeah, but, well, you know," he said, "there are some things you just don't talk about when you're . . . meeting someone. Death. Politics. The sordid past. Any clinical depression you might be getting therapy for. Let's add marriage while we're at it. Not a good topic to start with."

She looked at him. He liked the way her lips were glistening.

"Well," he said, "I'm doing just great with you here, aren't I?"

She smiled and touched his arm.

"You're doing fine," she said.

They both glanced around the bar. He observed a couple in a booth in a corner; floating tea lights in a dish lit their faces from below. She noticed three well-dressed women in a spirited conversation at a table for four.

The ambient music switched from the Mighty Blue Kings to Louis Armstrong.

"Well, since we've already mentioned sex, do you mind if I ask a question?" he said.

She shrugged and looked at him askance.

"Um . . . sure. Shoot."

"Do you *really* believe it's more important to men?"

"I don't know," she said. "How important is it to *you?*"

"You're skirting the question," he said, grinning. "I want to know the truth."

"And you suppose you'll get it from a woman you've just met at a bar?"

"Why not?" he said. "Maybe people we don't know are the best place to go for the truth." He sipped his drink. "No agenda."

"It matters to women," she said. "But not as much. Don't get me wrong—we like it. Sometimes a lot. We just don't define our relationships by it like you do. It's interesting that you'd ask that of me."

"How so?"

"Well, for one thing, you're clearly more experienced than I am," she said. "You also seem, I don't know, meticulous. Like you'd have answered something like that for yourself by now."

He studied her eyes for a moment.

"The truth," he said, "is that I already knew the answer. I just wanted to hear what you had to say."

She raised an eyebrow.

"Are you trying to pick me up," she said, "or piss me off?"

"Of course I'm trying to piss you off," he said, winking at her. "What better way to get a woman's attention in ways she won't admit to liking?"

She laughed.

"You really believe that?"

"Of course," he said. "What women say and what they really want are diametrically opposed. Only dictators are less reasonable."

"Wow," she said. "Are you sure you're not in your twenties?"

He touched her lightly on the elbow.

"Just making stimulating conversation, my dear."

She shifted on her bar stool.

"Hear it from me as we sit here drinking twelve-dollar cocktails in a room of nice-looking people," she said. "You *can't* define a relationship by the sex. Not ever. Narcissism is easy to hide when people are getting off. You *can't* hide it when you're sitting at a breakfast table on a Sunday morning with no other sound but percolation."

It hurts, David. Please . . . make it go away . . . make it go AWAYYYY . . .

He looked down.

"What's wrong?" she said.

He looked back at her.

"Nothing," he said. He forced a smile. "Perhaps you're right. About sex. And relationships."

She was silent.

"But it doesn't change our curse," he said.

"Curse?"

"Our obsession for stability when we're dating and variety when we're married."

"So you *are* married."

"I didn't say that," he said. He slipped his free hand into his pants pocket.

"Your face is flushed," she said. "Is there something you want to tell me?"

He looked her straight in the eyes.

"Actually, there is," he said. "You're beautiful. I mean, painfully so."

"Well, thank you," she said.

"I mean it," he said, his voice dropping. He moved one step closer to her. "You are lovely."

"Thank you," she said. Her voice had fallen as well.

The bartender strolled over.

"You two doing okay?" he said.

"I'll take another," the man said. "You?"

She shook her head.

"I'll wait."

The bartender nodded and moved away.

"So, what *are* we doing here?" the man said.

"How do you mean?"

"Well, we're two successful, attractive professionals, right? Yet here we are, cruising the Loop on a Friday."

"What's wrong with that?" she said. "Are you intimating we're . . . lonely?"

"It's too bad we can't have both the safety of marriage and the fire of an affair for all of our lives," he said. "It's crap that the fun has to end."

She slapped her knee.

"You *are* married!"

"Would you please stop with that?" he said. "Really."

She chuckled.

"If you're not married now, then you have been," she said. "Either that, or you're married with issues."

He sipped his drink, set the glass on the bar, and slipped both hands into his pants pockets.

"I think now I really can hear some air squeaking from our balloon," he said. "My fault."

"Oh, stop being silly," she said.

"I'm serious," he said. "It's amazing how the nuances of conversation can dictate . . . well, *this*. It's quite a dance we engage."

"Who says we're not still dancing?"

He thought it over.

"You're right," he said. "We are adults, aren't we? We're not just kids looking to get loaded and laid. We can actually discuss life's issues. The real ones. We've both filled our bags and dragged them by now."

"Oooh," she said. "I like how you said that."

He laughed.

"Hey, I'm a creative director. I can turn a phrase once in a while."

He smiled.

"I do have to say I'm surprised you're here alone," he said. "There's a lot of . . ." He looked around the bar. ". . . possibilities here."

"But I'm having so much fun with you," she said. "You're interesting."

"Interesting," he said. "To the mature woman, is that better than *hot?*"

"Whoever said interesting wasn't hot?" she said.

"Good point," he said. He retrieved his martini and sipped. "So what would you say if I *was* married?"

She sipped her own drink and looked down.

"Well," she said, looking up, "I'd enjoy your company for the rest of our time, and then go home without you."

"*You see!*" he said, stepping back and raising his arm. "Why would any guy want to admit that he's married?"

She scrunched her eyebrows.

"Umm . . . because he is?"

"Yeah, but then the mood is destroyed," he said. "Completely."

"That's one way of looking at it," she said. "You could also say that if a man's afraid to say he's married because he's afraid it'll stop a woman from flirting with him, he probably shouldn't be married."

"Nonsense," he said. His face went dark for a moment. "Marriage is impractical."

"We're back to that, I see. How so?"

"More than six billion people on Earth," he said. "And we're supposed to pick and stick with just one, what, forty, fifty years?"

"I think it's beautiful."

"Of course you do," he said. "You're a woman."

"Statistically, men marry faster after divorce or a death than women do," she said. "Explain that."

"All people marry for one reason," he said. "And that's to have someone witness their lives. It doesn't matter if you're eighteen or eighty. We need someone to acknowledge we're here."

"That's cynical," she said.

"If we could get away with changing lovers without having to deal with the emotional mess and our conscience, we would," he said. "We're wired to want both variety and stability and to crave one when we have the other. It's twisted and cruel."

He put his non-drink hand on his hip.

"So," he said. "That guy over there has been checking you out the whole time we've been talking."

She glanced over her shoulder.

"Who?"

"That guy, over there," he said. "The one wearing the black Pierre Cardin shirt at the other end of the bar. Someone should remind him the eighties are over."

She waited and then turned slowly on her bar stool to look.

She spun back around.

"That guy?"

"That guy," he said.

She blushed.

"He is . . . kind of cute."

"He belongs in a John Hughes movie."

"Jealous, are you?" she said.

"Should I be? I haven't known you long enough yet."

"But you're working on it,'" she said. She smiled and sipped her drink.

"That's confident of you," he said.

"Please," she said.

A couple seconds of silence.

"Besides, you shouldn't be jealous," she said.

"How so?"

"Because you *are* married," she said.

"I thought we already covered all of that."

"There's a tan line on your finger. If you want to work other options, you really should remember to take the ring off. Women notice things like that."

He looked at his left hand, spread the fingers, and slipped it into his pocket.

She winked.

He sipped his martini. "So much for being meticulous."

"I think it's funny," she said. "Cute."

"Cute," he said.

He sat on the bar stool behind him.

"You sure you don't want me to introduce you to Jake Ryan from *Sixteen Candles* over there?"

They both glanced at him.

"I'm sure," she said. "So how long have you been married?"

"A few years," he said.

"What's she doing if she's not out with you?"

David please make it STOP

"She usually goes to the movies with a couple of her friends on Fridays. Dinner."

She drank her Cosmopolitan. It was almost empty.

"Look," he said. "You sure you don't want me to move on? I mean, I feel like an idiot right now."

She touched his knee and smiled.

"I'm sure," she said.

His face relaxed.

"Okay," he said, "I wasn't exactly telling the truth. She's on vacation. Same friends."

"What do I care if she's at the movies or on vacation?"

He looked away and then back at her.

"I don't know."

"Easing your conscience with a little bit of honesty?" she said.

He looked down, thought, and smirked.

"I guess."

He glanced around the bar again. The young man in the Pierre Cardin was looking their way.

"That guy's still eyeing you even though the woman he's with is hot," he said. "You should be flattered."

"Right," she said. "Flattery is the grease on the skids to emotional hell. Why do you think so many women are crazy? I think I'll ride it out with you tonight."

She shifted on her stool.

"So, any kids?"

His face became dour.

"No."

"Why not?"

He shrugged.

"Dunno," he said. "It just never . . . went that way."

"I know," she said. "It's a personal question. None of my business. It's also a personal decision. Kids aren't for everyone."

He looked at two young men speaking to each other straight across the bar from them.

"And not everyone can have kids," he said.

He looked backed at her.

"I know," she said. "Life's funny that way. There are messed-up people who can have all the kids that they want, and there are wonderful people who can't have one."

"Not fair, huh?"

She shrugged.

"A lot of things aren't fair," he said. "Life's not fair. Marriage isn't fair." He looked her up and down. "Sex isn't fair."

"I think everything's as fair as it can be," she said, "considering that we're the only ones trying to make sense of the chaos. Chaos would get along just fine without people."

"That's an interesting thought," he said.

"I have a few here and there as well."

She smiled.

"That's a stunning dress you're wearing, by the way," he said. "I do understand why Pierre over there would rather look at you than his date."

She looked down at herself.

"You don't think it's . . . too much?"

"Well, truthfully, yes, I do. But then, if I had the power that women do, especially women who look like you, I'd wear it too. Keep it on the rest of the night, and you might get your proposal from a tycoon. Or at least a partner at a law firm. Then all your problems will be solved."

"It didn't work for Jackie O," she said. "And who said I have problems?"

He sipped his drink.

"We all have problems," he said.

"Even those of us out having fun for prices that could feed a Third World family for weeks?"

"Even those," he said.

"There's an easy explanation for that," she said. "For problems."

"What's that?"

"Relationships."

He chuckled.

"Of course," he said. "Women will always bring it back to that."

The bartender set another martini in front of him. The man glanced at him and nodded.

"I swear," he said, "women could watch another five thousand talk shows, read just as many magazines, burn another ten years rehashing it all with their friends, and never lose any interest. It's perfect idle chatter, because it's one story with infinite plots and no end."

"Explained like a man."

"We have a much different concept of time and how it should be spent."

"Right," she said. "Like drinking beer in dark bars all day and watching football, including teams you don't even care about."

"That's how we relax after killing ourselves to keep women like you happy," he said. He smiled and gently tapped her on the elbow.

"Well, you're right about one thing," she said.

He raised his eyebrows.

"About the subject having no end," she said. "The relationship equation is worse than pi."

"And it proves we're all nuts," he said. "Each last one of us."

She laughed and sipped her drink.

"Why do you think that is?"

He looked down, thought, and looked back up at her.

"Because all of us want to be treated as exclusively important, but not all of us want to reciprocate. If you have two people feeling that way at the same time, which is pretty much most relationships, well, there's your crisis."

She looked away, tilted her head, and nodded.

"It'd be one thing if we could all just get along as a big social family and avoid the problems of romantic idealism," he said. "But no. We all have to obsess over soul mates. We have to have sex like we're lions at lunch. And once we have sex with someone, we walk into their insanity whether we know or like it or not."

"So happy, married people who go to church and hold hands and read to their children and have loving sex are insane," she said.

"You *especially* have to look out for those," he said. "They're hiding something."

"Man, you *are* cynical," she said.

"Not cynical. Just realistic."

"So you don't believe in soul mates."

He smiled and laughed through his nose.

"It's a bloated fantasy of the Western hemisphere."

"Wow," she said. She puckered and whistled. "*Someone's* got a hang-up or two."

"Hang-ups, shmang-ups," he said. "We invented soul mates to fight the truth that all relationships are a pain in the ass and no one is meant just for us. At least not in the Hollywood way. We're all too selfish and complex to be soul mates."

"Okay, now I'll come out and say that if you weren't so charming and safely *unavailable,* you would have really turned me off by now."

He shrugged.

"I tell it like it is."

"Why hold back when subtlety's no longer useful?" she said.

He looked up and cocked his head.

"Is that Cowboy Junkies they're playing?"

She listened.

"I do believe you're correct."

"That's an interesting switch," he said. "I like it. We need some *mood* in here."

"They're so beautifully maudlin," she said.

"I'm not sure it'll help anyone in here get laid, though," he said. "Too pensive. Aims too high above the waist." He paused. "But it's good stuff for the heavy heart pretty much everyone's in here to hide."

He waved two fingers at the bartender.

"Like the music!"

The bartender glanced at him and gave a thumbs-up.

"Have you ever wondered if our choice of mate is just a Band-Aid for our own pathology?" the man said.

She reflected.

"Could be. I never thought of it that way."

"Take a close look at any couple," he said, "and you'll notice each person is the prescription for the other person's issues. Seriously. Pay attention. You'll see exactly what I mean."

"So your wife is the pill that you pop for your problems?"

He sipped his drink and turned his lips in.

"Must be," he said.

"I don't have a boyfriend," she said. "Does that mean I don't have any issues?"

"To the contrary," he said. "It might mean you have too many."

"Thanks," she said.

He raised his martini glass.

"My pleasure."

A moment of silence.

He looked around the bar.

"Looks like the place has filled up a little more," he said.

She surveyed the room as well.

"Looks that way," she said. "More people like us. Looking to become someone's prescription."

She winked.

He looked her over.

"You know, now that we've made it this far, I think I'll say that you really should cover up," he said. "That dress, I mean."

"Oh? And why's that?"

"Well, it *is* a little too much," he said. "Most of the guys in here, well, they might get the wrong idea."

"Wrong idea?"

"You know what I mean," he said. "Do you want attention for who you are or . . ." He looked at the supple skin of her shoulders. ". . . for how you present? You do understand the message you're sending, don't you?"

"What's wrong with wanting to look nice?"

"Nothing," he said, "as long as you're honest about what you're signing up for. Don't complain about the dogs when you're the one blowing the whistle."

"How paternal," she said. "You sound just like you're my . . ."

Their eyes met and stayed still.

"So where did your wife go for vacation?" she said.

"Arizona," he said.

"Phoenix?"

"Scottsdale."

"Same thing," she said.

He shrugged.

"So, any children?" she said.

His face flattened.

"You already asked me that," he said.

"You're right," she said, smiling. "Sorry."

"No kids," he said. He half-turned in his stool and looked away.

She leaned toward him and tried to see his face.

"Am I touching a soft spot?"

He turned back around.

"What about you?" he said. "Do *you* have any children?"

She set her glass on the bar.

"I told you I don't have a boyfriend," she said, "which also means I'm not married."

"That doesn't mean you don't have children."

"No," she said. "I don't. Have children."

He shrugged.

"Okay," he said. "No surprise. You don't strike me as the type."

"Oh?" she said. "And what exactly is the type?"

He looked her over again.

"You know what I mean."

"No," she said. "I don't."

"I don't know," he said. "You just seem like . . . you'd be better at being maintained than at maintaining."

She took her glass from the bar.

"Well, if you had any lingering hope of impressing me, you may have just sounded the death knell."

"Impress?" he said. "I thought we established our status as highly unlikely to happen."

She raised her glass in a half-toast.

"Indeed," she said. She sipped the last sip and set the glass back down. "So since we've made ourselves personal and unlikely to happen, I can ask you why no kids."

"Damn, you really are striking, you know," he said. "You remind me of . . ."

Her eyes narrowed.

". . . I don't know. Someone," he said.

"So was not having kids a choice that you made?" she said.

"Shouldn't this be about the time I tell you to go to hell?"

He winked at her.

"Why don't you?" she said.

No answer.

"Most women want children," she said. "I believe I might want them someday. If I can even have them."

"That guy is still looking over here," he said.

She shrugged.

"He's starting to annoy me," he said. "Want me to go over there and say something?"

"Please," she said. "First, he has that beautiful woman with him. Second, I'd be embarrassed for you. I appreciate the offer, but I'll be fine."

"Who said it had anything to do with you?" he said. "Maybe *I* don't like it. Maybe I don't like the *way* he's looking at you."

"Well, then, I'd say you're either very macho or very protective."

He stared at the man.

"He's even looking at me now," he said.

She studied his face.

He finished his current drink, set it on the bar, and picked up the next one.

"What would you say if I told you I haven't had sex in three years?" he said.

She looked away and bit her lip.

"I don't know," she said. "I guess it'd depend on why."

"I mean, what's a man supposed to do?" he said. "Even Christian virtues have their limits."

"It's that bad, huh?" she said.

He looked at her.

She searched his eyes.

"Why does being married mean I have to forget about what makes me human?" he said.

"Being married might be one of the only things that make us human."

It hurts, David. Please . . . make it go away . . . make it go AWAYYYY . . .

"Damn it, if that guys looks over here *one* more time."

"So you've made it this far without being a father," she said. "Think it'll stay that way?"

He grinned and shook his head.

"Okay, this is officially the strangest conversation I've ever had in a place like this," he said. "We should be having it over coffee and cigarettes at a diner at two in the morning. One with dirty Formica counters and tabletops."

"Why?" she said.

"Why what?"

"Why are people so afraid to have honest conversations about themselves?"

"If you're so concerned about deep and meaningful discourse," he said, "why are you dressed like that drinking Cosmos in a bar like this one? There's got to be book clubs out there."

"It's sad," she said, looking away, "that we have to hide so much of who we are when meeting a person." She looked at him with even greater focus. "Why is that a rule in keeping someone's interest?"

He rose and leaned against the bar.

"That's because if people see who we are, and we see who *they* are, none of us would bother with each other. Other people's problems are too much fucking work."

He sipped his drink.

"So what would you do if you found out, say, tomorrow that your wife was pregnant?"

"Man," he said. "What's with you and these questions? I'd say it's none of your business."

"No, really," the woman said, leaning forward. Her eyes were large and sparkling.

"You are so . . . familiar," he said.

"What would you do if you found out you were going to be a father?"

His face colored. He looked away.

"I don't know," he said. "I'm not worried about it."

"Would it be an intrusion on your life? One you couldn't live with?"

He stared at her silently with darkening eyes.

"You must be set in your ways by now," she said. Her face tightened and narrowed. "But could you change if you had to? Could you move far enough beyond yourself to live for someone else? Someone who loved and needed you?"

"Good God," he said.

He looked around.

Light reflected from the wristband of an expensive watch.

A man whispered into a woman's ear.

The music changed to something slow and moody by Coldplay.

"I think I've had enough of this conversation," he said. "I say we call it a night."

She grasped his wrist, but not too hard.

He looked at her hand and then deeply into her eyes.

He covered her hand with his own.

"I . . . ," he said.

She slipped her hand away and returned it to her lap.

"I believe that each of us is the author of the life we inhabit," she said. "There are some things, perhaps many things, that are way beyond our control. You can put God's will somewhere in there too. But most of what we deal with or don't is because of the choices we make."

She crossed her legs the other way.

"We are the living, walking sums of our actions and decisions," she said.

He glared at her.

"I think I'll close the tab," he said.

He stood against the bar and cupped his mouth with one hand.

"Excuse me!"

The bartender's back was to him. He was serving a small pack of fresh-faced professional Asian women.

"I've enjoyed most of this," the man said, glancing sideways at her. "You're smart and attractive. I honestly wish the best for you."

"What would you do if your wife was pregnant?" she said.

He set down his drink and cupped his mouth with both hands.

"Excuse me!"

The bartender now attended to two finance-looking men.

"You'd think a place like this would have a little more help," he said.

"If you really break it down, *we* have all the power."

He glanced at her sideways again.

"What? Who?"

"Us," she said. "The living. The ones of us who made it here."

"Uh, okay," he said. "If he doesn't look over here soon and bring me my check, his tip isn't a nickel over fifteen percent."

"If we're here, in the world, making decisions, we have total control," she said. "A god's control. But those who don't make it here, into the world, they have a voice too. Some people just can't hear it, because some people take it away from them."

"Excuse me, goddamn it!" the man shouted above the bar noise.

The bartender glanced backward and squinted, looking annoyed. He resumed speaking with the two men.

"Everything we say and do and think comes back to us somehow," she said.

It hurts, David. Please . . . make it go away . . . make it go AWAYYYY . . .

He spun toward her and looked at her solemnly.

"I know you," he said.

"Some people choose to live for themselves," she said. "There's still a price for that."

"I'm going to pay the bill and then I'm going to leave," he said. He finished the rest of his drink in one gulp.

The bartender rang up his current sale and looked their way. The man waved violently. The bartender nodded but then turned to serve somebody else.

"Asshole," the man said under his breath. He leaned hard on the bar with both hands and hung his head.

"Your wife's name is Joanna," she said.

He didn't look up.

"She's not on vacation."

He closed his eyes.

"You've never figured out if you really love her."

He breathed deeply. His back rose. He stood straight. His eyebrows were now thunderheads.

"Who *are* you?"

"She has Gestational Trophoblastic Disease," she said. "She contracted it many years ago."

Wrinkles formed around his eyes.

"She had malignant cells in the tissue that was developing into the placenta during her pregnancy," she said. "The doctor predicted an almost certain miscarriage."

The man cupped his hands to his mouth again.

"I . . . WANT . . . MY . . . FUCKING . . . CHECK!"

The bartender attended to the same customer, a fifty-ish blonde woman in jeans, a red button-down blouse, and a thin black leather jacket.

"Rather than have to go through the miscarriage, she opted for another procedure," she said. "An *elective* one concerning the embryo." She paused. "You acted concerned, but deep down you were relieved. You never wanted the responsibility." She paused again. "You'd just been going along with it because following the script of marriage and children was making you feel normal and accepted. You were too afraid of being single and alone and unrecognized."

He slammed his palm, bumping one of the two empty glasses. It tipped over, rolled off, and broke against the floor. Several people including the bartender stopped talking and looked their way.

"*I want my check! SOMEBODY BRING ME MY CHECK!*"

"The elective procedure aggravated your wife's original condition," she said. "A few years later, a partial hydatiform mole formed in her uterine lining and grew into the muscle layer below. Surgery could only partially remove it."

The man grabbed the other empty glass and threw it toward the bartender.

It smashed on the floor by his feet.

He looked at the shards and then at them. His eyes were those of a deer at the edge of a late-night road.

"*My check! I want my check, you dipshit!*"

The man fell forward onto his elbows on the bar. He ran his fingers through the sides of his hair.

"She soldiered on for quite a while," the woman said, leaning closer to his ear. "Longer than expected. Years. But then the bad cells came back. They completed a full hydatiform mole. A full-blown choriocarcinoma."

She touched his arm.

"Now she's bleeding badly in her pelvic cavity. The cancer has metastasized into her lungs."

He buried his face in his hands.

When he looked back up, the bartender was on the phone and still looking his way.

"All of that on top of the ovary she lost to endometriosis," she said. "The last one that could have given her any hope after the elective procedure."

"Who the hell are you?" he said.

She slipped her arm around his shoulder and rested her forehead against his temple.

"The tiny bumps forming on her urinary tract early on weren't looking very good either," she said. Her voice was a hardened feather next to his ear. "They've got to be really nasty by now. All things considered, I can't imagine she's going to live very much longer."

She drew her head back.

"And the pain, David," she said, softly, "the *pain.* "

A hand like a vice gripped the back of his arm.

The bouncer—a short human bull in jeans and a tee-shirt and sport coat—turned him around.

"I'm afraid you'll have to leave," he said.

The man looked at him hard.

"Not yet," he said. His eyes were wide and glassy and darting. "I'm not done yet."

"You'd be amazed by the things a fetus can see and remember," the young woman said. "Even after it's been discarded."

"I'm sorry, sir," the bouncer said. He was still holding the man by the arm. "You damaged property and nearly injured someone. You'll have to leave. *Now.*"

The man tried to slip his arm free.

The bouncer gripped it tighter.

"Let's go," he said.

He began guiding him toward the entrance.

The man let himself be led several feet. When the bouncer's grip relaxed, he yanked his arm away and dashed back to the bar.

She hadn't moved.

"I'm sorry," he said, dropping to one knee before her. *"So sorry, my dear, my darling little . . ."*

He took her hand in both of his.

"I didn't mean . . . it's not what you think . . . I was just so . . . *young* . . . and . . ."

The bouncer grabbed him hard by the shoulders, whipped him around, and shoved him toward the door again.

"Out!"

The man tried to return to the woman.

The bouncer bear-hugged him from behind and lifted his feet from the floor.

The man wiggled, flailing his legs.

"Let me go! You don't understand!"

He twisted and squirmed, but couldn't turn enough.

"I'm sorry!" he screamed up into the air.

The bouncer carried him the rest of the way out and released him on the sidewalk. Several smokers scattered.

"If you come anywhere near this establishment, we'll have you arrested," the bouncer said.

The man sprang to the wide front glass window. The top of the interior cherry-wood shutters was taller than he was. He tried stepping onto the window's thin concrete outer ledge.

The bouncer stormed toward him.

"I said get the hell out of here," he said, pointing down the street.

The man looked at him with the same wide and glassy eyes.

Then he stepped backward, turned, and walked away to his left.

He continued straight for a while.

The lights and sounds of downtown became the dark and watchful silence of fading-brick buildings and lonely parked cars and barren lots sequestered by fences.

He walked faster, aiming for the alley one block ahead on the opposite side of the street.

Once within its concealing canal, alone with the shadows of choices, he lay on the dirty, bumpy ground, pulled his knees to his chest, and closed his eyes.

LEFTY'S GREEN ROOM

Name's Parker Hill, and I can't really write for shit. Hell, I can't speak all that well neither, unless maybe it's to tell you what drugs I used to sell, or why I still carry a gun.

But this here's a story I felt I had to try to set down. For you, and for me. Maybe it just stayed in me all these years, fillin the cracks of my mind so I might have some peace and some truth before I go to the grave.

Not bein a man of the quill, I had to think long and hard about it all. What I should write and how. Where I should start. When to begin. Hell, why you should care.

I'll bet I drank a thousand beers and smoked five times as many Winstons before it hit me:

I had to write this because it's about the color in your head. Mine too.

And that color has *everything* to do with who we are and how we live in this world.

It all starts with Melvin "Lefty" Savage. He came out cryin on April 19, 1947, in a delivery room at the Kensing County Hospital about nine miles north of my home town of Colton, Indiana. His dad wasn't there for the delivery because he was busy gettin loaded half a block down at John's Tavern. And if you knew Frank Savage like most of us did, you'd know that he was in the bar as soon as his wife went into labor. News like that meant all-night "on me's," and the drinkin cult of Colton wasn't the kind to ask why he was *here* rather than *there*.

Twelve pounds, five ounces, Lefty was. As my buddy Tommy James would later say, he almost wrecked the garage in pullin out of it. Word was Lefty's mom screamed enough to peel the paint from a battleship. You knew as soon as you saw him he'd claim his share of physical space.

You also needed just one look to tell he'd never be as good-lookin as Dennis, his older brother by two years. Lefty's face was wide, his nose was pug, and his eyes were real deep set. Most people could tell you he looked like the kid of a caveman.

Lefty and his mom were let out the usual week or so after the birth. Her sister, Lefty's Aunt June, drove em home. Mr. Savage wasn't available on account he was too hung over to make the drive. When Mrs. Savage walked through the front door with that swaddled beast of a boy in her arms, he bawled her out for wakin im up. Then he just stared at the kid.

"You sure it's mine?" he said.

"Yes," she said.

"Well, then, there must have been one ugly son of a bitch on your side of the family," he said.

Even little Dennis looked at Lefty kind of funny. Dennis didn't have much to worry about in the Savage house, because as I said, he was easy on the eyes. He was charming as well, even at two. Nature had given im all that he needed to keep his dad off of his ass.

Unlike Lefty, who was just a week-old bundle when the rest of his life turned to black.

Far as I know, his dad never even held him, or fed him, or changed his dirty diaper. He *did* come up with plenty of words and names for him that you might find hard to believe, especially if you're a woman with a child.

All the while, as the years passed, Lefty grew bigger and taller and stronger. Dennis got better lookin, kicked ass at sports, and scored plenty of premium poontang. Mr. Savage drank more and lost a lot of jobs for bein a fuck. He made just enough to buy booze and then use what was left to pay the bills that mattered. Mrs. Savage hung out and kept her mouth shut.

While Dennis ran the football, hit the baseball, and slipped his hands into the best bras at school, Lefty sat in the dark in the basement, where his dad preferred to keep him.

Now you and me both know the world can be cruel and confusing, and I've done my part to keep it wrong. But even I never understood how low you have to go to torture your own. That takes a special kind of hatin yourself, and Lefty's dad had it.

The really hard beatings started when Lefty was about three and ran until he was six. At six, he graduated to the belts and shoes and two-by-fours. At about eight, his dad brought him down to the musty hell hole where Lefty spent much of the time that would make him who he was.

I didn't see that basement for myself until Lefty and me met in high school. It creeped *me* out, so I can't imagine what it was like for a kid.

The one time Lefty took me down there was to show me his secret stash of comics behind a concrete block he could wiggle out of the wall. He loved comic books but couldn't have em in the house unless he wanted his dad's foot in his ass up to the knee.

It was an afternoon about a month into our sophomore year. Early October 1963, I believe that would make it. Lefty was suspended from school. Mr. Savage was workin some crap two-day job and the missus was in bed checked out on pain medication. Lefty led me down the stairs into a blackness that sucked light like a vacuum. He of course knew his way in. I had to hold out my arms to guide myself.

Once on the floor, he pulled the chain to a bulb. He said his dad didn't let it be turned on, not ever, unless he said so. The light it threw was like wet sand. A couple cockroaches ran behind a soggy cardboard box in the corner.

In my view, at that time, that basement was the world's graveyard for old tools, empty gas cans, and bicycle parts. Some bulgin mystery boxes and hip-high stacks of twine-tied newspapers as well. I also saw some fine web work by a spider the size of your thumb.

It was a goddamn Shangri-la of worthless shit.

It was cool down there too. I'll bet the temp never climbed past sixty-five, except for maybe high summer. And the smell—like wrung-out rags that never dried all the way.

I couldn't stand bein down there for more than fifteen minutes. Lefty'd spent half his life.

But all that don't amount to nothin, you see, because there were the *pictures*. Everywhere, on each inch of wall with a flat and open surface. Created with whatever he'd been able to find. Pens, pencils, nubs of crayons, bits of broken concrete, paint from cans with rusty bottoms. Even old lawnmower oil.

Much of the art was still in good shape, even where you could tell his dad used assholes and elbows to get rid of it. While he didn't or couldn't rub or scrub or erase it as well as he would have liked, Mr. Savage *did* do a good job of smearin it here and there. But some of it, especially the carved stuff and the parts with oil-based paint, wouldn't budge. I'm sure those earned Lefty two times the typical ass-whippin.

To know what I saw, and how I felt, you have to first realize that these here bones don't have a lick of art in em. Not unless you count the one that can make a few kids, which it never did.

And while that time down in Lefty's basement didn't and couldn't change who I was or would become, it left me with somethin. Maybe it was a seed in my heart that made me think I could be more than what I believed I was, or am. Those thoughts might not be *true,* but goddamn if they ain't a beautiful thing to consider.

Quiet houses with puffin chimneys on gentle, rollin green hills. Faceless people playin and prayin, huggin and talkin, formin themselves a town. Herds of dreamed-up animals runnin through plains or lyin down to sleep. Angels and demons sittin together on boulders and green mountains. More angels watchin it all from silver clouds. Planets and stars I'm sure weren't real outside of Lefty's head.

It all told one big story that left you to decide what it was.

It was colorful, man. Imaginative. Original. *Detailed.*

And he'd done almost all of it down in the dark.

As I said, I didn't know or even meet Lefty until high school. I'll explain why that was later. No one called him Lefty then—the reason for it hadn't happened yet. He was still just Mel Savage. It was that sophomore year at Colton Central, which started early September 1963. Just a little before the Beatles took over and the Kennedys had their bad day in Dallas.

We were in the same fourth-period beginner's English Composition class. I still remember the teacher, Mr. Lewis. He's the one who came right out and told me I couldn't write. He particularly hated how I tended to drop letters from words. I of course then had to tell im he was full of shit, even though the bastard was right.

Lewis gave me three detentions for that "lack of respect," which was too bad for him, because I was expectin a whole lot more.

About the only thing I could hang my hat on in English Comp was that I wasn't the worst writer in the class. That was Lefty's title belt. And if you can believe it, Lewis like an ass lick sat dunces number one and two next to each other at the back of the room. Later on, we naturally pissed him off more than once. A few times we thought he might even shoot straight from his FBI suit like a bottle rocket. Nothin left on the floor but a pressed white shirt and black shoes, socks, pants, belt, tie, coat, and quarter-inch haircut.

Even though Lefty and me sat side by side, we didn't talk at first. He didn't speak up in class, neither. He mostly just sat quiet, to himself, lookin stupid but still big and scary in that simple way of his. He was *always* drawin in his notebook. He also looked up just enough so it seemed like he might be payin attention to whatever scrotum-head was talkin about.

The thing I had to get used to with Lefty at first was his size. At sixteen, he was already six-foot-two and at least two hundred pounds. It wasn't a soft and mushy two hundred, neither. He had wide shoulders, big arms, thick legs, and big hands, like bear paws.

I don't know where he got it, because his dad wasn't but five-nine, maybe a buck-sixty when he wasn't full of booze. His mom wasn't no Amazon either. And it's not like his parents fed him all that well—or at least his dad aimed not to. I'm sure Mrs. Savage slipped him what extra she could at the risk of a punch in the eye.

Lefty had to have had a Jolly Green Giant or two somewhere down the fucked-up family line. I also learned later on that he came up with ways to make himself stronger during all of those dark and lonely hours in the basement.

The first time me and Lefty had an actual conversation was around the last week of that September. It was across the street from the main parkin lot at the back of the school. That's where the burn-outs like me hung out at lunch and sometimes durin classes too. The teachers knew we were there and probably what we were doin. Of course they didn't like it. They also couldn't do shit, because it wasn't school property. They could bark and holler and maybe even come over, but so what. Worst they might do is call the cops. We got pretty good at breakin up as soon as we spotted a cruiser.

On the day that me and Lefty first really talked, I was out there on our corner with my buddies Tommy James and Rich Redoux.

We were shootin the shit and wonderin if we should even go back to class. Tommy looked across the street and back-handed me on the shoulder. Lefty was lumberin toward us.

He walked right up and stood there, lookin each of us over. I half-expected somethin weird out of him, especially when he didn't say nothin at first. Then he opened his mouth, and I'll never forget what he said:

"Boob says, got a cigarette?"

Me and Tommy looked at each other and almost cracked up.

"Come again?" I said.

Lefty's face was dead serious.

"Boob says, got a cigarette?"

I smiled at him, waitin for him to let me in on the joke.

"You want a smoke?" I said.

He nodded.

I pulled out my pack and gave him one. He popped it in the corner of his mouth.

"Boob says, got a light?" he said.

303

Me and Tommy glanced at each other again. I still didn't know what to make of it. I elbowed him and shrugged. He flipped open his Zippo.

Lefty leaned into it, puffed, and drew back his head in that slow and patient way of his. He inhaled real deep, held it, and blew it in a jet away from us.

"Boob says, thank you," he said.

Me and Tommy and Rich all stood there for maybe half a minute or so, and then we started talkin again. We were still tryin to get used to Lefty just standin there, watchin us, uninvited. You know the feeling. He was quiet—almost too quiet, like there was a whole lot of shit movin around far beneath the surface. He was just smokin his cigarette, lookin around. Checkin out the trees, the birds, the cars, his shoes, my shoes. The cigarette ash on the ground, the shapes of the clouds in the sky. Pretty much everything.

As I've suggested, if you'd seen him for yourself, you'd have thought he was as smart as raw steak. But out there on the corner that day, I had the idea there was a whole secret universe inside of him. One that only he could see. Lookin at Lefty that day made me think of those words about still waters, and how they run deep.

At least he was still most of the time. When he wasn't, it was the worst kind of opposite. I figured that out fast on that same September afternoon.

Most students ate their lunch in the cafeteria. A few walked off campus for a Coke and a sandwich. Others had cars that their parents had paid for. I refer mainly to the jockasses and the cheerleaders they got to feel up. A lot of em lived in the nicer neighborhoods on the far north and west sides of Colton. The ones with the professional breadwinners—bankers, company managers, department heads, dealership owners, salesmen breakin five figures.

Those of us from the south and east sides belonged to the masons and mechanics. The machinists and plumbers and painters and landscapers. The World War II veterans fightin the murder they couldn't forget with booze they couldn't give up. If *we* drove our own wheels, it was because we worked two jobs outside of school. Either that, or we made the most of the jalopies that our dads gave us after buyin another car one level up on the piece-of-shit scale.

Lefty was one of us. He showed us all how blue his blood ran that day we were out on our corner.

A white Chevy Corvair convertible full of jockasses peeled into the lot across the street. I knew that car pretty well. It was always parked at the Shake Shack about a mile from school.

They piled out, laughin and shovin and wrestlin and dickin around like they usually did. At the same time, this short little Mexican girl was crossin the lot with a couple of textbooks hugged close to her chest. She was just lookin down, shufflin along, mindin her own business. I still see her clearly in my mind, even after all of these years. Straight hair down to her shoulders. Pink sweater with buttons. White shirt buttoned up to the chin. Tan skirt that came halfway between her ankles and knees. White tennis shoes.

One of the jacks—as I also liked to call em—saw her and said somethin. She kept walkin, so he said it again.

When she reached the sidewalk, the jack, Buck Thompson, ran over and blocked her way. Buck was a senior and the starting tight end. She tried to move around him, but he wouldn't have it. He stayed in front of her wherever she went.

Next, Bob Mulligan—another senior, inside linebacker—came up from behind so they made themselves a Mexican sandwich.

We're all watchin the action now. Lefty draws deep on his cigarette, squints, and gets real, *real* quiet.

The girl's still tryin to go around or to a side to get away. But they're not gonna let her. None of it makes any sense to me. Why bother? They all got girlfriends and futures. The white-boy school administration loves them too. Most of them are gonna go on to places like Notre Dame or IU-Bloomington or even DePauw down in Greencastle. These dudes have no reason to act like dicks and mess with a Mexican chick other than that they're just too fuckin bored with bein privileged.

The other two jacks, Tom Sodek (junior, fullback) and Phil Barrelli (senior, wide out), get close but don't do nothin yet. They're just laughin in that way of knowin they won't be on the hook for most of the things they do in their lives.

Bob grabs the girl's ass. She drops her books and swipes backward at his hands. I'm pretty sure she's cryin.

"*Déjame sola!*" she says—which probably means piss off or somethin like it.

"Wassa matter?" he says. "Don't like white meat on your taco?"

Rich elbows me.

Lefty squints harder, takes one more drag on his cigarette, and pitches it to the ground. He slides off his jacket and hands it to me.

"Boob says, hold this, please," he says.

I do.

He looks both ways and then crosses the street, rollin up his sleeves while he walks.

Rich elbows me again. I nod. We barely know Lefty yet, but we *are* sure we like him better than the bench-press boys. We'll back him up fast if he needs it. Even if it means we get hit back hard and then suspended.

Lefty's fingers are twitchin. His arms are tensin up. He's built but not athletic—not like the jacks. But he's got that *think hard before you scrap with me* look about him, even at sixteen years old.

Tom and Phil see Lefty comin their way. Tom, who's closer to Bob, bumps Bob on the shoulder. Bob ignores him at first because he's still havin fun with the girl, but then he too sees the guided missile closin in. He nods at Buck, who leaves the girl to square up with Lefty.

Lefty reaches Buck and stops.

"Got a problem, friend?" Buck says.

The other three come close behind him.

"Boob says, leave the girl alone," Lefty says.

Buck spreads his shoulders. His eyes go dark and his face puckers up.

"The hell with you," he says right at Lefty's face, and I'd bet a new pack of Winstons that his breath smells like burgers, onions, and Peppermint Certs.

Lefty don't flinch.

"Boob says, let the girl be on her way. She ain't done nothin to you."

Buck grins and looks back at his buddies.

"Are you for real?" he says. A pebble of spit hits Lefty under the eye. "Anyone told you you talk like a retard?"

The other three chuckle and cross their arms over their chests.

What happens next is so fast I would of missed it if I hadn't been watchin so close. Lefty's right hand shoots up and out like a beam from a flashlight.

He hits Buck in the jaw with a *smack!* we can hear from across the street. Buck stumbles back.

When he shakes the stars and figures out what's goin on, his face gets even meaner. He lunges like Lefty's holdin a football.

Lefty catches Buck and throws him with a quick twist to the side. Lefty's face goes red, his eyes go wide, and his body looks like it's pumped with a few thousand volts. He tags Tom Sodek with a right and follows it with a left-handed haymaker that busts Bob Mulligan's lip.

Barrelli swings and catches Lefty flush in the temple. Lefty's way too crazy to care. He spins around and I hear a *whack-whack-whack-whack!* Barrelli's blood splashes Lefty's shirt, and then Barrelli drops.

The other three leap all over Lefty, get him to the ground. Now it's *their* turn to pound on him good.

I fold Lefty's jacket, set it on the grass, and nod at Tommy and Rich. We start headin to the parkin lot.

Two teachers bolt out from the school. Their black ties are floppin around and their open sport coats are flappin like wings. Their black shoes go *clack! clack! clack!* on the sidewalk.

It's Mr. Ray (biology) and Mr. Sanborn (algebra). Both of em are supervisors durin lunch.

Mr. Ray pulls Buck off of Lefty and grabs Tom by the shirt. Tom's still throwin punches but then he lets up. Sanborn grabs Mulligan with both hands and yanks him off as well.

"What's going on here?" Mr. Ray says.

I've almost forgotten about the Mexican girl. She's still there, watchin from the grass by the sidewalk that leads into the school. She's picked up her books and is holdin em close to her chest again.

Buck tries to get away from Mr. Ray so he can take another charge at Lefty. Ray holds im back.

"Whoa, whoa!" Mr. Ray says. "Knock it off! What's going on here?"

"Burn-out loser just came over and picked a fight!" Buck says, pointin at Lefty around Mr. Ray, as if Lefty's lucky Mr. Ray's in the way.

Mr. Ray keeps one hand on Buck's chest and looks back at Lefty, who's on his feet again. He's a little scuffed up, but he don't look too bad. He might even be ready for another round.

Sanborn turns on him.

"Did you start a fight with these boys?" he says.

Lefty only looks at him. He hooks his thumbs in the pockets of his jeans. His shoulders relax. He ain't even breathin that hard.

"You come with me," Sanborn says. He steps forward and takes Lefty by the arm.

Sanborn thinks they're already movin but gets jerked back when Lefty don't budge.

Lefty looked at the Mexican girl. She looked back at him.

Sanborn pulled on Lefty's arm again—harder this time.

Lefty let Sanborn lead him away.

Mr. Ray looked at each of the jockasses. Then he said:

"You boys mind yourselves now."

They all nodded at him. A couple said, "Thanks, Mr. Ray."

He went back into the school. The Mexican girl followed him in.

The dicksticks all hung out a little longer, talkin, actin a little bit fidgety. None of em looked at each other for long. I myself believe they all knew what none of em would come out and say. A sophomore burn-out loser had just given em all a good fight.

The administration kicked Lefty out of school for a week.

From that day forward, I knew Lefty would fit in with us fine. If he so chose it, that was.

He'd fit in with us at school, and *especially* outside of it.

Dennis Savage. Now there's a study for the ages if ever there was one.

His dad was angry and drunk and violent and always out of a job. His mom was a sweet lady but also the worst kind of co-dependent. His younger brother was a quiet, lonely, dumb-lookin dreamer his dad wished had never been born.

His house was a dark, dreary, smelly old place in a rougher part of the south side of town. Painted white, covered with soot. Yard full of weeds and litter and dirt patches. Black and rusty '47 Ford Super Deluxe up on blocks. Cats, rats, and raccoons always sniffin around.

And despite all of that, Dennis was the *shit*. At least at school and inside the limits of Colton, Indiana, population 16,742 accordin to the sign out on Route 36 headin south into town from Hensley.

Clean cut. Good lookin. Smart. Funny. *Real* good at sports, especially football. He was Colton Central's starting tailback. Ran for near 1,500 yards and scored 14 TDs his senior year, the year I got to know Lefty.

Dennis was the center of attention in the classrooms and hallways and at the cool parties on weekends. He hung out strictly with the most popular types.

He steered clear of his brother and anythin else that might let people in on the misery he came from. You wouldn't even know that him and Lefty was brothers unless somebody shook you and told you, and even then you might not believe it. They had no family resemblance. Their personalities were nowhere near the same, and they never spoke but for a few cold and fast words at home. I also know that Dennis never brought his buddies or especially his poontang anywhere close to the house.

Not that Lefty wanted it that way. As me and him became better friends, I came to believe that deep down he loved his older brother, and sometimes looked up to him too. He wished they could at least try to get along better.

It's not even that Dennis was mean to him, or looked down on him—that would all show up later on. In high school, he just saw . . . past him. As if he wasn't there. Lefty was what you'd call an "inconvenient truth" Dennis had to avoid lest it mess his personal style. He couldn't *afford* to like his brother, at least not out loud or in public.

Yet for as well as he managed to hide from his life's shittier details, Dennis was still an apple from an old and twisted tree. And you know what they say about how far the fruit will roll. His dad's soul was as nicked and gouged as the top of a desk in a fourth-grade classroom. And as I've said, even though Mrs. Savage had her moments to be loving and kind, she was worthless overall. Aware of it or not, she let her husband pack her boys' bags with heavy issues they'd always have to carry.

The good Lord at least gave Lefty some tools to deal with his pain. He really could have been a good neighbor if he'd been treated and raised a different way.

Dennis, I'm not so sure about. Even in high school, he had that what-you-see-ain't-what-you-get way about him. Northern Indiana's law-enforcement community will tell you that I'm not to be trusted on a lot of things, but trust me on this one. I've spent my share of time in correctional facilities, which means I got to know an all-star cast of con-men. The really good ones—the ones who could sell your mom's own apple-pie recipe back to her for a grand—come in different shapes and sizes, and what they want is all over the map, but most share one thing in common. Their minds are computers, and even less human at that.

I saw that in Dennis. He had that *face*. The one that said I know you're willin to risk gettin screwed over later if I win your trust right now.

He could talk hard with the guys and soft with the girls. But he laughed without a belly behind it. He also walked like someone was workin the switches and levers behind the machine.

Most of all, it was his eyes, man. You know what those gates swing open to. He looked at you long enough so you thought that he meant it and short enough so you couldn't see all the way in.

My own dad, who's been gone for a while now, once said the Good Book talked of me and you as glasses to be filled. How we fill that glass determines our character. I've still never read that book, but I heard the sense in what he was sayin, even back then. He was a drunk like Lefty's dad, but I do believe my father spoke as well as he could for the other Father. We're *all* empty somehow, and emptiness is pain, because it leaves us no choice but to look into ourselves and face what should be there but ain't.

Then there are those like Dennis, whose glass was worse than empty. That glass with no bottom can't ever be filled, neither. Plus, when you're that way, you make *other* people fill it for you. You do that by stealin what they're willing to give. Their love. Their trust. Their patience or compassion. Their *understanding*. By keepin the focus on you and your sorry-ass ego, you make sure the glass don't go entirely dry.

I don't remember too much of what I learned before droppin out after sophomore year. I *do* recall one thing from Mr. Sawyer's astronomy class. I think it stuck because it explained a lot of people I'd have to keep an eye on in my life. People like Dennis.

It was about black holes in the universe. Sawyer said black holes are these places in space with this thing called an "event horizon." If you fall past the event horizon, the gravity gets so goddamn intense that nothin can escape it. It even swallows light, which is why you can't see the middle of the black hole unless it's actin with or bumpin into stuff outside the event horizon, like gas from other stars, which is what you see when that swirly spiral thing starts movin all around it.

Sawyer said that on the subject of black holes in space, Einstein wrote that when enough mass gets packed into a small enough area—sort of like your ten shit pounds in a five-pound bag—all of space around it gets seriously bent out of shape and warps toward the center. *Everything falls in.*

So there you have it. Dennis was a glass with no bottom that became a black hole in Colton. He came off of the line ready to damage in wily ways. His mom and dad helped twist the parts that made him. They gave birth to the monster, fed it, raised it, and tightened the neck bolts before it left to leave skid marks on society.

He started fights, cheated on girls, told lies without a twitch or a blink. He got the attention he wanted.

I'm tellin you all of this because to appreciate Lefty's tragedy, you have to know his brother too. Beyond bein about me and you and the color of our heads, this here story's about brothers, and how they can be so different in spite of their blood. He'd never come out and say it, but Dennis admired Lefty in his own ridiculous way. Dennis was selfish but not stupid. He knew his brother had a gift. He also knew Lefty had more stacked up against him than Dennis ever would. Where life did nothing but give Dennis things to take, it made Lefty dig down to find out what he might give.

Dennis saw in Lefty what he could and would never have. He *had* to know that Lefty was a better person. At least I think so. And that would have made it harder for him to look in the mirror when he was all alone and not on stage.

And that, I believe in my heart, is why him and his brother would wind up dead on the very same day.

*T*he five days of Lefty's suspension went by faster than an Indy rear-engine stock block Buick V-8. Probably because I spent three of those five English classes gettin high with Rich and Tommy in Tommy's peesa shit 1950 Chevy panel truck. Tommy was the only one of us with a license *and* wheels. He was able to buy the truck cheap with what he earned workin nights and weekend days at Roger Stukey's scrap-metal yard. He turned seventeen the first week of October, makin him the oldest sophomore. He was held back his freshman year for doin only about 20 percent of his homework.

Me and Rich were sixteen. His birthday was late August and I'd just turned in September. Unlike Tommy, we didn't work much. We didn't have much legitimate money past what we picked up at a small job here or there.

So we made up for it by getting goddamn good at stealin.

Each unexcused absence while Lefty was out earned us each two detentions for a total of six. Of course that couldn't color piss, because throwin detentions at us was like addin fifty bucks to the national debt. Man, I *liked* my time in detention. It allowed me to dwell upon life's greater issues, like poontang. I got to know more than a few naughty girls who were also regularly assigned the forty-five after-school minutes in Dick Chase's Spanish classroom starting at 2:30 p.m. I never did thank the administration for getting me laid so many times.

On the day that Lefty got back, first week of October, he was already in his chair when I walked into English Comp. He looked like he might have a few more marks on his face than I remembered, but I wasn't gonna ask. He stopped doodlin in his notebook as soon as I turned into the aisle. He nodded at me, and I nodded back. It was like we'd been pals for a while.

I parked myself next to him and just looked forward at first. Lewis wasn't in the room yet.

"How'd it go?" I said after a minute or so.

He just kept drawin. I glanced sideways to see what all the pencil-scratchin was about.

It was the Mexican girl he'd got himself kicked out for. And damn if that drawin wasn't as good as a photograph. Every line in her face. Every lock of her hair. Even the fuzz and the lint on her sweater.

"Boob says, how'd what go?" he said, close to a minute later.

I turned a little and looked at him.

"Your suspension," I said.

He kept a straight face and stayed busy with his drawin.

"Boob says, I like it better here than at home," he said.

Lewis came into the classroom. As usual, he walked like he had a javelin goin from his ass to the back of his head. I would have loved to see him try to dance. Some people say how you dance is a sign of how you are in the sack. A lot of professional white men have to be really lousy lays. Either that, or their wives don't know any better. Especially wives married to teachers that dress like they're from the FBI.

Lewis set his black briefcase—what other color would it be?—on his desk, clicked the latches, and opened it. He removed a stack of papers and his copy of the paperback book the papers were supposed to be about. I myself didn't know what the book was about. Guess for yourself whether or not I wrote the essay too.

He scooped up the essays and started handin em back with their grades on em. Took him close to five minutes to do it, just as you might expect from a bureaucrat workin on the taxpayer dollar. Although, come to think of it, I should probably mind what I say, because the taxpayers have spent a lot on me too through the years.

Lewis put Lefty's essay face down on top of Lefty's notebook, which he'd already closed. Lefty turned it over, and I looked.

He got a B-. Not bad. At least for him it wasn't.

Of course when Lewis made his way back to the front of the class he stared at me for a second. I do believe I was the only one who didn't get a grade on the assignment. Oh well. Send me to hell for it.

"Clearly most of you *did* read the book," Lewis said. He crossed his hands behind his back and then came down my aisle again. He stopped at Lefty.

"Mr. Savage," he said. Lefty looked up and then away from him. "While you do not write particularly well, you did express one of the more meaningful insights about personal resistance to government control in Orwell's *1984*. Would you care to share that view with the class?"

Lefty kept lookin forward. His hand was flat on his essay with the circled red grade.

"Mr. Savage?" Lewis said.

Lefty sat straight and looked at Lewis.

"Boob says, no matter what the government gives to or takes away from the people, it can't ever own us as long as we love something more than we love it, or any institution for that matter."

My eyebrows went up.

A few of the other kids giggled. Lewis gave Lefty a funny look too.

"Very good, Melvin," he said. "Please continue."

Lefty stared into space for a second.

"Boob says, the government of Oceania could not own Winston's soul until it figured out what he was most afraid of. Once they knew what that was, they used it to make him swear off his feelings for Julia. She was the love in his heart that kept him from total loyalty to Big Brother. Boob says, once they could scare and intimidate him enough to make him give up even secret love, that's when they knew they could pack up and never worry about him again."

Lefty folded his hands on his desk. He looked down, and then up.

"Boob says, nothing can own or destroy or betray us as long as we have even just one thing that's beautiful inside of us, no matter how powerful the enemy is."

A few more snickers around the room.

"Very good, Melvin," Lewis said. "Well stated." He still wasn't sure if he should laugh or get angry. "But I'm also going to have to ask you to refrain from that kind of language in class."

Lefty looked down, looked up, and shrugged.

"Do you understand me, Melvin?" Lewis said.

Lefty shrugged again and nodded.

"Then why don't you continue with your summary," Lewis said. "There's much more to it."

Lefty paused.

"Boob says . . ."

Lewis came closer to his desk until he was loomin right over im.

"I asked you not to use that language!"

Lefty scratched his face.

"Boob says, what did I say that was wrong?"

Lewis's face pinched and turned a little red. Now he *was* pissed off.

"Say it one more time," he said.

Lefty glanced at me and then back at Lewis. I honestly believe he didn't know what the hell Lewis was so upset about.

"Boob says, say what?"

Lewis turned darker red. He pointed down at Lefty's face with his FBI finger.

"That does it!" he said. "To the principal's office you go!"

More giggles and snickers.

Now Lefty's face went red, but it was more because he felt like he was the one bein left out of the joke.

"Boob says, what did I do?"

Lewis went even darker red. I loved it. It made his pale-white ass-face look like a beet, or a wine stain.

He grabbed Lefty's arm and yanked it to lift Lefty out of his chair, but Lefty didn't move. He was too big and strong.

I saw a bead of sweat on Lewis's temple. His nose scrunched up. He pulled on Lefty's arm again. Lefty pulled his arm away—hard. I don't think Lewis had any idea what was comin. Not like I did.

"Boob says, you better not touch me again."

Lewis just stared down at him. I do believe that *he* believed his black suit and crew cut were supposed to have super powers that got kids out of their chairs.

Usually, those things were enough. But it all meant shit to Lefty.

I just kept on likin im more.

Lewis took one step back.

"Up, and to the principal's office," he said. This time, his voice didn't sound quite so official.

Lefty looked at him a little bit longer, just for good measure. He glanced at me. And funny, because in that one second, I knew exactly what he was thinkin, and what we were gonna do.

I nodded at him.

He slid his notebook and essay from the desk and stood up. He moved forward, but Lewis was still in the way. Lewis looked him up and down with that face that says "you're a punk." I was kinda hopin he might push Lefty's red button right there.

Instead, he stepped to the side and let Lefty go past im. We all watched Lefty leave. After he was gone, Lewis went back to the front of the room and kept talkin about Eurasia and Oceania and Newspeak and what have you.

I didn't hear a word. I was too busy thinkin about Lefty and the subject of payback.

*T*hree detentions. That's what Lefty got for rubbin Lewis the wrong way on his first day back from suspension. *Insubordination,* they called it.

And so there we were. Me, Rich, Tommy, and Lefty, killin time in Dick Chase's Spanish classroom at 2:30 p.m. on that very same day.

We were up and out as soon as the hand hit 3:15. Went straight to our corner for a couple of smokes. I'd already filled in Rich and Tommy about the day's events, so they knew somethin fun was up. It was just a matter of what it would be.

Rich and Tommy thought Lewis was a dick just like me and Lefty did. But they were still also warmin up to Lefty. To them, he was way too new to be trusted and, truth be told, a little bit weird. They hadn't passed many words with him. But they trusted me, and *I* was cool with Lefty.

"What do you think?" I said, drawin deep on my Winston. "Should we do his tires?"

I blew out and flicked a few ashes.

"Sugar and sand in his gas tank? Paint his windows? Cut his telephone wires? Dog shit in his mailbox?"

I dragged and flicked more ashes.

"Change the lock on the door to his classroom?"

Tommy lifted the collar on his black leather jacket and stuck a hand in his jeans pocket. The air in Colton was cooler that early October. Had a little more snap.

"Fuck it," he said. "We ring his doorbell around midnight. When he comes out, he gets the baseball bats."

I thought it over.

"Not bad," I said. "Not bad. Dangerous though. Could wind up bringin the heat."

I looked at Lefty, who'd been dead quiet.

"What do you think, Mel?" I said. "This is your gig. What do *you* say we do?"

Lefty looked at me, and then at empty space somewhere over my shoulder.

He drew on his cig, blew out, and thought a little longer.

"Boob says, I know a way to hit him even harder."

Rich and Tommy looked at each other and then at me. They still didn't know what to make of how he talked. I shook my head real quick and waved them off.

"What's that, Mel?" I said. "What you got in mind?"

"Boob says, he keeps his bottom desk drawer locked," he said.

"How do you know?" I said.

"Boob says, because I was the first one in there one day and I checked it out."

He dragged, blew out, and squinted at me through the smoke.

"Boob says, I think it might be fun to find out why he locks it."

I looked at him a second longer and then at Rich and Tommy.

"Works for me," I said. "How we get in?"

"Boob says, the lock on one of the windows to the janitors' station is busted. It'll slide right up if we mess with it right. We can crawl in, and there's a key ring on a wall hook by the head janitor's desk. I'll bet we find a key that gets us into Lewis's room."

I thought about it.

I was also tryin to get past how come he knew all of that and I didn't. It seemed like somethin that should have already been in my head.

Man, there was a lot we could do with it.

An awful lot.

"Let's do it," I said.

Wasn't a breathin body in sight when we got to Colton Central in Tommy's panel truck at about 10:30 p.m. Saw just a few empty cars parked here and there.

We parked about two blocks down and made our way back by stickin as well as we could to the shadows. We'd also all dressed in dark colors so not to attract the late-evening stroller or Colton black-and-white roller with a siren on top. Wore gloves too, because while they didn't have the high-tech forensic shit then, they could and did dust for fingerprints.

The janitors' station was garden level at the back of the school, makin it half above the ground and half under it. If you got down on the grass and looked through the windows, you could see all the desks and lockers and cabinets.

Lefty showed us which window was busted. It was open in less than a minute.

I stuck my head in. There was a desk about three feet down we could land on. I gave the thumbs up and then wiggled feet first through the window, which was about four feet wide and two feet high.

I dropped to the desk, makin a boot print on a paper and knockin the phone off the hook. I put the phone back in the cradle once I reached the floor.

Up behind me, Tommy was already through. His fat-booted feet crashed on the same sorry paper. Rich followed Tommy, and Lefty came down last.

Lefty went straight for the keys. Me, Rich, and Tommy made quick business of openin drawers and checkin out desktops for anything of immediate value, mainly legal tender printed in green. By the time Lefty dangled the key chain, I'd already helped myself to five or so bucks in loose singles and pocket change, plus a decent watch I was sure I could sell. Rich scored two packs of cigarettes and—funny shit—a full metal whiskey flask with the Colton Central logo on it. Tommy found a few dollars and a titty mag, which he rolled into a tight tube and stuck in his back pocket.

We followed Lefty into the hallway and took a right toward the staircase at the end. About halfway down, I heard water drillin metal. I turned around, and wouldn't you know it, Rich was takin a piss on somebody's locker. Specks of spray were bouncin from the force of the stream.

"Aw, for Christ's sake, will you come on?" I said.

He looked at me sideways and smiled.

"I'm pretty sure this here's Tom Sodek's locker," he said. "Or at least, it's close enough."

He finished his business, zipped up, and jogged to catch the rest of us. We were already through the door at the end of the hall and on our way up the stairs.

Up on the first floor, the main floor, we went straight to Lewis's classroom, which was close to the stairway. Lefty tried about fifteen keys of what had to be fifty before one turned the lock. He opened the door, and the four of us walked right in.

First we kicked and turned over most of the desks and threw a few chairs. Tommy grabbed a piece of chalk and wrote LEWIS SUCKS FAT DICK real big on the blackboard.

Lefty went to the bottom drawer of Lewis's desk and started workin on the lock with a paperclip. I myself never had much luck with paperclips on locks. You'd have thought Lefty did it for a livin. The lock opened up for him like a loaded freshman female with a senior date on prom night, and Lewis's private stash looked Lefty right in the face.

I walked over to him.

"Boob says, check this shit out," he said.

He took off his gloves, reached into the drawer, and pulled out a pair of panties. Red silk.

"Jesus H.," I said. "Whose are those?"

Lefty put them on Lewis's desk and kept diggin in the drawer. He found a stack of maybe twenty instant photographs. I slipped off one of my gloves and flicked open my Zippo so we could see em better. All we had besides that was the moon through the windows.

"Well, would you take a look at that," I said, leanin closer to the top picture.

It was one hell of a Polaroid moment in color, which was new that year.

In the picture, Lewis was wearin a pink bra and pink panties. Both lace. His eyes were up, his chin was down, and his hands were on his hips like he was Betty Boop or some shit. He was wearin Betty Boop make-up too. And damn, was he a hairy son of a bitch without his FBI suit.

"Whachoo got?" Tommy said, steppin around by me and Lefty. Rich followed close behind.

They both checked out the picture. I looked back with a big and goofy smile.

"Is that *Lewis?*" Tommy said.

"Shore is," I said. "Let's see what else we got, Mel."

He reached into his coat for a smoke and leaned toward me without lookin. I lit him up with my lighter.

He puffed to get it goin and then slid the top photo to the back of the stack. I closed the Zippo. We'd look at the rest of the pictures by moonlight.

My heart was racin. You see, it wasn't just Lewis in those pictures. The first five or so were of him in different poses—some frontal, some with his hairy white ass to the camera—but the next few after those were of another dude. Probably the guy who was takin the pictures of Lewis. Except this other dude wasn't in his underwear like Lewis was. He was wearin a nice white blouse and a red skirt. His make-up was neat and careful too, not like Lewis's Betty Boop mask.

"I can't believe this shit," Rich said.

Me neither. And why would Lewis keep them in his desk at *school?* Did he think his drawer was the door to the fuckin Federal Reserve Bank or somethin?

If he kept stuff like this at school, what would we find in his *house?*

"I say we keep em," I said. "That'll give im a jolt in the morning."

"We can tape 'em up on lockers," Tommy said. "Or in the cafeteria, or right outside the principal's office, or . . ."

"Boob says, no," Lefty said in that low and even way of his. The way he spoke, you'd never imagine he had so much rage in a cage that was ready to blow—unless of course you saw it for yourself like I did, includin the very next day.

"What do you mean, Mel?" I said. "You got a better idea?"

Lefty drew on his cigarette and ashed in Lewis's drawer.

"Boob says, we leave the stack and take just a few," he said. "That'll spook him even better. When he figures out the drawer ain't locked, the first thing he'll shit over is the pictures. When he sees they're still in there, he'll think at first he's okay. But when he looks through them later, and it hits him that they ain't all there, he'll need a goddamn ambulance."

Me and Rich and Tommy all looked at each other.

Rich shrugged. So did I.

"Works for me," Tommy said.

"I like it," I said. "Gives us more time to play with his head."

I put my Zippo back in my coat pocket.

Lefty popped his smoke back into his mouth and sorted through the pictures again. He kept five—three of Lewis and two of his pretty buddy. He put the rest back into the drawer.

"What else he got in there?" Rich said.

Lefty dug in and moved a few things around.

"Boob says, papers, stapler, some mail, black leather gloves, breath mints, candy tin . . ."

He pulled out the tin and took off the lid.

Me and Tommy leaned closer.

No candy or breath mints in this bitch. Just five-dollar bills, folded in half.

"Count it up, Mel," I said.

Cigarette still danglin from his mouth, he flipped through the notes.

"Boob says, forty bucks," he said.

Me, Rich, and Tommy looked at each other and smiled.

"So, ten bucks each," I said.

I clapped him on the shoulder.

His head snapped toward my hand like I'd clamped live cables to his ears. I pulled it back by reflex so fast it almost swung behind me.

"I say we take the panties too," Rich said. "For the flagpole out front."

All of us cackled.

"Boob says, sounds like a pretty cool idea."

He swiped the panties off the desk and tossed em at Rich. Rich caught em with both hands at his belly.

"Alright then," I said. "Let's head out."

Lefty ground out his cigarette in Lewis's drawer and then slipped the butt in his coat pocket. He handed me the cash, put the lid back on the tin, and set it back where he'd found it. He closed the drawer and stood up.

Me, Rich, and Tommy turned toward the door.

Out in the hallway, we realized Lefty wasn't with us. I went back to take a look.

And when I saw what was up, I laughed so hard my asshole hurt. I even fell down in the doorway.

Rich and Tommy ran over.

"What's so funn . . . ," Tommy said, and then he saw it too.

Pants around his ankles, shirt and coat hiked up, face all tight and pinched, Lefty was droppin a deuce right onto Lewis's chair.

Tommy hit the floor right behind me and howled even louder than I did. Rich bent over with his hands on his knees and his back heavin up and down.

Lefty wiped himself with a paper from the desktop and then tossed it on the floor. He put his gloves back on and came toward us.

Me, Rich, and Tommy were still blockin the doorway. My face had tears on it.

"Aw, man," I said, pushin myself back up. "That was beautiful. Just beautiful."

We all went back into the hallway. Lefty closed the door and locked it with the key from the ring.

We made our way back down the stairs and through the lower-level hall to the janitors' station. Lefty put the key ring back on the hook, and then we each climbed out through the window. Lefty was last, so I reached in and grabbed a hard hold of his hand. I pulled while he slid up and out.

After he closed the window, the four of us jogged toward the front of the school. A few cars drove past out on the main road. Each time, we dropped flat to the ground so not to be seen.

When we reached the flagpole, Tommy lowered the flag, which of course was lit from below, put the panties on the snap hook, and then raised it back up.

We hauled back to Tommy's truck. It was tough to run because we were laughin so hard.

We were *still* laughin after we drove away—except for Lefty. He just sat there, mellow and quiet, thinkin.

I was already lookin forward to a good night's sleep. I even hoped I might dream about Lewis cleanin the deuce from his chair while we spent his forty bucks.

I glanced at Lefty again. His face was calm, but there was also something real serious in it.

Maybe he knew his dreams would be different from mine that night. Or maybe he wouldn't dream at all, or sleep. Maybe his dad would be up, drunk, waitin for Lefty to get home so he could throw a few of the punches that'd make him feel better.

Or, maybe, just maybe, Lefty, in that weird, wise way of his, already knew that he'd be done at Colton Central High School in less than twenty-four hours.

*T*he crap was already fresh on the fan bright and early the followin morning. Two Colton cruisers were parked right out front. When me and Tommy walked into the school, you could feel the buzz of *somethin's up*. Everyone was talkin and whisperin and lookin around.

We saw a cop with a couple of teachers. A few freshmen were tryin to listen.

"Parker!"

Rich was comin our way from up ahead.

"You guys gotta see this," he said when he reached us. His eyes were all lit up.

I looked around for Lefty but didn't see any sign.

"Lewis's room?" I said.

Rich smiled and nodded.

I nodded too. We followed him until we got to the four doors that let on to another hallway runnin left or right. We turned left toward the action.

At first, too many people were gathered around Lewis's room for us to see it. We got a little closer and then bumped our way to the front. Two cops were talkin to Lewis and Dr. Streetum, our principal, right outside the door. People referred to him as doctor, and he liked it. He had a Ph.D. in one thing or another. Education, I think. Or maybe it was Bureaucratic Bullshit. He reminded me of that dude who got to bone Marilyn Monroe even though all he did was write plays.

Streetum looked like he was jawin the most. Lewis looked like he was really pissed off. His face was red and his mouth was tight and turned in. His arms were real stiff too.

I pushed and shoved to get a better look into the room. A couple of janitors were puttin the last of the desks and chairs back into their rows. Lewis's chair was gone, surely bein cleaned of the paperweight that Lefty'd baked just for him with his ass.

The clock high on the wall of the hall said 7:22 a.m. That gave me three minutes to get to my class on floor number two.

I elbowed Rich and glanced at Tommy.

"I'm off," I said. "Catch you boys at lunch."

I cruised to the same stairs we'd used the night before and made it to Howard Ephraim's Biology class with at least a minute to spare.

Ephraim. Another crew-cut American patriot with a chip on his shoulder and a corn cob crammed up his ass. He was a marine who'd served in Korea. He fuckin *loved* to remind us we were spoiled pussies who couldn't appreciate the freedom he'd fought so hard to provide. I guess he preferred not to notice what was pickin up in a booger-shaped country called Vietnam around that time. But I'm sure it shut his mouth soon enough. I can still name the boys from Colton who died while fightin the NVA and the Cong.

Besides a frog sliced open, about the only thing of interest to me durin that first period was the Colton cop who showed up at the door. He removed a few students—myself not included—to ask a few questions out in the hallway.

Next two classes were Shop and Health. Pretty low key other than a few whispers about the Lewis Incident. I didn't hear my name among any of it, but I did hear Lefty's. Word about his run-in with Lewis the day before had been makin its rounds. He had to be a reasonable suspect.

I couldn't wait until period four. The suspense was freakin killin me.

I even got to Lewis's room with minutes to spare.

Lefty was already there. I smiled like a cartoon cat. He nodded and kept a straight face, but I knew he was grinnin a little inside.

Lewis, I noticed, was *not* there yet. Also, by then you'd never have guessed we'd worked the place over just the night before. They'd cleaned the place up pretty good.

The bell rang. I glanced at Lefty. He was sketchin again. It was another picture of the Mexican girl. Even though he hadn't seen her in a bit, his latest work was even better than the last one I'd seen. It was like she was always posin for him live in his head.

The rest of the kids in the class were kinda quiet.

Five more minutes went by. And then, as if he was bein chased by the Russians, Lewis flew into the room and swung the door shut. He slammed his briefcase on the desk, looked us all over, and then came around and stood in front of the class.

"I'm sure many of you are aware by now that this classroom was vandalized last night," he said.

He crossed his hands behind his back. His pissed-off eyes were bulgin like a bug's behind his FBI glasses.

"Dr. Streetum and the authorities are busy with the investigation," he said. "As am I." He looked at me and Lefty. "And believe me, we *will* find out who's behind this."

He stepped toward our aisle.

"Mr. Savage?" he said.

Lefty didn't look up. He just kept drawin. The room got even more quiet. You could hear Lefty's pencil on the paper.

"Mr. Savage?" Lewis said again. "Do *you* have any ideas about who might be responsible for violating my classroom?"

Lefty still didn't say nothin.

"Mr. Savage?" Lewis's voice had a bit more bite to it this time.

Lefty stopped, thought, and then went back to drawin.

331

Lewis was about to start talkin again, and then, straight out of nowhere:

"Boob says, a man reaps what he sows."

"Come again?" Lewis said. "Did you have something to say to me?"

The pencil just kept skatin over the paper.

"Boob says, you're an English teacher," he said. "You've heard of the Bible. Maybe read some of it too." Lefty still wasn't lookin up. "Boob says, no man gets what's not coming to him, unless he's just unlucky."

Lewis's face went even redder than I'd seen it so far. He reached Lefty's desk in three long strides and jabbed his finger at his face. Lefty looked up at the finger, but not at him.

"*I've had enough of you!*" Lewis spat.

All I could do was watch. I would have loved to cold-cock that bastard right on the chin, but it was Lefty's show now.

"You *are a student in* my *classroom, and* I *will not tolerate this disrespect! Do* you *understand me?*"

He jabbed with the finger again. It came about an inch from Lefty's nose.

"*You* know *something, Savage!*" Now his lips were wet, and his eyes were shakin in their holes behind the glasses. "*I want some* answers, *and I want them* now! *Speak up! Who did it?*"

I glanced around. Everyone was frozen. One kid even looked pale.

The finger was still in Lefty's face.

Lefty put his pencil in his notebook and closed it. He leaned across the aisle and put it on my desk.

Then, before I could blink, he whipped around, grabbed Lewis's finger, and snapped it. You heard the *crack!* It gooses me out to this day.

Lewis screamed and fell back. He crashed into a desk behind him. The red-haired girl shrieked and jumped right out of it.

Lewis covered his hand and bent over. He opened his mouth to scream at Lefty, but Lefty was already out of his chair. He grabbed Lewis by his suit and threw him to the floor. Lewis tried to get up but couldn't. Lefty was on him hard, poundin his face.

The kids sittin close by cleared out. Lewis's arms and legs were flappin around. He kicked over a chair. I saw some blood on the floor by his head.

Lefty was like a surgeon, man. All steady nerves and crazy focus.

A girl to my right started cryin.

The door flew open and two teachers ran in. Both of em leaped on Lefty. It took a choke hold to get im off of Lewis.

Lefty chilled out quick once he was up. The devil in his eyes disappeared too.

Lewis got to his feet and straightened his suit. He had the start of some bruises on his face and his lip was gettin fat.

The teachers, Mr. Trowden and Mr. Langston, held Lefty on either side. Lewis came up to him and got right in his face.

"I'm pressing charges," he said. "You're finished at this school."

Lefty shrugged. His face may as well have been on Mount Rushmore.

"Get out of my classroom," Lewis said.

Trowden and Langston tried to move Lefty toward the door. He wouldn't allow it at first, but then he did. Lewis followed em to the doorway and then he turned around.

"You are all to remain seated until I return," he said. "You can open to chapter three in your grammar handbook and begin working on exercise two, which will be your homework today."

He looked all of us over, real good. Then he left, closin the door behind him.

I was expectin everyone to talk it up as soon as he was gone, but they didn't. Most of em started workin on the grammar like Lewis told em to.

As for me, I just looked down at the cover of Lefty's notebook. I thought about what was inside of it.

I thought about him as well.

I'd never see him in that room or the school ever again. But he was my friend now, and we'd be meetin up again for sure.

We liked each other without havin to come out and say it.

And, as things would turn out, I still had so much more to learn from him and his pain.

Barely a month into his sophomore year at Colton Central High School, and Lefty's kicked out. For good. No chance for a pardon, or of ever comin back.

Of course Lewis, Streetum, and the dean, Frank Fuller, beat his brow behind closed doors to get what they could from him about the prior night's events. I wasn't there, but I had a good idea of how it went down.

Lefty would have sat there, a little slouched in his chair, mostly because he didn't give a shit he was in it. He would have kept a straight face while the administrators took their shots at grillin im hard, which was like tellin a corpse you're gonna shoot it.

He listened until he'd had enough of the noise. Then he fessed up to the crime and said he'd acted alone.

He did tell me more about it later on one night when we were drinkin beers up on a trestle over the tracks headin north past Hensley and Bracken toward south Michigan.

They asked him why he'd done it. He said it was because Lewis was a dick. That, and he didn't know how to teach George Orwell. Lefty didn't say nothin about the stuff in the drawer.

They asked him one more time if anyone else was involved. To *tell the honest truth*.

He said nope. No one else. Just him.

So they asked him, again.

He said no, again.

They stared him down to look for a tell on his face. He didn't give em one.

CCHS pressed their charges for b & e and vandalism, and Lewis brought his own for battery. Lefty got probation and community service for his offenses against the school.

The battery gave him bigger problems. I later found out, to no great surprise, that Lefty already owned a criminal record. One count disorderly conduct, one aggravated assault. The judge of course looked way down his nose at that. He gave Lefty nine months in the Kensing County Juvenile Detention Center.

All of these events also helped me figure out why I didn't remember Lefty from before that sophomore year.

It's because he wasn't *there* before that year.

He should have been, seein as how his family lived inside District 108. Hell, once I really thought it over, I realized I'd *never* known or seen Lefty before September '63, and we'd both lived in town all our lives.

Lefty explained all of that one too one night up on the trestle. Too ashamed of his odd-lookin son, Mr. Savage had decided early on that Lefty would receive his education at home. In other words, Lefty's mom gave him what supplies he needed to "learn" with while he was buried in the basement. She helped him as best as she could when Mr. Savage let her go down there, or when he was too drunk to notice.

The school at home thing worked up through eighth grade. After that, Lefty's dad was ready to have him out of the house. But he also didn't want him crampin Dennis's style at CCHS. Rather than have Lefty go to Colton Central, Mr. Savage got him transferred to St. Martin's Catholic High School in south Hensley—on a *scholarship* on account of his artistic ability. He could give a shit about Lefty's art, but it was a lot of booze money they were askin for. I'd always thought that if Lefty's dad could weasel a way to get his kid into a private school, he should have been able to hold a job for more than a couple of weeks.

Where CCHS was maybe a ten-minute drive from Lefty's front door, St. Martin's called for thirty through stop signs and traffic. Of course Mr. Savage made Lefty hoof it alone. St. Martin's didn't send a bus into Colton, and Mr. Savage would rather fail at bein sober than drive the bad seed from his spunk to school. He wouldn't let his wife drive Lefty neither.

And so Lefty had to get up way earlier than the rest of us to walk or ride a rusty bike to a place he liked less than we liked CCHS. He also couldn't play hooky. Bein private and Catholic and therefore expensive, St. Martin's had their own special truant officer. That individual also paid particular attention to those whose coin was bein flipped by the school. There was no way on God's blue stone that Lefty could skip without his parents bein aware by period two. And if that phone call came, fiery hell was the price that rang up. After all, it was the good Savage name on the line. Lefty told me that the phone rang twice because of his not showin up, and the result at home was what you'd expect.

At the same time, St. Martin's had no clue of what they'd signed up for when they'd said OK to Mel Savage. They had an idea of what he did and could do with his art. And while his writin basically sucked, they knew he was brighter than he looked. He was even half decent at science and math.

But they didn't know about the beatings, or the basement.

They started gettin pissed off at Lefty barely a month into his first semester. They were also free with the rod, especially when the target was as big as our friend. Lefty wasn't a problem that leaped right out, but he did have that funny way of talkin and sometimes of lookin at people. He was always quiet too, and that drew attention as well.

Most of the major issues had to do with other kids makin fun of how he talked. At first, he cussed at em. Then he pushed. Then, when it didn't stop, he kicked ass. If a teacher tried to break it up, he gave the teacher something to think about too.

That of course got him sent home, and that got him some close physical contact with his dad.

It didn't take long for Lefty to be permanently excused from St. Martin's Catholic High School.

Of course Mr. Savage lost his mind. The fists came first, and then the basement, sometimes without any food. That went on for a while until Mr. Savage realized he had to do somethin about Lefty's education before Colton came knockin. He finally gave in and let Lefty do some studyin with his mom down in the hole.

If Mr. Savage hadn't been tied to the rules of civilized Indiana society, he would have left Lefty to rot where he couldn't be seen. But, drunk though he was, he knew he *was* tied. He also wanted Lefty out of the house before long. He arranged for Lefty to enroll for sophomore year at CCHS after he'd met his freshman requirements from the schoolin at home.

And that's how Lefty wound up with us, before he got kicked out of there too.

I thought to maybe pay him a visit at home soon after Colton Central gave him the boot. Before the judge put him away. But then I figured it was even less a happy time than usual at the Savage house. Two expulsions in a year. His dad had to be piss blind and burnin raw. There was nowhere else to send im. Colton South, a smaller high school than ours, had been closed since '59 for "renovations" that were still bein renovated. It would be at least a couple years before it opened again. The next closest public high school was in Raymond fifteen miles east, and they didn't take kids from out of the district.

Mr. Savage and his son now had themselves another serious problem. They were gonna have to figure out what to do with all that space and time together again once Lefty was back. It was dialed up to get ugly.

What happened during that time is a major part of this story, and we'll get to it soon.

Autumn ended early in Colton that year. I guess winter was just that goddamn impatient. It usually is when it wants to bring you that freeze that turns your nuts into clinkin china by the second week of November. This one didn't leave us alone until mid-April. The leaves barely had their chance to change clothes before the frost came in for the kill.

The Colton Central Cougars football team finished 5-2 in the Saganack Eight Conference and 6-3 overall. Respectable, but not enough to rank in the state like they did in '62. They could have been 7-2, but Tom Sodek fumbled at the Eastern Heights five-yard line with less than two minutes to go in the last game of the season. Eastern Heights ran out the clock and won 23-17.

A few Cougars did make the all-conference team. Tailback Dennis Savage was one. That and his decent stats were enough to get him calls and letters from colleges. He went with Indiana State. Buck Thompson wound up at DePauw down in Greencastle. Bob Mulligan got a partial scholarship at Indiana Evansville.

Phil Barrelli didn't get squat. He was okay in high school, but not big and fast enough to cut it with the college coaches. I don't believe he even went on to college. Got his girlfriend pregnant summer after senior year and went straight into full-time work layin brick and buildin houses. That made im kind of a smudge on white perfection.

Wasn't much for me and Rich and Tommy to do once the early winter arrived. By December, the temperature stick didn't piss vertical red past thirty-five. That of course made our smokin corner a little less accommodating. We had to smoke our weed and cigarettes somewhere else or in Tommy's Chevy shit-panel truck.

We weren't into basketball or wrestling or student plays or anything else that high school serves up to busy the kids when it's cold and snowin outside. As always, the boys and me had to knock our noggins for ways to keep ourselves from gettin too idle.

We had to come up with our own indoor activities, and the less time we spent at home, the better. Me and Rich had to use our heads even harder on days when Tommy was workin or couldn't give us a lift in the Chevy.

In time, we got smarter about a few things, startin with the effort to meet other like-minded dudes. It didn't take much to find a few guys who appreciated beer, weed, pool, and creative ways of makin money. We also got better at organizing the money part.

I still credit those days as servin me well for when I'd really need the skills later on. We worked mostly on burglary, which if you ask me is the near-beer of felonies. Burglary's a whole different mindset than robbery, especially the armed variety. I know because I've committed that kind a couple of times in my life. On a personal level, if you have even a green pea of a conscience, armed robbery can fuck you up. To do it, you have to look straight into a soul for a second, and it sucks to see what's lookin back. If I hadn't needed the money bad right at the moment, I never would have done it.

But I digress. The days and months of that Colton winter passed like a foot-thick sheet of ice on Stanton Lake. When the weather finally got better, so even the birds were okay to come out, we came out too, and hung out on the corner again.

For me, it still felt different not havin Lefty with us. I hadn't heard a peep from him since he'd been sent to Kensing County Juvie. News about him had spread for a few weeks after all the action with Lewis, but when it died down, so did his name and his memory. It was like he'd never been there. The world simply moved on and forgot.

I bumped into the Mexican girl while Lefty was gone. She'd started followin me. I wasn't aware of it at first, but then I figured out that I was seein her face more than I normally would or should. Finally, one day, I think it was in late February '64, I decided to walk straight up to her.

She took off the other way, walkin real fast with her head down.

I jogged until I caught up.

She looked up at me. She couldn't have been an inch over five feet tall.

"Ukscyoosmee?" she said.

"You remember me?" I said. "From that day out in the parkin lot a few months back."

She didn't say nothin, so I said:

"You've been followin me for a while."

Still nothin. Just lookin up at me with brown eyes. Pretty eyes, actually.

She was attractive, but not in the instant way, like with the smokin-hot chick that ropes you in from any distance whether you like it or not. She got easier on the eye the longer you looked at her. Cute. Simple. It also helped if you had Lefty's renditions of her flashin around in your head.

"*Amigo*," she said. "Friend?"

"Right," I said. "Friend." I held my hand horizontal over my head. "I have a tall friend. He helped you that day."

She nodded.

"You like my friend?" I said.

She smiled and nodded again. I noticed her hair was really nice too, like she washed and brushed it a lot.

"Your friend," she said. "Where he is?"

"He no here," I said. "He gone. Kicked out."

"Kick?" she said.

What a drag, I thought. She was one of maybe five Latinos at CCHS. I think we also had about fifteen or so negroes. The rest of the kids in Colton were as white as an English ass in Alaska. Tough as it was for em in the 60s, at least the negroes had the language to work with. This little girl probably had to put in twice the time just to make the grade.

I moved my hands back and forth horizontal in front of me.

"No here," I said.

"He comes back?" she said.

"No," I said.

She hugged her books real tight and looked down.

"Maybe I see him again?" she said.

I stared at her for a few moments, and decided right there she was cool.

I smiled and nodded.

"Yes," I said. "But not now."

She looked a little confused.

"He's in a place he can't leave," I said.

A little smile and a shrug. Maybe she thought I was talkin about turtle doves.

"You'll have to wait," I said.

Her smile dried up a bit.

"Wait?" she said. "Long time?"

"A few more months," I said.

She looked at her feet. When she looked back up, she held out her hand toward me.

"*Gracias,*" she said. "Thank you. You please tell him I am Rose."

I shook her hand. It was soft and delicate, like a doll's.

She turned around and scuttled away. Once she was out of sight, I just stood there, in the hallway, lookin at the last spot where she'd been. Some dude ran into me by accident, and I didn't even tell him to watch it. I was too busy thinkin about her.

She was even more beautiful to me now, at least in the part of my head that pulls up faces. It was like Lefty's pencil was busy in there, fillin in all of the things I couldn't see with my eyes.

Once he was out of juvie and back in my scene as I expected he'd be, I'd try to get him and Rose together. On the surface, they made about as good a match as Bluto and Olive Oyl. But in that place that only the soul understands, they were as right as Archie and Betty.

I started headin toward my next class.

*T*ime came when my instincts reminded me I'd be seein Lefty again pretty soon. It was late spring '64, which finally moved through Colton with a fresh warmin wind of *Thank Christ*. If you're from the Midwest, you know exactly what I mean. Sixty degrees feels like South fuckin Florida. You throw open the windows and start thinkin about the shorts you haven't worn in over half a year.

I ran into a Rose a few more times before Lefty's release in July. Always, she asked me when she might see im again. And always, I gave the same answer, which was "hopefully soon."

She looked a little better each time I saw her too. It was clear she was spendin more time in the mirror, like she was gettin ready for Lefty to come home.

I didn't have any classes with Lewis that second semester sophomore year, which ended early June. The jiz bucket had given me a D in English Comp. You should have seen how he looked at me after Lefty was gone. He still couldn't prove that I'd helped trash his classroom or that I knew his dirty little secret, but his eyes always said there was chance I was in on it all.

He even gave me the *special* evil eye after he started receivin certain pictures one at a time through the mail in a plain, typed envelope with no return address.

One day in class before he got there, I saw that he'd changed the lock on his drawer. Bigger, better, stronger. Sometimes, when he stared at me with them dark and beady FBI eyes, all I did was look back and maybe crack a smile. What could he do?

I also saw Dennis a little more often during Lefty's hiatus. He was usually hangin out with his fellow future Republicans. Either that, or he was walkin with his arm around his girlfriend, Laura Dawson, who, I have to say, really was a hot piece of ass.

Him and Laura broke up a few times after high school. My own guess is that Dennis became an even better beaver trapper down at State. Him and Laura eventually married later on. We'll cover that more down the line here as well.

I know that Dennis saw me too, at least as much as I spotted him. But that's it. He *saw* me. He had no reason to speak to me, just as I had none to him. We tossed maybe thirty words total in our two common years at CCHS, and they were all your stock expressions. His only real knowledge of me was that I was friends with his brother. I think that's probably why when he did see me after Lefty got the boot, he eyeballed me a little closer than he otherwise would have.

We were different dudes in different worlds. I was suede and smoke and leather and beer. Long, greasy hair past the ears. The stain on the wall of a room that wasn't built for me.

Dennis, well, you know what he was. What's important here is that my connection to Lefty gave me peeks at the truths that Dennis had to hide. He knew that, and he hated it. The occasional longer look from him was meant to figure out if I might have *him* figured out.

I was the low-life stooge who might blow his cover and pull down the institutional pants he was destined to wear. And when those people are caught lookin down at their undies, they forget their make-believe status for a second, and it sucks.

It goes beyond even that. Folks also use institutions because they're a sure-shit way to get control over others. All of a sudden, Jane and Joe get to give orders and make decisions and steer the course of a life. You know what I'm talkin about too. It could be a bank, or a school, or a prison, or a police department. Jesus, look at Washington, D.C.

But the thing you got to remember is that for most institutional people, their weight drops by about 90 percent as soon as they step outside their four walls. The dude who kicks my foot at the gas station without excusin himself might be the CEO of Big Dicks USA. But he's also just a dude who kicked my foot at the gas station. I'll gladly tell him to bend over for a rear-end driver. He don't have his office or my job to protect him. At the gas station, he's a man. A person, no better than me or you.

I'll say the same goddamn thing about anyone we lift up over ourselves. Just because someone has a special talent or a bigger paycheck doesn't mean they're any closer to greatness. The world is full of beautiful genius stuck in the ghetto.

If only Dennis Savage understood any of that. It might have made him a cooler person, seein as how he came from humble roots. Instead he stuck by people who kept his image as he liked it.

The hell with it. Me and Rich and Tommy had other things to think about. We'd kept ourselves highly productive while Lefty was gone. We were gettin better at makin good money the socially unacceptable way.

We'd begun checkin mailboxes late at night for anythin good that might be in them. It wasn't exactly a cash cow, as most of Colton did gather its post at normal hours on a regular basis.

But there were those special times when people did leave their goodies outside. Whether they were old or lazy or just out of town I didn't always know. Most of their shit was postcards, magazines, junk mail, and personal letters, but we didn't care about that. Siftin through all of that was worth it when we scored a payroll or government check.

Tommy had a contact at a currency exchange just outside the northwest corner of Bruxton. For a cut of the action, the guy was willin to cash those checks. We all took turns at forgin em, and we never did our business *at* the currency exchange.

It got better. Tommy's contact had another contact with access to Indiana motor vehicle records. That way, we always had the state driver's license number printed below the forge on the back of the check to make it look like ID had been shown. Our forgery ring was a serious pain in the ass for the cops.

We kept that goin for a while to the tune of about fifteen hundred each, which was a *haul,* especially if you were sixteen in '64 without a real job.

The key for us was not to get greedy. Keep our hits short and focused and then move to somethin else. Don't sit too long where the cops would be sure to find us with time and some clues.

We'd also planned out how to handle the cash. No big purchases. No flashin bills. Spend it within reason over a period. Save a piece of it too. You have to admit, that was fairly sophisticated thinkin for a group of teenage burn-outs.

After removin ourselves from the forgery trail, we shifted to burglarizin liquor stores in Frankfort County, which was two counties to the east of Kensing. I'll bet we hit 75 percent of the retail suppliers, and I'll bet even more they were really pissed off. Even after the word was out and stores were bein watched, we still found our ways to get in and load the back of Tommy's panel truck with as much buzz juice as it could hold.

Of course the first thing we did once we had the cargo back in Colton was help ourselves to what was necessary for our own enjoyment. After that, we sold the rest to our county's very thirsty teenagers at beautiful black-market prices. Turned out to be one hell of an enterprise. It taught me a lot about sellin a product where the demand is always bigger than the supply.

Once again, we kept at it for just a few months while the stories made their way to the front of the papers. And right before the heat could get close, we ducked out, stashed our cash, and went back to the drawin board.

I should also mention that the attention from quality females started improving around then as well. We had the cash to reel em in and help em have fun so that *we* could have fun, if you catch my drift. But we also knew we had to keep our wits about it. We'd start beggin bigger questions from the girls and maybe other people too if we showed and spent too much.

Tommy had his job at the scrap yard to explain some of it away. With the cash pilin up wherever we could hide it, me and Rich soon faced the truth we'd need a front as well. We began runnin out of ways to bullshit about where a few twenty-dollar bills came from.

We both got a job at Bill Stokes's pool hall. It was a hangout where a select group of Colton's alcoholics went to fill up, shoot stick, play darts, and listen to the juke. There was also a little sit-down area for eatin Bill's fast food.

Rich washed dirty dishes in the back. I kept the floors and tables clean. I also emptied the ash trays, which was a shit assignment even for a chain-smoker like me. If the tips were right, I fetched drinks and cigarettes for a few people too.

Can't say I was in love with havin to be at a certain place by a particular time. I'd had enough of that at CCHS. Wasn't thrilled about havin to be accountable to Bill either. He was a cool guy, but he hassled me hard if I was more than five minutes late.

Me and Rich sucked up what we had to. Keepin the taller cash with a lower profile was way more important. We kept our mouths mostly shut and played by the rules as best as we could.

Some of you might recall another event that took place while Lefty was on ice at juvie. Most will say they can even remember where they were and what they were doin on November 22, 1963. Those of you who weren't here yet will have heard or read about that day at least a few hundred times by the time I'm writin all of this down.

As for me, I remember it was after lunch on a Friday. I was sittin in Mr. Slopek's Health class. We were talkin about the female reproductive organs, so of course I was dialed in for most of it. Toward the end of class, Dr. Streetum came on the P.A. and said that Kennedy had been shot dead in Dallas. He called an emergency assembly in the gymnasium. It was a tragic day for our country, he said. We needed to be together "as a group" and talk it out.

I of course did not attend that therapy session. Rather, I got an early start on the weekend by gettin high with Rich and Tommy out on our freezin-cold corner. None of us had to work that Friday, and Rich had some good weed he bought from a negro passin through from Indianapolis.

By late that afternoon, I was too stoned to notice that the whole world was losin its mind. It was a big deal, really big, and it stayed that way for a while. My own dad, who was usually too wasted to say anything, even had a few words on the subject. I didn't listen to any of it, though. I think I told him to shut the fuck up. The bastard didn't even vote.

Did I develop my own take on Kennedy later on, after all of the stories and theories and dirty laundry came out? I guess. What happened was sad, sure. He was our *guy*. But we also can't forget he told his lies and fixed his values and used his power to help out his dick and deep pockets just like anyone else at the top of the institutional food chain.

Lookin back on it even now, I'd still say he wasn't no king or prince of Camelot. He was a smart and connected and popular dude who wore out his welcome in the sandbox. The institutions will bring you in and move you up, and then, if or when you no longer fit, they'll tear you down and spit you out.

I know, because I'm a card-carryin institutional reject. The only ivory tower that even came close to makin me welcome was the Indiana state correctional system. That was simply because the law and the taxpayers agreed that was a good place for me to be.

Lefty was a reject of the system too. But because his older brother would always live and die by it, he would never escape it, not even when it did all it could to push him away.

W as about the third week of July, late afternoon, about a month or so after CCHS had let out for the summer, when I finally ran into Lefty again.

Tommy had to work at the scrap yard, but me and Rich had the day off from the pool hall, so we just walked around town and had a few smokes. We got bored and wound up headin to our corner by the school of all places.

Lefty was there when we got there. Just standin, quiet, smokin a smoke, lookin our way as we approached. He nodded toward us too.

I jogged over, grabbed his arm, and clapped him on the back.

"Hey, buddy," I said.

He drew on his cigarette, squinted, and blew out.

"Boob says, what's up," he said. "Hey, Rich."

"Mel," Rich said. His voice was clipped and his head was cocked a little bit sideways.

The trust just wasn't there yet. Just goes to show its delicate nature. A lot of times in life, someone breaks ours and then we return the favor by refusing to trust someone else. All it takes is a little abuse or betrayal or a broken heart or two to screw our relationships good. Even the ones we don't have yet are doomed. Especially those.

But still—as long as Lefty was okay by me, the other guys would play along. And deep down, Rich and Tommy knew that Lefty checked out okay. They just weren't ready to admit it yet.

Me and Rich both lit a smoke.

"It's good to see you again, Mel," I said.

Lefty just looked at me quiet.

"What do you say we get some beers and head over to the trestles later on?" I said. "Hang out. Catch up."

I waited for him to answer.

"Boob says, sure, Parker," he said. "Why not. Let's get some beers."

We kept chillin out until we finished our smokes.

And just as we did, the movie and comic-book shit showed up.

We heard the revvin and the peelin rubber first. Then we saw the white Chevy Corvair convertible with the top up. It pulled right up to the curb at our corner.

The doors flew open and the jockasses piled out. Buck Thompson, Bob Mulligan, Tom Sodek, Phil Barrelli.

Right after that, a black Ford Galaxy with a white hard top pulled up behind the Corvair. I couldn't see who was in it.

"Look who it is," Buck said, walkin up to Lefty. "Where you been, Boob?"

Lefty hooked his thumbs in the belt loops of his jeans.

"You got sent to Kensing juvie, right?" Buck said, chucklin. He looked back at his buddies. "They pump you hard in the ass up there, *Melvin?*"

Lefty glanced at the Galaxy.

"Boob says, at least you brought more back-up this time."

Buck shoved him with both arms. Lefty stumbled back, but caught his balance fast.

I looked at his face. The devil wasn't out. Yet.

It was there though, waitin.

Three more jacks had jumped out of the Galaxy. Now they were comin toward us too.

The first two were Tim Walrond, who had played safety, and this other dude I'd seen before but whose name I couldn't remember. The third one, a few steps behind them, was Dennis.

Buck shoved Lefty again. Lefty kept his cool. He looked at his brother.

Me and Rich glanced at each other and nodded that we were ready for go-time.

Okay.

Bob, Tom, and Phil came up so that Lefty faced a wall four people wide. Tim and the other dude came closer too. Dennis hung back a little, keepin some distance.

"So what do you say, pussy?" Buck said, and pushed Lefty again. "You ready for it *now?*"

Bob and Tom stepped forward. They saw me and Rich move toward them, looked at each other, and almost laughed.

But for all their strut, there was one thing that they didn't and might never have in a fight.

The bloody-black words *I just don't fuckin care* carved by a switchblade on their souls.

Buck cracked Lefty in the jaw. Lefty's head snapped to the right. He fell back and bent over.

And right when he looked up, I saw it.

The devil, off of its chain and out of its mind.

Lefty's face turned into a hell mask. He lunged at Buck and tackled him hard to the ground.

The other jacks just stood and watched at first. Lefty was on Buck like a red-hot iron blanket. The bench-press buddies didn't look at ease.

Lefty was smotherin im so much this time that I wondered if Buck could even breathe. Lefty was crackin im hard in the face too. Real hard.

Bob and Tom and Phil just kept watchin. They still didn't know whether to shit or shine shoes. When they figured it was clear their boy was gettin walloped, Tom finally jumped on Lefty's back and put him in a choke hold.

That's when I went into action.

If there's one thing you *can't* say about burn-outs like us, it's that we don't dress right for a fight. We tend to wear stuff we can use.

Like steel-toed black boots.

Before any jacks knew what was comin, the shinin tip of my right foot was in the side of Tom's face.

He screamed like a bitch and rolled off of Lefty.

Then, before I could make another move, it was *me* hittin the ground. One of the jacks had plowed me over from behind. My face was so flat I could taste the dirt in my teeth. Then the fists came, hammerin the back of my head. The blackout was speedin my way.

I heard a mud of noise and shouts and fuck-yous. A few more fists smackin and thumpin.

I waited for the lights to go out. It approached me like a tidal wave and then, bumps and bruises be damned, it pulled back.

I pushed myself up with what strength I had. Rolled over. The world was upside down. I was still seein plenty of stars.

When I got myself back to a blur, I saw two jacks kickin Rich's ass. Four were poundin on Lefty.

Dennis was still standin back at a distance, just watchin it all.

Wobbly though I was, I made it to my feet. Tim Walrond and his no-name buddy saw me and shot right over. Rich was still on the ground.

"Wha-whad, you foggers wanna go?" I said. My goddamn head was shimmy-shimmy shakin.

I tried to hold up my fists.

They must have seen I was worthless. They laughed and called me a dick and went back to the Galaxy.

Dennis looked at me a little longer and then he got in the Galaxy too.

Lefty was slowly workin his way back up to his elbows.

Buck, Bob, Tom, and Phil were walkin toward the Corvair. They stopped when they saw me up and almost back to my senses. One of em—had to be Tom, still pissed about my steel toe—ran back over and punched me full tilt in the stomach. Knocked me to my knees. Then he kneed me square in the mouth, and I tasted the blood right away.

I fell over slow to my side. The engines revved up, and both cars pulled away.

I stayed on the ground. When reality tried to find me again, I touched the blood on my mouth and then the egg on the back of my head.

I crawled over to Lefty, who was just now gettin to his knees. Rich took a little longer, but he found his way to his feet as well. His face was pretty mashed. His bottom lip was split, and both of his nose holes were rimmed with blood.

I put my hand on Lefty's shoulder.

"Good to have you back, Mel," I said.

I reached into my jacket and pulled out a flattened cigarette. Lit it with my Zippo.

"So how about them beers?" I said.

I looked him straight in the eyes. The devil was gone. It was only Lefty now.

"Boob says, yeah, let's go," he said.

Rich was tryin to move his jaw.

I gave him my cigarette.

"Here," I said. "You need it. More than me."

He took it, dragged on it, and winced because of his lip. He was gonna have a shiner too.

We left our corner and walked the mile or so to downtown. I scored our beers from Bill Stokes's nephew Bobby, who was twenty-two and always willin to contribute to the delinquency of a minor. Sometimes me and him worked together at the pool hall when Bill was doin his sister's son a favor. It's safe to say Bobby wasn't a model employee. Like us, he preferred makin his money with a little less effort and even less responsibility.

With our beers in a big grocery bag, we made our way to the abandoned garage over by the tracks, which were just over a mile outside of downtown to the north. Bobby came along. We'd hang out there until it got dark and we could climb a trestle without drawin attention.

We were all hurt pretty good, but it wasn't nothin a few cold ones couldn't fix.

Plus, for me, my spirits were high because Lefty was back.

We had a lot of catchin up to do.

"So," I said to Lefty. I had a lit Winston in one hand and a cold can of Schlitz in the other. "What'd you learn at Kensing County?"

We were sittin facin north with our legs danglin down from the trestle. Those trestles could be a bitch to climb sometimes, especially with a buzz in the dark. But the view and the quiet up there were worth the work. Seein as how we didn't spend much time in the gym, I guess you could say it was a way of keepin fit.

I was in the middle with Rich to my left and Lefty to my right. Bobby had split before we went up. Tommy didn't show at nine like he was supposed to. That meant he was either out with some dudes from the scrap yard or hookin up with Mandy Morgan again. She'd been sniffin around him for a couple of months. She was twenty years old and, word had it, very agreeable in pleasin a man.

My head still hurt like hell from the fight, but the beers and the weed were helpin me out. Rich was drinkin as best as he could with a busted lip. Lefty's black eye had gotten more colored and puffy as well.

You never woulda guessed he had one by the way he acted, though. He was real chilled out. Just sippin his beer and starin out at the tracks.

"So, how it'd go at juvie, Mel?" I said.

I hadn't mentioned it when Bobby was with us. It wasn't really his business.

Lefty rubbed his jaw and then looked sideways at me.

"Boob says, it was just time on the clock," he said. He looked forward again. "That's all they took from me. No big deal."

"Anybody mess with you?" I said.

Lefty spit and watched it sail down to the rocks and pebbles below.

"Boob says, sometimes," he said. "It happens. I took care of it when I had to."

I nodded. Sipped my beer.

"How about the stiffs runnin the place?" I said. "They ever mess with you?"

Lefty looked at me again, and this time he smiled a little.

"Once in a while," he said. "Mostly they let me be. Told me what to do and where to go. That was about it."

I stared at him, but not too long. That was the very first time I figured he could and did speak without givin credit to Boob. Maybe the months in juvie had rearranged some things in his mind. Either that, or he was even more complex than I was gettin to know him to be.

He spit and looked forward again. I looked forward too. I wondered right then what it'd be like to just say fuck it, climb down, and head all the way down those rails to wherever they went.

"How'd you spend the time?" I said. "The time you had to yourself, I mean."

"Reading," he said. "Thinking." His was voice deep and steady. I heard some faraway sadness in there too. "I drew when I could. When I didn't have paper, I just did it in my head." He sipped his beer. "Mostly, I thought about my green room."

"Green room?" I said.

"Yeah."

I waited for him to explain it. He didn't.

Rich lit another cigarette. A couple of whistlin trains made their steel racket in the distance.

"Say, Mel," Rich said. "You mind if I ask you a question?"

I looked at Lefty. He was lookin past me at Rich.

"Sure," he said.

"How come you say boob all the time?"

I gave Rich a *look:* "Hey, come on, man, is that any kind of thing to ask right when he got out of . . ."

"No," Lefty said. He put his bear paw on my shoulder. "It's okay, Parker."

He set his Schlitz on the platform and leaned back on his hands so he could see around me.

"I do it because I do it," he said, "and it means what it means."

Rich looked at me and then at him.

357

"Hey, man," he said. "I'm just askin' a question. You don't have to take it personal. It's just, well, a little unusual, man."

"You're okay with me because you're okay with Parker," Lefty said. "I'm sure we can keep it that way. You can ask me most things that you want. But if you bring that up again, I'll break your fucking skull."

Rich stared at him. Lefty stared back, calm as the woods after a snow.

"Whatever you say, partner," Rich said, but he was lookin more at me when he said it.

We all sat there quiet again. The weed was startin to wear off for me. The pain in the egg on my head came back a little.

"Let's all just be cool," I said. "We're gonna get along fine. Rich, stop askin the stupid questions. And Mel, don't get worked up about shit that ain't necessary. We're all friends here. Nobody means nothin wrong. Let's just take it easy and drink our goddamn beers."

Lefty looked at me, then Rich, and then forward again.

"Boob says, I'm cool," he said.

I raised my eyebrows at Rich.

"Me too," he said.

"Alright," I said. "Now, let's talk about makin some money." I sipped my beer. "Mel, while you were at juvie, me, Rich, and Tommy got pretty good at earning outside of a job."

I put my hand on his shoulder. He didn't look at it.

"I don't have talent like you, Mel," I said. "But I do believe there's somethin I'm good at in this life. You up for makin more in a week than an English-teachin dick bag pulls in a month?"

Lefty's face stayed blank and still, but I saw the little turnin wheels behind his eyes.

"Boob says, yep."

"Alright, then," I said. I let my hand slide from his shoulder. "Let's talk."

And so we did, deep into the night. With our legs danglin down and the occasional freight rollin north from below, we shared ideas, got more drunk, and looked up at the stars.

We dreamed, and grew a little bit closer. At least me and Lefty did.

It felt like home. The *real* kind of home.

I treasure those moments as much now as I did back then. It was a special time to remember before our greed and Lefty's horror at home led us all into the clink.

*T*ommy was the first to decide that summer that he was gonna drop out of high school for good. The scrap yard had offered him more hours at a good wage, and he liked the idea of addin to the cash we were already makin. Plus, his Chevy panel truck had been givin him problems that he himself couldn't fix. Mandy Morgan was really puttin out for him too, so each extra dollar he spent on her became a greater return on investment. Medical bills were also pilin up on his mom, and his dad lost his job on top of that. The family needed Tommy's extra income.

Me and Rich likewise decided that sophomore year would be our last at CCHS. Lefty was pretty much done with the system as well. As of summer 1964, all four of us were finished with public education. From then on, we'd be makin our own rules. Survivin *our* way, in *our* world.

That world had been treatin us well for a while. It also didn't take long for Lefty to become a part of it. It was him who suggested one night over beers and fresh weed that we look into the business of fake

IDs and documents. The taxpayers of Kensing County had made it possible for him to learn from some of the best young minds in the trade up at juvie.

By late August, we had ourselves a solid operation. Counterfeit driver's licenses, birth certificates, papers of citizenship, even medical reports for dodgin the draft. Pretty much whatever you needed to get past the government to get what you wanted. Tommy and Lefty took care of production. Me and Rich managed sales, marketing, and distribution.

In particular we built ourselves a quick list of beer-lovin minors who wanted to be twenty-one faster than natural time would allow. It became a market of bulls snortin to pay for the privilege to buy liquor and get into bars before the state said okay. The demand was so high we raised prices by 50 percent by the end of September.

We'd also agreed on one thing. To protect the enterprise, we'd keep the action away from Colton and its closer communities. It'd be a lot of extra money we were leavin on the table, but we had to resist the pull to bring it local. Doin so would have been like makin the rope, throwin it over the branch, and then givin it to the authorities so they could hang us.

To reach the markets that were farther out and therefore safer, me and Rich bought ourselves a car. At first we used it to make important contacts along the supply route. Those contacts then helped us develop our channels for the products that Tommy and Lefty created.

The procedure became so clean and efficient that we were bangin out as many as twenty driver's licenses in a day at fifteen green dollars apiece. That's three hundred 1964 dollars on days we decided to work instead of drinkin beers and smokin weed. We were earnin more than some of the white collars in north and west Colton, and we were teenage fuckin punks.

We put together a few other means of profit around that time too. Mostly nighttime burglaries of houses we knew would be empty of people. We got good at breakin into businesses late night as well. Made decent extra cash sellin all kinds of shit that we stole.

But none of that compared to the ID operation. That was our gravy. It got so we had to find even more new ways to hide the cash, both from our families and especially the law. It took *all* we had to keep a low profile, let me tell you. Money like that burned canyons in my pockets every time I talked to a chick or went past a store. It got even worse when I drove past new cars for sale.

That stretch of '64 was also a time of big ups and downs for Lefty. I got around to tellin him that the Mexican girl's name was Rose and that I'd run into her while he was gone. His face was straight as always, but I saw the light go on in his eyes. Seein as how I would no longer be enrolled at CCHS, I wouldn't get much chance to play matchmaker. But I helped him to think even more about her. That, I do believe, made him feel at least a little bit good.

And I guess that made me a little happier too.

He spent a lot of his free days just standin or sittin around downtown Colton. Mostly watchin, waitin, hopin he might catch a glimpse of her sooner or later. He didn't go near the school because of his expulsion and the possible cop factor that could follow his ignorin it. Neither of us knew Rose's last name, so we couldn't go to the phone book. For him, it would take some patience.

It paid off. He finally saw her one night about the third week of September. He was sittin on the bench under the elm tree at the corner of Franklin and Main. The one right outside John Martin's hardware and office-supplies store. As Lefty told it later on, he was lookin north down Main and smokin a cigarette when the 4:15 show of *Mary Poppins* let out at the Jewel Box, which was halfway between Franklin and Montaigne. He watched the crowd empty out onto Main. A few packs of kids and teenagers hung out in front. Some other people went for a walk because the weather was good. Most got into their cars and drove home.

You should have heard how Lefty set the scene for me. He told me of how the dark-gold sunlight kissed the trees and traced the buildings right before dusk. How the air was so clear that night it was like the earth had quit movin just so he could see and hear *everything*. A meltin scoop of vanilla ice cream by John Martin's storefront doorway. A pebble of broken glass lyin alone and forgotten at the edge of the sidewalk. Chirpy conversations the insects were havin where they couldn't be seen. Beyond all of that, the freights rollin away with metal clangs from the railyard.

That same early autumn clarity helped him single out Rose from a crowd of taller people between the Jewel Box and him. She was with another girl who looked like her and was about the same size too.

When they got a little closer, he flicked away his cigarette and got up to move toward them. Rose didn't see him right away because she was walkin with her head down as always. The other girl was the one who noticed Lefty first.

He stopped, and then they stopped, and then they all just looked at each other. Rose held a little red purse close to her chest with both hands.

Lefty walked up to her, pulled a folded piece of paper from his jeans pocket, and held it out. She stared at it for a second, and then she took it.

The other girl watched her unfold it. It was one of Lefty's drawings of Rose.

"B-Boob says, hi," he said.

She smiled.

"That's something I wanted to give you," he said.

She looked at it some more.

"What ees thees?" she said.

"Boob says, it's you," he said. "It's how I remembered you from the last time I saw you."

"How . . . how me you remembered?"

Lefty shrugged.

"Boob says, I remember lots of things." He tapped his head.

He looked down. She did too.

"Boob says, do you like it?"

"It's . . . beautiful," she said. "*Hermoso.* You draws very . . . well."

He looked up.

"I have more."

She smiled again.

"Boob says, maybe we could get together sometime and, you know, I could show them to you. Maybe we could see a movie too, or sit down for a Coke."

She kept smilin but didn't say nothin. Then she grabbed her friend by the arm.

"To you, I present my seester, Isabella," she said.

Lefty nodded at her.

"Boob says, glad to meet you. I'm Mel."

The sister nodded back but looked a little scared. He did after all have the handsome-caveman face and the height and the slabby arms hangin out from the sleeves of his tee-shirt. To her, he must've looked like somethin that'd talked the zookeepers into lettin it go.

"So, what do you say . . . Rose? Can I see you again?"

She held her purse even more tight and looked at her feet.

When she looked up again, her smile was bigger.

"Yes," she said. "*Sí.*"

Lefty told me that he then smiled too. I wish I could have seen it for myself. He never did smile that much, so when he did, you knew it was real.

"Boob says, great. I'll meet you here, at the corner." He pointed at the bench beneath the elm at the corner of Franklin and Main. "Friday night. Six-thirty."

She nodded. He stepped aside to let them pass. He watched them turn the corner.

And that was how he felt some happiness before his life went deeper south.

K eepin all of the cash on the lowdown became an even more serious problem. Our fake IDs alone pulled in close to a grand the first week of October.

I have to admit, the success was even startin to make us afraid.

We had to be even more careful about what we put in the banks. Well-dressed white people tended to look funny at a teenage burnout with a thousand bucks on top of a deposit slip. We had to spread it out *good*. We stashed a lot of it at home in places not even a cop dog would be able to find. We also buried some and made maps to keep track of it.

We did allow ourselves to enjoy spendin at least a little here and there. Some decent clothes, a nice meal, better boots. We bought better weed as well. Hookers proved to be another great way of dumpin disposable income without too many questions.

Of the four of us, Rich was havin the worst time controllin himself. It took shout-downs and even close to beat-downs to keep him in line. He talked big about a new car and even a house, but in the end he chilled out. He didn't want to land in a state-owned concrete closet any more than we did.

As for Lefty, he'd started seein Rose regularly, and she didn't inquire into how he could pay for the movies and dinners and banana splits. She also didn't ask much about the clothes, jewelry, and stuffed animals he got for her. As practicin Catholics, her parents had to have wondered what was up, but as far as I know, they never made too big a deal of it. Their daughter was happy with someone nice and polite who treated her well and who could pay for her. He even did and bought nice things for Isabella once in a while.

From my view, Lefty's success with the business at that time was nothin compared to what was comin out from his mind. The thought of it *still* blows me away.

He drew more landscapes like the one he'd made in the basement, only even more complex. He also created these kick-ass paintings of buildings that made me think of what ancient Rome would have looked like on a different planet. Then there was a portrait that reminded me of da Vinci's *Last Supper*, only the savior was Elvis and the disciples were burn-outs like us.

His work was showin a lot of extra *green* in it too. Green grass. Green fields. Green houses. Green skies. Green walls, chairs, and tables. Hell, even green people, only they weren't sick, or aliens. He was even usin more green in his pictures of Rose.

But if business, art, and love were workin out okay for Lefty, his life at home was their equal in bad. His dad was drinkin even more and workin even less, and without school or juvie or jail to keep em apart, the tension got way worse. His words with Lefty got sharper and meaner. The pushes and punches got more serious too. The hurt and rage were buildin a bomb in my friend.

Dennis of course had spent as little time at home as possible before leavin for Indiana State. Him and Lefty didn't speak much that summer, except maybe to say get out of the bathroom or it's your turn to take out the trash. Although he didn't mention it much, I knew that Lefty still wished Dennis and him were closer, or at least not like strangers from countries at war. I heard it in the way he said his brother's name—like a gash that could scab but never close.

I wanted to tell Lefty that even if him and his brother did spend more time together, they'd never get along that well anyway. Their hearts were just too different in ways that couldn't be changed. With Lefty, you always knew that once he trusted you, and let himself like you, you could reach inside him and touch something that made both you and him feel real.

His brother, as I've sort of explained, was more like the dressed-up doll in the store window showin what could be yours if you were willin to believe the display. It looked good, so if that was your thing, you ponied up and didn't care that there might not be anything beneath the plastic that was pullin you in.

Dennis wouldn't be around to hang out with anyway. He left for college early in order to practice for football. And as far as I knew, he didn't return for semester break or holidays.

He didn't even come home after the bloodbath at his house right before Thanksgiving.

As for us, October and November flew by that year, probably because business was boomin. If we'd just been a *little* more mature, we might have kept it up longer.

We'd carved out four major fake ID markets by early November. The waiting list grew and grew and so did the cash. The four of us eventually ditched our other schemes to focus a hundred percent on the big one.

We put all of our eggs in the one fucking basket. That was our first screw-up.

The second one was me, Rich, and Tommy quittin our jobs. We all got tired of bein bored and havin to listen to the boss. And by doin that, we of course pissed away our half a front for the cash in our pockets.

Screw-Up #3 was goin against our better earlier judgment to *not* do business in Colton.

So what made us get so stupid so fast? I can't answer that. Why do rich-ass CEOs steal from the same companies already makin em rich?

The first real talk of bringin our business to Colton came up one night around Halloween. We were all workin our way to a serious bender with a couple cases of Schlitz. I believe it was Tommy who got the conversation goin.

At first, me and Rich said forget it for the obvious reasons. Lefty kept silent on the subject. But once our buzzes kicked in, me and Rich found ourselves more open to the idea.

For one thing, we knew how bad the minors in town wanted and needed the service. It wasn't that they couldn't get booze. Most of em just had to beg those of legal age to buy it, and you and I both know that's a pain in the ass, especially when you bat zero on a Saturday night. We were in a position to help them scoot around the unfair restrictions on their ability to enjoy a beverage.

There was also a *shitload* of cash to be made, and we didn't have to go far to make it.

The goddamn greed had already started creepin in.

We stayed stuck on the concept even after our hangovers wore off the next day. And so we set up shop. My trusted better instincts were callin me all kinds of names, but I have to admit I kind of liked the decision at first. No hours and hours of drivin all over the place to make the money. No hassles with the dudes in the middle who thought their cut should be more. Just us, the four of us, workin with people we knew in a town that we knew, providin a service they were happy to pay for.

Word spread fast as fire too, so much so that I had to tell a few of our customers to chill out, shut up, and wait their turn. Colton's kids were wettin their pants when they held their own state license that was almost impossible to tell from the real thing. Our product was so good it was foolin even the cops. Shit, employees of the Indiana Department of Motor Vehicles couldn't tell if they were fake or not.

Pretty soon a lot of local minors were holdin cards that were issued by us. We were startin to attract the heat but couldn't feel it because of the money. Colton cruisers made snail-slow drive-bys past our houses at funny times of the day. Cops on foot gave us the *look* when they saw us in town. They didn't have nothin solid yet, but they knew that somethin was up.

Of course we were too rich and, typically, too buzzed to make the right moves at the right times. I think we were darin the cops to bust us. We'd done a good job of dodgin em so far. We knew that they were on to us, so if we felt the fuzz was gettin *too* close, we told ourselves we'd just destroy our equipment and deny every word of it. Then we'd look into somethin else and bring the cops back to square one.

Lefty was lyin low and keepin quiet as usual. He was hangin out with Rose a lot too. For a stretch, we saw him only once a week or so outside our "workin" hours to maybe drink some beers.

They'd found somethin in each other. He'd opened up and shown her who he really was. She liked him a whole lot back. I saw it for myself whenever he brought her over to hang out with me and Rich and Tommy. They could just sit there, not a muscle twitchin in either of them, and just listen, or watch, or *be*. His caveman face was always relaxed around her. The only other times I saw that were, well, when he was alone with me.

I particularly remember a talk we had one night in mid-November. The leaves were rust and red and yellow and the temperature was droppin. We were all in the basement at Tommy's house. His dad was asleep in the second-floor bedroom after a lot of cheap vodka, and his sick mom, who liked her wine but not every day, was snoozin right next to him. Tommy's older brother, Steve, had already moved out to live with his girlfriend. He'd knocked her up in the summer.

Me, Tommy, and Rich were drinkin plenty of our usual Schlitz. Lefty was slouched in the corner with his arm around Rose under a big-ass Beatles poster taped to the wall.

We started talkin about God, and fate. Hell if I know how it began.

Me and Rich and Tommy went a few rounds about whether God and Jesus were real and if so, then how come there were like a thousand religions and each one said the others were confused.

That's when Rose sat up.

"Jesus, he the truth!" she said. *"La verdad!"*

I leaned forward in my chair. I was pretty buzzed by then. My can was attached to my body somewhere by the end of my arm.

"Oh, yeah?" I said. "How so?"

"*La Biblia,* it say so!" she said.

That was when I saw the silver crucifix on the chain around her neck. Jesus's head was pokin out above the top button of her sweater.

"So what?" I said. "It's a book."

"Not just a book," she said. "Truth! *La verdad!*"

"Well, I'm glad someone around here thinks so," I said. "Beats pissin in a can, which I'll do right now if I can't make it to the hole."

I finished my beer, set it down, and started toward the dark bathroom doorway behind me.

"Boob says, she's right," Lefty said.

I stopped and turned around.

We all went quiet, and looked at him.

I sat back down even though my piss bag was ready to blow.

"What do you mean, she's right?" I said.

He slipped his arm from Rose's shoulder, sat straight, and leaned forward.

"Exactly what I said," he said. "Even if it don't apply to me and you."

We looked hard at each other even though I couldn't focus real good.

"No, man," I said. "What do you *mean?*"

Lefty looked down, thought for a second, and then looked at me again.

"I mean, Jesus is true, and so is God, but they ain't always been there for us as we'd want them to be."

"Melvin . . . ," Rose said.

She put her little hand on his shoulder. I knew right then they'd talked it over before. Or at least Rose had been talkin to Lefty about it, and he'd been payin attention.

He glanced at her hand, touched it real soft, and removed it just as carefully.

He looked back at me, dead serious, straight in the eyes.

"There is a God, Parker," he said. "We just can't see it or feel it because we're broken and pissed off. We don't want to work at findin' it either. It's easier to say fuck it and think we're too smart to believe in it."

I opened my mouth to speak, maybe to argue, but then I didn't know what to say.

"Boob says, isn't much reason to live if there isn't a truth, or a god who's lettin all this shit happen without some promise it's all gonna work out," he said. "And even if that god is there, that doesn't mean it won't pass some of us by."

He fell quiet and sipped his beer, a Pabst Blue Ribbon.

"If you were God, would *you* waste time on dudes like us?" he said. "Me neither. But He still does. If He didn't, we wouldn't have *any* hope, man. It'd be just us, fucked-up people like us, making a goddamn mess of the place." He looked off to the side, and then back at me. "All of us need some hope. At least enough to look for our green room."

There he went again with that green stuff.

"Green room?" I said.

He stared at a spot on the floor. His eyes glazed over. If I hadn't been so loaded, I might have told you that I saw his tears.

Rose rested her head on his shoulder. He kept starin at the floor.

"Boob says, if we do find our green room on our own," he said, "I'll bet you God will be in there, chilling out, waiting for us. He'll light a smoke for us and tell us everything's cool."

I glanced at Rich and Tommy. They were as skunked as I was. I highly doubt they were tuned all the way in.

My bladder was cussin in Korean by then. I remember wantin like holy hell to drain it, but somethin kept me stuck to the chair. Maybe it was the weight of the thoughts in my head, or of the rocks of doubt in my heart.

We all sat in silence a bit. It wasn't weird. In fact, drunk as I was, I could say even then that it felt like we were a real family, thinkin different things and not always agreein but still able to share the space that we had. You know you're at home when you don't have to talk all the time and you won't get thrown out for bein yourself.

Hell, if we'd known right then that our lives would change for good inside a couple of weeks, we might have stretched that time together much later into the night.

We'd never get to feel that way again.

*I*f you can believe it, the end of the world for four kids from Colton began with a glass of milk right near the end of November 1964.

Lefty's dad's drinking had gone from really bad to pure insane. We're talkin beer for breakfast, vodka for lunch, and whiskey for dinner with maybe a sandwich to help push it down. By middle October, his body quit on his brain after years of fightin the good fight. His hands had started to shake, his blood pressure could drive a locomotive, and his already nasty depression dropped lower and made his temper even more wicked. An ulcer broke out in his belly too.

Public aid could help him only so far on account of his not havin any insurance. One of Colton's family doctors, Dr. Traynor, even took pity on him and tried to help out at no charge. He also warned him hard of what would happen if he didn't let go of the bottle for good.

Of course Mr. Savage accepted the favors and advice and said thanks. Then he went right back to the liquor store. About the only thing he did to help himself was drink more milk for the ulcer.

It was milk he was drinkin on that day in late November, a Wednesday morning. Lefty was sittin with him at the breakfast table while Mrs. Savage made the eggs and toast.

As Lefty explained it to me through letters later on, his dad was in a mood as foul as hell's outhouse because of the ulcer. The pain was so out of control he hadn't been able to take down nothin *but* the milk that week, which multiplied his misery by two.

Mrs. Savage served Lefty his food and then sat down with some for herself. After Lefty finished, he started drawin in his sketch book. It was another picture of Rose. The mornin news spoke at a low volume from the kitchen AM radio.

Lefty's dad watched him draw for a while, and then said somethin highly unfriendly. Lefty, who'd just about had it with him by then—as in one inch left of the rope—said somethin right back.

He'd been gettin more bold and defiant with his dad of late. Part of it was the freedom he felt from bein self employed. Another part was that he was still gettin bigger and more powerful, so much so that his nut-house dad had started to think twice about some of the moves he made against him. He sure as shit couldn't and didn't lock him in the basement anymore.

But beyond even that, I believe, Lefty had become harder to beat down at home because he loved someone now, and that love had made him grow even harder to break on the inside.

All the same, Mr. Savage didn't like bein talked back to, especially when his ulcer was stark-ravin mad. He cussed at Lefty and jumped from his chair. Lefty jerked back and knocked over his dad's glass of milk. *That* made Mr. Savage lose what was left of his mind. He stood over Lefty and screamed like he wanted his vocal cords to come undone.

Lefty didn't move, even with his dad's acid-smellin breath and spit flyin in his face. His mom was already cryin.

His dad balled his fists and held em up. When Lefty still didn't move, Mr. Savage stormed out of the kitchen.

He came back a minute later with a sketch book that he took from Lefty's bedroom. It was full of pictures of Rose. Mr. Savage said Lefty's art was shit and so was he. He fished some matches from a kitchen drawer and set the sketch book on fire.

Lefty leaped from his chair, knockin it over, and grabbed for the sketch book. His dad backed away with it while the flame kept lickin it up. When the sketch book was more than halfway ruined, he stamped it out on the floor and looked his son straight in the eye.

"Damn you and your drawings for pussies," he said. "At least your brother will be a man to respect."

The furnace light behind Lefty's eyes went up. The demons kicked open the door.

He grabbed his dad by his old flannel shirt and threw him to the floor. His mom begged for him to stop. He kicked his dad in the face. Lefty kicked him harder, and then harder. Mr. Savage howled and clawed at Lefty's legs. His mouth and nose were bleedin good. Lefty pulled him up with his left hand and cracked him square in the jaw with his right.

Mrs. Savage ran from the room. Lefty looked back toward her. In that one second, Mr. Savage snatched a meat cleaver from the counter. His eyes were deadly now.

Lefty inched toward him real careful with his fists up. They stalked each other in a circle until Mr. Savage's back was to the table.

Lefty told im to put down the cleaver. Mr. Savage said I want you out of this house right fuckin now and you're never comin back in. You're ugly and stupid and a total disgrace to my name. If I could do it again I'd make sure that you'd never been born.

Lefty lowered his hands. The furnace flames went down.

Mr. Savage lunged with the cleaver and caught him on the upper left arm. It cut through Lefty's shirt but didn't break the skin.

The flames kicked on again, and Lefty dove at his dad.

Mr. Savage jumped out of the way. Lefty crashed into the table. He fell forward over it and braced himself on his right arm.

His dad came at him and brought the meat cleaver down so hard and fast it whistled.

Lefty looked down and saw that his right hand now had only the thumb.

His brain filled with voltage and the siren went off in his ears. He grabbed the tipped-over glass from the table and smashed it on his dad's head. A gash on his scalp poured blood like wine over his face.

Mr. Savage dropped the cleaver. His eyes rolled up. He fell back against the frigerator door, and slid down to the floor.

Lefty pounced on him and pinned him with his knee. He snatched the cleaver and raised it.

And then, lookin down into his dad's faraway eyes, he brought it down thirty-six times. At least, that's what the police reports said later on. I doubt Lefty was keepin count at the time.

Whatever the tally was, it did the job. Mr. Savage was here with us no more.

All pissed and partied out, Lefty's demons slid back into his heart and closed the door. The fire in his eyes disappeared. His face relaxed. Pushin with his good hand, smearin the blood on the floor into a pre-school project, he scooted on his butt to the cabinet door beneath the sink and sat against it. He looked at his stump of a hand. His breathin started to slow.

A few minutes later, his mom tip-toed back into the kitchen, and all the A-plus angels in heaven couldn't have made her ready for what she saw in there. Lefty just looked at her, long and deep, and then he closed his eyes.

He didn't move an inch, not even when the cops and the medics showed up.

The blue boys barged in, guns out, and told him he was under arrest. The medics tended to his hand while the cops watched real close, and then the cops took him away.

And all of that was just act one. I'd swear even now that the moon and the stars and even Aztec fuckin sun dials had lined up to round up the four boys from Colton.

News of the slaughter spread fast. Me and Rich and Tommy called each other to discuss what we ought to do next.

But the Colton cops had already decided that for us.

You've heard that whole thing about six degrees of separation. Well, in this case, I would have called it six degrees of luck that sucks ass. Turns out a kid from Colton we'd made a license for was the son of a second cousin of a Kensing County sheriff's deputy. The kid's dad found it and busted his balls, and the kid told him where he got it. The second-cousin deputy then of course caught wind of it, and he had contacts up and down the Colton Police Department.

The Colton cops dug around on us some more. I've already mentioned they were highly suspicious, especially after we brought business local. Pretty soon they had themselves a full script of information with our four names as stars in the show. A few cold-case files for unsolved burglaries came out for a cameo too.

They'd been plannin to bust all four of us *that day.* They rounded up me, Rich, and Tommy all at about the same time just a few hours after Lefty's arrest. I was takin a whiz in the bathroom when they showed up at my house. I believe Tommy was gettin high in his basement. Rich wasn't home to say hi, but Mrs. Redoux let the cops know where to find him. Rich got roped while he was still in line at Bob Miller's grocery store six blocks down. He was buyin stuff for the stew his mom was gonna make for dinner.

It blew at the time, but I had to laugh about it later. It still makes me chuckle and shake my head once in a while. All we had to do was *not do business in Colton.* We could have made our money a little bit longer, packed up, and then moved on to another way of makin it.

Instead we got stupid. Not a good recipe for young guys who'd rather get drunk than read the paint on the ceiling of a cell.

In the end, we screwed ourselves. Anyone can outsmart the world for a while, and help themselves to everything in it. But hear me now and don't you forget it. The world is wiser and stronger and more *right* than any of us, and it deals with those who hurt others and live for themselves, and who take more than their share.

*T*he whole thing made noise in the regional news. In Colton, it was the only news for a while.

The cops came down hard once they had us all in custody. It didn't take long for them to get what they wanted.

Of course they nailed us for the fake IDs and documents. They also got us to confess to three of their unsolved burglaries.

Lefty was already cooked because of the murder. Now he had the other charges too.

All the trial stuff started in March 1965. I got to know jail cells and the Kensing County courtroom better than my bedroom at home.

And to boot, the state decided to try us all as adults even though Tommy was the only one legally so. Lefty would become one in April. The "calculation" and "sophistication" of our offenses had earned us all the right to be grouped and potentially locked up with the big gorillas.

Colton thought we were total losers. They would have rather forgotten about us, but they couldn't look away from us either. We were the four-car pile-up they rolled past at five miles an hour.

All four of us each got four years for the IDs *plus* two years for the burglaries. No parole. We'd also be sent to different prisons to keep us apart. The county judge said we ran "too great a risk" to become "conspiratorial recidivists" if allowed to stay together.

Lefty of course had way bigger problems beyond those.

To make matters worse, he'd started goin berserk. Spittin, cussin, throwin food. He even pissed on a guard that was walkin past his cell.

In time Lefty got so nasty in so many ways that he had to be transferred to a solitary cell. Up until his murder trial, he wasn't allowed to step out except to take a shower with two armed guards watchin im try to use the soap with one good hand. His meals were passed through a slot.

The authorities thought they were keepin im under control while teachin him to behave. What they didn't know was that they'd made im at home, just as his dad had done for most of his life. Stickin Lefty in solitary was like gettin back at a cockroach by trappin it under a dirty plate.

They also gave him hell for drawin pictures on his cell wall. By some Houdini kind of magic, he'd smuggled in the nub of a green pencil. I myself can't imagine how. He was workin on a mural when the slot of his door opened and the guard figured out what was up. When he refused to hand over the pencil, he pushed the "go" button for the riot squad to come in and get it.

Now it's important to remark on one thing you may have already figured out for yourself.

He'd been drawin on the wall *with his left hand.*

More than that, from what I heard later on, the partial mural was so damn beautiful that the jailhouse guards didn't try to erase it. For all I know, Lefty's work remains on that wall to this day. If it is still there, I hereby declare it a holy gift to all of those who've spent their lonely time with it.

Lefty's trial for the murder began in May '65. The local media was all f-in over it. Chicago and south Michigan sent their own reporters too.

The prosecuting D.A. was a tall and skinny Hoosier yup named William Smith. He looked like a toothpick for a fairy-tale giant. He always wore bow ties, and his black hair was clipped so close to his head that his cow licks stuck out like tiny porcupine needles.

He was also a snarlin bulldog with brains in the courtroom. I once heard that he'd finished near the top of his class at the IU-Bloomington School of Law. Plus, he had a hate-on for the dregs of society. Dregs like Lefty Savage. He didn't give a half-cooked shit about how Lefty's life might have made him a problem. He saw only a killer with some seriously bad marks on his social report card, and he meant to persuade Indiana to kick his law-breakin ass.

Lefty's public defender was gonna help his client try to squeeze through a plea of not guilty by reason of self-defense. He also knew Lefty was lookin at possibly long and hard time. His bigger hope was to get the jury to shave a few years by takin em deep into Lefty's childhood. He meant to show that Lefty's life was a dark and lonely road leadin straight to the loss of his fingers. Lefty was a gifted and sensitive artist, he would argue, and when Lefty's dad destroyed the hand with which he'd learned to draw, he gave Lefty no choice but to put his own end to the pain and abuse. And if he hadn't done that, his dad would have surely killed *him*.

Of course Smith the D.A. said let's break out the box of tissues and while we're at it the orchestra too. The world's full of sad stories about kids who were abused, but most of em didn't hack their daddies *thirty-six times* with a cleaver. No, Lefty was a case of evil nature usin imperfect nurture as an excuse to rage upon the world.

I wasn't there to see the trial, of course. I was busy waitin for my transfer to maximum security in Bixel in northeast Indiana. According to what I gathered while warmin the county cot, it was a prancin-pony show of witnesses and evidence. The D.A. loaded the stand with every hostile talkin head he could find. That included two shrinks who'd "determined" Lefty was a "psychopath." Former jockasses Buck

Thompson, Bob Mulligan, Tom Sodek, and Phil Barrelli showed up as well. Even Mr. Lewis had a chance to sound off.

The public defender called up Lefty's mom and Rose to speak of his better nature. He also brought in his own shrinks who said—in their own terms—that the state's head-doctors were full of fly-flecked shit. Lefty wasn't a psycho, but rather a "deeply traumatized victim" who'd been through the most vicious kind of cruelty before he finally snapped. He suffered from anger, anxiety, *and* depression, but he could still be healed. Most important, he did have a conscience, as well as compassion for others. He could love and be peaceful and contribute to society if not provoked by daily hatred and violence. A cold cell in the middle of guns and guards and the worst of humanity wasn't going to help him. He needed "intensive in-patient care from mental-health professionals."

Dennis took the stand as well, and *that's* what I'm pissed I had to miss. Even though he was the D.A.'s witness, no one—maybe not even the D.A.—could have told you what he was gonna say under oath. Dennis wasn't *for* Lefty . . . but he wasn't all against him neither.

And wouldn't you know it, he didn't move left or right about his brother while bein cross-examined. His words didn't help, and they didn't hurt. They were just there, carefully spoken but spoken without care. Short answers. Blank face. Flat voice. No emotion.

Lefty had trouble with or without his brother. D.A. Smith was whoopin ass with the jury, especially when it came to describing the murder as it occurred. He put the whole place under a spell with how he told the Savage story right down to the blood splatter beneath the kitchen clock. He also showed the crime-scene photos, which weren't real pretty. By the time he was done, a few jurors were starin at Lefty like he'd killed Spanky from *Our Gang* instead of his lunatic dad.

The public defender did what he could. He didn't have the D.A.'s power to pull people in, but he was smart and straight-on. He made a good case as to why someone like Lefty would have cracked like a branch from the tree of what's real.

The jury convened for more than a week, and word was that things were gettin tense behind their closed door. Rumors of a hung jury spread fast.

Even the D.A. was startin to sweat. The defender might have planted just enough doubt to sway at least one person, and that was all he needed for a mistrial.

Now, here's where things took a big turn. Not bein schooled in the law, I can only explain it as I understood how it happened.

Smith had been lookin for murder in the second degree. When he thought he might lose it all to a hung jury, he pulled the judge and public defender together and offered a deal to make sure he could drop at least half a hammer on Lefty. If Lefty would change his plea to guilty, he'd reduce the charge to voluntary manslaughter.

Lefty would also have to agree to one other thing.

Smith had his connections in high places, so he knew things many people didn't. One of those things was that right around that time, the Life Sciences Department at Ballard College in Pinkton, Indiana, was puttin together a project that had somethin to do with "biosocial and behavioral photobiological research."

The head of the team and department was Charles A. Sumner. His friends called him Chuck. That meant Smith called him Chuck.

Smith and Chuck had been on the phone a lot as of late. It was during those conversations that Smith figured out he might still guarantee himself a conviction, even if it was a lesser sentence. That mattered everything to him, because he'd never lost a trial. Not yet.

Plus, his buddy was workin on something big, and he needed just the right guinea pig for it. Smith knew he might have it for him in Mel Savage.

That's just how it could go back in '65 in Colton.

The maximum sting for voluntary manslaughter would have been fifteen coins in the can. Smith offered Lefty seven years to run *concurrently* with the other convictions he was sharin with us. No parole.

If he pled guilty and signed on for Ballard College Chuck's special "research."

"The Effect of Color on Mood and Aggression."

That's what they were callin the project.

And right beneath the title: "Innovative Treatment Techniques for the Violent Mind."

Innovative Treatment Techniques. That's the part that jumped out at me at the time. What the hell was that supposed to mean? I'm sure Lefty knew, because his defender wanted every detail before they said yes to a deal.

Clearly they could have said no without further questions. The rumors of a hung jury favored them most of all.

But that's still all they were to both sides. Rumors. Either the D.A. or the defender stood to lose big dependin on whether or not they were true.

Lefty accepted the deal.

None of us had much to celebrate that spring of '65. It would be years before any of us could touch a cold beer and a warm woman again. Time would get cruel and turn into brick.

Perhaps the only thing to look forward to—the only thing that kept us all from hangin ourselves with our bed sheets—was the money. A big share of it was still out there, safe and waitin in creative locations away from any authorities that might have an interest. And on the back end of our hard time, the stacks would still be tall and cool and green. They'd welcome us home, get us drunk and laid, and maybe help us move further from the past.

Yes, thank God. At least there was the money.

Because without it, I'm afraid, our hope just might have run out.

Prison. What a brilliant idea. Round up all of the apples that don't belong in the basket and drop em into a box full of worms. Let time forget about them, and then roll em back into society bruised, pissed off, and even more rotten at the core.

Surely I understand the *why*. I just don't see the *what for*. Most people are decent and hard-workin, and they figure out how to get through their lives in spite of their struggles. The dudes in prison *can't* get through it, and don't. I guess most of us convicts deserve each other, just as good people who play fair with the law deserve to live in peace and without fear.

I broke the law, and the law broke me back. One minute, I was drinkin and smokin and countin my cash before steppin out to shoot pool and maybe pick up some poontang. The next minute, I was sleepin in state-issued pajamas on a hard bed with a blanket I could have used to blow my nose. I didn't much like my time on the institutional toilet either. Nothin like makin unholy noise with your ass because of the diet and havin a whole cell block crackin up at your discomfort. Better yet when guards and goons walk by and see you about to blast off.

Prison's the place for fixin the problem without havin to cure it. Curin it takes a lot more effort and patience and grease from the elbow than the racin rats can afford. Better just to round us up and stick us in. Problem out of sight, problem out of mind—until of course it shows up again to make off with the whole picket fence instead of just a few slats.

All we do in prison is get better at what you put us in there for. We get trained in new trades by the experts. Share ideas. Figure out the things we did wrong to get caught. Let our hearts harden past what's human because it's the only way to survive. You cannot have compassion for your fellow man when you're surrounded all day by crazy fucks who feel *nothing*.

It started for me day one at the Peterson State Penitentiary in Bixel, about a half-hour north of Fort Wayne and fifteen minutes from the Ohio border. My cellmate was a guy named Leo Rankin. Went by Lee. It was his third trip to the pen, and he was only twenty-five. This time it was for aggravated battery.

"It could have been worse," he said to me that first day. "I was ready to carve the bastard up, but his old lady cracked me good with a beer bottle while I was beatin' his ass."

Lee pulled his hair apart and showed me the scar on his scalp.

"And I'm gonna beat your ass too," he said to me, "if you don't abide by a couple of rules."

I didn't find his rules acceptable, so I told him to get shanked.

He punched me in the side of the face. I shook it off and hit im back. We wound up wrestlin down to the floor. A guard walked by but didn't do nothin.

I'll bet we went at each other for a good five minutes before we both got tired out. We let go and sat on the floor to catch our breath. We both had some shiners and scrapes.

"You're still gonna do what I say," he said.

"Hell I am," I said. "I'll smash your face even harder if I have to."

He crawled into his bed for a snooze.

We got testy sometimes after that, but he never tried to push his way on me again.

And that was only *my* first day. I had to wonder how the others might be holdin up. Tommy'd been sent to Bisping Correctional Center in Casper. Rich was at Pawanee Correctional in Pinkton Falls. Lefty would be payin his social bill at max-security Harrison State Prison, about thirty miles north of Indianapolis.

I wasn't worried at all about Tommy. He was nuts and tough enough to fend for himself. He'd take a few punches in prison, but he'd never wind up anyone's bitch.

Rich I wasn't so sure about. He'd always had a softer side, and I don't mean in the same way Lefty did. Rich held up fine when he was with us. But without us, alone in a house full of ravin-mad animals? Hell, one time I almost prayed for him.

Of the four pens, Harrison had by far the roughest rep. That's where Indiana trucked some of its biggest tickin time bombs. If I ever felt sorry for myself at Peterson, I thought of Lefty's lot with the worst of the misfits. The rapists and sadists and spree killers. I reminded myself that no matter how bad it gets, someone *always* has more problems than we do. That right there pulled me through plenty of nights when I might have . . . well, when I thought I might not make it.

I learned about Lefty's life in prison through the letters that he wrote—also *with his left hand*. The correctional administration opened and read em all, so of course me and him had to be careful with content or else the letters wouldn't find us.

It was also through our letters that Lefty picked up his nickname. It was me who started it. I called im Lefty in a letter because I said he was gonna have to do more than draw and write with his good hand from now on. He was gonna have to get better at pullin his pony southpaw too.

He thought that was funny shit. And from that point forward, he signed all of his letters as Lefty.

We also worked out a few codes for sharing information that might not get past the screening. That's how I learned some things about Lefty's "project." He told me most of the rest later on, after he was released from the system.

So here's how I understood "The Effect of Color on Mood and Aggression: Innovative Treatment Techniques for the Violent Mind"—

The state—surely backed by the feds, but never outright verified—wanted better ways of dealin with its most wanted and sometimes the mentally ill. In other words, how could authorities get people to either talk or behave if they wouldn't in spite of the tactics?

Chuck Sumner and his buddies at Ballard had stepped in with a theory. They said the color of a room figured into how hard or easy someone under question or treatment would be. A religious man ready to share his faith by means of high-grade explosives would be more likely to "cooperate" under interrogation if he was in a dim-colored room instead of a bright-colored room.

They also said people were "affected by the near infrared and long ultraviolet range of the electromagnetic spectrum." Colors had a "major influence on the endocrine system" that "regulates mood and metabolism." They "excited or reduced agitation." "Both the academic and law enforcement communities" should "pay serious attention" to the possibility that "significant effects on human behavior may be produced by artificial lighting or interior color selections."

They were going to measure the "precise effect of color" on "particular biochemical mechanisms in the body."

Some of what I'm sharin with you goes beyond my letters with Lefty. I read up on the subject later on too. I still have my notes and pages in a drawer around here somewhere.

The researchers' plan was to put Lefty through tests in a 10' x 10' room set up just for the project at the prison. According to them, anything bigger could muck up results because "not every subject would be sure to react."

The "subject" also had to be either alone in the room, or there with just one other person. More than that would create a "diffusion effect." That meant "too many other colors and stimuli would compete with the primary color and reduce the monochromatic effect."

The test room wasn't to have any windows either. Just a door, a table, a chair or two—all white. The walls and ceiling would be white as well.

The color of the room and its objects would be controlled by lamps on tracks along the edges of the room. Two tracks above, two tracks below.

The floor would be dark brown.

They'd monitor Lefty's breathing and heart through special pads stuck to his chest and measured by remote. It was some kind of new technological shit that'd been provided for the experiment.

All of it would be watched and recorded by a camera in each corner of the ceiling.

That bein said, the tests on Lefty began with a red room.

It was just Lefty and one of Sumner's assistants in a lab coat with an ID badge. Sumner's boy also had a clipboard and a pen.

The assistant began by askin questions from a form. Almost right away, the red room made Lefty get jumpy. Blood pressure went up. Breathin got faster. His right knee started to bounce.

His answers got short and snappy—yep, nope, maybe, what's it to you?

The assistant looked up and down between the subject and the clipboard and scribbled his notes.

Then the assistant began clickin his tongue. Rubbed his nose over and over. Changed his position in his seat every ten seconds or so.

It all pissed Lefty off worse inside the red room.

The cameras watched from the corners.

The lab coat kept on fidgeting.

Lefty finally leaped across the table, threw the lab coat to the floor, and slugged im in the face so hard the guy's glasses flew off. He even grabbed the pen and tried to stab im with it. The door flew open against the wall. Two guards pounced on Lefty, still snarlin and red in the face.

And so it went for the log book. Red Room Day One—"Not likely to calm the boy down." That's how I would have wrote it.

The next time they brought Lefty in, the room was purple. No assistant this time. Only the table and a chair. A couple of typed pages stapled together on the table.

At first, Lefty didn't bother to read em. He just sat there, thinkin and lookin around. Not so bad. At least not as bad as the red room.

Ten minutes went by, and then fifteen. He got a little restless, mostly because he was bored. He picked up the pages.

He finished readin and set em back down. He felt a little uneasy, and looked that way too, but he didn't get worked up. Just sat there, silent and still. He bit at the thumbnail on the hand that no longer had fingers. His eyebrows scrunched. His forehead crinkled up.

The typed pages were about the plea agreement havin been later determined invalid. But, he still had to complete the experiment *plus* serve the full fifteen years he would have been given for voluntary manslaughter. On top of that, his mom had suffered a stroke and was now paralyzed on the left of her face.

It was all bullshit, of course. Just somethin they put together to see how he'd react. He did react, but not as they might have expected. If they'd had him read it in the red room, someone might have gone home without a head.

When they brought him back in a week later, the room was orange. Once again, no one in there but him. One chair, one empty table. Just Lefty, and orange.

Didn't take long for him to get cranky. Started chewin on his left-hand fingernails. Tappin his foot. His breathin and blood-pumpin went up a bit.

Then it got goofy. They started playin a tape of Benito Mussolini through a small speaker mounted over the door. Lefty listened to the spaghetti speech for a few. Then he stood up, went to the door, and pulled down hard on the speaker.

It didn't move, so he wrapped his bad hand around his good hand and gave his best yankee-doodle-yank. It got looser.

He kept at it until the wall mount broke, plaster and all. He ripped the wires from the back of the speaker and threw it on the floor. Then he stomped the livin shit out of it.

After all of that, he simply sat back down. His breath and blood came back down, but he was still a little edgy.

The lab coats left him in there. Fifteen minutes. Twenty.

When it hit twenty-five, he got up and started bangin on the wall. "That's enough!" he said.

No response. Just orange light.

Five more minutes. Ten.

He scratched at the wall with his left hand until his fingernails started screamin.

The coats let im carry on that way for a little bit longer, and then they opened the door.

Lefty spun around with his back heavin and his teeth bared.

"Do that again," he said, "and I'll rip you to pieces."

The coats nodded and took some notes. The cameras checked it all out from the corners. Two guards entered the room, cuffed Lefty, and led him back to his cell.

And so it went for a while. Much like mine and Rich's and Tommy's, Lefty's life was a daily drill of eatin and sleepin and watchin your back. Figurin out what to do with all that time to fill up your head. For all of you who think the day ain't long enough, you're wrong. Twenty-four hours is a *lot* of time, man.

Lefty didn't write much about how he got along with the convicts at Harrison. His cellmate's name was Joe Burton. He was servin an Old Testament life span for multiple rape and attempted murder. That's about as much as I knew.

What letters Lefty wrote went only to Rose, his brother, and me.

I kept his letters in a neat stack with a rubber band around it. I looked through em with regularity, especially at night, when the pain in my mind was the worst. Some of the letters had sketches of Rose. Others had drawings of me and him. Some were pretty funny too.

He also sent me sketches of places where we used to hang out in Colton. One was a perfect portrait of downtown, right down to the sale signs in the windows.

A few other pictures were of the visions he'd been seein in green.

I still believe those letters and pictures were what saved me in there. When all you live with is metal and anger and concrete, you forget about the rest of the world and the good people in it.

And when that happens, you can only hope you know someone who can help keep you out of the thickest part of the dark.

*T*he next time they put Lefty in the room, it was blue. A different lab coat was in there with him too.

The coat started the session with general small talk. How are you? How are you getting along in prison? Any thoughts you'd like to share about the experiment so far?

Lefty gave his short but pointed answers.

The lab coat lit a cigarette and then offered one to Lefty.

They both leaned back in their chairs, smoked their smokes, and simply took it easy.

The lab coat chatted with Lefty. Said his name was Roger. He talked about his favorite sports teams and music, as well as some books that he liked. Lefty listened. After a while, they even laughed and sat with their legs stretched out in front of them.

The cameras rolled in the corners.

Roger ground out his cigarette, slipped off the coat, and hung it over the back of his chair.

Then he cracked Lefty in the face.

Lefty crashed backward. His cigarette flew out of his mouth.

"Asshole," he said, rubbin his jaw and crawlin up to sit on the floor. "What'd you do that for?"

Roger rolled up his sleeves, walked around to Lefty's side of the table, and held up his fists.

"How about another kiss?" he said, and swung straight down. The punch stung Lefty in the eye.

Lefty cussed. When Roger didn't come at him again, he stood.

"Damn you," Lefty said.

Roger lowered his fists.

"You're right," he said. "That was rude of me."

He went back to his chair, put his coat back on, and sat down. He shook out a cigarette, lit it, and offered another to Lefty.

Lefty collected his chair from the floor and sat back down at the table. Roger lit his smoke for him.

"Boob says, thanks," he said.

Roger raised his eyebrows. Lefty just smoked.

"Boob says, I've enjoyed the time," he said.

"Likewise," Roger said.

Lefty set his cigarette on the edge of the ashtray.

Then he stood up, leaned across the table, and grabbed a left handful of lab coat.

"But hit me again, and I'll rip your fucking eyes out of your head."

Roger held up both palms and shrugged.

Lefty let him go and sat back down again.

They hung out for a little bit longer. Then the guards came in, cuffed Lefty, and led him out.

Back in his cell, Lefty laid down on his bed. He was feelin the smacks to his face but also the bliss from the blue.

Sometime later, he sat up to write a couple letters. One was to me. The other was to Dennis.

I wrote back. Dennis didn't.

Didn't matter. For even as Lefty set his pen to the paper, Dennis was already well down the road that would put them against each other in the worst imaginable way.

Y ou know my take on institutions. At the same time, I know they have their purpose. We might not always like or agree with em, but made as we are, we need em.

Dennis Savage sure did.

Like a lot of people, he felt at home with systems made up of structure, control, competition, and rewards. His love of that made all the right people fall in love with him, and that right there might have been his greatest strength of all.

As anyone could have predicted, Dennis was a Big Man on Campus at Indiana State. Studied criminal justice. Put together some respectable numbers in football. He didn't light up the field or set any records, but he did start as halfback in three of his four years down there. He got an A+ in poontang too.

After college, he married Laura Dawson, his high-school sweetheart. She'd stuck by him even though she was all the way up at Michigan State. They got married at the Pleasant Valley Baptist Church in Colton. Funny, because Dennis had about as much religion in him as Jesus had patience for tax collectors. They had a baby girl not long after that.

Dennis was accepted into the Indiana Law Enforcement Academy straight out of college as well. After finishing that in the standard three months, he applied with the Kensing County Sheriff's Department.

They of course walked him right in, said welcome home, son, and made sure he sailed through his three months of training in the field.

By spring 1969, he was set to shoot through the ranks. He was so damn popular that many believed he'd make sergeant in well under ten years, which as I understand it is climbin the cop ladder with a tank of nitrous oxide strapped to your ass. The department loved him, and the county loved him too.

Somehow, some way, people always managed to look past the family he came from.

He made a decent paycheck for a young guy. Got himself a three-story, four-bedroom Victorian house on an acre in Blanchard, a nice little town two to the east from Colton. Him and Laura also had a second child, a son, Timothy.

A few Kensing County papers and magazines even wrote feature stories about im.

But as you and me both know, the person we show and the person we are ain't always the same.

Peterson's internal information network made me aware that there was the Dennis Savage that the county knew, and then there was the one that *we* knew.

I started hearin his name soon after he joined the force in '69, and mostly in ways that didn't flatter the man.

Word had it he shook a lot of people down before lettin em go for a price, which was usually cash or personal property or other highly un-cop-like arrangements. One story had him bangin a dope dealer's girlfriend with the dealer's permission in exchange for no arrest. He'd swing by the house without any notice, have his romp in the bedroom—almost always when the dealer was home—and then tip his cop cap on the way out. That went on for a few months, and then Dennis busted him anyway.

The whispers about corruption of course trickled into the sheriff's department, but they didn't add up to squat. It was always a low-life's statement against Andy Griffith's, and you already know whose record was perfect in those particular contests.

Dennis Savage looked like he had it all.

But his lies were overweight, and just like anything else that just can't stop, they'd keep on goin until they burned and bottomed out.

*T*he next time they tested Lefty, they had him in a pink room.

This time, he had more company—*two* lab coats, in spite of the risk of the "diffusion effect." Sumner must have had a special reason for it. They both carried clipboards. The room also included a cart with shiny instruments that looked sharp and unfriendly.

The lab coats began by just starin at Lefty. Then, every fifteen seconds or so, one or the other would glance at the cart.

Lefty's breathin and heart rate were high until about five minutes in. Then it began to drop.

Both coats started speaking with im, and neither was nice. They asked and said shit that would make most men get surly. Lefty didn't pay attention to all of what they said, because relaxed though he felt, he remained fully aware of the flesh-carvin tools.

At one point, he asked if he could lie on the floor while they kept talkin. They said okay, so he got down and stretched out.

A few minutes later, he felt the edge of a blade movin lightly back and forth just above his right ankle. It wasn't cuttin into the skin. Just touchin it, movin across, makin itself be known.

His heartbeat kicked for a second but then went back down and stayed steady.

A foot started nudgin him at different places on his body—shin, knee, shoulder. All Lefty did was glance up a time or two at the coat who was doin it. The coat even squatted right by Lefty's head and acted as if he might spit in his face.

"Interesting," the coat said, and then he sat back down in his chair.

Both him and the other looked up at the cameras before writin on their clipboards.

Lefty didn't care for the pink room. While it kept the demons down, it silenced somethin in im too. Something important. It was like he was just a body with a mind that was barely awake.

I once read how the law used pink in other experiments like Lefty's several years after he died. I'm sure the article's still around here somewhere. It had to do with how pink made it hard to get worked up because your heart muscles can't race fast enough when it's all around you. Sometimes prison authorities used pink rooms on inmates who were freakin out, even those who were color blind.

Another thing they tested on Lefty a few times was how long it took for a calming color like pink to sink all the way in. Most results wound up near fifteen minutes. They also figured out the effects stuck around for about another thirty minutes after he was removed from the pink room.

Only problem was, once the color's effects drained out and his head returned to normal, his mood was way more foul. Both Lefty's cellmate and a prison guard got the ugly end of it at different times when Lefty was comin down from the color. Those earned him stints in solitary without light.

I'm sure he thought about Rose while he was back in the dark. She'd been standin by him so far. To my knowledge, she didn't even hold another dude's hand while he was gone. She came to visit him every couple months too.

I've never even come close to a love like that, and I've had my share of relationships. I've also had my chances to be true. To be myself and open up to someone who might care enough to help heal the pain.

But I just couldn't do it.

From what I gathered during those years, Rose graduated from CCHS and then earned an associate's degree from the Kensing County junior college. She worked hard and went to church and practiced her English until it got real good. Even got herself a job as a receptionist for a small law firm in Camden, which is about fifteen miles southwest of Colton.

Most of all, she waited for her boyfriend to come home.

So I guess you could say that all in all, the experiments on Lefty gave the lab coats the results they were lookin for.

They tested their colors on him a bunch of times over the course of a year.

A few of those times, for reasons unknown, Lefty reacted different to a color than he had before. But in general, the conclusions were mostly the same. The only two colors that did nothin at all to him were yellow and brown. Don't ask me, because I couldn't tell you why. Neither could Lefty, if he were still alive to talk.

Overall, that worked out okay for Harrison State Prison, because Lefty's cell, like most others there, was painted yellow. They obviously hadn't consulted any lab coats before they picked from the palette, because yellow can upset the violent, the insane, and the overly sensitive. I know that because I read about that too.

The other colors they tested on him were white, black, and green.

For the white, the base color of the testing-room walls, they simply turned off the lamps. After all he'd already been through, it made him even more nuts than orange and red had done. Even I could have called that one. White was the extreme other end of the black in which he'd always lived. It's a damn good thing he'd never been to a doctor's office in his life. Can they make those places any whiter, man?

When they tested the black on him, he didn't react, but it wasn't the same kind of no-show as with the yellow and brown. Those two were just fog horns makin noise at a deaf man. The black was aiming the racket at someone who could hear it but was simply stone-cold to the sound.

The last color they tested was green.

If black was one end and white was the other, then you could say that green was the perfect half between the two. It mirrored the opposites back at themselves and so canceled them out, which left itself a balance. A head without extremes.

No pain, no pleasure.

Neither happy, nor sad.

No regret for the past, no worry for the future.

It made his mind pure and clean and quiet.

Where with white and black he tuned out in opposite ways, the green room made him tune *in*. With perfect clarity too—so clear he didn't even have to see anything, because all that he needed was already inside him.

The coats tested the green room on him multiple times, and his response was always the same.

It stripped away everything save what made him at peace.

And just as with the other colors, the effects from the green stuck around after he was out of it, only longer.

As for me, I spent most of my 2,190 days of incarceration in white and gray and black and yellow rooms. They were all the same to me. I just couldn't *feel* things like that. Not in that way. Not like Lefty.

I got out about a year before Lefty did. At the time, I thought that maybe if I got lucky, and if society would allow it, I'd have a new chance to look for a "green room," or at least somethin like it. Somethin that fit Parker Hill and made him at ease to the point where he'd want to *contribute*.

The main question of course would be whether I'd act on that chance.

What do you think?

You're right.

*T*he world had changed like a bitch by the time Indiana let me out in spring 1971. Dick Nixon was ending the trade embargo against China. The Communists were returnin the favor by lettin us stop in to play ping pong. Gas was thirty-six cents a gallon, and a decent new car went for about four grand. Our national ass was fillin even more of the sky in Vietnam.

Hell, we'd even sent fuckin men to the *moon*.

People were doin way more drugs as well, especially LSD and pot.

I myself had soured on grass. I'd been away from it for six years, and I just didn't miss it. Before my sentence, I smoked so much that the soil that made it was probably gettin pissed off. Now I could barely stand the smell of it.

But I also wasn't an idiot. I'd sell it to serve the great demand in the market. I'd move a lot of LSD too. Plus, there'd soon be a small but lucrative heroin trade runnin between me and Detroit. A negro I'd met in Peterson—or *black* dude, if you were on board with Lyndon B. J.—had some good connections. After hangin out with im on the inside for a couple of years, I knew I could trust im. Even my cynical gut said he checked out.

I had the plan, the product, the markets, and the ideas. All I needed was my team.

It was about three months on the outside before me and Tommy got in touch. We hadn't written or spoken at all since we were sentenced.

At the time we re-connected, he was havin a hell of a time findin ways to make a dime. His uncle had tried to set him up workin on cars at a full-service garage, but the owner fired him after just two weeks upon finding out just who he had hired.

I let him know that everything was cool and that the money would be okay again.

Once we were back together, we looked up Rich as well, but he wouldn't have anything of it. He'd had a real hard time at Pawanee Correctional. The prison apes had kicked his ass a lot, and he even got raped a few times. His experiences had brought him to Jesus, and it was a relationship he intended to keep. He didn't respond to our calls to his parents' house, where he was stayin until he got back on his feet. We stopped by a couple of times. His parents refused to let us in or even say where he was.

I found out later on that he joined a new Protestant church where Keeler's Pharmacy used to be on the west side of Colton. He also met a Christian woman there. They got married and had three Christian children. One of his new friends at church got him a job drivin trucks for a moving company. He started teachin Sunday school and became an assistant pastor.

The Lord really does forgive, folks.

There was the Vietnam situation to think about too. Lefty wasn't sweatin the draft because of his hand, but the rest of our numbers were still there to be pulled from Uncle Sam's hat. Only Tommy's was called, and he was declared unfit for duty because his feet were too flat and his spine was slightly curved. His recent membership in the Felony Club didn't go over well either, which is kind of funny when you think of all the other roughnecks and ghetto rats the Pentagon rounded up to run through the rice. The poor have permission to die.

Rich's number stayed in the hat, and so did mine.

Rich had turned to the Truth, and so the Truth had jumped in to protect him, or so I still believe.

I also believe that Providence decided to cover *my* ass for a separate reason. God didn't want me to die yet. In His own mucked-up way, He had a different plan for me.

Come 1971, about the only plan in my mind was makin tall cash. This time, I'd focus on just one business, the drugs. I'd also keep my inner circle smaller and tighter than a hummingbird's ass.

No more gettin spread out with side jobs to make extra cash I didn't need. No more shady connections in the chain of distribution. And I wouldn't do a lick of business within twenty-five miles of Colton.

My specialization brought about greater sophistication, and that led to income that could warp a man's mind, or at least a burn-out convict's. But that much money also attracts every sniffin breed of human rodent close to the trade. In time, those rodents wanted to either move us out of the market or wiggle in for a piece of the action.

Me and Tommy and the two other partners we carefully picked all learned fast that a gun was a better friend than a dog.

The violence was the one thing I *hadn't* thought much about even though I was fresh spooned from the stew where they make it. It's not that I was ever one to back down from a fight. I might even use a bat, or a two-by-four. I also still wore steel-toed boots. But when it came to knives and guns, I'd just never had the stomach. That shit brings you to a scary line in your mind, and once you cross it, you can't ever go back.

My idea at first had been to at least try to do business the right way. The professional way. But as you're aware, my industry isn't exactly known for its rank on the scale of ethical conduct. We eventually got caught with our pants down during an LSD deal. Two negroes showed me and Tommy loaded weapons instead of the cash they were supposed to exchange for the acid. Still seein ourselves as real businessmen, we of course had no weapons. They made off with our product at a 100 percent discount.

We also had to keep an eye on two market players who were known for their weapons as well. One was the nephew of a Detroit mob guy. The good thing was only one of our heroin zones bumped against his. When we knew his people were workin a deal, we simply stayed clear. He let us do our business when it didn't mess with his, and we of course let him do his. It got tense only twice, and nobody ever got hurt.

Then there was Renaldo Kane, an Irish–Puerto Rican pain in the ass. He ran a smugglin and distribution outfit out of Michigan City. He did deals in at least half of our markets, so it was just a matter of time before we both started gettin annoyed.

The way I saw it, I was an Indiana home boy and he was a transplant out of New York who'd done time in three different states. Him and the psychos he kept on his payroll had a reputation for serious violence, but me and Tommy couldn't let that get in the way. We had to make a living, and it was *our* turf. He made his threats, and his people talked tough and waved guns in our faces, but hell if he was ever gonna run us out.

We just had to watch him real close. He was way more trouble than the dude in Detroit. I never in my life intended to kill anybody, but if I had to, I would have killed him.

And then there was Deputy Dennis Savage of the Kensing County Sheriff's Department. It didn't take long for me and him to start eyeballin each other. Whenever he saw me, no matter how near or far, he gave me the eyes. *I've got a read on you.*

It was one of those things where, once you see a certain person, all of a sudden they show up everywhere, and almost always when you couldn't predict it. I still recall two times when a county cop car filled up my rearview and tailed me for miles. The more I looked into the mirror, the less I could tell who it was. It was like I was bein chased by a fuckin shadow that knew how to drive.

But I was sure it was him.

The first time he showed up to give me shit right from my front door was November 1971. I remember the Indiana wind bumpin hard on the windows of my apartment that night. There was a loud knock on my door. And then another, and another. The last one was like a sledgehammer, so I knew it wasn't no Jehovah's Witness.

I looked at the clock. It was like two in the morning. I was still full of the vodka I'd finished with the chick lyin naked in my bed. I pulled on a tee-shirt and jeans from my dirty laundry and made my way to the door.

When I opened it, the light from the hallway spilled around the shape of a man. He was slender but solid with thick and wide shoulders. His bulky black-leather cop jacket made him look even bigger than he was. He was also wearin shades even though it was hours before the sun would wake up. His hand was restin on the butt of his gun in the holster.

"Can I help you?" I said, squintin. The light was brighter than it should have been because my veins were still eighty proof.

He stepped forward, into my apartment, bumpin my shoulder on the way in. He went to the center of the front room, turned around, and stared at me.

"Close the door, Parker," he said.

I closed it, rubbed my eyes, and turned on a lamp.

That's when I figured out it was him.

"Dennis?" I said.

He just stood there. His hand was still on his gun.

"Want a beer?" I said.

He didn't say nothin, so I moved for the kitchen to get one for myself.

"I didn't say you could go anywhere," he said.

I stopped and spun around at him.

"Excuse me, *Dennis,*" I said, lookin im square in the sunglasses. "Unless you got a warrant, I'd like to know why the fuck you're in my living room at two a.m. without an invitation."

His face was chiseled stone. His chin tilted up a little.

"You run a drug trade from here through South Bend and all the way up to Detroit," he said. "I know what you're selling, what your routes are, and who your partners are. So here's how it's going to be, Parker."

His hand was still on the gun.

"You're going to pay me one thousand in cash per month," he said. "I'm going to pick it up from you, right here, on the first of each month. You can expect me around midnight. If you're not here to open the door and hand it to me, the payment goes up to twelve-fifty."

I glanced at my pack of Winstons on the coffee table.

"You mind if I have a smoke?" I said.

He shrugged.

I grabbed the pack, shook one out, and lit it.

"What makes you think I've got money like that?" I said.

"Shut up, Parker," he said. "These are the rules. You'll follow them, or you'll go straight back to prison."

I motioned around the room with my arm.

"Does this look like a mansion to you, Dennis?" I said. "Come on. A grand?"

"You have it, and you'll pay it," he said. "And your first payment is due right now."

I almost bit on my cigarette. Buzzed as I was, I thought to punch him in the face. Hard.

He glanced at his watch.

"It's twelve after two. You have three minutes to pay me, or it goes up to twelve-fifty."

I looked hard into the sunglasses. Not even a trace of the whites of his eyes.

"You're serious," I said.

"You have two minutes and forty-eight seconds," he said.

Man, did I wish Lefty could have been there to see and hear what I did. Sometimes, you just can't find a bigger problem than right inside your own family.

With my cigarette bouncin in my mouth as I ran, I bolted back to my bedroom. It was as dark as a cave except for the moonlight slicin in around the closed window shade. I hopped the bed toward the closet and bumped the naked chick on the way over. She woke up and said somethin.

I told her to keep her mouth shut. My closet was two slidin doors. I ripped one open and yanked on the chain to the overhead bulb. My cigarette was still bouncin so much that I ashed on myself. I dug through some shoes until I got to the shoebox in the back. I was too stressed out to remember how much was in it, but I knew it had more than a grand.

I knocked the lid off the box and grabbed two packs of twenties bundled as 500 bucks. Then I told the chick to shut up again, ran around the foot of the bed, and hauled ass back to the front room.

He was still just standin there, like a marble statue in a museum at nighttime.

I realized my cigarette was somewhere else but in my mouth. Probably in the bedroom or the kitchen.

"Here," I said, and handed the cash out toward im. "You satisfied?"

He just looked at it.

"What?" I said.

"How do you expect me to carry it?" he said.

My arm dropped to my side.

"Gimme a break," I said.

I looked around the room. There was a brown-paper take-out bag on the floor by the coffee table. It had oil stains from the beef and fries I'd wolfed down for dinner, but it'd have to do. It was two in the fucking morning, man.

I scooped it up, jammed the cash into it, and held it out to him again.

"You happy?" I said.

"Watch your mouth, Parker," he said, takin the bag. "This situation can turn on you at any second, so mind your manners."

He went to the door and opened it.

"Next payment's due at midnight on the morning of December first," he said over his shoulder in the doorway.

He shut the door behind him.

After that, I just stood still right where I was. The adrenaline cooled out, and I remembered the booze still left in my tank. There was no way I'd fall back asleep, so I fetched a Schlitz from the fridge and lit another smoke. Turned on my 13" black-and-white and flipped through off-air snow until I hit a rerun of *The Mod Squad*. Then I parked myself on the sofa.

Sometime later, the chick came out from the bedroom. She was wearin just her panties and one of my dirty tee-shirts. She said why not come back to bed.

I said give me a few minutes.

She nodded and left me alone.

I drank two more beers. Smoked a few more smokes. Finally, I stretched out on the sofa, and fell dead to the world.

I drifted into the dark of my dreams. On the way down, I called out to Lefty in my head.

I asked him to please come in there, and help me make it more green.

Six months passed. They can go by pretty fast—unless you're in prison, that is. They sure moved quick for me on the outside. I filled it with business and booze and as many women as I could find to please me for a while.

I even worked some legitimate jobs to help keep the cops from lookin at me.

Of course I mean cops except for Deputy Dennis, who continued grabbin his monthly grand. Right at midnight, first day of each calendar page.

The day I first saw Lefty again was May 15, 1972. We'd hadn't written to each other since I got out. He didn't know my current address, but I did find out through some investigation that he had been set up in temporary state housing meant to keep him warm while he looked for his own place and a job.

Once I knew where he was, I gave him a call. We talked for a while, and I let him know that he didn't have to deal with the state's roach hotel. He could crash with me for as long as he needed.

He said okay.

To make room for him, I had to kick out the chick who was stayin with me at the time. Amy. Nineteen-year-old waitress I met at a diner in south Hensley not far from St. Martin's Catholic High School.

She wanted to be an actress in Hollywood. Christ—don't they all? Her dad split when she was nine, and her mom booted her from the house when she was only sixteen. I felt kinda bad that I was joinin the list of reasons she couldn't trust no one, but then I got over it. Lefty was back, and we had a lot of catchin up to do.

I drove out to pick him up from the housing project in Brownlee, which is about an hour and a half from Colton. Dark brick, darker windows, a few stray cats in the courtyard. A half-dozen dudes with dirty eyes and filthy fingers drinkin from brown paper bags on the sidewalk. It was probably a step up from prison, but I don't imagine too many white suburban Christians walkin past very often, not even in the daylight.

I might have missed him if it hadn't been for the good-lookin caveman face you couldn't mistake or forget. He'd lost some weight, and he wore a different expression. Sort of vacant. The look of someone who'd just had dynamite removed from his brain.

He was starin off at somethin to his right when I pulled up to the curb in my new dark-green Challenger. I leaned across the seat toward the open passenger window.

"Lefty!"

He looked my way, let it register, and nodded. Then he grabbed the suitcase at his side and strolled over to the car.

I parked it and got out. Ran around the back and gave him a hug.

"Good to see you, man," I said.

He nodded again and kind of smiled. I opened the trunk and set his suitcase inside.

"Let's go home," I said.

We both got into the car. I started it up, lit us a couple of Winstons, and hit the gas.

"So, how you doin, man?" I said.

He was coverin his bad hand with his good one in his lap.

"Black Dog" by Zeppelin was on the radio. I turned it down durin one of Page's fat guitar licks.

"You look like you dropped a few pounds," I said, lookin sideways real quick. "You quit eatin or somethin?"

He scratched his bad hand and plucked his cig from his mouth with his good one. The smoke he blew out made a foggy sheet against my windshield.

"You look pretty lean, man," I said.

He just squinted, smoked, and stared ahead.

We drove another mile or so. I turned onto the highway.

Now the radio was playin Pink Floyd. Somethin from *Meddle*.

"Boob says, how are you making money these days?"

I didn't answer right away.

"LSD, grass, heroin," I said. "I work straight jobs here and there too."

He ground out his cigarette. He didn't ask for another.

"Why?" I said. "You want in? There's room."

He covered his bad hand. Looked out at the trees and signs and buildings blurrin by outside the passenger window.

"Boob says, sure. Maybe."

I glanced sideways again.

"You still in touch with Rose?" I said.

"Was," he said, still lookin out the window. "Until about a year ago. She stopped writing."

Up ahead, about a hundred yards off to our right, a deer stepped out from the trees. It had a thought to cross the road right where I was speedin toward.

I passed it. A couple seconds later, I saw it jog across the highway in my rearview mirror.

411

"Don't sweat nothin," I said. "You're home now. You're with me. Rich checked out so he could move in with Jesus, but Tommy's still around. We'll help you get back on your feet."

I clapped him on the leg and felt a thin, square bulge in his left pants pocket.

He looked at me and then moved up in his seat so he could slide out whatever it was.

It was a little book with a red cover and a title in gold letters. I leaned closer to read it:

New Testament

And right beneath that:

Psalms / Proverbs

I sat straight again and looked forward with both of my hands on the wheel.

"Looks like you've been doin some readin," I said.

He ran his left thumb over the cover.

"Boob says, yep."

"Well, I guess it's better for the mind than titty mags."

Another stretch of rollin rubber and silence save for the radio.

"You ain't gonna run off with Rich, are you?" I said.

"Boob says, Rose sent it to me," he said. "About a month before she stopped writing."

He flipped the pages with his thumb. I glanced down and saw, real fast, a whole lot of ink. All verses he'd circled or underlined.

We drove for a while. A tall sign came into view on our right—DICKIE'S Exit 171. I knew it to be a bar and restaurant connected to a liquor store.

"Let's get a beer," I said. "I'm buyin."

I pulled off at the exit and drove around to the frontage road. About a quarter-mile down, I parked in the lot with the four other cars in front of DICKIE'S. The windows were boarded and the paint was flakin from the building, but the OPEN sign was up on the door. That's all that mattered to me.

We stepped inside. There was a wall board full of really old food 'n drink specials to our left. A cash register and "Please Wait to Be Seated" sign straight ahead. A door in the wall leadin to the liquor store to our right.

We crossed over to the bar, which ran along the far left wall of the restaurant. It was separated from the dinin area by a half wall. A Milwaukee Brewers game with bad reception was playin on the black-and-white next to the bartender's register. We grabbed a couple stools and sat down.

The bartender looked at us and raised his eyebrows.

"Two Schlitz," I said.

He nodded and cracked open our pint cans.

"We'll run a tab," I said when he set em down in front of us.

And so there we sat, drinkin our first cold one together in years. We talked. Watched the game. At times, we didn't say or do nothin at all. Just thought to ourselves, and looked around.

After a while, it hit me that Lefty was more relaxed at DICKIE'S than he'd been in the car.

I thought it might have to do with his little red bible. He'd placed it before him on the bar. It looked a little funny there among the glass rings, beer puddles, and overflowin ashtrays.

I leaned back and lit a Winston. An old couple was eatin meatloaf and mashed potatoes in the dining area behind us. Two drunks were spittin while they spoke far to our right at the bar. A forty-lookin

413

female was drinkin somethin clear on the rocks by herself a few seats to our left.

I stared at the walls, which I hadn't really yet noticed because the light was so low.

They were covered in wallpaper that was startin to peel and bubble out in a few spots.

Forest-colored wallpaper, old and faded.

We stayed for a couple more hours and had a few more beers. Hell, in time, even I started to feel Lefty's peace, like warm bath water movin gently inside of that room full of green.

A man might be out of the prison, but that rarely means the prison's out of the man.

Lefty was now set up in the front room of my apartment. One night early on when I got up from bed to take a piss, I peeked in on him while he was snoozin on the sofa. He might have been countin some sheep, but he slept like he was still in the joint—stiff, out of place, rarely all the way under because part of his mind was always tuned in to the danger. And when he was awake, he *always* stayed in the front room except to relieve himself, grab food or beer from the kitchen, or step out somewhere with me.

The first couple of weeks, pretty much all we did was hang out in the front room. Drink Schlitz, watch TV, snort a little coke. Talk about prison. I also let him smoke some of the weed I had for sale. I didn't enjoy the smell of it in my apartment, but the situation wasn't about me right then. It was about him, and makin him feel okay.

One night I even offered to score us a couple of hookers so he could get the years of tension out, but he said no thanks.

We didn't do any smack. I might have been sellin a rickshaw load of it at a spectacular profit, but I'd sworn to myself long before that I'd never, ever use it. I wouldn't even try it just once to find out how much it's supposed to get you off. I'd seen both the front and back ends of usin, and I'm not sure if the back end even qualifies as humanity. It's a wood-chipper for the soul, and it don't turn off no matter how many times you flick the switch. No way, man. Not me. I couldn't cross over into that black of a nightmare.

Whenever I left to either do a deal solo or clock in at a legitimate job, Lefty just stayed glued to the sofa until I got back. Read his little red bible. Wrote letters to Rose he didn't mail. Drew in the sketch book that I bought for him one night on the way home from sellin LSD.

He didn't yet know about my arrangement with Dennis. He would, though. Soon. The first of June was comin up fast.

Tommy dropped in a few times, but only when I was around. Even after the years in the joint, him and Lefty were still neither warm or cold to each other. Just . . . there.

One night, while Lefty was drunk and asleep on the sofa, I found myself starin at his suitcase. He had just the one to his name. It wasn't that big, and it had barely anything in it. Two shirts. Two pairs of pants. Two pairs of socks. Three pairs of underwear. Toothbrush and a comb. One pen and one pencil, unsharpened. A legal envelope full of old letters from me and Rose, as well as a bunch of his drawings.

That was it. It was a bona fide case of a man's possessions tellin the tale of himself. He had no home. No money. No family, especially since his mom had been diagnosed with breast cancer about a year before his release. She'd sold the house in Colton and went to live with her sister, June, who'd moved to northern Wisconsin.

Lefty was a real-deal wanderer now. All he had was me, his pain, and the gift God had given him for reasons known only to Him.

By May 31, I still hadn't yet spoken of Dennis to Lefty. Truth be told, I still didn't know how to handle it. Should I give Lefty the heads-up and tell him that his brother was the worst kind of scumbag now? Should I make sure he was somewhere else at midnight on June 1? Or, should I let em both see each other after givin Dennis the cash?

I didn't decide, which I guess was my decision.

June 1 came around, and like German clockwork, the knuckles rapped on the door. I popped out from my bedroom with the cash in the brown paper bag.

Lefty was drinkin a Schlitz and watchin a rerun of *Hawaii Five-O* on the 18" color Emerson I'd bought brand new the day before. The thing was a goddamn beaut.

The lamps were off, so the light from the Emerson was splashin and flickerin all over the walls like liquored-up ghosts.

I crossed the front room with the bag. Lefty never took his eyes off the TV. I looked back at him and opened the door.

There was Dennis, hands on his hips, shades on his face, and his authority fillin the doorway.

"Hello, Dennis," I said.

His jaw moved and he peered around me. He must have seen the feet up on the coffee table behind me.

"It's Officer Savage to you," he said, steppin forward and grabbin the bag from my hand.

"You're right," I said. "I keep forgettin that part."

His shoulder bumped me on the way in. Once he was past me, he stopped and stared at the couch.

Lefty looked away from the TV and saw the cop starin down at him.

"Lefty, I'd like you to meet Deputy Dennis Savage of the Kensing County Sheriff's Department," I said.

No sound but the TV for a moment.

"What is he doing here, Parker?" Dennis said with his back to me.

"He's a free man now," I said. "Don't you have tabs on all of that?"

I walked around him, snatched my Winstons from the table, and lit one up. The smoke joined the party of flickerin ghosts in the room.

"I know he's out of prison, Parker," Dennis said, still lookin down at Lefty. "What's he doing *here?*"

"Well, for the time, he lives here, Dennis. I mean, Officer."

Lefty covered his bad hand with his good one.

"I see," Dennis said. He turned around. "You do understand that raises the rent."

I looked away, thought it over, and shrugged.

"Nope," I said. "I let the landlord know. He's cool. Rent stays the same."

"No," he said. "I mean your rent with *me*. We're looking at two convicted felons in one bush, Parker. That changes the price."

I looked at him real hard. My mouth puckered into a little "o" while a chuggin train of words pulled their freight through my mind.

"You better take off them sunglasses, Dennis," I said. "Or you might not see my fist hittin your fuckin face. And besides, the sun went down a few hours ago."

He gave me his cocky cop smile that flashed his upper teeth.

"That'll cost you five hundred," he said. "Go get it."

"Don't have it," I said. I drew from my cig and blew the smoke right at him.

"Make it six hundred," he said.

I didn't move.

"You have one minute, or it's seven hundred."

I looked a second longer, shook my head, and then moved past him toward my bedroom.

"You can also add five hundred for your new tenant," he said to my back. "That's eleven hundred."

I stopped. My mind went red with rage. All I could see through it was the .45 semi-auto in my bedroom.

"That's enough, Dennis," Lefty said.

I turned around. Lefty was already up off the couch and approachin his brother.

"What gives you the right?" he said, real slow and even.

"Sit back down, Melvin," Dennis said, "or so help me I'll ruin the rest of your week."

Lefty stayed still.

"Why didn't you ever write back to me, Dennis?"

The changin scenes of *Hawaii Five-O* were throwin more electric paint at the ghosts slidin around on the walls.

"I must have sent you fifty letters," Lefty said.

"You have twenty seconds to get the other eleven hundred," he said without lookin at me.

I bolted back to the bedroom and grabbed the rest of the cash. Now he really was diggin deep into my pockets. The fuckin rent was due too.

I returned with part two of the payment. He stuffed it into the bag.

"The least you could do is say thanks," I said.

"Don't talk to me like I'm some kind of thief," he said. "You're a *drug dealer*, Parker. A drug dealer with a record. People know it, and they're watching. You're safe right now because of *me*. You have no idea what would happen if I stepped out of the way."

"Right," I said.

"Boob says, have you talked to mom?" Lefty said.

Dennis nodded toward the little red bible on the coffee table.

"What's that, Melvin?" he said.

Lefty glanced at it and then back at him.

"What does it look like?"

"It looks like they fed you Jesus and you ate it," Dennis said. "I understand. Why you need it."

He looked from Lefty to me and back again. Then he shook his head.

"It's all such a waste," he said. "This. All of it."

He turned for the door.

Lefty grabbed his arm and spun him around.

Dennis tensed up. He almost dropped the bag, but switched it to his left hand before it fell. His right hand went to his holster.

"*You* tell *me*," Lefty said. "What *should* I live for?"

Dennis almost smiled, but stopped himself.

"Well, Melvin, I guess that *is* the question, isn't it," he said. "I honestly hope you figure it out."

He pulled his arm away from Lefty's grippin hand.

"Unfortunately, at least in this world, you're a criminal, and worse than that, a killer," he said. "Our father's dead because of you."

Lefty's face stayed still.

"You never loved him, Dennis," he said. "You didn't care for him any more than you do about anybody else. Except for maybe yourself."

"You don't even know me," Dennis said. "Your opinions mean shit."

His hand was still on his gun.

"Let's save the family and morality speeches and stick to the truth," he said. "You are where you are because of who you are."

Once again, he looked back and forth between me and Lefty.

"I don't owe either of you anything. I've already been way too easy on you, *Parker*. You really don't know how bad it can get."

Oh, yes, I do, I thought but didn't say.

Lefty turned around and picked up his bible from the table.

"There's a lot in here you ought to know, Dennis," he said.

Dennis smirked.

"Please," he said.

He moved toward the table and pointed at it.

"There's, what, six empty beer cans and the roach of a joint right here! The *Bible? Salvation?* You're lucky I don't arrest your stupid ass right now."

"Then why don't you?" Lefty said.

Dennis went quiet.

Lefty stared into the sunglasses and then glanced down at the brown paper bag.

"Because you got what you came for," he said.

Lefty rubbed the thumb of his good hand over the bible.

"We have to believe in something that's better than we are, Dennis," he said.

Dennis's hand drifted down from his gun.

420

"Right," Dennis said. "You're right. If we don't all go to church on Sunday, there is a chance we could turn out like you."

"Or you," Lefty said.

Dennis looked at me.

"See you next month," he said.

He went to the door and opened it.

"Fifteen hundred, July first," he said over his shoulder.

"Damn you, Dennis," Lefty said.

Dennis looked down, at the floor. His back was still facin us both.

"No, Melvin," he said. "Damn *you.*"

He stepped out into the hall. And just before he closed the door:

"Nice TV, Parker. Business must be good."

Then he shut it.

Lefty went back to the sofa and lay down. He was still holdin his bible. Close to his chest, in his good hand.

I watched him and then turned off the TV. The ghosts disappeared and the room went dark.

"Good night, Lefty," I said.

I turned around to head for my bedroom.

"Good night, Parker," he said from behind me.

And that was how we left it.

I know how to be good, and so do you. We all do. It's written inside us the second we shoot from the chute. Maybe even before that. The Christians and Muslims and Jews and Hindus and atheists and even the witches worshippin trees can fight all they want about who's right and what's wrong. It don't change *my* truth, in my eyes, in my heart.

It's simple, really. First we figure out we're here. Next, who got us here. In time, we also figure out the world's bigger than we are and that it really doesn't care all that much about us. And once *that* becomes clear, we hope hard and fast that certain people and ideas will make it all a little easier to get through.

Usually it's mom and dad that help us out. If they're no good, we look up our friends. If they're just as useless, then maybe we'll try ourselves. And if we suck at hangin tough too, which we usually do, that's when we find our religion, right there, where it's been all the while.

As for those who *don't* find their religion after trial by flames—like me—they *blame* what they can on religion. It's an easy assignment.

People like that tend to do what I do, and make the choices I've made. Because if you can write off most people and things and even your faith, it's pretty easy to live only for yourself even though society might not like it.

But don't get me wrong. We can argue all we want about God. We can bitch about why He "ain't here" or why He lets some shit happen. But there's a secret piece of me and you, way down, that knows things just won't ever be right unless we believe that He's around.

I drink and smoke and do drugs. I sell an illegal product that harms people. I've told lies. I've hit men with the idea of hurtin em bad. I sleep with as many broads as I feel like, and sometimes I don't even remember their names while they're lyin right there next to me.

I'm not what you would call a good person.

But in my heart, I cry. No one knows that but me and now you.

I cry because life gave me an excuse to be selfish and I took it.

I let both my doubts and the darkness out there get in the way of my hope.

And goddamn it, I'm still not ready to change. Maybe I never will be.

I've even called on God to explain *me*. He still hasn't coughed up an answer.

Maybe He's waitin for me to do the work. To find those answers we're born with.

Yeah, I know how to be good. Maybe even happy.

But like I said, I ain't ready.

I'm still too proud and pissed off, and the anger still lets me feel like I'm in control.

Seein as how I'm a pain in the ass, He must have a reason for keepin me here.

Hell, I think you might already know what it is.

*L*efty joined the business just shy of three weeks later. It was him who told me he was ready one day while we were both sittin on the sofa drinkin beers. He wanted in.

He'd already gone to one interview with a concrete business that the state system's job-placement program had set up for him. That's all it took to make up his mind. He knew inside of five minutes that not even a blue-brained second-shift manager with a lazy eye and a scar on his face would treat him like a normal clock-punchin human. Lefty walked out before they had the chance to kick him out.

Until then I'd been glad to support him while he struggled slowly to his feet. I kept him fed and buzzed and sheltered and high. I bought him clothes and art supplies.

There was only one thing I wanted to ask him when he expressed interest in my work.

"What about that?" I said, noddin toward his little red bible. It was next to an empty bottle of Schlitz on the coffee table.

He stared at it.

"That will be fine," he said. "Nothing in it is going to change because of what I say or do."

That's when somethin in *me* jumped up. I was surprised by how strong and instant it was.

"You sure, Lefty?" I said. "I mean, it's okay if you still want to try somethin else. Somethin a little less . . . well, you know."

He looked at the floor and then back up at me.

"Boob says, nope, I'm sure."

I pushed myself up from the sofa and sat on the edge of the table to face him.

"But Lefty, I'm sellin *drugs*," I said. "I could wind up back in the pen." I set down my beer bottle and leaned forward with my hands on my knees. "Especially if Dennis changes his mind about our arrangement. You sure you want in on that? You still have a chance to go legit."

I looked to my side at his bible again.

"At least, well, at least you can find some hope, even if it's just in a book, man. You don't have to shut off the rest of the light in your mind."

He stared at me, real hard, straight in the eyes.

"Boob says, I know exactly what you do, and where it could wind up. I said I wanted in, and if I didn't mean it, I wouldn't have said it."

I stared back at him, just as hard. I was really close to cryin, or at least to losin a tear.

Damn this world we fuck up for ourselves.

"Lefty, you *do* have somethin in yourself to live for, and hope for. Way more than I do. You have a gift, and it might even still give you a chance to save your soul and do somethin with your life. Look at all the artists who ever lived, man. Just about every one of em had serious problems. They used their gifts to get rid of some of their pain, and even to touch other people while they were at it. You could still do that. Even with your past."

I lit up a Winston.

"Boob says, thanks, Parker," he said. "I understand what you're trying to do, and what you're meaning to say. But sometimes a gift is just a gift, and nothing more. I want in, and that's the end of it."

I blew dragon smoke through my nose, set the cig in the ashtray, and took a sip of beer.

Then I hung my head and looked down at my feet.

"I wonder how that mural's doin," I said when I looked up again. "The one down in the basement."

"Couldn't tell you," he said.

"Well, I sure hope whoever lives there now ain't painted over it, or let their kids get to it with crayons and shit. That thing was a goddamn masterpiece."

He shrugged and sipped his beer.

"Well," I said, "I still think about what you did down there. Sometimes, at night, when I'm lyin in bed, I see it again in my mind, and it makes me feel that some things can still turn out okay."

He thought it over. Then he shrugged again.

I glanced at the sketch book to my right by the edge of the table.

"You mind?" I said.

He didn't say nothin, so I took it as okay.

I picked it up. The first thing I opened to was a two-page spread of a section of the same basement mural I'd just been talkin about. The scene was just as I remembered it. Better, actually. All that was missin was some of the color.

"You need any more pens and pencils?" I said. "If you want, we can get em tomorrow. I'd be glad to see you finish it."

He considered it.

"Boob says, thanks, Parker," he said. "If you're willing, that'd be fine."

He sipped his beer.

I sipped mine.

"Okay," I said. "You're in on the business. We'll get you started this week. I gotta deliver some smack in Indianapolis. You'll come along for the ride. I'll bring you on a few more deals after that. You can hang out and watch and, if necessary, maybe back me up. We'll talk a lot. I'll tell you all that I know. When you honestly feel like you're ready, and I believe that you're right, I'll send you out on your own. Smaller ones first. You'll work your way up."

I picked my Winston up from the ashtray. It had almost burned itself out.

"I'll also get you a gun."

His eyes moved, but his face was picture-still.

I clapped him on the leg, smiled, and turned on the TV. Sat back down next to him. We watched a few shows and drank a lot more beer.

Later on, even after I'd tied on a good one, I couldn't help but hear a tickin clock in the back of my mind.

A second hand, countin down the minutes, one by one, to a day that had to happen.

J ust as I'd expected, it didn't take Lefty long to get a feel for the trade. We delivered the heroin in Indianapolis and got paid without so much as a sneeze. Here's the package, thanks for the payment, see you next time. In, and out.

Lefty came with me on three more deals after that. Two LSD, one heroin. On the way to sell the smack, he asked me where I got my shit. I told him about the negro I knew in Detroit. My main supplier. I drove there every one or two months to pick up the shipments I'd sell.

After those deals, both of us agreed he was ready to be on his own. A guy from Bruxton wanted four ounces of weed. I sent Lefty to complete the transaction.

I also gave him a Browning hi-power 9mm automatic.

"So how'd it go?" I said as soon as he got back.

It was late. Real late.

He looked at me in that deep-eyed caveman way.

"Boob says, fine," he said.

He sat down next to me. *McMillan and Wife* was on the tube.

"You mind?" he said, reachin for one of the two cold cans of Schlitz I hadn't opened yet.

"Go ahead," I said.

He grabbed one and cracked it open against his left leg. The colored pens and pencils we'd got him at the art store were on the table too. He put the can between his legs and gathered up his supplies, includin his sketch book. Then he leaned back, and started to draw.

McMillan and Wife came back on after a commercial, but I was still too busy watchin him work. Studyin his eyes, his face . . . and especially his left hand. Damn if it didn't glide around just like the other one used to. Lines came to life. Funny-lookin details added up and made beautiful sense.

I watched him for a long time. He didn't mind.

At some point—I don't remember when—I even caught myself feelin happy.

Business got even better during the next few months. I welcomed the increase in revenue, especially now that I was into Dennis for fifteen hundred a visit.

At least I was still payin normal rent for my apartment. Truth be told, even with Dennis diggin into my earnings, if I saved long enough, I might have still afforded the twenty grand or so to get a decent house. Buy some okay furniture too. But ownin a permanent address with public records and paperwork ain't the best thing when you own guns without a permit and move narcotics to cover your bills.

Lefty got more and more solid bein out on his own. Soon enough, I had him settin up deals on my behalf.

Dennis maintained my payment schedule perfectly. And each time he collected the bag, he looked at Lefty less.

Lefty tried findin Rose again without much success. Her family wouldn't give him any information. I myself believed she was probably married with a new last name. So, he plowed through phone books, called lots of wrong numbers, and wrote letters that went to all the wrong places. He'd also been readin the letters she'd sent while he was at Harrison. A lot of nights, that was how he went to sleep.

He was also drawin *all* the time. It was like the Renaissance, only in Colton. He was now buyin his own pens and pencils and sketch books with the cash he was makin, and he was workin through all of em fast.

He drew all kinds of shit. Birds and airplanes and angels. Planets and stars in every shape but round. Rivers of flames in the sky. Rows of houses as white as Indiana Protestants. Mellow, hangin suns that painted the world in a coppery light.

A flat map of the earth with musical notes bent into the shape of the continents.

He drew lots of faces as well. At first, he made a book of just women, with most of em lookin like Rose. But in time, the more he drew, the less she showed up in his work. She might have still been in his heart, but she was finally startin to leak from his brain.

He continued workin on the mini of the mural from the basement too. He re-created the whole thing left to right over five two-page spreads.

He was also takin his time with colorin it. He filled in bits and corners and sections real slow and careful every few days.

At night, we stayed up later together. Thinkin deep, talkin out loud. Sometimes we just sat there, sayin nothin, watchin the reruns until they shut down.

When we did talk, the split between us was an even fifty-fifty at first. But the more we kept at it through those weeks before he died, the more he opened up, and the more I shut up so he could air it all out. I still believe he said more to me in that short time than he had to all other people combined in his life up until then.

He talked about his family, especially his mom and Dennis. He didn't say much of his dad, other than that he had always wanted to love him. That it broke his heart that his dad refused to let go of his rage at the things that were his own goddamn fault.

He talked about his time in prison, and the experiments. How some of the tests they ran on him still made him think and feel in ways he didn't understand.

He spoke a little of Rose, and even about his art.

He covered just about everything he had on his mind, and in time, I realized I might be the only person who would ever know that much about him. He knew even then he wasn't gonna make it to the seventy years or so that most men might have a chance to expect.

He wanted just one person to hear him out in case he had to go.

It had to be someone he trusted enough to maybe figure out why he'd even been born.

It had to be someone who cared.

Someone with love enough to let him say what he needed before his time was up.

And that, damn it all, would come around right too soon.

I'm gonna do the best I can to recount what was goin on right before January 1, 1973, the day that Lefty died. While the time still exists in my mind, that one day always charges in and shoves the rest of my memories out of the room.

Business was still really good. Our heroin supplied the demand. The pot and LSD were still a hit too, especially with the college kids readin the poets and listenin to Floyd. They were the same ones who thought Nixon's parents were genius for namin im Dick.

And speakin of the parents, I was sellin dime bags to some of them too. The put-together professional types who were either miserable or in denial about somethin beneath the good-lookin veneer. Even the privileged need to escape from themselves once in a while.

By the middle of December, me and Lefty had pulled even deeper into our own, well, society. I don't know how else to say it. We spent *all* our time together, more than we ever had. We didn't talk much to other people beyond what was needed for business. That included Tommy, who was definitely feelin squeezed out. He still stopped in, but he never hung out for long.

Me and Lefty learned plenty more about Dennis as well, mostly from another Kensing County deputy who depended on us to hold up his addiction to coke. He liked to party with us too, and when he did, he spilled a whole lot of beans.

Dennis shook down *everybody*. He was also wily enough to keep his arrest rate high while makin sure certain people stayed out of the joint and deep in his pocket. People like me. For every three lawbreakers he bagged for the public, he might keep one on the street for plans of his own. Some other deputies in his department knew what was up, but they didn't talk. He was way too tight with the right people.

He also hadn't lost his taste for the skirt. His family had no idea just how much koochie dad enjoyed on the side. No surprise. It was just another built-in bonus for those who love power and live for themselves. Dudes like that will always have worshippin women who are ready to lie down.

Turned out he was a heavyweight drinker and gambler too. He'd even fallen into serious debt with a couple of bookies who had a hate-on for him but couldn't do nothin because of who he was.

So that was my greater knowledge of the man who came to collect from me just as the annual calendar was ready to flip. I was drinkin vodka and orange juice and lookin out my front window when the cruiser crept in and parked in the lot.

The knock came as soon as the minute hand hit the hour. I wasn't even payin attention to the countdown on the TV. Lefty was watchin it, though. The lights were off too, so the electric paint and flickerin ghosts were swirlin on the walls again.

I looked at the empty bottles of Schlitz on the coffee table. Me and Lefty had already finished enough to open us a goddamn basement bowlin alley. We'd been drinkin since seven o'clock.

The knock came again, harder.

I glanced at Lefty, and then I answered the door.

There he was, all shoulders and big-dick bravado.

"Hi, Dennis," I said. "Happy New Year."

"You're not holding the bag," he said.

I looked at the tumbler in my hand.

"Oh, yeah," I said.

I looked back at where I'd set the cash on the lamp table.

"It's over there," I said.

He shrugged with his palms out by his hips.

I turned around real slow to get it. My knee bumped into the coffee table on the way. I said shit. An empty bottle fell over and rolled onto the carpet. I grabbed the bag and brought it to him.

"Here," I said.

He held the rolled top with one hand and supported the bottom with the other.

"Bag's wet," he said. He held it up and sniffed it. "Beer."

"Okay," I said. "So what?"

"Get me a new bag," he said. "I can't carry this one."

"Christ," I said.

I was halfway to the kitchen when Lefty stood from the sofa. I stopped and looked around. He was movin toward the doorway.

"Boob says, you don't need a new bag," he said. "Take the one he gave you, and then get out of here. You have what you came for."

"This isn't your business," Dennis said.

"Yeah it is," Lefty said.

A couple seconds of quiet. I could have weighed it with my triple-beam drug scale, man.

"Sit back down," Dennis said.

Lefty lunged forward and grabbed him by the cop jacket with his good hand. He yanked him inside and slammed the door shut with his bad hand.

Dennis dropped the bag of cash. He didn't lose his shades though. The electric paint and TV ghosts started swimmin on those as well.

"You just made a big mistake, Melvin," he said.

His face was tight and pinched. He snapped his holster open. His cop jacket squeaked.

"I'll shoot you right now, so help me," he said.

"You're no good, Dennis," Lefty said. "For anyone."

They were standin about two feet apart.

Dennis slid his gun from the holster, turned off the safety, and held it halfway up.

"I will shoot you if you don't shut up and sit down," he said.

Lefty didn't obey.

"What you've done with your life ain't right," he said. His voice was fallin a bit. "You don't even have it in you to be a brother, or a son."

Dennis smiled. His white teeth flashed through the dark.

"You're a loser," he said. "And a felon, and a killer. You ruined our family. It's *you* who won't ever amount to shit. So don't bother wasting your breath passing judgment on me."

"Boob says, yeah, I'm what you say, and maybe more," Lefty said. "But my life was written that way. Yours wasn't. Dad made this world a bad place, and so have you. You could have made a lot of things better. But your heart is just like his."

Dennis pointed the gun at Lefty's face.

"Parker, get my bag," he said, lookin straight down his arm. "Get it *now*. Or I'm going to waste your buddy right here. And if I do that, I'll have to end you too."

Lefty grabbed Dennis by the wrist so fast I barely saw it. The gun went off. The bullet punched the wall behind the TV. I dropped to the floor.

Lefty swung his left arm around Dennis's neck and threw his hip into him. Dennis's feet left the floor and crashed into the coffee table. The beer bottles scattered with a bitch of a racket.

That's when I saw Lefty's gun, the 9mm he got from me. It was still on the table.

Dennis fired again. The bullet went through the ceiling. Dust puffed out through the hole.

I couldn't decide what to do, man. A big part wanted to leap on Dennis. A bigger part said bad idea. I kept my face pressed to the carpet.

They continued wrestlin hard. Bottles were clinkin and clankin. I heard the *smack!* of a fist.

Dennis cussed and growled. Lefty hit im again, and again, and again.

I looked up. Dennis's face was a mess. His shades were on the floor by the lamp table.

Lefty pinned im down with his right knee and cracked im again in the side of the head.

Dennis stopped strugglin.

Lefty waited. When Dennis still didn't move, he lifted a little of his weight from him.

Dennis's gun came up again. Lefty hooked the gun hand with his right arm and reached back for his own gun with his left hand.

While he was doin that, Dennis slipped his arm free.

Now they were both pointin their guns at each other's faces.

"Let go of it, Dennis," Lefty said.

"No way," Dennis said. His words were damp from the blood in his mouth. "Your sorry life is over, Melvin. You're either going back to prison for a *long* time, or you're going to die. Decide which one sounds better."

Lefty went quiet. I craned up my neck from the floor.

"Then let's go," he finally said. "Let's both do the world a favor."

He fired into Dennis's head a bunch of times, fast and furious.

The bloody mess was all over my fucking floor, man. Lefty got off im, real slow. He moved backward until he bumped into the coffee table. He sat down on the edge of it.

Then he looked at me.

"I love you, Parker," he said. "More than anything else."

He raised his gun to his left temple.

"Lefty!" I screamed. *"Don't do it!"*

His face relaxed. Even through the dark, I saw the peace in his eyes.

"Wherever it is we wind up, I'll be there waitin for you," he said.

He fired.

He fell sideways and to the floor. His bad hand landed on his brother's leg.

I crawled over and pulled him to me.

I held his head to my chest, and for the only time in my life, I cried so hard I lost my breath.

*T*he scene was absolutely filthy.

Two ex-convicts and a cop in a drug dealer's apartment. Two of that assembly now dead, most notably the one with the badge. Matter and splatter all over the carpet and furniture. Bullet holes in different places. Empty bottles everywhere. Tall cash in a beer-stained bag. Illegal guns and more questionable cash on the premises. A shitload of drugs with intent for sale in the bedroom.

Of course I was scared and freakin out. So much so I completely forgot I was drunk.

I had to think straight, man. Cover all of my bases and angles before the thousand flashin lights showed up outside.

First up, I had to de-contaminate what I could of the scene. Fast.

With my heart playin African bongos, I grabbed the cash bag and bolted to my bedroom. Emptied my dark-blue canvas dirty-laundry bag onto the floor. Changed out of my bloody clothes and shoved em in. Then I stuffed the guns, drugs, and all of my cash in there too.

I cinched it shut, cruised out of the bedroom, and hauled ass out the back door.

I took the stairs three at a time down to the alley. With the bag's drawstring looped over my shoulder, I scaled the chain-link fence between the alley and the trees on the other side. Then, pumpin with adrenaline and lookin at it like it was just another trestle, I climbed one of the taller trees as if I was a bear on high-grade blow. More than halfway up, I tied the drawstring *real* tight to a branch close to the trunk.

Climbed back down, ran back up to my apartment, and snatched a big brown-paper grocery bag from the cupboard under the sink. Filled that with every last one of the empty beer bottles. Ran back down to the alley and got rid of the bag in the Dumpster.

My neighbors' windows were lightin up like fireflies.

Ran back up to my apartment to clean up anything else that I could.

By the time the cops showed up, all that was left to make my life a bitch were the bodies and the two guns that had made em be dead. That, and the blood and bullet holes, of course. Still ugly, I know, but at least I'd saved myself a few more tough explanations.

The hard knock came, followed by the command.

I opened the door, held up my hands, and stepped back.

The cops charged in with their guns up.

I was flat on the floor gettin cuffed inside of ten seconds.

With my cheek rubbin the carpet, I moved my head and looked at Lefty.

His eyes were open and lookin at me.

I'm still sure, even now, that I heard his voice in my head, and it told me that I'd be okay.

*T*hey busted my balls pretty hard back at the cop shop. A gallon of coffee and a temple of crumpled Winston packs later, they still had nothin on me.

I told them what happened, over and over. And then I ran through it again. The story didn't change to trip me up because I really was just a couple lies short of the truth, and I could remember each time exactly what they were.

Dennis knew his brother was stayin at my apartment. They'd been arguin about different things lately—I didn't mention the extortion of me for obvious reasons—and this time when Dennis stopped by, it got hotter than usual. They screamed and pushed and cussed, and Lefty closed in to clobber him good. They'd been fightin and arguing since they were little, I explained.

Dennis pulled out his gun. Lefty drew his own and killed him at close range. Then, knowin that his life was done from there, he sat on my table and finished himself.

What more could the cops say about that? The evidence backed what I said.

They searched every square inch of my place. All they could find was a couple of pot seeds and some faint coke residue—not enough for a bust. They even searched the alley and the garbage. They found the beer bottles, but big deal. They *didn't* climb any trees or shake any branches.

The badges stressed me out and made me lose sleep, but they couldn't hold me on charges.

In the end, the books were closed and filed on what they could prove.

Murder-suicide.

So here I am, an ex-convict well past middle age. Never married and not about to re-think it. Still drinkin and smokin too much but not about to die from it yet.

Yeah, I've had a tough life. I won't serve you any excuses. That would just make me another cliché and take away from this here story I finally took the trouble to write.

Maybe my life was what it was so that *I*, Parker Anthony Hill, might learn a few things to pass along in my own words. When you get down to it, I guess we all have a few pennies to pitch into the piggy bank of wisdom.

Wisdom that includes the fact that the world exists in spite of us.

Nurture is more important than nature.

It's our pleasure that causes most of our pain. That includes the pleasure we get from drugs. They're here to stay and make money for people like me because they're a faster fix to the soul's problems than faith is. Now read that first sentence again.

Crime is just a way of sayin we might have played by the rules if we'd believed the rules would have done right by us.

Shit like that.

And just like Lefty said, sometimes a gift is just a gift, and nothing more. Just because you got one, it don't make you special or guarantee you're gonna stand out.

It does mean you have one extra choice not available to many others, and if you're smart about it, you might find a way to use it to touch other people and color their minds.

Maybe even color em green.

I've got other ideas and wisdom pennies that you'd think would keep me away from most of my trouble.

But as with a lot of us, there's a difference between what I know and what I do.

It didn't help that I kept dealin drugs and breakin laws well after Lefty died. That experience should have snapped me out of it, but it didn't.

The law could and should have hit me way more often. I did have to sit in jail here and there. But for every one time they brought me in on charges or locked me up, I got away with a hundred other things.

I think I know why.

God was done usin men to punish me a long time ago.

He wants me to sit in judgment of myself. To stew in the knowledge of my actions and choices until I confess I am the author of myself and most of the things that happen to me.

That way, with no one to blame but me, maybe I'll even decide I can change.

Maybe.

But pride's a tall wall to climb. I'd rather believe I'm fine as I am. It's easier that way.

As for right now, I'm doin okay, or at least as the world would define it. I have my freedom. A couple close friends, includin Tommy when he's around.

I have my mind and my health. A nice TV. Beer and cigarettes. Books to read once in a while. The Pacers and the Colts and the Hoosiers.

I'm still gettin along fine without Viagra. I've even had the same legitimate job for a while.

Then of course there's the cash. I earned a pile from my years in the drug trade, which I finally got the hell out of a little while ago.

Plus, there's still a tiny bit left from what we'd stashed in '63 and '64 before the state locked us up. That includes both my share and Lefty's. He'd told me where he'd hid his durin all of our late-night talks.

I went back to his old house in Colton to get it a few months after his funeral, which was attended only by me, Tommy, and the funeral director. I paid for it. Dennis of course received a hero's tribute complete with all the cop ceremony and twenty-one guns. A few hundred people showed up for that one. Mrs. Savage didn't make it down for either.

When I knocked on the door of the old house, a guy of about thirty or so opened it. He had a son and a daughter, both little, one by each leg.

I told him who I was and where I'd come from, right there in Colton. I explained my relationship with the family that'd lived there. I even handed im my driver's license.

I also showed im the sketch book of Lefty's that I'd brought—the one with the mini-mural of the big one in the basement.

I asked if I could go down and see it. Made up some bullshit about how I was startin to make a photo journal of my life and times in Colton.

He stared at me and the digital camera hangin from around my neck. Then he said okay and let me in.

Once inside, I didn't linger long, although I did notice how much had changed. A couple other families had given the place a different vibe. No more feeling of pain and sadness that was gonna drop on you like a wet blanket retrieved from the garbage. No smell of too much alcohol.

It felt much more like . . . well, family. Full-time employment. Kids that got along and would someday do their homework. Even a whiff of spiritual faith. There was a stainless-steel cross on the wall above the TV.

With the guy watchin me, I made my way to the basement door at the back of the house. I had to pass through the kitchen. The two kids ran up ahead of me, straight to the nice-lookin wife at the sink. She stopped washin dishes and looked me over.

Her husband was a few feet behind me, in the doorway. He told her who I was and what I was doin there.

I nodded and forced a smile. She eyeballed me as if I were the rotten, young ex-convict I was.

I wasn't there to win people over. I went to the basement door and opened it.

The stairway was as dark as I remembered it. I looked around for a switch, but that didn't prove to be a modern addition. So, just like old times, I went down as well as I could.

When I reached the floor, movin by the light tricklin down from the stairway, I went to where the chain to the overhead bulb should have been. It was still there, and I gave it a yank.

Dim light flooded the basement. When I turned around, the guy was standin right there, at the foot of the stairs.

He chatted me up. I knew the drill. I stayed chilled out and let him say what he wanted for as long as he liked until he was satisfied he'd done the right thing by lettin me in.

He went back upstairs after about five minutes.

The basement had been made a lot cleaner. Just about all of the shelves looked like they'd been replaced inside the last few years. A lot of the junk and wet boxes and scrap-shit was gone.

But the mural—holy miracle that it was—was right there, on the walls, the same as it had always been.

I stared at it and took it all in just as I had that first time in '63. Then I took close pictures of it in sections.

And when I was done doin that, I went to the spot that Lefty had told me about.

The concrete block I'd be able to remove. The one on which he'd painted a figure in a green robe.

I squatted, set my camera and the sketch book out of the way on the floor, and looked back toward the stairs again. Nobody was there as far as I could tell—not even the edge of a shadow. I *could* tell that the guy had left the door at the top almost all the way open.

I could also hear the wife sayin something to the kids. She was still in the kitchen.

It was a risk, man.

I drew a big breath and let it out. Located the block's chipped-away top corners Lefty had described. The block was big and heavy, but it would slide right out if I did it right.

The corners were slightly sanded too—Lefty's work from before. I was to hook the two middle fingers of both hands into the corners and pull on an even plane. It'd take some muscle and patience.

I looked back toward the stairs again.

My heart was a fuckin melon about to explode.

I hooked my fingers and pulled. It made a low grating sound, and then it cooperated.

Right before I pulled it out the rest of the way, I looked closer at the art that was on it.

My breathin got caught.

I had to be sure I was seein it right.

I pushed the block a couple inches back into the wall and stepped away from it.

I looked at it longer, and then I closed in again.

The figure Lefty'd painted on it—the one in the robe—was a major piece of the mural, but at the same time it wasn't a focal point. You'd have a hard time explaining it unless you saw it for yourself.

It was like the figure was *right there*, ready, waitin to be found. It made me think of . . . I don't know—God, or somethin like it. Someone or some*thing* important. But you'd miss it if you weren't lookin at it the right way. No shit. It struck me as new because it'd been about ten years since Lefty took me down to see the mural.

Guess I hadn't been lookin at it the right way.

And for whatever reason, Lefty hadn't included the figure in his miniature.

I couldn't describe the figure's features to you because, well, it didn't really have any. It wasn't male, or female. Just a bigger person-like shape with holes for eyes plus a nose and a mouth. Long, grayish hair that fell over the shoulders.

It was like Lefty had made it plain so that we'd complete it ourselves, in our own minds.

The thing that is bigger and greater than us. That's lovin us no matter what we say or do, and that's watchin with compassion and givin us strength even when we run and hide.

I had to look it over even closer after that as well, mainly because of the loops and swirls Lefty had painted in the hair.

I traced em with my finger, and figured it out.

Boob.

The loops and swirls spelled *Boob.*

Boob as in the Boob that said whatever was right to Lefty accordin to the private relationship between him and his Maker.

A clock started tickin real loud in my head. I had to wrap it up fast, or the guy or especially his wife was gonna know for sure that somethin was up. I'd been down there close to fifteen minutes, and I'd be blessed if they gave me even five more before they came back down.

Real slow and careful, I slid the block all the way out.

I was startin to sweat, mostly from the nerves.

With my back straight and my thigh muscles workin, I set the block on the floor.

After wipin my head with my forearm, I looked into the space. Almost stuck my head in.

Then I saw it, right there, about a foot and a half behind the wall.

The green plastic yard bag that Lefty had tied shut with a knot. Right next to the stack of comic books he'd hidden from his dad.

I reached in and pulled it out.

That's when I *really* felt like my pants were a pool around my ankles. Now my heart was bangin the Indiana U marchin-band bass drum.

I looked up once more at the stairway.

Still no one.

Something Big and Powerful had to be watchin over me, man.

I untied the bag and peered in. Almost all large bills in packs, just as Lefty had said.

I slipped off my coat and lifted up my baggy shirt. Removed the toothpicks I'd cut in half and connected at intervals to the two bands of duct tape tied sticky-side-out around my stomach and chest. I put the toothpicks in my pants pocket. Then I stuck the packs of fifties real close together to my front and sides. After that, I unbuttoned my jeans—a tighter pair—and slid the thinner packs of hundreds down the inside of each leg. I cuffed each leg real tight to make sure nothin could slide out before I got back to the car.

Only two bulky bundles of twenties remained. I slipped those into my jacket's inside pockets.

I was gonna make it out with *all* of the cash.

I buttoned and zipped myself up. Put the empty yard bag back into the wall.

Then I bent down, wrapped my arms around the block, and lifted the bitch back up.

Slid it back into place.

Stared at Boob again.

The mural was speakin to me differently now. I'm tellin you, man, what it meant and said to you depended on how you felt at the exact moment when you were lookin at it.

It depended on the color of your mind.

In that final moment, as I took it all in for the very last time, I thought about the curse of genius, and how hard it must be to carry, especially when it's stuck with nowhere to grow.

Most of all, I thought about green rooms.

I've tried to help myself find mine. Each time I feel a pull to say or do somethin that's good, or true, or real, somethin that doesn't come from my pride or my anger, I open Lefty's sketch book with the miniature mural.

And add my own touch of green usin one of his pencils.

I don't color it as often as I should, but at least I'm havin a go at it.

As for you, I don't know how far ahead or behind me you are on the pathway to heaven or hell. My guess is that you're better off than I am, but you still have work to do.

I realize my résumé ain't as good as John the Baptist's. But if you can forget the source for a minute, maybe you'll spot somethin in all of this that you can use. Certain things that hold up regardless of who or where they're comin from.

If you go back to the start of this here story, you'll see I said I couldn't write for shit. Hell, I know I still drop letters from words all over the place. Maybe I'll get around to fixin that one of these days. What I *have* learned is that maybe I can write, a little. Maybe we're all better at somethin than we think we are.

Maybe all it takes is the courage to reach into the dark for the beauty that's hiding in there.

Melvin Savage did.

I miss you, Lefty. I miss you with all that I have for a heart.

I hope you're coolin out and takin it light with Boob inside your green room.

But even more, I pray, for all of us down here, that someday we might meet you there.

ABOUT THE AUTHOR

Jonathan P. Davis is a writer of both fiction and non-fiction. His previous published work includes *Life, Inc.* (AuthorHouse, 2006), an existentialist fantasy novel; *Stephen King's America* (Bowling Green Popular Press, 1994), a book-length thesis on recurring themes in the popular author's work; and ghostwriting for a young-adult horror/suspense novel. He is also a songwriter and musician and an award-winning business and marketing freelance writer.

27687443R00266

Made in the USA
Lexington, KY
22 November 2013